This book has been donated

in memory of:

Sharon Ash

EVERYTHING YOU CAME TO SEE

EVERYTHING YOU CAME TO SEE

A Novel

Elizabeth Schulte Martin

Skyhorse Publishing

First Edition

This is a work of fiction. Names, places, characters, and incidents are either the products of the author's imagination or are used fictitiously.

Skyhorse Publishing books may be purchased in bulk at special discounts for sales promotion, corporate gifts, fund-raising, or educational purposes. Special editions can also be created to specifications. For details, contactthe Special Sales Department, Skyhorse Publishing, 307 West 36th Street, 11th Floor, New York, NY 10018 or info@skyhorsepublishing.com.

Skyhorse® and Skyhorse Publishing® are registered trademarks of Skyhorse Publishing, Inc.®, a Delaware corporation.

Visit our website at www.skyhorsepublishing.com.

10 9 8 7 6 5 4 3 2 1

Library of Congress Cataloging-in-Publication Data is available on file.

Cover design by Erin Seaward-Hiatt

Print ISBN: 978-1-5107-2404-4
Ebook ISBN: 978-1-5107-2405-1

Printed in the United States of America

For my mother.

EVERYTHING YOU CAME TO SEE

First Act

In the mornings, people aren't in the mood to be entertained. They walk a wide arc around me, they avoid my eyes and the coffee can I have out for tips. They have to get into one of those gray-glass buildings and they don't have time for some kid with greasy hair who refuses to get a real job. But I have a long reach. I have a million tricks to close the distance.

In this act, I hook the audience by offering someone an apple. If they reach for it, I pull it away. Today, the guy I hooked was a tie-wearing, briefcase-toting business man with a Tom Selleck moustache, and when I pulled the apple away, he actually looked a little surprised. I don't know why. Here I am in whiteface, eyebrows arched up to my hairline, and he expects some kind of serious transaction to go on between us? No, no, guy. You've mistaken me for someone who doesn't wear spandex bodysuits on the street. I'm not the someone who's going to give you a snack-on-the-go and make it easier for you to get right to your boring job. I'm the someone who's going to make you late. I delay reality. I don't feed it to you.

This morning, with Tom Selleck, I spun the apple on the tip of my finger, Harlem Globetrotter–style, then balanced it on the tip of my nose. Two more people stopped to watch, and I offered him the apple again. Before he could get his hand on it, I popped it twenty feet into the air. At this point, the guy got mad, which was perfect, because people who won't stop to watch someone's amazing physical agility

1

might still stop to see a potential fight. I bounced the apple around like a hackey sack. Heel-toe-knee-hip-elbow. I kept it knocking against all the edges of my body, got a nice rhythm going there, then let it hit me in the crotch. Everybody, especially Mr. Selleck, laughed.

All in all, about five people stayed to see the act to the end, which is pretty successful busking for me. I drew those five people into the space between themselves and the apple, and closed that space with a snap, and locked it, so they'll never see another apple without thinking of me.

Also, I made a dollar fifty.

Christiakov told me writing down my ideas for acts was a good habit to get into, so I'm giving it a shot. The rule I made for myself is that I'll write five, then I can say that I tried. I've never written an act down before but, lately, I forget my ideas, even the details of the shows I've already done. I'm too distracted by other things—like how to get to St. Louis. Like the letter that showed up a week ago in my PO Box. Like a backpack full of potholders.

So, I'm going to take Christiakov's advice, and this apple act counts as the first.

It's midnight and I'm hiding under a table at a McDonald's where this girl I know is the manager. I'm eating a paper-thin cheeseburger and a really badly bruised apple. I'm so tired, I just want to stare at the wall and not even chew, let this burger disintegrate in my mouth. But once I make a rule, I try to follow it. Rules keep you out of trouble and, even if they don't, if everything falls apart, in the end you can say, "I did what I was supposed to, so you can't blame me for the way things turned out."

That sounds bad, I guess. I should get a new motto. "Laughter makes the world go 'round"? "Love makes a family"? "A tomato is not a vegetable; it's a fruit"?

Oh, well. Some people are born clowns, and the rest of us have to work at it. My own mother thought I was a stick-in-the-mud and, one time, she actually said so. I think I was six. She made a bet with my brother: if she could make him laugh, he would owe her his first month of wages at his first job. We were eating dinner, some sort of noodle with gravy on it that we spun on forks with wooden handles. No sign of our father.

Andre said, "What do I get if I don't laugh?"

And she said, "A Corvette."

And my brother clenched his jaw. "You're on," he said.

My mother went back to eating her noodles. Every so often she would make a face, cross her eyes, burp. My brother kept his face tight as a drum. We were good at that. Being real tough shits. My mother was never intimidated by our tough-shittiness.

So, she picked up her plate with one hand and pulled out the neckline of her blouse with the other. With a deadpan stare at my brother, she dumped the whole plate down her shirt. Andre fell out of his seat laughing.

But I was scared. I said, "You wasted all that food!" I watched the doorway; I was sure the worst would happen.

My mother peeked down at the noodles in her shirt. "William Henry, you're a real stick-in-the-mud sometimes," she said. "Besides, if you wanna be pragmatic, what's the price of a few noodles to the price of a Corvette? Honestly, kid."

If it weren't for my mother, there would be a place for me in one of those gray-glass buildings. I wouldn't have minded that sort of life, not even a little. It's the ghost of her that keeps me from following rules like "Don't sleep in a McDonald's" or "Don't walk barefoot on a city street wearing lightning-blue lipstick and flying an imaginary kite."

Now the only rules I have are the ones that I hold myself to:

One. Breathe.

And two. Stretch.

And three. Write.

And four. Keep going.

Five. Open wide. Eat this reality so someone else doesn't have to, so someone else has a story about why they were late to work. It's when I can do this that I feel her the most. Like she's hovering in that space between me and an apple and a stranger, waiting for me to close the gap.

3

CHAPTER I

St. Louis
April 1990

CALEB HAD A SPECIAL WAY of interviewing candidates, which involved getting to know them as little as possible on a personal level. He had a list of questions he never updated or deviated from, and he tried to keep eye contact to a minimum, in case his interviewee was prone to interpreting eye contact as an invitation to go on tangents about their childhood, their last marriage, or their substance abuse problems. The template interview was the fair way to do things, since the more he got to know performers, the more they generally frustrated him. They were criminally narcissistic, unhappy people. If it weren't for them, his job would be just like any other business manager's. He would take inventory, hire the employees, choose the dates, crunch the numbers, count out the register, call it a day.

But circus business was not like any other business, namely because the performers were not like any other people. The boy who sat across from him was supposedly twenty-four and had several years of performing experience, though his splotchy stubble and overeager, damp handshake pegged him at about eighteen. His application said his name was William Henry Harrison Bell, and the fact that he blushed when Caleb said his full name aloud assured Caleb that it was his given name, and not some kind of terrible pseudonym. Caleb noticed that he was antsy and smelled like he had slept in his clothes, which were all frayed around the edges. He needed a new pair of shoes; the tongues lopped out of his Converse high tops, and half the rubber on the toes had peeled off.

"Could you just call me Henry?" the boy asked.

"Of course," Caleb said, drawing a line through the three other names.

The boy, Henry, was a candidate to fill the position of "clown." There were two open clown positions, in fact, and in order for the performers to have enough practice time before shows began in June, Caleb had to make the hires by mid-month. It was April 5. He had already done fifteen interviews, and none of the candidates so far had been satisfying.

"So, first," Caleb began, "can you do any sort of aerial stunts?"

"I can do everything," he said, leaning back and smiling, pleased with his answer, no doubt certain that Caleb would be pleased with it, too. His eyes were soggy and hopeful. Delusions of grandeur and an iron deficiency.

Goddamn performers.

Caleb had worked for Feely and Feinstein's International Circus for ten years, hiring the talent and managing the finances. He made sure everyone got their checks and submitted their tax forms. He kept track of their sick days. He took the receipts for their travel expenses and made sure the talent got their travel schedules and all their paper work up to date. Considering the circus was a mobile one, which traveled to about ten different cities every summer, managing the travel alone was a heavy workload.

When Seamus Feely, his childhood friend, offered him the job, he had said, "Caleb, how would you like the most boring job in the circus? You'll have your own office."

At the time, Caleb was thirty-seven years old and managed the Louisville Hanky Panky Party Shop. He'd asked, "Why would I want a boring job at a circus when I can keep the boring job I have now?"

And Seamus said, "Well, there's the office thing. Like I said. And you won't get a lot of lip from the talent, because they don't know anything about tax forms or work visas, so they'll do what you say, and they'll respect you. You'll meet interesting people. You'll wear a suit."

It had seemed like a move up. Before he'd been sidetracked by death, by money, and by an endless parade of needy weirdos in his life, he had once wanted to be a museum curator. He'd gone to college for this, majored in art history, and had barely grown his beard out and learned to eat cereal for two out of three meals a day when his father got sick. He left school to take care of his dad, and by the time he died, Caleb couldn't remember what was so important about school. In fact, he couldn't seem to drum up a reason why anything was important but continuing to breathe, to eat, to shit, to ward off nonexistence. Living itself was success, and bully for him, he kept on succeeding, day after day, and there was no sense in taking risks that would only complicate the goal. He did his own mediocre paintings and worked wherever he could, until he ended up at the Hanky Panky Party Shop, a place with a horribly frank combination of supplies for bachelor parties and children's birthdays: G-strings and plastic Mickey Mouse flatware.

Managing a circus was a lot more like being a museum curator than selling Magic 8-Balls to grown men and edible bras to little girls. And besides, he missed his native St. Louis. Louisville, Kentucky was not the same, even if the two cities did happen to be named for the same French guy.

So here he was, in a wood-paneled office in a portable building on a big desolate stretch of dirt in St. Louis, interviewing some transient high school dropout, and wearing a very nice suit that was too tight around his arms.

"Do you have experience with animals?" he asked.

"I don't like animals," said the boy, pulling his worn-out shoes underneath him, so that he was sitting cross-legged in the chair. He couldn't stay still—Caleb kept thinking that any moment he would lean back just a bit too far, hit the wall, and knock down the framed print of Beckmann's *The Acrobats* that Caleb's wife had given to him two Christmases ago.

"You don't like them, or you're afraid of them?"

As soon as Caleb asked this question, he knew he shouldn't have. It opened a space for the boy to squeeze in personal details. Fortunately for Caleb, the boy only shrugged, as if he didn't know the answer.

"So go back to the aerial stuff, then. What exactly do you have experience with?"

"Aerial silks. I've done stuff suspended, on a hoop. Never tried the trapeze, but I could probably do it."

Caleb made notes on his clipboard. Few people claimed to be as well-rounded as this kid, but it was obvious he was stretching the truth. Caleb started to doubt the wisdom of even letting the boy come in for an interview—he had no tapes, no portfolio. But the applicant pool was shallow, and he had decided to interview anyone who applied, even if they seemed like a long shot. And then, of course, the boy had the Russian's recommendation, which Caleb couldn't ignore.

"Ever been shot from a cannon?" This question wasn't on the list, but Caleb was bored with the conversation, already convinced that the boy would be a bust, as they were all busts.

"No. Once I jumped out of the bed of a truck, though. It was moving pretty fast at the time."

"Okay." Caleb pretended to write "no" beneath the imaginary question. He took a deep breath. "So, tell me about your act."

"Well. I mean. I'm just going to show it to you, right?" said the boy. His eyes had dropped, and Caleb knew that he had succeeded in sounding so uninterested that the boy lost confidence.

"Yes. But I want to know where you got the idea for it. How did you come up with it?"

Here, he brightened again. As the boy talked about the inspiration for his act, his admiration for Charlie Chaplin and Jackie Chan, Caleb still found himself only half-listening. It had been a long afternoon, searching for new clowns. The last two that worked for him were good, two Finnish cousins, not a word of English between them. They'd gotten an offer from a circus in Finland, and how could they resist a position that would take them back home? Caleb didn't hold it against them, even though they'd left him in the lurch. Adrienne told him to see it as an opportunity, and he tried to take his wife's advice because she was always right about these things, about ways of seeing.

Caleb interrupted the boy, who was still talking about Jackie Chan.

"All right, then. Let's see your audition. Follow me," he said.

The boy sprang up from the chair and picked up his prop trunk, which had rested near him during the interview. He knocked it against the wood paneling of the office before stepping out into the hall.

Outside, the squat portable building that housed Caleb's office was a small rehearsal studio with a rounded roof. Clustered near it were the blue-and-white trailers that carried the circus from city to city during the summer. They were rusted around the windows, and the roofs peeled up at the corners. Someone driving by who didn't know that this was Feely and Feinstein's International Circus might think this was a depressing place, and they might not be wrong, not on this particular day. Once the tent was up, though, the lot would stop looking like a good place to get knifed by a hobo, and more like a child's craft project, shoddily put together, but charming. Or so Caleb liked to think. The sky would get blue again, the kids would come, and everything would smell like funnel cake.

He led the boy into the studio, which had wooden floors, badly in need of refinishing, covered partially by forest-green rubber mats. Mirrors hung along the walls on either side, and the room was damp, smelling slightly mildewed. Caleb probably could have gotten rid of the smell with a little Pine-Sol, but he liked it.

"Don't mind me. Just relax and do your stuff," said Caleb, as he unfolded a metal chair close to the stage. He sat, clipboard and pen in hand, careful not to smile.

The boy closed his eyes.

Caleb watched as the boy then opened his trunk and took out a plate of spaghetti covered in plastic wrap. It was real, the meat and spice pungent and fresh, probably from one of the Italian joints on The Hill. Caleb had no idea how the boy had managed to keep the sauce from leaking out all over the rest of the props, and then realized that he probably hadn't. The boy uncovered the plate and placed it and a fork on the mat, took his place behind the plate, rolled his neck a few times, and took off his shirt to reveal a face painted upside down on his back in permanent marker. Then, he flipped his ass in the air and tucked his knees next to his ears so that the marker-drawn face turned right-side up.

9

"Don't worry, I'll clean up when I'm done," he said.

For a second, hope crept up on Caleb and he thought there might be a slender chance that the boy would be as good as he said he was, a thing that people would pay to see. *God, kid, if you could just be* good, *please be good.* If people didn't start paying to see things, then this season would be Feely and Feinstein's last.

And this was the other reason, difficult to admit for Caleb, that he had taken to getting to know his interviewees as little as possible—if the circus fell apart, and odds were it would, Caleb did not want to feel the weight of the lives he'd undone when he fired them all.

HENRY HAD COME TO THE circus with a prop trunk, a letter from his brother, and the black spiral notebook where he kept his ideas for sketches. He'd had thirty dollars, but he spent it on a plate of spaghetti and a room at a motel where even the front-desk clerk looked like a hooker. This was the first time he had auditioned for anything, and he was terrified. He also hadn't eaten in a very long time—the thought of the spaghetti wrapped in a grocery bag in his trunk made him salivate like a thirsty dog.

The wind blew so hard as he searched for the circus grounds that he had to crouch and pin his map down in order to read it. His map was hand-drawn on a napkin by the hooker motel clerk. He'd asked her if she knew where the circus was, and she said, "Yeah, I been there once."

He followed her directions to what looked like an abandoned trailer park. At the entrance was an electric sign, cursive letters filled with little, red, unlit bulbs that said FEELY AND FEINSTEIN'S INTERNATIONAL CIRCUS set above a metal arch. Henry walked beneath the arch, toward the cluster of trailers. He lowered his head and pressed against the wind, the pulse of air rushing past his ears, deafening him before subsiding into stony quiet.

When he lifted his head, he saw a man standing next to a huge white horse not twenty yards away. Henry froze. The man was short and muscular with translucent hair and eyelashes. His skin was probably once just as fair, but now it was the kind of ruddy tan that people with his coloring only achieved working day after day in the sun. His eyes were an unusually light shade of blue, and he wore a shirt with no sleeves and black work pants splattered with drying mud. The horse beside him must have avoided the mud that the man had not because it was spotless, nose to hoof.

Henry had never been this close to a horse. He'd visited a friend once, when he was very little, who lived on a farm and had goats and cows. And he'd gone deer hunting a couple times with his brother and Will Miller and nearly brushed shoulders with a doe that had sprinted past them. But the only horses he'd seen were from car windows, as he drove by their pastures. They were far in the distance, flicking flies, indifferent to Henry. This one was only a few footsteps away and looking right at him.

"Can I help you?" asked the man who held its reins.

"Hi," said Henry. "Are you Mr. Baratucci?"

"No," said the man. "I'm Lorne. Who are you?"

"I'm Henry Bell. I have an audition."

The man seemed to consider this for a moment. He said something that Henry couldn't quite understand because the wind kicked up again and silenced him. Then the man raised his wiry arm and pointed to one of the trailers.

"Thanks," said Henry.

The man nodded and jerked the horse's bridle, leading it away. When it moved, he could see the muscles undulating beneath its skin—just one neck muscle, Henry thought, looked larger than the biggest muscle in the human body. In spite of how firmly Lorne held its reins, the horse still craned its great neck to look back at Henry.

His hand was slick with sweat when he offered it to Caleb Baratucci, this hawk-nosed, green-whiskered man he'd been told to find. But he did the best he could to be cool, be sharp, be older—so the man didn't ask questions. He did not want to spend another night under a table at a McDonald's or in the bed of some idiot girl or lying in his prop trunk, half-awake all night for fear someone might shut him in it and bury him. He wanted a cozy trailer or train car, to wake up to the same faces more than one day in a row. He wanted someone to mash up some potatoes for him and slop them onto a plate once or twice a day—he'd eat it like it was birthday cake.

The manager didn't ask questions about where he came from or where he'd worked before or why he wanted to join a circus, thank God, but he also didn't laugh at the act. The manager gave him a "We'll be in touch" and another cold handshake, and, that fast, Henry was alone again, outside in the cool, wet air, in a strange city. It should have devastated him. He had one more night at his motel and no money to go anywhere after that, no idea where street performers did their busking or how to get there. He should have felt hopeless, but he didn't.

Without anxiety to keep it stifled, hunger ripped through him straight up his gut, a slash of pain. He realized he was shaking. Had he been shaking when he performed? If he had, it would be no wonder the manager hadn't laughed. He knew he had to eat or he would black out, so he opened his prop trunk to see if there was any spaghetti sauce to scrape up.

He pulled scarves and grease paint aside, rifled through red rubber noses and stained spandex. And this was when the miracle happened. He felt a hand on his shoulder and when he jerked around to hit whoever it was trying to push him into his prop trunk and bury him, he saw the tallest woman he'd ever seen, wearing cutoffs and holding what looked like sandwiches in white wrappers in her arms. The woman had high cheekbones and full lips, which pulled back into a smile. Her blond hair was long, freshly washed and staticky, clinging to her back, except for a few oppositely-charged strands that lifted themselves off her shoulders. She was something out of a fairy tale, queen of the giants, a post-cake Alice.

The giant pried the electrified strands of hair from her face. "Hi. You must be one of the clowns. Sorry to startle you."

He stood up straight. "I didn't know anyone else was here."

"Just got here," she said. She offered him one of the paper rolls in her arms. "Sandwich?"

"Don't you want it?" asked Henry.

"No," she told him. "I went overboard at the deli. I got these poor boys for half-price, ten of them. I can never look at another poor boy. Here, take it." She waved the sandwich at him. She must have taken great care to have beautiful hands, he thought. Her nails were long, squared, freshly enameled, looking hard as jewels. Her hands themselves, though, were large, easily big enough to palm a regulation-size basketball. She moved them daintily in spite of this, and the skin he touched as he took the sandwich from her was soft.

He unrolled the sandwich from the paper in a clumsy way and devoured it in front of her. She didn't try to make conversation with him while he ate but pulled a pack of cigarettes as thin as sucker sticks from her purse. As she stood there, watching him, smoking her cigarette and smiling, he wished he could stop eating and say something to her, something grateful or funny.

She had deep dimples in her cheeks, which for some reason looked strange on someone of her height. Her clothes were all tight, fitting her badly and wonderfully at once, and her breasts were huge, big as fat cats curled under her T-shirt, stretching the words "Southern Blue" across her chest. When he finished, she offered him a cigarette.

"No, thank you," he said.

"You want a stick of gum?" she asked.

"What kind?"

"Big Red. I only chew Big Red."

"Oh, man, that's my favorite," said Henry, holding out his hand. "It's so juicy and super cinnamony."

She unwrapped the gum before she handed it to him. He couldn't remember anyone ever doing this for him, certainly not a stranger. In fact, strangers usually held out the pack and let him get his own piece. He considered that she might be coming on to him, but while it was hard to pin her age, he felt certain she was several years older than him. It seemed more likely that she was just weird.

She said her name was Adrienne and asked what his was.

"William Henry," he said, and then added, "Harrison," and then added, "Bell."

"That's a hell of a name."

"Yeah."

"It's very nice."

Henry noticed that one of the rings on her finger was a wedding band. Cheap-looking silver, like his mother's. A poor woman's wedding band.

"Your mother is patriotic, then?" she asked, dragging from her cigarette.

"I guess. She liked the Fourth of July."

"Are your brothers and sisters named for presidents?"

"Just me. My little brother is named after Frank Zappa, but his name is just Frank, not Frank Zappa."

"I love that," she said, smiling and grinding the ember of the cigarette into the ground with the toe of her canvas shoe. She tucked her purse in her armpit. "Alright," she said, "I need to go. Hope I see you around."

"Yeah," he said, "thanks for the sandwich."

She turned and walked toward the building with the rounded roof he had just come from, her hips swaying with her enormous strides.

"Hey," he said. "It's just Henry, okay? People just call me Henry."

It was the second time that day he'd been called by the name that had only ever been used by his mother, and it didn't sit right with him.

"Yep. Got it," she said, and kept on walking.

WHEN HE FINALLY GOT BACK to his motel, he took a hot bath. The ink and spaghetti sauce on his back soaked off, turning the bath water the color of vomit.

He dried with one of the thin motel towels and searched for a space big enough for him to stretch out. There were things that needed to be worked out, toxins that were settling in his muscles and organs; toxins caused, for example, by the circus manager. Henry still couldn't believe he hadn't been impressed by the bit, even though Henry had perfected it, studied the movements of his facial muscles for weeks and then spent hours with his ass in the air and his knees tucked next to his ears as he practiced mimicking those movements with the muscles in his back. His body was wrecked from practicing it.

Then there was the toxin caused by regret and hunger. He wished he'd had the wherewithal to get that giant woman's number, and maybe ask for another one of those poor boys for the road.

In the space between the end of the twin bed and the television, he sat down on the rug, legs straight out in front of him, and folded himself in half. The carpet was rough and coated with a mixture of humidity and nicotine that had settled into the fibers. The whole motel smelled like semen and stagnant water. There was hardly any room to stretch, even though the only things Henry had cluttered the room with were his prop trunk, his own body, and a grocery bag that held a change of clothes, a toothbrush, a spoon, and the letter from Andre.

He'd gotten the letter several weeks ago, and Henry had still not answered it. He was beginning to doubt that he was even capable of writing Andre back. With every week that passed, Henry thought of a thousand more things that he could absolutely not live without telling his brother, and so the very idea of starting to write became impossible. There was just too much to say.

The last time Henry saw Andre, he was twelve. Andre was seventeen. His brother left at night with nothing but a duffel bag, and Henry had watched him go, too small to keep him from leaving, too afraid to wake their father so he could stop him. Besides, it had seemed so unreal that part of Henry figured a cop would drag Andre home before he even got out of town. His brother did not get caught, though. Henry spent the next two years thinking his brother was dead, occasionally finding himself doubled over with stomach pains in the school nurse's office. He'd thought this all the way up until he'd received the letter, in fact. But the stomach pains were the worst in the beginning, when he was first getting used to the idea of his brother not being in the world, and they didn't even begin to subside until Christiakov, his Russian clowning teacher, taught him to stretch.

Christiakov said that if Henry couldn't stop himself from being anxious (which created the toxins in the first place) he ought to at least be able to stop the physical pain that the toxins eventually caused.

And so Henry stretched in his smelly motel now and told himself he would get to his brother's letter as soon as everything wasn't so uncertain. Moving onto his hands and knees, he lifted his back leg and grabbed the ankle with his left arm, making a hoop of these appendages that strained his spine again but relieved his stiffness. He knew just when enough was enough, like a violinist knows how to tighten the strings on an instrument to produce the right note. It was all about balance.

CHAPTER 2

In June, Caleb arrived at the circus grounds on the first official day of the season. Adrienne accompanied him, as she always did, having baked about four dozen thumbprint cookies to welcome back the performers. They parked in the lot, which wasn't much more than a muddy hole at the moment, and Seamus met them at the busted sign that marked the entrance, smirking as he shook Caleb's hand.

"Well, hello," he said. "Are we ready for this?"

"Don't say 'we.' You sound like an asshole."

"Fine then." He continued to smirk, obviously not the least bit bothered by Caleb's insults. He was used to them, for one, and for another, Caleb knew Seamus didn't care if he came off like an asshole or not. "Are *you* ready for this?"

"Yes," he said, though he felt anything but ready. At least he had hired the clowns: a young woman from the West Coast, and, at Adrienne's urging, the high school dropout. There was nothing left to do on that front but pray, and since Caleb wasn't in the habit of that, there was nothing left to do but hold his breath, watch, and see if two weeks was enough time for the two newbies to figure out how to work together.

Seamus turned to Adrienne and reached up for a one-armed hug, avoiding her plate of cookies.

"How's my girl?" he asked. "Beautiful as ever."

"You're so full of crap, Seamus. Do you want a cookie?"

"No, thank you, though I imagine they're wonderful. Watching my figure."

Caleb rolled his eyes. Because of his father's investments, Seamus was now reasonably well-off and had the luxury of taking good care of himself. He looked nearly as fit as he had as a teenager when he and Caleb had lived in Dogtown and spent their every free minute playing baseball. Caleb thought if he had Seamus's money he'd have a bit less of a gut, too, but he also had Adrienne and would never have turned down her cookies, no matter how much money they made.

Seamus owed his good position in life largely to his grandfather, Alastar Feely, and the 1904 World's Fair. The neighborhood where Seamus and Caleb grew up, Dogtown, got its name from an incident that occurred during the Fair. According to that legend, Igorot tribesmen from the Filipino exhibit would sneak into the neighborhood of Dogtown and steal dogs from the residents, mostly blue-collar Irish families, the fathers of which were often absent, working long days and nights. The Igorots ate the dogs, which St. Louisans found disgusting, but the fact didn't stop them from going in hoards to the Fair's Igorot village.

While it was true that the Igorots ate dogs, and obtained them from that neighborhood, it was not the Igorots who did the actual stealing of the dogs. It was done by a very young man, Alastar, the son of a bricklayer who lived in the neighborhood. An Igorot tribesman knocked on his door one night and asked, in battered English, about the availability of dogs for hunting and eating. Alastar, who did not want to be a bricklayer like his father, explained that all the dogs around here were pets, and if the tribesmen got caught taking them from people's yards, they could be in a lot of trouble. If they wanted dogs, Alastar said, he could provide them, but not for free. They would have to pay for their meat with work. After the Fair was over, Alastar wanted the men to stay on for a few months as an attraction in a show he was assembling himself.

The tribesman agreed, perhaps because he wasn't exactly sure what he was agreeing to, and Alastar brought them dogs upon dogs—his neighbors' dogs, his cousins' dogs, dogs he knew by name, whom he untied from trees and made off with in the night. Meanwhile, he bought a realistic-looking mermaid tail for a woman in his neighborhood whose husband had died, and who was scrambling for money. He also purchased a preserved fetus from a medical school, outfitted it with shark's teeth and clay horns, and attached a modified rubber toy snake for a tail. And this was how Alastar Feely began his circus—with one sideshow of small, muscular brown men, a mermaid, and a demon baby.

By the time Alastar died, the circus had ten good freaks, two elephants, and three pretty trapeze artists. Alastar passed the circus on to his son, Conall, who partnered briefly with the Feinsteins, grew the troupe into its heyday, and passed it on to Seamus Feely. Who really didn't do much with it at all.

Caleb, Adrienne, and Seamus slid between the flaps of the circus tent, which Caleb had paid a team of ex-cons (in cash) to erect. Inside, they found the performers already at work. Lola, Remy, and Chuck, who made up the Flying Delaflote family, were on the trapeze. The Nigerian fire-eater, Azi, had a woman on each shoulder, Vroni on the left, Jenifer on the right, and each woman had a lit lantern on a chain that they spun until they were white wheels of light. Lorne, the trick-rider and animal handler, rode the horse around the ring at a trot, back arched, chin lifted, the pale blue color of his eyes made all the more otherworldly looking by the way the lighting was rigged at the moment. He kicked his commands into the horse's sides with his heels.

Lola fell from her brother's grip then, shrieking and giggling as she dropped into the net. Her fall distracted Lorne, who nearly slipped from the horse's back.

"Christ, Chuck, you have the hairiest forearms! I can't hold on because I can't stand to touch them. Shave! Please!" she moaned.

"Always has to fucking scream when she falls," Lorne said, shooting Lola a glare. The aerialists ignored him and continued arguing.

"I am *not* shaving my forearms," said Chuck. "It will itch like fucking death. I won't do it!"

Caleb had known the Delaflotes for five years. They were French-American and he never got tired of hearing them curse and insult each other in French accents.

Remy shouted from the scaffolding, "Hey, look at this guy! Nice of you to show up, Baratucci."

Seamus chuckled, stroking his chin with his gloved fingers. "What a bunch of consummate professionals."

A loud crash kept Caleb from returning either Seamus's or Remy's snarky remarks, as the lantern Jenifer was swinging hit the ground. The lamp oil spilled, creating a small ribbon of flame that snaked along the dirt floor.

"Oops!" she said, jumping from Azi's shoulder and running for the fire extinguisher.

"Way to go, butterfingers," said Vroni, who remained perched on Azi's other shoulder.

"Well, get off your ass and help me put it out!" said Jenifer.

The newly hired clowns, Henry and Kylie, had, up until now, been holding their own quiet rehearsal in the north corner of the tent, away from the hub of action. Kylie paused for a moment to watch the scene, but Henry motioned for her to continue. She seemed annoyed but went back to their practice.

Kylie, whom Caleb had offered a job shortly after hiring Henry, was a graduate of a theatre program in San Francisco that offered a clowning arts "emphasis." She was the first college graduate he'd ever hired, and her audition and portfolio had both sparkled, in Caleb's opinion. And here was this guy, who Caleb suspected was not even out of his teens, trying to boss her around.

A short woman with a helmet of white curls rushed toward his wife then. "Adrienne!" she shouted. Adrienne, who seemed a little pleased with all the chaos, was nearly knocked over by Sue, the circus's poodle trainer.

"Adriennnnne!" the rest of the performers yelled out together, unable to resist doing their best Rocky impersonation.

Adrienne thrust her plate into Caleb's hands to hug Sue, whose dogs swarmed and circled them as the two women embraced. Sue was in her early forties, only seven or eight years older than Adrienne, though the white hair made her look older. Adrienne and Sue had been especially good friends when Adrienne was still performing with the troupe as the resident giantess, taking lunches together, coming up with weird hand jives to pop music, teasing Azi by occasionally replacing his lighter fluid with glitter-spiked Kool-Aid.

Adrienne pinched one of the white curls on Sue's head. "Still wearing your hair like this? I though you wanted to be a brunette."

"Ah, people think it's funny," she said. Caleb offered her a cookie, which she took.

"You could wear a wig," said Adrienne. "It's not all about the audience."

"It *is* kinda all about them, Adrienne," said Caleb, thinking about their tight budget, his duty to make the circus stop hemorrhaging money. He hadn't told his wife about their precarious position yet because Adrienne was Adrienne, and it made her an absolute lunatic to have something to say and not be able to say it, to want to take an action and not be able to take it immediately. Playing card games with her was like being in hell—she always went out of turn, always blurted out her hand. She couldn't know about Feely and Feinstein tanking. All the performers would know within the hour, and the sinking morale would seal the circus's fate.

He felt guilty, though, keeping it from her. These were her friends. Besides, Adrienne may have had a big mouth but at least she was honest, almost 100 percent of the time, and he wished he could be honest with her in the same way.

Sue waved off the suggestion of a wig. "They give me headaches. Besides, this is me, really. It's authentic."

Again, their reunions were interrupted by noise. Someone laughing—but not a laugh that Caleb was familiar with. He turned to see Azi, bent forward, hand at his mouth. He straightened quickly when he realized he was getting looks, especially from Vroni and Jenifer, whose eyes had narrowed, cat-like and disapproving.

He let out one last muffled chuckle, and then Caleb saw the source of his entertainment. Henry was pretending to sleep standing up, while Kylie tried to keep him from slumping to the side. When she would finally get him propped up, his knee would cave beneath him, and he would topple, stiffly—but when Kylie caught him, his body went soft as a worm's, impossible for her to hold on to. It was disorienting to see a body move like that, and the only possible reaction was to smile at how weird he looked and how miserable Kylie seemed.

Adrienne linked arms with Sue and moved toward the clowns to get a better view. She'd advocated for Henry to Caleb when he was considering whether or not to bring the boy on. He'd told her that the boy was talented, but that he had a bad feeling about him, like he might also be crazy. Adrienne had given him a sidelong look. "Oh, and suddenly crazy is a problem? Is he a good clown or what?"

Of course, Adrienne was right. He *had* to hire the boy. To let him go would be negligent, and Caleb was anything but negligent. He couldn't have cared less that Henry seemed like he could use a break. If that was all Henry had to offer, Caleb would've told him to take a hike. What Caleb couldn't turn away was an excellent clown. During his audition, the boy had stabbed himself in the back with a fork for twenty minutes, splashing spaghetti sauce all over the stage and twisting his cartoon-back, never slipping out of character. It was absolutely bizarre the way he could move his back like a face, and funny, too. Caleb had needed to pinch his mouth closed with his hand to keep from laughing.

Any decent clown could play to an already excited crowd, but from Caleb's perspective, the clown's primary job was to stir the energy in a room of people who were not yet engaged with the show. Which was exactly what Henry had done at his audition and what he was doing at the moment, drawing all the energy in the circus tent to him and Kylie.

When they finished running through the skit, Henry held up a hand to acknowledge Caleb. He noticed Adrienne, too (because who couldn't notice her), but he turned away quickly and ran to guzzle water from a hose that someone had stolen from the animals' quarters and hauled into the tent.

"Good job, Caleb," said Adrienne quietly, before liberating herself from Sue's side and stepping forward to extend her hand to Kylie.

"Oh, I'm . . . I'm really sweaty," said Kylie.

"That's okay," said Adrienne, and Kylie reluctantly shook her hand.

"Hey. I'm Kylie," she said, the red flush beneath her freckles deepening.

"Adrienne."

"I've heard about you," she said.

Caleb smiled. Adrienne no longer performed, but she was still Feely and Feinstein's queen.

Adrienne told Kylie that she looked forward to seeing their show, then went to greet Henry, who had his back to them all, overly focused on the hose. She laid her hand on his shoulder and bent forward to say something that Caleb couldn't hear. Even though he didn't quite catch Adrienne's words, he assumed she'd complimented him because he saw the boy's mouth form a "thank you" before he looked away from her. Though he hadn't known Henry very long, Caleb recognized that the boy was being uncharacteristically humble and evasive and he felt a jolt of jealousy.

But the feeling subsided quickly, and he felt so ridiculous for entertaining such an idea that he laughed out loud to himself.

"Are you finally losing your mind, Caleb?" said Seamus, landing a light jab in Caleb's shoulder.

"I think so."

"What are you giggling about?"

"The clowns, I guess."

"Yes, I think they'll do great. I'm going to talk to that boy, see what kind of act he wants to do. Could give them quite a bit of ring time if he's got a good plan," Seamus mused.

Caleb thought it was unfair to ignore Kylie, who was also pretty clever in their skit, but he nodded and said nothing about it, knowing that Seamus had already made up his mind. Henry did seem to be the one directing the action. Besides, he didn't want to argue with Seamus. He was sold on the clowns, and Caleb was too satisfied by that to split hairs over who did the selling.

AFTER ADRIENNE HAD FINISHED PASSING out cookies and Caleb made a game plan for the year with Seamus and the rest of the performers, he and Adrienne called it a day. In the closed space of their car, Caleb could smell

Adrienne's magnolia bath powder. It wasn't an unpleasant scent, but it made him slow down. Caleb couldn't quite explain how, but the flower smell meant trouble, maybe because she used it as a kind of aromatherapy for when she felt down.

"Adie, is there something on your mind?" he asked.

"Hm," she said, as if she was trying to recall. "I haven't felt so well, lately, I guess."

"Like . . . physically?"

He hoped, he really hoped that she hadn't convinced herself again that she was pregnant. It was too sad for him to see her fantasize about the realities of her biology taking a vacation. He knew when they got married they would not have children, and he was entirely at peace with it. She, on the other hand, seemed deeply grieved by this fact, and he had tried to fabricate some comfort for her. "The universe will work something out for us," he'd told her once, but she'd taken it as a prophecy. Saying it had made him feel guilty, made him feel he encouraged these fantasies that always ended up hurting her.

"Yes. I feel weird, I guess, physically. But also . . . Nancy called and told me that Curtis is coming to town. And that he asked for my address."

"She didn't give it to him, did she?"

"She said she didn't."

Curtis was Adrienne's ex-husband, and while Caleb tried not to vilify a man he'd never even met, the things Adrienne told him about the guy made him seem like scum, like absolute shit, shaped to resemble a human being. Which was probably how everybody's wives' ex-husbands came off, but Adrienne never actually bad-mouthed Curtis. Still, he came off like a creep in subtext.

At the red light, Caleb stroked the soft white hairs on Adrienne's forearm. "He doesn't know where we live, he doesn't know where you work, he doesn't know anything about us."

"I know. It's all in my head, but I don't like the idea of him here," she said.

"You're right. It's in your head. There's no reason not to feel safe. You got me, all right?"

She sighed dramatically, and her unintentional insult made him chuckle.

"I see. You're saying that I'm not a mighty protector?"

"It's not that."

"I see how things are," he said.

"No, you're totally a mighty protector. I feel very safe," she assured him. It was funny to hear from her, given that she was almost seven-and-a-half feet tall, riding in the car completely folded over so her face hovered an inch above the dashboard. She realized this, too, and smiled back at him, which was what he'd hoped for.

Caleb happened to know that for protection, in addition to his mighty self, Adrienne had a sleek little handgun in a hatbox on a shelf in her closet. It was the one thing she was not honest about, the one thing she kept hidden. Caleb had found it and, perhaps having to prove to himself it was real, he'd taken it to the range one day while she was at aerobics. But he never let on that he knew about it. In her heart, she was a pacifist, and he knew she wanted him to think of her in these terms, as a woman who believed that birds and trees and car keys had souls, and everything was precious and that there was never a need for any sort of destruction. The notion that she counted an expensive killing tool as part of her personal property did not fit into the image.

And this was just as well, because Caleb preferred not to think of this part of his wife, either, the part that was anxious—and armed.

CHAPTER 3

BEFORE OPENING NIGHT BEGAN, HENRY sat in his trailer at something like a dressing table (it was really a metal shelf, where someone might keep their tools in a garage). He rubbed a thin layer of white grease paint over his skin and dabbed a flesh-colored shadow beneath his cheekbones. He lined his eyes with black and pinched his nose into a rubber bulb that was as shiny and red as a maraschino cherry.

He'd been sleeping in that trailer for the past three weeks, and he planned to keep sleeping there until the circus headed out of town. Of course, he'd expected to sleep in a trailer, but he had thought that the trailer would be air-conditioned and connected to some kind of water supply. Right now, his trailer was neither of those things, because no one lived in the trailers until they started moving. The other performers lived in St. Louis during the winter and had apartments, and so there was no reason to spend the money making the trailers habitable when they were still performing shows locally. Henry had not yet gotten a paycheck and had no money for an apartment. It would have been no problem, if it wasn't so unseasonably hot.

It was almost time to go on, and so he stretched, but Caleb interrupted him before he got very far.

"Here's a revised order for the acts tonight," he said, trying to catch his breath. He looked for a place to put a blue scrap of paper, dropping it eventually on Henry's dressing table among dirty tubes of makeup, a magnifying mirror, and a handful of toys that came from several years' worth of Happy Meals.

"Thanks," said Henry, not looking up from his stretch.

"On a scale of one to a thousand, how much does that position hurt your nuts?"

"Five," said Henry. "Until you distract me, and then it's more like thirteen."

"I just spent an hour photocopying this set list, and another hour running around giving it to people in this weird heat, and you've got something snarky to say to me because you're in the middle of your special breathing exercises or whatever?"

When Henry didn't respond, Caleb lingered in the doorway, scratching his beard and jingling the change in his pocket.

"Sorry, I don't mean to be rude," said Henry, thinking he might be waiting on an apology. "It's just, I gotta go sit on my neck in a minute and I don't want to go on cold."

"No, no, you've got a right to be annoyed. Seamus is the one who changed the order at the last minute, though, not me."

He was halfway out the door, but then popped his head back in. "My wife says to break a leg, but she couldn't make it tonight. She isn't feeling well."

Henry raised his head. At the rehearsal, she'd encouraged him. He could smell the cinnamon from the gum in her mouth when she'd said his comic timing was impressive. "I love how patient you are," she'd said. "I can't wait to see your debut." The giantess wanted him to succeed. He'd looked forward to having one person in the audience rooting for him and not secretly hoping for him to make a mistake. Now she sent her apologies through Caleb.

"Oh. That's too bad," said Henry. He tried to hide his real disappointment behind polite disappointment. "Is she okay?"

"Oh, y'know. Women have these mysterious headaches when they'd rather not be somewhere. She'll recover."

THE SHOW STARTED WITH THE Flying Delaflotes. Caleb watched as Lola entered the ring first in silver underwear and a space helmet. The speakers quaked with *Also sprach Zarathustra* as she ascended the scaffolding. It was Seamus's policy that the show should always start with the most beautiful girl and the most dramatic music possible. Lola was beautiful, with her honey-colored curls and her aerialist's body, but she seemed to have a hard time getting up the ladder with the helmet on. She had to lean her head back to keep it from clanking against the ladder, and even so the helmet hit the metal ladder twice, making a sound as loud and open as a brass bell. Caleb squirmed in his seat as the people around him fanned themselves with programs and looked at each other for a clue as to how to react.

Lola's brothers, Remy and Chuck, followed her to the top of the scaffolding in their own silver leotards and space helmets. As the trumpets swelled, all three removed their helmets with a flourish because, thank God, it would be impossible to do an aerial act with them on. Those were Seamus's idea, too, or the Delaflotes, who waved now with rigid arms and forced smiles, would never have agreed to it.

But when Lola finally took her trapeze and flew, she did look like something stellar, a white-and-silver flash against the dark of the tent. Between the hands of one brother and the hands of the other, she seemed free from the normal rules of physics. When her body went up, it stayed up for an impossibly long time; while she tumbled, she was a swirling galaxy, a child's sparkler cutting runes into the darkness.

Later, the clowns would do their transitional improv, Caleb's favorite circus tradition. The kids wouldn't miss a beat, climbing that scaffolding in their own space helmets, clank-clanking all the way to the top.

Caleb felt it so keenly, the whiplash, the breathlessness of being jerked between the beautiful and the absurd. He shared this only with Adrienne, but in these moments, watching these performances, he felt a sense of relief that he had not become a museum curator. No gallery could generate this kind of dynamism, nothing still and contained in such a space could move him as this did.

BEFORE HE LEFT HIS TRAILER, Henry closed his eyes. He kept his hands on the grain of the wood paneling until he found the door, groped for the handle, and opened it. This was a game he played as a kid, the blindness game, where he pretended that he had suddenly lost his vision and tested himself to see if he could enjoy the world without it. Now he did it because he was nervous and couldn't bring himself to meet the eyes of strangers—not yet, not until he was performing, safely in the skin of his character.

He stepped out of the trailer, eyes still closed. The night air was cool. The smell of fried dough, the sound of drunken voices, and the giggles of children led him toward the tent.

He heard a man say, "What's with the clown? Is he high or something?" Popcorn crunched beneath his feet, and he ran his hand along the side of the tent until he felt the opening. A large hand pulled him inside.

"What is wrong with you?" asked the owner of the hand.

Henry smiled, though his legs were still shaking. Even with his eyes closed, he knew the hand belonged to Azi; only one person in the troupe had hands so massive. Azi also had the biggest muscles Henry had ever seen, though his high cheekbones and thin, arching eyebrows made him look strangely delicate from the neck up. He drew the eyebrows on; as a fire-eater he had burnt his real eyebrows off repeatedly, and they now refused to grow back.

Henry could feel the fire-eater's face in his, now, examining his closed eyelids. The animal handler and trick-rider, Lorne, was there, too. Henry could hear the soft sighs of the circus's one and only elephant, Tex, and Tex didn't leave her pen without Lorne by her side.

"I don't want to see. Put me onstage, Azi," he said.

"What? You can't go on with your eyes closed," said Azi, clutching Henry around the shoulders, holding him in place as if he might run out and embarrass the circus.

"I'll open them, I promise. The first step I take out, I'll open them. Just point me in the right direction," he said.

"Just put him out, Azi. Clowns're supposed to fall on their faces," said Lorne.

Henry had to laugh because this was Lorne trying to be helpful. There wasn't a hint of irony in his voice. To him, a clown's job was simply falling on its face.

Azi made an irritated grunting noise and shoved him forward. As soon as Henry felt the fabric of curtains brush over his arms, he opened his eyes. His limbs stiffened into the limbs of a tired farmer as he walked into the ring.

He still couldn't see the audience. The lights illuminated the ring, but the bleachers and the people in them appeared only as a vaguely shifting darkness. It was so different than performing on public streets, where he could watch his audience's every raised eyebrow, every slight nod. He didn't like to see anyone before performing but to not see an audience *while* performing— this seemed impossible. How was he supposed to read them?

Across the stage was Kylie, wearing the costume he had designed for her, a patchy circular skirt over bare legs, her tan skin made up to look dirty with gray smudges of makeup. She was still behind the "shanty" prop but already puckering her face in preparation for her role. She looked pretty, in spite of the goofy costume, with thick brown hair in a high ponytail and a spatter of freckles on the crest of her cheeks. He could see her waiting for her cue, taking measured breaths, activating her confidence.

Henry made his way to the middle of the set, looking dog-tired, and sewed imaginary seeds in dirt that covered a raised platform. Beneath the dirt there was a thin mesh that could be punctured when the stagehands sent up the carrot sprouts.

As Henry planted his seeds, he listened to the audience. They were so quiet. Someone opened a package of candy, and it sounded like someone tearing open the side of the tent. They remained silent as Henry made a show of wiping his brow, miming the ache in his joint.

Henry heard popcorn between teeth. He was waiting for just the right moment to cue Kylie onto the stage, the moment just before their anticipation turned into fury or fear. That was the secret to comic timing. A piece of candy hit the floor, a man coughed. A sigh floated up from the middle of the room. *Yes*, he decided, *those are sounds of frustration.* He put his hand next to his mouth and mimed a shout at the shanty prop. Kylie came into the ring with a heavy step, a surly sneer.

Under her makeup, her face glowed with fervor. She plopped her empty plate proudly on the table and got the first quiet ripple of laughter out of the audience. Good for her. One half a laugh was all he needed. Just one snowflake to start an avalanche.

She patted his cheek: *Eat, old man, eat.* The touch, so often rehearsed, felt sharper tonight, more smack than tap.

They had worked on this skit for the last month, and during that time, Kylie had experimented with how much to touch him during their act and in what ways. At a certain point, Henry had gotten to thinking she was not experimenting with her role so much as experimenting with the touch itself. When the scene was over, he would find her still holding on to his wrist. But then, when he would tell her to hold this or that pose a bit longer, or even tell her that she had done something well, she would get angry. She'd say, "Sorry, I was taught *never* to be inert for so long," or "Thanks, I'm glad I've met your standards." She never stayed after rehearsal but left in a rush, as if there was somewhere more important that she needed to be.

Where's the food? Henry mimed.

By the time he was upside down against the hay bale, the audience was guffawing, sputtering out trumpet laughs and whacking their knees. Henry thought, then, his back twisted under the warm lights, staring out into an undulating darkness of bodies, that he was very comfortable. It felt like when he was little and had stretched out on his bedroom carpet, projecting himself into the worlds between his fingers. It was exactly as yellow-bright and soft now as it had been in that imagined world, the laughter full and musical, but muted, as if the whole tent was lined with pillows.

AFTER THE PERFORMANCE, HENRY WAS flanked by Caleb and Seamus Feely. In his excitement, Seamus was more red-faced than the first time Henry met him, but he wore the same polo shirt and Dockers, an unnecessary sweater draped over his shoulders. He whacked Henry's sore back, pulling him into his side for a one-armed hug. Henry stood stiff, trying not to cringe.

He kept saying, "This kid! This kid knows his audience. Don't he, Caleb?"

Not far from the trailer, the audience departed, energized and noisy, the children chasing each other, sword-fighting with the white paperboard cones they'd eaten cotton candy from. Azi sold slap bracelets, and the children all whacked them onto their wrists with a pop, wincing as they admired their new jewelry. Azi had told Henry he expected to make more selling slap bracelets than he made performing and suggested that Henry also find something to hock post-show.

Caleb smiled at the unwanted hug Seamus imposed on Henry now. "Yeah, he knows his audience." Caleb was still wearing the suit he'd worn earlier and shiny patent leather shoes. It occurred to Henry that these clothes, the suit, the Dockers and polo, were Seamus's and Caleb's costumes, and that this hugging and encouraging and so forth was also a show.

"Good job, Caleb. You can find 'em, you can sure pick 'em. This kid! Wow. What a great operation we've got here," said Seamus.

The last time Henry had seen Seamus was when Henry proposed the farmer skit. Seamus asked Henry to "give him the trailer," and Henry had fumbled through a description the best he could. When he finished, Seamus nodded and said, "That's perfect. Something cute for the kids." He'd seemed more excited about the fact that the skit was written and finished than the skit itself. And now here he was, tucking Henry into his armpit, like this was their mutual project, the fruits of some long, fraternal collaboration.

When Henry didn't smile or say "golly, thanks," Seamus tried a different tactic. He spun Henry to face him, holding him by his arms. He was still smiling, but there was no kindness around his eyes. "You keep that coming."

Henry wanted to knee him in the testicles. He didn't like being told what to do, and he definitely did not like being touched, especially not by a guy like Seamus, who pretended to be friends with people while using them like tools. But then he thought of the warm lights, the singular way laughter sounded in that tent. "Yessir," said Henry, and Seamus nodded.

Caleb waited until Seamus was gone to roll his eyes. "Good job," he said. "You made the boss happy."

"Thank you," said Henry.

They watched as two boys went by, the older one walking behind the younger and smirking as he tossed pieces of popcorn at his head. He made swooshing noises. "Fireball! Fireball!" he said. The younger boy cradled a Teenage Mutant Ninja Turtles action figure near his chest and said evenly, "Quit it. Quit it. Mom, tell him to quit it. Quit it, Sam."

"They liked it, too," said Caleb, nodding in the direction of the boys. "So. It's all downhill from here, I'd say. Right?"

"Tell Adrienne I hope she feels better."

Caleb paused for a moment, then nodded. "Yeah, yeah, sure thing."

HENRY FELT EXHAUSTED. ALL HE wanted to do was curl up on the thin cot in the trailer that he'd dressed in. He needed to clean up, though, and brush his teeth, which meant he had to go to the animals' quarters and get some water.

The animals' quarters were in a small, stuffy barn that smelled like piss and hay and, faintly, of Lorne's Old Spice deodorant. The camels and the white horse were already in their pens eating dinner when Henry got there to draw his water. The camels, Izzy and Ichabod, chewed their hay, ignoring Henry. Those two were friendly enough, more interested in food than anything else in the world, which Henry found understandable. When the white horse saw him, though, she stopped eating and watched him with what seemed like curiosity, and a little suspicion, as he balanced the hose over the side of his bucket to fill it.

"Hey, horse," he said. He called her this, though he'd learned her name was Ambrosia. When Henry asked Lorne what the hell kind of name Ambrosia was, he'd replied, "It means some kind of treasure. Or something. And she's my treasure. She's a special animal." Henry was pretty sure he was wrong, so he'd looked up the word later, and found out that ambrosia was food for gods—treasure of the edible sort.

As Henry filled his bucket, Ambrosia released a puff of air through her nose that sounded a little like indignation.

"What?" asked Henry. "You want some?"

He walked toward her pen, and she took a step back. When he peered over the gate, sure enough, her drinking trough had not been filled yet. He slung the hose over the edge, spattering her with water. The trough began filling, the water landing with a loud, bright *smack*.

Henry heard Lorne's growl from just outside the barn.

"C'mon, now. C'mon. Time for rest. Don't you wanna rest?" he said. Henry heard a noise like the muffled tick of a clock and Tex's heavy footfalls carrying her into the barn.

Lorne was pink and sweating. He was still dressed for riding: white suit, sequined vest. One of his hands pressed against Tex's hind flank, and the other held a long wooden pole that ended in a silver hook.

Lorne startled when he saw Henry, even though Lorne had seen him here nearly every night for three weeks, getting his bucket of water. When he realized Henry was giving Ambrosia a drink, he muttered a breathless "thanks" that sounded more annoyed than grateful, but he had his hands full just trying to get Tex to take a step.

"She never wants to get in her own pen at night," Lorne explained. "She wants to get in Ambrosia's stall with her." He pushed Tex, then waved peanuts in front of her, which she snatched from his palm with her trunk without taking so much as a step.

"You can't sleep together. You're side by side, it's close enough," he huffed, pushing her again. When she still would not move, he swung the hook into her flank. She finally took a couple of steps, looking back at Lorne over her great shoulder. The hook was the thing that made the ticking sound, the sound of it being stuck in her flesh and then plucked out. Henry looked down, focused on the water pouring down into Ambrosia's trough, wishing he could close his ears.

He thought Tex was perfectly reasonable for not wanting to sleep alone.

Back in his trailer, Henry locked the door behind him, shut out most of the lights, and closed the blinds. Noises bubbled in from the grounds outside as he scrubbed his body with cold water from the bucket and changed into a T-shirt and a pair of thin boxer shorts. He washed the makeup from his face with Noxzema and brushed his teeth. The drawer by the sink where he kept his toothbrush and Noxzema was also where he kept his brother's letter. The surface around the sink was littered with makeup and toys and wadded-up tissues, just like his dressing table, but the drawer was empty, except for the letter. He pulled the envelope out now and set it on top of a compact of red face paint and a set of false rainbow eyelashes. As he brushed his teeth he rested his fingers on the letter. This was his habit, his nightly routine. It felt too sentimental to read it over and over, but just to rest his fingers on it as he went about his business, that seemed alright. The paper envelope was starting to thin from the humidity and his touch. He tried not to smudge the return address, which he needed to be able to read when he wrote his brother back. Which he had every intention of doing.

When he finished, he tucked the letter and his toothbrush back into the drawer and prepared for his evening stretch. As soon as he was situated on the floor, he heard a light tapping at the trailer door. *Probably kids*, he thought. *Probably think they've found a little pocket of mystery, the home of a gypsy who would read their palms, or a set of Siamese twins.*

Henry released his breath, reached his fingers up into the air. The muscles in his neck were all clenched around his vertebrae. The euphoria of performance was wearing off, and it was painful to sit up straight. Sometimes this pain lasted a long time and sometimes it went away quickly.

The tapping came again. Henry got up and moved to the door on the soft balls of his feet, making no sound. "Who is it?"

"It's just me. Open the door," said a woman's voice.

"Adrienne?" he whispered. Maybe she'd started feeling better. Maybe she'd come after all, and seen his performance, and wanted to congratulate him.

"No, it's Kylie."

Henry unlocked the door. Kylie stood there wearing a sundress, holding a bottle of Jack Daniel's by its neck. He should have known it wasn't Adrienne. Kylie's voice matched the rest of her, pinched and girly and small, all the things that Adrienne and her voice were not.

"I came to celebrate," she said.

Henry didn't say anything.

"Well? Can I come in or what?"

"Sure," he said and moved out of the way so that she could get through. "Adrienne? You mean big Adrienne?" she asked, looking for a place to put the whiskey. Since there really was no place, she set it on the floor, and then sat down next to it. "Can we turn on the lights? Wait, were you going to *bed*? We just did a kick-ass show, and you're going straight to bed?"

"I don't have any money to party." He shrugged.

"But it's the start of the season," she said, as if that fact made his empty pockets irrelevant. "Everyone is going out. Jenifer and Vroni. Those high-wire guys. Azi. The Delaflotes. Poodle-lady. Even the crazy trick-rider. They're all going."

"I don't really know all those guys very well yet. They might not want me to come out with them."

She smiled, then, and it began to make sense, the sundress and the booze, and her hand on her hip—the girl-clown was flirting with him.

"I don't know them that well, either," she said. "Obviously. Since I just referred to what's-her-name as 'poodle-lady.' And then just now as 'what's-her-name.'"

Henry sat down next to her. "Are you going?" He liked that sundress on her. It was the first time he'd seen her wearing regular clothes, not a costume or a sawdust-covered unitard. Her legs and arms had little green bruises on them from falling during the show. One or two bruises were unavoidable, but she was covered in them. She didn't know how to fall right, a fact that annoyed Henry, especially since she wouldn't take his instruction on how to do it correctly.

"I think we should hang together," she said. "Since we had so much success as a team." Her lashes lowered, the corners of her mouth curled up shyly, and he thought she seemed like a caricature of herself, an innocent girl acting like a porn star acting like an innocent girl. Actors never stopped acting, not really. Even sincerity looked contrived when an actor wore it.

Her insincerity annoyed him, too. But the freckles were charming and it had been too long since he kissed a girl, and he found himself leaning forward. Her lips were warm, and she smelled of the outdoors, but not of post-performance sweat, sawdust, or the animal musk that permeated the grounds. She'd cleaned up, too, somehow.

"You've already brushed your teeth," she said, as if this tickled her.

"Lucky you," he said.

"You're like a little old man."

"I'm a creature of habit."

Henry knew bodies—he'd studied them carefully, his own and others. He studied the ways they could move, and the things they could say without words. He knew Kylie's body was saying "go," so he went, even though it was almost certainly a bad idea. To shut up the inner voice that told him to stop, he moved faster than he normally would. He pulled her to her feet while he kissed her and pushed her into the wall of the trailer.

Her legs encircled his waist, and she was still acting. He supposed she was used to making this face or that and just getting what she wanted. She had crossed the country in her grandfather's Mercedes, or so Henry had heard, and he believed it because he had seen the Mercedes, shiny and as unreal-seeming as a sleeping unicorn in the Feely and Feinstein lot. Her grandfather gave it to her as a gift because it was old and he had plenty of other expensive new cars, and probably just because she had made some face that had undone him. Things came easily to Kylie, and she probably thought that Henry would be another one of those things, a naïve boy who would stop giving her hell at rehearsal and share his spotlight in exchange for a more private kind of attention.

He fumbled at the buttons on her sundress, determined to see her act falter, make her snort or cry out or say something she didn't want him to hear her say. Make her stop acting. If he could do that, then he could let go of the thoughts that were making him so lonely. Even though he felt at home under the lights of the circus tent, Adrienne had not come. His brothers were not here and likely never would be. The disgust he felt at Seamus's praise and the hook in Tex's hide served to remind him of what an outsider he was here.

But if he could see what this girl was about—maybe that would drown out everything else.

He caught the hem of Kylie's dress in his fingers and slid it up her thighs.

The more skin he touched, the more he knew that beneath her fake attraction was real attraction. He could feel it in the muscles that she was not controlling as consciously as the ones in her face, the ones he felt in her lower back and in the legs that tightened around him. She dug her heels and chin into him. This was where he had her. She couldn't make her body tell lies, but Henry could make his body do whatever he wanted. This girl was green as grass.

She pulled the dress over her head herself, and he carried her to his cot. Holding her up was killing his back. She smiled up at him as she landed on the cot and undid her ponytail.

"You're strong," she said.

Henry said nothing but peeled away her underwear, little things, striped like a piece of Christmas candy. Carefully chosen. Beneath them, he found a star, the center of this green girl, a tattoo in blue. It meant something to her. And so he stopped and traced it with his finger like he was considering it, like he wanted to know what secret it represented, though he didn't especially care. That little movement took only a few seconds, but it sucked the actress right out of her. When he looked back up at her, she was transformed. Her face was made unpretty with panic and lust. He pressed his chest to hers and felt her heart thundering.

It didn't feel wrong to have drawn out that real Kylie at first. It was good to be held so close, to feel so needed. But when he pulled back and saw her limbs spread out, naked and delicate as the violet petals that he and his brothers used to crush and rub into their skin when they wanted war paint, he felt disgusted. Wasn't it unfair of him to demand something unrehearsed from her, when he had no intention of giving her the same? He searched for sexy images in his brain to replace the one of the soft nude thing in front of him. Girls in G-strings holding their tits like dessert cups in front of them. Girls in roller skates. Cindy Crawford. Sharon Stone. Adrienne. Yes,

Adrienne, the giantess. He could never push a woman that big into a wall, couldn't take a single thing from her that she didn't want to give. A woman like Adrienne would envelop him. She was the seventh-largest woman in the world, he'd heard, which meant any lie he could tell with his body would be irrelevant. They would both know who was holding the cards, and that would make things simple, gentle, direct.

Nothing like this.

When his body finally forced him to let go, he kept his face turned away from Kylie, because the soft, glazed look of anybody in that state was the most vulnerable of expressions. He gulped, though, trying to catch his breath, and the noise gave him away. She pulled his face back to her and kissed him, and for the brief duration of that kiss, it was as if they were just two people who liked each other, and neither one was taking advantage of the other.

They redressed without speaking.

Henry filled a jar with water from the sink and turned his back to Kylie while he drank. He was the first to say anything, asking her if she wanted some water.

"No, thanks," she said.

"But you've sweated all your water out," he said.

She shrugged and tugged a loose barrette out of her hair. "I was thinking we might have a little of that whiskey. Cap off the party, you know?"

"I don't drink," said Henry.

"Not even a little bit?"

"No."

"Really? Why not?"

Henry refilled his jar. "Because I'm an athlete."

Kylie rolled her eyes and peeled the plastic from around the top of the bottle. "Oh, well. Excuse me then. By all means, you must stay pure."

"You shouldn't drink, either. You have to be in good condition to do this shit or you'll ruin my show," he said. This girl had been to a real school, and they hadn't taught her how to take care of herself. Didn't teach her to drink water, didn't teach her to fall.

She opened her mouth, and Henry thought she was going to tell him to go and die, but she didn't. She unscrewed the lid and took a drink straight from the bottle. Because Henry read bodies, he saw, in the way she raised the bottle to her lips, in the way she swallowed hard and shuddered at the burn of it, that she was biting back regret, and he was surprised by how much this stung. *I'm a dick*, he thought. *I'm Seamus.*

He walked around to where she sat, and she took another swallow of whiskey.

"Let's be friends," she said. She was back to playing at being sexy and cavalier, but it wasn't irritating to him anymore. He wanted to say something nice but he couldn't, so he offered her his empty jar, thinking, *for Chrissakes, at least keep track of how much you're poisoning yourself right now.*

"It isn't just your show, you know," she said, pouring herself the drink.

"Nope. You're right. It's Seamus's show," he said.

"Right. Seamus's show. I saw him congratulating you tonight. Tousling your hair, 'oh, way to go, slugger! That's m'boy.'"

Henry kept his mouth shut, embarrassed.

"He didn't congratulate me. He didn't even look at me," she said. "This clown business is a goddamn boys' club. Actually, the whole circus is."

There was nothing to say to that, either. It hadn't occurred to him before, but yes, when he thought of girl clowns, he thought of children's parties, not big tops, not spotlights.

"How am I supposed to get to Ringling Brothers' if I can't even get Seamus's attention here?"

"Why would you want to work for Ringling Brothers'?" he asked.

"Don't tell me you don't."

"I don't. They're just a big Feely and Feinstein. Nothing innovative. I'd be background noise to the elephants. You'd be invisible."

Kylie considered this, swiping the tip of her finger over the rim of her glass. "I got the first laugh," she said.

"You were supposed to get the first laugh. That's what I meant to happen."

"Still," she said.

And Henry was sorry for her, which still felt to him a bit like love. "Yeah. Okay. You got the first laugh."

The Farmer Show (A Pantomime)

This farmer (who I will play) has just planted a row of carrots. You see the carrots, their green parts make a leafy line in the center of the ring. He dusts off his hands and dabs the sweat from his face with a big red hanky and calls his wife to bring him dinner.

The farmer is so tired. He's so hungry.

The wife comes out now. She looks dirty and nuts with her hair all in little knots around her head, so you think the life of a farmer's wife isn't so easy. She slaves away and watches all their little kids, who aren't in the show, but who you figure are probably running around outside or something. Offstage, that is. The wife brings him an empty plate.

The farmer gets mad. He does all this work, all day, and for nothing. His wife keeps gesturing, it's there, it's there on the plate! *But he thinks,* why would she do this to me? Does she hate me? She must hate me.

Of course, it's his fault that there's no food to eat. She cooks what there is. The farmer knows that, and he knows it's his fault, in his heart.

And none of this is said either. It's got to come through in their gestures, in the way they move around each other.

The wife stands her ground. She puts her hands on her hips to say: There is food on that plate, and you will eat it.

The farmer holds his hands up: Do you expect me to eat with my hands?

The wife dashes offstage and brings back a magnifying glass and some twee-zers.

The farmer starts to fume. The wife goes right on eating her teeny tiny food happily with her own tweezers and magnifying glass.

The farmer throws his magnifying glass at his wife, who ducks and throws her magnifying glass back at him. He arches his back like he's doing the limbo to dodge. It goes on like this, like a dance, objects flying everywhere, until the wife finally cuffs him in the chin. She knocks the farmer against a bale of hay, upended with his legs splayed apart in the air. She scolds him by shaking her index finger at him and stomps away.

Then, the farmer cries. But his stomach keeps rumbling, which causes him to startle every time he hears it. This is what I've been practicing the most for this act, changing my face fast from sad to surprised, so watching me is like watching sped-up film, a little Benny Hill homage. The audience won't know what to feel for the farmer; should they pity him or laugh at him? My bet is they choose to laugh, that they might even laugh harder to drown out that urge to feel sorry for him.

In the end, the farmer finds out he has a magical ability to make the carrots grow. He spends the rest of the skit trying to convince his wife of his new powers— whenever she comes onstage, he can't make the carrots grow. It's like the carrots hear the farmer call her and they stop growing because they don't want her to know his power. But she's clever and she's not going to let some carrot outsmart her. She sneaks out and "catches" the green sprout of a carrot top growing. The two of them then pull an enormous carrot from the ground, and the act ends with the farmer's wife hefting the tip of the carrot upward so that her husband can take a bite.

CHAPTER 4

Edgefield, Indiana
April 1978

HENRY HAS A CLEAN ROOM of his own with thick, bright-yellow carpeting. He stretches out on his bedroom floor sometimes and spreads the fibers apart with his fingers. The space between the pieces of yarn in his carpet becomes huge, big enough for him to fit into, big enough for him to live in, its own sunny otherworld.

Cassie is his neighbor, and on Saturdays she drags him past where the yard ends, into a wild acre that no one calls "yard," and so no one mows. Cats live there, and snakes, and spiders, and stubby gnarled trees that are all tangled into one another.

Cassie is in second grade with him, and she's the only girl who's really a bad kid, a girl who picks fights with boys and has a horror movie laugh, a high-pitched, ragged giggle. The only sound he's ever heard that was uglier was a bag of rusty nails being dumped into a bathtub. The girls are afraid of her. The boys are afraid of her, too, so they make up reasons to avoid her that are not fear—they say she's dirty, that she has head lice, and a type of fungus that comes from not washing properly on the back of her neck. It's true, her clothes *are* dirty, and her hair hangs in dull clumps, like she may not have gotten all the soap out of it. But that isn't why they avoid her.

In the field, Cassie holds Henry by both arms and stares him straight in the face. They hear the faint whistle and chug-a-lug of a train in the distance, probably from Chicago, probably carrying steel and covered in painted-on words that Henry struggles to read when the train goes by. She holds him firmly, her small fingers squeezing so hard that his skin pinches between them. He tries to twist out of her grip—the only time anyone holds him like this, it's because they intend to give him something other than a kiss, something like a talking-to through clenched teeth or a head-butt.

But Cassie is stronger than him. She mashes her lips into his and opens her mouth, which forces his open as well. She tastes like metal and sesame seeds. Her tongue is all over, slapping against the backs of his teeth and the roof of his mouth. It's like he's taken something from her, hidden it in his mouth, and her tongue is on a mission to take it back.

His teeth close around her tongue. It isn't that he doesn't like the kiss, and it isn't even that she's hurting him, squeezing his arm. He bites her because he thinks it might be funny. He can't laugh, because his jaw is otherwise engaged with the biting, but he will be able to save the moment and tell it later to Andre, who will definitely laugh at the meanness and the justness of the bite.

Cassie shrieks and tries to pull away, but his teeth are still clamped down on her tongue. Her scream rushes directly into his mouth, down his throat, and rattles inside his lungs. All her sounds are rusty nails scraping the bottoms of things. He unclenches his jaw, right as she pulls back her fist. She busts him in the cheek, and he trips backward. A branch scrapes his back as he falls into a bed of wet, dead leaves on the ground.

"You bit me!" she says. Her voice is shrill. She spits pink saliva onto the ground and moves toward him. He hurries to get to his feet.

"Why don't you shut up before we get in trouble?" says Henry. She begins backing away from him, positioning herself to claim innocence if anyone comes. If they did, it would be curtains for the two of them. Kissing was probably like cussing, an offense of the mouth, so their mothers would wash their tongues and teeth with soap. Which would be better than being ratted out to their fathers, especially Cassie's father, because better the devil you know than the devil you don't.

Cassie must be thinking the same thing because her mouth quivers from the strain of holding in another screech. She has blood in the crevices between her baby teeth. "Why did you do that?" she says. Fear of punishment turns her into something delicate. Her green eyes become glassy with tears, and he is sorry for her, which feels a little like love.

He hears the gravel crunching in his driveway and looks toward the house, expecting to see his father's truck. Instead there is an unfamiliar van creeping up to the house, shiny and clean all over, a lacquered cotton-candy blue. Its lights are on, even though it's daytime. A man gets out wearing a tan leisure suit. He's wearing sunglasses and has a thick brown beard and moustache.

"Who's that?" asks Cassie.

"Don't know," he says.

The man has a cigarette, which he holds between his lips while he takes a small briefcase from the passenger side of the van. Henry can't see his face. The man shuts the door to the van and walks toward the front of Henry's house. Henry hears the screen door swing open and for a second he feels afraid for his mother, for Andre and baby Frankie. But Andre is up the road at his friend Will Miller's house for the afternoon, and anyway, his mother would never open the door for someone she didn't know or wasn't expecting.

"Let's spy," he says. "Let's go get a look in his van."

"Why?" Cassie asks.

"Because I want to. I played what you wanted to play." Henry grabs her by the arm and starts walking toward the van. "After this it'll be your turn to pick again. Okay?"

They tiptoe across the gravel as if there were any way to keep it from making noise. In the van, he sees mostly junk, but not normal-person junk like soda cans or old shopping bags. It's strange junk, carefully arranged. Most of the van is filled with boxes covered in floral paper and stacked five or six high. There are different sizes of these boxes, but they are all covered in the same flower print.

"Okay. I guess he's not a bad guy," says Henry, but he is not entirely convinced.

He doesn't tell Cassie this, but Henry suspects the man in the van might have some news for his mother about recent UFO activity, which they needed to discuss privately because they didn't want to scare him and the other kids. Three weeks ago, while Henry and Andre were practicing their kung fu on the back porch, Andre told him about a spaceship—how he saw it out his bedroom window, the white gleaming belly of it, which looked like the smooth white holding tank of Edgefield's water tower. His brother had waited, sweat in his eyes, for Henry to say something about the aliens—that he had seen them, too, or that he believed him or that he thought Andre was a big fat liar. But Henry didn't know what to tell him. Andre seemed to need Henry's help, and the idea of being needed by his older brother had startled him into silence.

Henry remembers Andre's confession now and thinks the bearded man with the slick van is just the sort of person who would drive around the county warning citizens of an alien threat.

The gray afternoon darkens into evening, and still his dad doesn't come home, and neither does Andre. The game Cassie plays with him is "chicken," an extension of their earlier game. Henry loses: he will look but he won't touch. By the time the van pulls away and his mother calls "Kids!" he's told Cassie "no" three times. She wants him to put his hand between her legs, and if he says "no" one more time, she says he's dead because she's going to kill him. So when his mother calls again, he goes without a word, because he can't say no, and he's too embarrassed to say good-bye.

He hides in the hall closet instead of going to his room. The closet is lined with clothes that he and Andre have grown out of or worn out. His mother has plans to repair them or send them to the Salvation Army, but she doesn't get around to it. They just cushion the bottom of the closet for Henry when he hides.

He twists himself into a space between the floor and the lowest shelf, leaving the door open just a crack so that the light can get in. He can see his mother moving in the kitchen through the crack. She's making chili, he can tell. He hears the beef sizzling in the skillet and smells the armpit scent of the spices. His mother moves fast and makes a lot of noise, smacking the spoon against the rim of the pot, running the water, listening to a staticky radio station—the blades of her knives make rapid thumps against the cutting board. She sings. And dances. Henry likes it when she dances but cringes a little when she sings. Frankie's head bobs in and out of the frame of Henry's vision, too. He pulls every pot and pan out of the kitchen cabinets while their mother cooks, and she leaps over colanders, pivots on cookie sheets.

One of Henry's toy cars is in the closet, left here on purpose for just such an occasion of having to curl up with a guilty stomach. He likes to swipe his thumb in circular motions over the hood. It comforts him when he can't stop feeling bad, when there is a magnet in his gut that pulls all his thoughts to it, and there his thoughts sit, all tangled in his stomach. The purple paint on the hood of the car is worn off from all his rubbing, revealing a thumb-sized oval of bare metal. He rubs it vigorously, now, feeling guilty, thinking of Cassie's skinny white legs, and the way they met each other at her crotch. A line, as thin and short as a hair from his own head, marked the division between the left side of her body and the right, and the rest was skin. It didn't bother him to see it, but it was a surprise he wasn't ready for.

His mother peeks into the closet. Her head has a halo of stray, curling reddish hairs that have been loosened from her braid by the steam in the kitchen. Her cheeks are pink. Her chest, just below her neck, is flushed as well—she is all pink, except a little green bruise the size of a raisin beneath her collarbone. She looks like she's in a good mood, but her eyes don't focus on him. They dart around the closet, and she rubs her palms on the front of her pants like she's trying to dry them off.

"Henry, don't you want to play in your room?"

He shakes his head. No, he would not like to play in his room. His room is a place where he only allows himself to feel good.

She reaches inside the closet, smooths his hair. Her hands smell like onions and lavender hand lotion. When he looks up, her eyes finally settle on his, and he thinks that she might know something is up. She opens her mouth, and he knows the words that will come out: *What did you do? You look guilty as sin.*

But she doesn't say this. Something retracts the words back down into her. She swallows them, her throat bobs. He knows she must have magnets inside her, like he does, that are pulling bad feelings down into her belly. They pull down the reprimand on her lips, too, because she sees the question in the curl of his frown: *What have you done?* And because she doesn't want to be asked this question, she doesn't ask it of him, either.

"Well," says his mother, pulling her hand away. "Supper's about ready. I'm making chili and cornbread."

"I knew it."

"Because the onions stink, huh?"

He nods, smiles his happiest fake happy smile at her.

"You get out of the closet when you hear Daddy pull in, alright?"

"Okay," he says.

She closes the door almost all the way. Frankie, who has crawled up behind their mother, peers in and laughs when he sees Henry's face. "That's funny, huh?" says their mother. "Brother is hiding." She pulls Frankie back with her into the kitchen.

When Henry hears the crunch of wheels in the driveway, he tucks the little car back in a corner, determined not to touch it anymore that evening, and comes out of the closet. His father walks in the front door and wipes his feet. He has a paper bag in one hand and a blue-and-silver can of beer in the other. His mother comes and kisses his father on the cheek before going back to the kitchen.

"Hi, sweetness. Hey, Frank," he says.

Frankie bangs out a song on the refrigerator door with a spoon and ignores him.

"Hi, Daddy," says Henry. He keeps his back against the closet door.

"Hi, buddy," he says. "You want a present?" He holds out his paper bag.

His mother calls, "Don't give him candy before dinner, Andre."

Henry walks to the paper bag that his father holds out to him and peers inside. There is another can of beer and a box of Bottle Caps.

"Do I get my choice?" Henry asks.

He gets the reaction he hoped for. His father's big chest heaves with laughter. His older brother really does look like him—Andre the junior and Andre the senior are both tall, both broad in the shoulders. Handsome, according to his mother and his aunt. But when Henry looks at his father, he mostly looks at his mouth and his crooked, bright-white teeth and how his lips lie over them. His father's mouth tells Henry what he needs to know about how to act.

"The candy is for you, buddy," he says.

Henry takes the candy out of the bag and shakes the box. He hears the pieces, imagines the tangy purple and orange, the cola that, amazingly, really tastes like cola.

"Thank you," he says.

"You're welcome," says his father and hugs him with one arm. Henry makes himself stand still. "And now I'd better wash up. Filthy hands are no good for eating," he says, holding up black-smudged fingers.

"Eww," says Henry, because he thinks his father expects him to. His father makes hitches for mobile homes. Henry doesn't think of it as dirt or grease but just as the regular color of father-hands.

Henry takes the candy to the kitchen and holds the box out in front of his mother. "Can I have this?"

She wipes her hands on a dish towel. "After dinner," she says. "And you have to share with Andre."

When she says his brother's name, she becomes still. He'd forgotten Andre, too. He isn't in the house; he's still at Will's, probably eating burgers and drinking cans of RC with the Millers. His mother breaks out of her frozen state and grabs him by his arm. He feels Cassie's fingers in the places where his mother's are now. There will be four bruises like piano keys on his arm, he can tell. Cassie started them, and his mother's grip assures them.

"You need to get your brother," she says, likely thinking of the last time Andre came home so late from the Millers'. "Go as fast as you can, and when you come home, come in through the cellar door and then walk up from the basement," she says.

He runs down into the basement and then back into the April night, using all his strength to push the cellar doors up and open. When he runs his feet barely scrape the ground. His mother lets him help, lets him move, fast and light over to the Millers' house, and this is why he loves his mother. She makes plans, she gets ideas. She lies, and he loves her for that, too.

The reason he has to do this, go fast, go now, is because his father wants everyone home when he is or it hurts his feelings. He takes offense, if he gets home and finds one son in the hall closet and the other at the neighbors'. He feels they are avoiding him. This is what his mother explained after the last time Andre was out late, and they'd *all* gotten in trouble, and had the strangest punishment ever: his father pushing Andre onto the couch, covering him in a blanket, and then sitting on him to make him stay put. He sat on him for a long time, while Andre yelled that he couldn't breathe. His father said that wasn't true, that he couldn't make so much noise if he couldn't breathe, and that if he'd shut up for half a second, well, he might believe him that he couldn't breathe and get up. Andre started to cry and their mother told their father to stop, that was enough. Andre never cried, was immune to groundings and whippings and being yanked around—Henry marveled at it. But his father wouldn't get up, because his mother was sort of being punished, too, for letting Andre stay out so long. The more she begged, the more his father mashed Andre's head into the couch cushion, until Andre did stop crying, and moving, and their mother, with a final *meep*, pressed her hands over her mouth to keep her voice from coming out.

Henry hadn't been able to stand still, pacing back and forth, watching. When he heard that *meep*, he felt a giggle rising up in his throat, even though it wasn't funny. He didn't think it was funny at all. In fact, he thought his brother might really die, and he was terrified, and yet his chest was bouncing with laughter that he couldn't let out. If he made a noise, it would only draw attention to himself, and then he would be in trouble, too, and he was not immune, not like Andre. He cried at the lightest slap, the threat of a raised voice.

His brother was let up then, sucking in air, white and walleyed as a fish. Andre tried to run but couldn't even get out of the living room before he fell, panting on the floor, looking around like he didn't know where he was.

When Henry gets to the Millers', Andre is taking a one-handed shot at the basketball hoop over Will's garage door.

"Andre!"

"What?"

"Dinner! Dad's home."

Will Miller is much shorter than Andre, a blond boy who blushes easily. His hair sticks to the sweat of his forehead. "You gotta go?" he asks Andre.

"Yeah. I do," he says. "I'll see you Monday."

Henry and his brother walk to the end of the Millers' yard and hear the screen door slam as Will goes inside his house. They break into a run at the edge of the property.

"Up through the cellar," Henry says as he overtakes Andre. The moon is covered with clouds, and so the only lights come from their neighbors' porches.

When the two of them reappear at the top of the basement stairs, they hide their breathlessness, and their mother says, "No tomatoes down there? Well, sit down, and we'll eat it as it is."

LATER THAT NIGHT, HENRY FINDS he has to go back to the closet. He climbs out of bed and pads across the thick yellow carpet of his room and down the stairs to the hall closet, where he feels around in the dark for his car.

His fingers brush against the baseboard as he searches beneath the cast-off clothes until he runs into something smooth—some hard, cool object. He would swear that it hadn't been in the closet when he was here only hours ago. He stands on his tiptoes and reaches high, groping for the chain that turns on the closet light. Henry squints in the light of the one bulb and digs beneath the coats.

He finds a floral-print box. It isn't exactly like the ones he saw in the van earlier but it is similar. It has a gold latch, which he immediately flips up.

There are two tiers inside, like in his father's tackle box, the upper tier nesting in the lower tier until the box is opened. Arranged on these tiers are compacts of colored powder, tubes of lipstick. There are words printed on the tubes and compacts, but they are written in cursive, which Henry can't read yet. There are gold-ribbed tubes in the box as well, and Henry thinks at first that they are bullets. Eyelashes sprout from a pair of plastic eyelids. His mother doesn't wear this stuff. She just looks regular most of the time, no extra eyelashes. Sometimes she wears lipstick, but not this color. A small round box with the same floral pattern sits on the lower tier. He pops the lid off and finds folded plastic bags inside it. Nothing in them. Just a tint of blue on the plastic.

There's a stack of photos, too, beneath this bag, though he doesn't get to look at them because a sudden terror of getting caught seizes him, and he reburies the box beneath Andre's corduroy coat. His guilt is replaced by paranoia, a sort of spirit that grabs at his ankles running up the stairs until he can cover them beneath his quilt.

The Act You Do When You Want
A Bed To Sleep In

This is another act I've already done. Lots and lots of times. Kylie made me think of it, so here it is, number three.

I usually did this one at dusk, when it looked like if I slept in the park one more night, I'd get picked up, because a cop kept nodding at me too casually, like, "Don't mind me, I'm a friendly officer who doesn't suspect for a second that I've seen your mug on the side of a milk carton."

Right when I needed her to, she'd appear, some college girl in perfect white Keds and pink hoop earrings. I'd coax her into handing over those Keds and juggle them. Then, I'd add her earrings. Then, a book from her backpack. I'd toss them around and make it look like a big effort, and when I returned it all to her unharmed, she would smile, and I would "slip" out of character and smile back. She would feel special, and the rest would be easy.

I did try to live in a motel once, but my neighbors were all owl-eyed and yellow-fanged and full of drugs. I heard their children's bodies hitting the floors and the walls, and I couldn't stay because it made me think of Frankie.

Nothing is worse than thinking about Frankie. Nothing could land me back at home faster than that kid. So I don't think about him.

The college girls always had a good place to stay, and I kept crashing with them even after I'd turned eighteen and didn't have to worry about getting picked up. It was nice. I'd wake up buried beneath a mountain of someone else's security blankets: stuffed bears and elephants and yarn-haired dolls. These things would all smell like the girl who had invited me home, like apple lotion and Exclamation perfume. And sure, I usually slipped out before she woke up, but I'd leave a note, and I never felt cruel.

Real cruelty takes time, and I didn't stick around long enough for that. Sure, it isn't nice to perform your way into a girl's bed, it's not strictly honest or professional. But there are worse things a guy could do.

CHAPTER 5

St. Louis
June 1990

ADRIENNE WAS TRAPPED IN HER bed, paralyzed by sleep. Shadows moved around her house, clicked doors open, shook the plumbing. She wanted to investigate the noises, but no matter how hard she tried, no matter how many times she said, "I am going to wake up, now," she could not pull her eyelids apart to make it happen.

Finally, she managed to pull back the white coverlet and kick her legs over the side of the bed. She padded on bare feet to the kitchen, thinking she had heard the pantry door swing on its hinges. The air rushed out of her chest when she saw her ex-husband there, spreading peanut butter on a piece of wheat bread, not even using a plate. She didn't say anything, only turned on her heel and stalked back to the bedroom to get her gun out of the hatbox and say what she had longed to say to him for years: "Get out of my house, or I'll kill you." But halfway to the bedroom, she realized that she was still in bed, sleeping, only dreaming she had gotten up. She woke up for real this time with her heart in her throat, able to move, but afraid to. Her sheets stuck to her. The coverlet was heavy over her body.

It was just an accidental nap, she told herself. She'd had a migraine and had fallen asleep.

She missed the first show of the season. She was in bed instead, having nightmares. That was what happened.

Feeling oriented again, Adrienne propped herself up on her elbows. The migraines had been happening more often and they were taking longer to pass. *It's stress*, she thought, *it's because you're anxious about Curtis coming to town. It's almost time for your period. You've had too much caffeine lately.*

Whenever she had a migraine, she had to make a list of all the things that it could be that were not tumors in her brain.

Two months ago when she'd first started getting the headaches more frequently, she also noticed her breasts were a little swollen. For a few bright hours after she made this discovery, she believed she might be pregnant. Later, she didn't know why she'd jumped to this conclusion, but as soon as the thought had occurred to her, she started cleaning the house, vacuuming and dusting until she was sweaty. She daydreamed, while she worked, of a white bassinet in the living room, a Winnie-the-Pooh mural in the guest room. Caleb kissing a bald baby head before he went off to work. A drawer full of tiny socks.

It was extremely unlikely that she would be pregnant. She'd always had irregular periods, even after the surgery to remove the tumor that leaned against her pituitary gland. This was the tumor that had caused her to grow and grow and grow until she was what she was. She had it removed many years ago, but the doctor had warned her that things would never be quite right for her as far as her hormones were concerned. There was too much chaos in there for the elegance of fertilization and gestation: no well-timed release of an egg, no ordered, predictable cell growth. No baby could live in her body.

But that was nice, she'd thought. It had felt real enough.

Now, as she reached for the remote on the nightstand and flipped on the television, she found it difficult to believe that *she* could stand living inside her body. Her migraine was beginning to subside, but she ached in strange ways, in her joints. It felt like she had bruises deep under her skin, on her bones.

On the news, the anchor was talking about a plane that had crashed. Everyone had died. Two hundred and twenty-three people. Which meant there were thousands more people mourning and having nightmares and shivering every time a plane flew over them. At the same time, these people would search for quiet moments when they didn't have to think about the dead or imagine their final, awful minutes. They would hope to lose them-selves in a conversation about something else, a dumb movie, a gin and tonic and a basket of onion rings at happy hour. They would push the dead away so that they could be alive.

Her blue-and-yellow macaw, Richard, who had been perched on the headrest of the bed, opened his wings and hopped down onto the pillow next to Adrienne. The blue feathers around his neck ruffled as he tried to catch his balance. She closed her eyes for a moment to shut out the light—the sound of the television comforted her, but the flash of the screen threatened to bring her headache back full-force.

"Hi, Richard. Sweet bird. Sweet boy," said Adrienne.

"Sleepy head," he said.

"Yes, I know. Mama's a sleepy head."

He blinked at her, cocking his head to one side. She petted his neck, and he stretched toward her to give her a better angle to rub him with. "That's the stuff. Peanut butter and jelly," he said.

She used to think his voice was creepy. She thought the fact that he made human sounds with a reptilian tongue made the words sound not-quite-right. He was originally purchased as a part of her act when she was the Amazon Woman at Bill's Caribbean Steakhouse in Louisville, and even though she fed him, and he helped keep her act popular, they were not friends. They barely touched each other when they were not onstage. He had lived with her, though, for ten years straight now. She could only imagine that he somehow loved her with his little tree-nut-sized brain. This was why she let him sit on the bed, even though his claws piqued the coverlet. That, and Richard would very likely outlive her. He was forty-seven, thirteen years older than she, but parrots could live to be a hundred, and she could not. And so after she was gone, Richard would still be walking around, sliding his face across the floor, eating pasta and peanuts and carrying memories of her in his head. She wanted the memories to be good ones.

This was what she was thinking when she heard keys in the door and the smooth mechanical shifting in the lock. She bounded into the living room, checked the peephole, and then undid the chain when she saw it was Caleb. She returned to the bedroom, Caleb following her.

"How was the show?" she asked.

"Fine," he said, taking off his tie.

"How were the new clowns? Was Kylie nervous? Did you tell Henry to break a leg?" She repositioned herself on the bed, and Richard drew closer and began preening himself.

"They were fine, too. Seamus liked it. That's all that matters."

"You said it was all about the audience," she said.

Caleb sat in a white wicker chair by the door and slipped off his shoes. "Well, they liked it, too. Everybody liked it. Everyone lifted them up on their shoulders and carried them to their trailers. And then they did the same thing to me for finding them."

"They did?"

"No, not really. But it was fine. Why are you even worried about it? Didn't you say you weren't feeling so great? You should let yourself rest."

Adrienne shrugged. She waved her remote at the television, where a reporter in red lipstick stood in front of an airplane that was so blackened and twisted it looked like a giant fly, crushed by a swatter. The volume was low, but she left it on.

"In other news, we went out for a drink after the show—well, everyone but the clowns, who are broke, and Seamus, who's a non-participating asshole—and Lorne punched Remy in the eye."

"You're joking."

"Not at all," said Caleb, massaging his own feet. "Remy had, like, two beers, and you know what a lightweight he is. He said something about the camels screwing each other or something, and he would not let it go, and finally Lorne was like, 'They're brother and sister!' and punched him right in the eye."

"Oh my God. And Remy didn't retaliate?"

"He *tried*, but Azi basically put him in a bear hug until Lorne left. You should have seen it . . . or maybe you shouldn't have. God, Azi's strong. Remy was so pissed he almost cried."

"Are you writing up Lorne?" she asked. Richard nudged her hand with his beak to let her know he would like to taste her fingernails, please. She held her hand out and he closed his beak gently over the tip of her index finger.

"Eh. Honestly, it was kinda funny. 'They're brother and sister!' I mean, Remy had it coming."

Adrienne was more worried about Lorne. He did not quite connect actions to consequences in the way that most people did, even though he seemed reasonably intelligent and he'd always been kind to her. She remembered a time that he had offered to take her coat when she arrived at the circus, which she thought was so polite of him. But rather than hang it up, he threw it on the ground—not maliciously, but because he really didn't know what he was supposed to do next. Adrienne had chalked this up as "kinda funny," but now that she thought about it, Lorne had seemed irritated at the last rehearsal as well.

"He can't go around doing stuff like that," she said.

"Alright, alright, I'll say something. Don't you go lecturing him."

"Why not?" she asked.

Her husband smiled, apparently amused that this wasn't obvious to her. He crawled into bed next to her still partially dressed—T-shirt, suit pants, and sock-feet.

"You're so nice all the time. It'll be too harsh coming from you. Besides, I'm his boss."

Richard moved to make room for Caleb and squawked to express his distaste.

"Yeah, yeah, yeah," said Caleb, offering his own fingers to the bird in supplication. "Anyway. Are you feeling better?"

Adrienne reached for the remote on the nightstand and clicked the power button. The images of talking heads and hideous plane wreckage collapsed into a black screen.

"Yes," she said. "I feel much better."

She tilted her chin to meet his lips with her own, feeling the pulse of her migraine thrumming in her temples, not excruciating, but constant. She wasn't lying. She did feel better. She just didn't feel like herself.

Notes For A Show About An Angel

I'd like to forget about the farmer show. It gets laughs, and Seamus likes it, but after performing it a couple times, it's already feeling so cheap. Just another show about people getting hurt. I love the laughs, I do, but goddamn, do people laugh at anything else?

I'm thinking about all those Chaplin bits Christiakov made me watch. There's this skit called One a.m., and it's, like, half an hour of Chaplin, drunk, trying to get up to his bed. It's him falling down the stairs, getting in fights with himself, getting eaten by a bed that folds up into his wall. And yeah, it is good, because Chaplin was good, but the story is stupid. A drunk trying to get up to his bed? Who cares about this guy? Who cares if he ever makes it? The audience can laugh, laugh, laugh, but the show never makes you feel any different about drunk Charlie. Nothing moves inside you.

But what if it's not a drunk trying to get to his bed, but an angel that's trying to get back up to heaven? What if the person struggling is innocent? What if they are holy? I could probably rip off a lot of the blocking from One a.m., but it would be such a different show from Chaplin's if I just slapped a set of wings on Kylie.

I'll have to teach her how to fall so she doesn't bust her skull.

I want to see. I want to see if I can make people laugh because they want good things to happen for someone. I want to see if I can take all this schadenfreude and burn it.

CHAPTER 6

Two weeks had passed since opening night, and they had run the farmer show a total of six times. Henry was already bored of it, ready to move on. But performing in a circus was different than busking on his own—he couldn't just change things up when he wanted, and that frustration, along with the heat, and the guilt he felt over his brother's unanswered letter, had him feeling pretty crummy.

The letter was the first thing Henry thought of when he woke in his trailer, in sheets drenched in sweat. It was the last thing he'd thought of before he fell asleep with towels soaked in ice water draped over his neck and wrists. Andre, Andre, Andre. Back from the dead.

In so many words, Andre's letter said:

Dear Henry,

I am working in a factory packing recordable cassette tapes in a city you have never heard of, in a country you didn't know existed. I'm sorry that I left you alone. But just think of all the times you left me alone. You and Mom. You could have helped me but you didn't. Now, I am staying in this country you didn't know existed for a while, but I'll be coming to the States for a few weeks and I need you to go back to the house with me.

Your brother,
Andre

P.S. I called home. Hung up whenever Dad answered, but finally got Frankie. He gave me your PO address. Wouldn't say much else.

He knew Andre expected him to write back—he'd been careful to print the return address neatly on the envelope as well as in the letter itself. Henry was anxious that he would miss him if he waited too long to reply, but at the same time, he didn't want to see his brother at all. The letter also forced him to think about the possibility of more letters—he imagined a day when a letter, making the same accusations, would arrive from Frankie: *Why didn't you protect me?* After all, he'd set up the PO Box a year ago, with the express purpose of giving Frankie a way to reach him. Henry had written a letter to Christiakov, telling him he couldn't stop worrying about his brother, and Christiakov had set up the address, sent the information to Frankie through his high school, and continued to pay for it each month. Frankie hadn't written him once, though, and Henry wondered if he had, if he would have ignored him, as he had so far ignored Andre.

He let his fingers graze the envelope as usual as he washed up for rehearsal, but what was a soothing ritual a week ago had become a painful habit, like biting his nails down to the quick. He put the letter back in the drawer and turned his thoughts to angels with gauzy wings swooping across the center ring. He would try to convince Kylie that they should do the angel show instead of the farmer show. He would get her support first and then go to Seamus for his approval.

Kylie had been civil enough to him in spite of what happened opening night. She kept insisting "we'll be friends," even though her friendliness came off a little strained. During rehearsals, they argued, and outside of rehearsals, they were too polite. But even if she wasn't exactly his friend, Kylie was a reasonable person. She would definitely see the merit in this new act.

Henry grabbed his notebook and hurried out the door of the trailer, wearing jeans and his clown nose and carrying his shoes and shirt along. He needed to feel the air on his skin. The miserable heat was getting to him.

WHEN CALEB LEFT HER THAT morning, Adrienne was asleep in bed, naked, except for a slender white gold bracelet he'd bought for her. She was sprawled out, taking up nearly the entire bed, her left leg draped over a pillow, her right arm spilling over onto the nightstand next to the bed. She was bent at all the right angles, at all the right joints, and Caleb wanted to paint her, with the light just as it was, coming through the blinds in white stripes.

If someone were going by appearance alone, they would never accuse Caleb of being an artist, or even someone who could appreciate the difference between a Rembrandt and a paint-by-number. His dark suits and receding hairline probably evoked "insurance broker" or maybe "compulsive gambler," but every other Sunday, he was at the Saint Louis Art Museum, wandering, his hands clasped respectfully in front of him, a well-behaved spectator.

He liked the Modernists. There was a beautiful collection of Max Beckmann at the museum, and he could stand for the whole afternoon, quietly looking at one Beckmann piece after another and feeling like if Beckmann weren't dead, there might have been someone in the world who would have understood his way of seeing things. Even though managing Feely and Feinstein was a far cry from being an artist, or even a curator of art, Caleb had come to realize the job as one that required a certain kind of sight—insight, maybe, or perhaps more accurately outsight, the ability to see the thing as strangers saw it: with their hearts, and from a great distance.

Beckmann had seen the circus the same way that Caleb did. *Akrobaten* and *Der Traum* looked like paintings of dirty toys dumped into a frame. All the clothes and objects looked as if they were once cheery, bright colors that had become dull and waxy with use. The people in the paintings seemed propped up at strange angles like marionettes. It was at once nostalgic and nightmarish, and when Caleb watched his own performers in the ring, this was exactly what he saw.

Once, early in his marriage, he brought his brushes and canvas to the museum and tried to recreate the *Portrait of Valentine Tessier*. The woman in the painting reminded him of Adrienne, the way she gazed off to one side, and it wasn't quite clear if her expression was flirtatious or suspicious. She was tall and blond, cat-eyed with high-arching brows, sophisticated and surly-looking.

Caleb had started a lot of paintings but had never finished a single one. Mostly he was glad for this, because artists, like his performers, seemed self-absorbed and pathologically unhappy. A high price to pay for good hands. But sometimes, when he saw Adrienne like she was now, he wished there was some way to share it with someone, to show them what it was like to see her in the morning, through the lens of his love, beautiful and sleeping and draped in light.

He shut the door and let her rest though she had been sleeping a lot lately. She had an appointment to go to the doctor and find out if her headaches were just headaches, or something else. Some-unmentionable-thing else. She'd told him, holding his hand in bed before they fell asleep, "This has happened before. It's always a false alarm," but she must not have really thought this, because she'd eaten nothing but hot coffee and pickled herring since she saw the news about that plane going down.

BECAUSE THE CIRCUS WOULD BEGIN its tour in one week, Caleb's first order of business for the day was to get signatures on travel paper work. When he arrived at Feely and Feinstein, Caleb found things not going as smoothly as they had started. It was unseasonably hot and the performers were so sweaty they were sliding right off their equipment and each other.

Henry was all worked up. It seemed he and Kylie had been arguing for quite a while before Caleb had walked in. Henry paced around Kylie, who stood with her arms crossed. His movement stirred the dust from the dirt floor and made everything look mired in a dreamy, gritty haze.

Remy, whose eye was still mottled purple from the jab Lorne had taken at him at the bar, was talking to Azi on the opposite side of the ring, both of them politely trying to ignore the clowns' argument. Lorne, however, sat on the first set of bleachers and watched like he was attending a matinee. He seemed to have a stake in all this, too, but Caleb wasn't sure what it was.

"If you think the show needs to be 'enlivened,'" Kylie said, "why *don't* we put in the horse? It requires hardly any extra work and hardly any extra money."

"Because. Horses. Aren't. Funny."

The girl ticked reasons off on her fingers: "The horse is available. The horse is trained to perform. A horse doesn't require us to learn entirely new stunts and new choreography. A horse doesn't require new props or costumes."

"She's a very good horse, Henry," Lorne said. "I can get her to do about anything you'd like. She's the great-great-great-granddaughter of the Horse of a Different Color—you know, from *The Wizard of Oz?* A very special animal."

"Fuck your horse!" Henry shouted. "Why don't you do your job, Kylie, so the horse can be a horse and not a prop?"

Lorne shook his head, flattening his thin hair in even, angry strokes. Then, Kylie spotted Caleb.

"Caleb, tell him. Tell him he's an idiot," she yelled.

Caleb held up his hands to indicate that he was not a part of this argument. He didn't moderate fights, period, because there were too many of them and getting involved only dragged them out. Seamus was officially the artistic director, and he'd given Henry a bit of power letting him script the farmer act. It was up to Henry to hang on to that power, if he could.

Caleb told them, "I don't give a shit if you have a horse in your show or not, as long as it doesn't cause any legal problems."

Kylie looked miffed at this response, but rather than argue with him, she continued yelling at Henry. "You're not listening to me. I *can't* learn a new show," she said. "I'm still learning the one we do now. I'm not comfortable being more than a few feet off the ground in the silks. I'd have to learn this all from scratch." She reached for Henry, but Henry pulled away with a fierce jerk of his shoulder.

"Then I'll climb it. I'll be the angel," he said.

"Or we could just do the *totally successful* act we've been doing!" she said, moving close to him again.

Jesus, Caleb thought, *you've got to stand down a sec, kid.* Just when he thought he might have to break his own rule and step in, Azi walked over and stilled Kylie by resting a hand on her shoulder.

"Henry," he said. "There's no sense in arguing about it before you talk to Seamus. Getting the costumes and props you want—that means money and time he must agree to."

Henry stopped shaking. He sat down, folded his hands around his knees. "Alright," he said. "I know. It would be a lot of work."

The conversation was over then because the German girls arrived to help Azi with a hoop of flames that was rigged to combust clockwise but wouldn't light past six o'clock. The clowns sat silently. They really did look like dirty toys in a frame, their sweaty skin smudged, their anger straining the angles at which they held themselves.

IN HIS OFFICE, CALEB SPENT too long staring at the summer itinerary. The tour dates were in an arc of cities across the Midwest and Great Lakes regions: St. Louis, Galesburg, Chicago, Indianapolis, Fort Wayne, Toledo, Detroit. The map on his desk showed little red rings around these cities, making a chain from the Mississippi to Lake Ontario. Two months on that little red chain had never seemed long to him before but, looking at it now, the chain seemed to stretch out unreasonably far from his home and wife. And this year there was an extra link in the chain that would take him even further. Feely and Feinstein could only call itself an "international" circus because of an occasional appearance in Toronto. This year was a Toronto year.

He had a scheme to capitalize off this show in Toronto: as part of his strategy to resurrect the circus, he intended to pilot a new kind of show, one without animals, with a focus on showmanship. He thought he would find the most receptive audience for this in Toronto, where the shows billed as *cirque* had plots, beautiful costumes, masterful staging, and human-only casts. And they sure drew a crowd, sans animals, sans freaks.

The Toronto show would not be a tent set up in a mall parking lot. Instead, they were booked at a club known for fringe performances: the campy, the lewd, the bizarre. He didn't want Feely and Feinstein to play to audiences like that every night, to young people who had stomachs full of craft beer and an overly developed sense of irony, but he wanted to show Seamus that they were versatile, that they could put their show on any stage with just a few adjustments. He knew exactly how the show would work, but kept the exact plan and venue under his cap, where he seemed to be keeping a lot of things lately.

It was in Toronto, watching such a show five years ago, that he'd met the Russian. He had white hair and friendly eyes, a lanky body that made it hard to place his age. They stood next to each other in the audience, and whenever one of the performers did something exceptional, or the plot took an unexpected turn, the Russian would elbow Caleb and say, "How about that, my friend?" If anyone else had done this to Caleb, he would have found it irritating. But there was something magnetic about the white-haired man, who introduced himself, after the third or fourth elbow to Caleb's ribs, as Luka Christiakov.

They'd gone to a bar and Caleb drank black and tans while the Russian, an old clown, drank water. They talked circus, and Caleb told him all about Feely and Feinstein. How, when he worked out the season's budget, he was always convinced it would be their last year of operation. Somehow, though, by pennies and the skins of their teeth, they made it through one more show, one more week, one more season. And he told him about the Feelys themselves, how Seamus persisted that there would always be a place for the circus as it was. How Seamus was just like his old man, Conall, in that one way, resistant to anything new.

They talked about the nouveau movement. If Beckmann shared Caleb's vision of the circus as it was, then Luka Christiakov shared Caleb's vision of what the circus could be. No elephants. No canned music. Just skilled performers and a darn good story.

When they left the bar, the Russian had told Caleb not to worry, that things would turn up for his circus. "This world bends to belief, and money follows imagination. Baratucci, this only sounds like optimism. It's the heaviest of truths, but you'll work it to your advantage. I am sure of it."

Now here they were, a few months from what would almost definitely be the death of that Feely baby. And here he was, still pushing for something new, hoping it would save them. Those bickering clowns were more *cirque* than *circus*, and that was no accident on Caleb's part. They would fight for things because their youth and their training compelled them to, especially Henry. It had to be contained, or it would blow up in Caleb's face—but that will to fight was necessary for the show.

ADRIENNE CAME TO HIS OFFICE later that day. She had to duck down to clear the doorway. Once inside, she made the whole room look laughably small, and Caleb felt like he was a child in a tree house, only playing at the business of adults with his desk and his papers.

"I brought you a sandwich," she said, dropping a plastic bag on his desk.

He took out a sub wrapped in white paper. "Did you eat?" he asked her.

She shrugged, bundled her hair up in one hand then let it fall over her shoulder.

"You have to eat. How am I going to feel okay about going out of town if you don't eat?" he said.

"I've been feeling nervous. I just want to sleep and smoke and take baths."

Caleb could tell that she was thinner this week than last, her jaw and cheekbones more pronounced than usual. And she hadn't done her nails. Last week's polish was flaking off at the cuticles.

She saw the map lying on his desk and cocked her head to look at it. "How long will you be in Chicago?"

"A weekend," he said, chewing his sandwich. He offered her a bite, but she shook her head.

"I can't," she said.

"Adie," he said, "I don't know what to do with you."

69

"You don't have to do anything with me. If something needs to be done with me, I'll do it."

"I wish you would come with us. You could follow in the car and sleep in my trailer." He offered this even though he knew she would refuse.

And indeed, Adrienne snorted and rolled her eyes. Two people in a tiny bed in a tiny room in the heat. He knew this was not her idea of comfort. What she wanted was for him to stay. He considered telling her that it was his last chance to save his circus, but even that sounded like a lousy excuse.

"We'll get a motel," he said.

"That would be ridiculous. You might as well quit your job. We'd spend half your salary on motel rooms."

"You want me to quit my job?"

Adrienne didn't answer. Something had caught her eye on the other side of the small cobweb-covered window of his office.

"Is that Henry?" she asked.

"I don't know. Is he sulking?"

Adrienne frowned. "It is Henry. Why is he going in that trailer?"

"Probably needs a nap after fighting with Kylie all morning," said Caleb. He slipped the map into a drawer in his desk.

"Fighting?" she said, still staring out the window. "Is he living in there? In that hot nasty trailer?"

"He doesn't mind it. He's happy for a space."

"Caleb, how could you let him stay there? It's got to be a hundred and twenty degrees in that thing!"

"It cools down at night. Besides, he likes the heat. He says it's good for his flexibility."

Adrienne clenched her jaw and stared at him. He knew she believed in the generosity of his spirit. She believed she knew him better, as his wife, than acquaintances who would jump to the conclusion that he was a curmudgeon. He knew that to have this belief challenged, to think that the general opinion of her husband might be truer than her own understanding of him, made her furious.

"Adrienne, what am I supposed to do? There's nothing in the budget to put him up somewhere else. He should have planned better before he ran away from home."

This was meant to be a joke, a funny thing to lighten the mood so they could have a pleasant twenty minutes together while he ate his sandwich. But Adrienne balled up one of the clean napkins on his desk and tossed it at him.

"You don't *plan* to run away. For one thing. He's just a kid, and you're letting him live in a death trap. It doesn't even have a window AC unit."

"Lots of kids live in death traps," he said. "I'm not *letting* it happen. There's just nothing I can do about it."

"We have a guest room. We aren't doing anything else with it."

"Are you serious?"

Adrienne lit one of her long cigarettes.

Of course she was serious.

"Okay, I understand that you're just trying to help him out, and that it isn't fair that he has to sleep in that thing. But he isn't a puppy. He's twenty-four years old and he's my employee."

"You know damn well he isn't twenty-four. And you leave in a week, anyway. *One* week. It's not going to ruin your professional relationship. And so what if it does? This is a circus. It's supposed to be a family. You're the only one in a suit."

She stood but had to keep leaning forward since she couldn't stand up straight without putting her head through the ceiling. "I'm going. I just want you to think about it. It's one week."

"It's our last week together before I leave."

Her voice softened. "I know. But we should be generous."

Caleb watched her leave through his window. As she walked to the parking lot, she passed Azi and Lorne, stopping to kiss their cheeks. She had to bend down in a significant way for Lorne, though she could reach Azi's bald head by simply tilting her chin down. *She* was generous. Everyone knew it.

He liked that she saw him as generous, too, but it wasn't accurate. He turned away people who poured their hearts into their auditions, and people who looked hungry, and people who had loneliness written all over their bodies, simply because his outsight told him they were not the best thing for Feely and Feinstein. The only possible exception to this was Lorne, who wasn't so good, but who was a bargain, a guy who did four jobs for the price of one. No, Caleb was not generous like Adrienne. Adrienne could never think of a man as a "bargain."

But that was fine. If Adrienne managed the circus, it would have gone under a long time ago. Henry could stay right where he was.

HENRY WALKED, ENRAGED, BACK TO his trailer after rehearsal. The fight with Kylie and Lorne had taken a lid off his composure. He tried not to "show his ass," as his mother would have called it—he tried to talk himself out of his anger. He told himself that Kylie was just incompetent and that Lorne was just strange, but it felt like they had ganged up on him, even Seamus, whose will was carried out by his employees so well that, even though he was hardly around, Henry could feel his absolute control over every show, every tent corner and costume stitch.

The problem was really that the angel show was extra work that no one wanted to do but Henry, so they'd bullied him out of his idea.

He was in his head, not paying attention, and found himself in the path of a camel. It was Izzy. He could tell by the small, circle-shaped chunk cut out of the edge of her ear.

Lorne, who was walking the camel, his T-shirt soaked in sweat, yanked Izzy out of Henry's path.

"Excuse me," said Henry and redirected himself.

"Hey, clown?" he asked.

"Yes?" said Henry and kept walking.

"You afraid of horses?"

Henry spun around to face him but kept walking backward. "No. Of course not. I'm in that barn smelling her every night, aren't I?"

"Then why don't you want Ambrosia in the show?"

Henry watched Izzy chew something that she was imagining eating or maybe had regurgitated. "It isn't about horses or no horses. It's that I want to do a whole different show."

"Well . . . Seamus isn't gonna let you do a new show. I can tell you that right now. So you should consider using Ambrosia, alright? You should just consider her."

Henry wanted to scream. He had absolutely no idea how to work the horse into the farmer act without making it seem forced. He didn't know how the dilemma had become "either we do a new act, or we incorporate this fucking horse for no reason." Oh, wait, yes he did. Because Lorne had butted in and insisted that the horse would be a marvelous addition, and Kylie thought, *Here's a way not to learn anything new.* He was filling with toxins, a boiling, poisonous anger.

"Well? Will you think about it?" asked Lorne, and Henry's anger suddenly diffused. Lorne's tone was more pleading than insistent, now. The more he talked to Lorne, the more he felt the man had some deep misunderstandings about the world.

"I will think about it," said Henry, his voice lowered.

Lorne took this at face value, immediately brightening. Henry was blowing him off, and most people would have bristled at this, but Lorne thumbed his suspenders and smiled.

Inside the trailer, Henry stripped off his clothes and lay on the cot in front of the fans, one blowing out, one blowing in. The sheet beneath him became soaked with his sweat almost immediately.

When he could not relax, he got his brother's letter out, and lay back down, resting the envelope on his chest. When Henry took a breath, the letter rose on his chest. He told himself that it was paper, light as anything, and that there was no way it could be crushing out his breath. He was strong. He could tighten his muscles and protect the bones and organs they surrounded. Azi, who had to be 220 pounds at least, maybe more, had stood on Henry's chest before, and the lungs within him kept filling and emptying, as if there were nothing pressing on them at all. The letter was just a letter, he told himself. But the feeling of being crushed would not go away.

The letter was no longer a comfort, and he no longer had the planning of the angel show to distract him from the responsibility he had to answer it.

He wrote and revised this in his head, over and over, and never got anything on paper that was the kind of thing to send to a brother. "Dear Andre," it would begin, "When I sit down to write your letter, all I can think of is Dad hitting you with a chair leg. I think you were ten. I remember wondering where he got the chair leg from, because we didn't have any broken chairs.

I can't stop myself from wishing I could be him in that moment, knocking the wind out of you. I'm sorry. I don't know what's wrong with me."

Now, in an attempt to slow his racing, anxious heart, he even wrote a few lines on the back of a Feely and Feinstein flyer: *Dear Andre, I'd like to see you*, and then a few lines that he scratched out, then a few more. *Dear Andre, Guess what? You were right. I'm a traitor.* He started over. And started over. *Dear Andre, Dear Andre, Dear Andre.*

He gave up, shoving the letter and the flyer back into the envelope. He put his clothes back on. He looked for things to cover himself with. If he could not get out from under this, he would let himself be buried. He would help this slow smothering along.

CALEB WAS THINKING HE SHOULD paint Adrienne as herself. Not with her as Valentine Tessier and him as Max Beckmann, but as himself, the artist, Caleb Baratucci, and her, the subject, Adrienne Lee Baratucci. He walked the circus grounds that afternoon imagining this and inspecting the trailers, cataloguing the damage that was already accumulated on the vehicles so that he could record any damage sustained during this season's travel.

Azi hollered at him, caught up with him. "Baratucci. Lighter fluid. You know we need it?"

"You're joking."

"Use a lotta lighter fluid, man," he said.

Caleb sighed. "Alright, alright."

The fans were running when he reached the screened windows of Henry's trailer. From where he stood he could see the boy's feet. He was lying in the cot, which was right under the window. As he walked further, though, he saw that it was only his feet that were uncovered. The rest of him was under a blanket pulled over his head. He wasn't moving. Caleb could not see his chest rise or fall through the turning of the fan blades.

He went to the door and knocked. No answer. He yanked at the door, but the stupid kid had locked it. As if that were any type of privacy when his windows were wide open. He ran back to the screens.

"Henry, what are you doing?" he shouted.

When the boy didn't answer, Caleb pinched the mechanism that held the screen in the window and it fell forward. He pushed the fan inward. Only when the fan hit his legs did the boy jerk upright. Caleb hoisted himself up with his arms and dipped his chest toward the cot, gravity pulling the rest of his body through the window. Henry was under not one blanket, but two, and a large piece of plastic that had been stretched over the window on the opposite side of the trailer.

Caleb pulled himself back into a dignified position, snatched up the plastic, and threw it into a corner. "Goddammit, Henry." What was this idiot doing, lying under blankets and *plastic* in this weather? He knew Henry believed his body was full of toxins—was he dumb enough to think he could sweat them out? Breathing hard, Caleb glanced out the window to see if anyone had been walking by during these last embarrassing moments, if anyone had seen him looking so desperate, a pathetic, frantic man trying clumsily to squeeze through a tiny window.

"What the hell are you doing? It's three hundred degrees in here. Are you trying to kill yourself? Are you trying to ruin the show for everyone?"

Caleb reached out to pull the rest of the blankets off him, and Henry raised his arms to shield himself. His hair was so saturated in sweat that it looked like he'd just held it under a faucet. Caleb put his hands down. He hadn't intended to hit him, but the boy's reaction made him feel almost as guilty as if he had.

The boy pushed the blankets off. A smudged envelope fell on the floor next to the cot, and Henry fumbled for it. His clothes stuck to him and seemed to make it hard for him to move. He couldn't manage to pick the letter up and fell off the cot.

Then Caleb knew. This was not about sweating out toxins. This was the opposite. This was surrendering to them.

Caleb replaced the fan in the window. He went to his bucket and filled an olive jar with water. He offered it to the boy but did not feel generous.

CHAPTER 7

Edgefield, Indiana
November 1978

HENRY MEETS THE SPECIAL AGENT, the one with the van full of floral boxes, one more time. The night it happens, it's snowing in Edgefield and he is lying in bed thinking about how much he wishes he were the favorite. He wants to be everyone's favorite: his mother's favorite, his father's favorite, God's favorite. He envies the all-white kittens in litters of tabbies. He envies red popsicles.

The wind rattles the windows of his bedroom. A train's howl can be heard above the storm in the distance, chugging, cutting through the icy air.

He should be the favorite, he thinks, because he's noticed that he's better than most people at a lot of different things. For one, basketball: he played with Andre and his buddies, Will Miller and Bud Stinson, all seventh graders, and he made six baskets, even though they were way taller than him.

For another thing, he could make his body into interesting shapes. Several months ago, he'd seen children on a television show doing backbends and tried it himself in the living room. It was too easy. He walked his hands back toward his ankles. His arms followed, and so did his torso, until his chest planted on the ground and he grabbed his ankles. He propelled himself forward with the muscles in his lower stomach, so that he became a wheel and rolled. Once he felt like the wheel was impressive enough, he called his mother into the room.

She looked ragged. She was putting Frankie's pants back on him for about the eighth time that day. Their well was dry, and so she had just come back from the neighbors' with two ten-gallon buckets of water that she pulled in a red wagon, which was not their toy, but belonged to another neighbor. "What do you need, William Henry?" she asked.

"Watch this move!" he said and made his human wheel for her. When he righted himself, he saw that his mother's sleepy eyes had widened. She stood very still and held her hand, clenched in a fist, at her chest.

"Holy guacamole! I thought you were going to break your neck."

He touched the part of his body that concerned her. "Nope. Neck's fine," he said. "I made that move up. Good, huh?"

Later that evening, they watched *Drunken Master*, with Jackie Chan, who, their father pointed out several times, "does all his own stunts." Andre sat next to their father's recliner, both of them hypnotized by the swiftness of Jackie Chan's moves. While the smiling, muscular hero on TV whacked guys in the nuts, dunked them in vats of water, and bonked them on the backs of their heads, his mother traced the veins in Henry's arms with the tips of her fingers. He loved this touch—the light graze of her fingers, but not so light that it tickled.

"You got some talent, you know?" she said.

And Henry had thought, *This is what it would be like to be the favorite.*

He turns these thoughts over in his mind as he tries to sleep. His mother's favorite is Andre. His father has no favorites. *God's favorite is Jesus*, Henry thinks, readjusting his head on the pillow, and too bad that's already been established and there's no way to go back on it.

He is on the edge of sleep, when, inside Henry's body, something falls and the impact of its landing jolts him awake again. His mouth feels dry and sticky, and there is a full pitcher of red drink in the fridge. If he's quiet about it and doesn't turn on the lights or leave the refrigerator door open too long, he probably won't wake up his father, who fell asleep on the couch during *Charlie's Angels.*

He walks carefully down the stairs, listening to each footstep's echo against the stairwell. Each one is a password, getting him safely from one moment into the next. At the bottom of the stairs, he can see into the living room. He passes his father, who is breathing steadily, whistling a little when he exhales. He is in the position he often sleeps in—arms folded over his chest, legs crossed at the ankles. No blanket, even in the cold weather. His hair spreads in a halo around his head.

As Henry walks through the kitchen door frame, he can see into the laundry room. There is a man-shaped creature standing by the washing machine. The light from the porch outside outlines his lanky suit-clad figure.

Henry stands motionless. The suit makes Henry think that this man is a special agent. He knows what Andre has told Henry, about the extraterrestrial ships that hover just above the tree line at night. Why is he doing their laundry?

Henry tries to steady his breathing as the man moves toward him. No, he isn't doing their laundry. The fluttering light from the television in the other room begins to illuminate him and Henry sees that the man's suit is ugly, pink, not what he would expect from a special agent. But this is part of the illusion. His face is long and slender. He has coarse brown hair and a beard.

Henry is hyperventilating. He knows this word from school, from when Cassie did it on purpose until she passed out. The man reaches for him, putting his hand on Henry's shoulder. He feels the weight of this hand all the way down in his knee joints. The man says something: "Be still." Or, "Be quiet," maybe.

The kitchen suddenly fills with sound, like one of the Chicago-bound trains jumped its tracks and ran right into the house (as Henry always expected it one day might). Henry's knees nearly buckle beneath him at this sound. The agent staggers back, toward the laundry room. Henry can't slow his breathing. All he can think is to get away, get away. He hears his father say, "Don't move."

Henry wants to run. But he doesn't know if his father's directive is meant for him. His voice sounds like it is meant for everyone. He wants the whole world to stop moving, every last person had better listen and be still, or else. Henry's body tells him otherwise. It tells him to run, to hide. He stays frozen in place, unable to decide. He turns his head enough to see his father, who has a gun leveled in their direction, a rifle that Henry has seen only once or twice before. His father isn't much of a hunter. Slowly it dawns on him that the sound that filled the kitchen moments earlier came from this gun.

Footsteps down the stairs, into the living room. Mom. She will tell him what to do.

The agent is standing still in front of him. Henry smells something coppery and knows it is blood. He checks himself and the agent for holes and doesn't see any. He waits for his mother to give him an order, to explain what is happening, say something soft to their father to calm him down. But she is just standing there in the living room, white as chalk, one hand over her mouth and the other twisting the fabric of her nightgown. Like someone has flipped a switch, he feels the pain now, a burning sensation on the top of his head. Something oozes down into his eyebrows.

From upstairs, Frankie begins to call for someone to get him. He's two, but he's still afraid to walk down the steep stairs himself. "Mommy? Mom?"

When his mother finally says something, it doesn't sound like her. "What the hell is going on? You put down that gun, Andre!" Her words are so muddled by fury and panic that they sound like animal noises. Henry was ready to run to her, but he's confused again. She seems as dangerous as his father with his gun, as dangerous as the agent.

"Who are you?" his father is saying.

"Please," the agent says in a raspy voice, "please, don't shoot again. I'm not here to rob anybody. She knows me. Tell him, Rylan."

Now his older brother's voice comes from the living room. "Dad, stop." His voice is even. It seems only Andre understands what this is all about. He touches their father's arm. "Let me get Henry."

Their father knocks Andre back with his elbow before he pulls the trigger on his gun again. This time the agent runs, stumbling over the mound of laundry toward the back door and out of the house. Their father chases him.

"You never listen! You never listen to anyone!" his mother is screaming in that animal voice, calling out after their father, who is long gone. And then it seems she can't sustain it, and her words drop into a breathless sort of moan, and Henry can't understand what she is saying.

Andre, who is still on the ground, rubbing his chest with the fleshy edge of his hand, glances up at their mother, then lowers his head again, trying to catch his breath. Frankie is wailing upstairs: "Get me up. Get me up. Get me up."

Purple shadows are growing at the edges of Henry's vision. He sees his father's legs move past him. His mother is on the floor, and Andre is beside her. The purple shadows turn into a bright wave of sunshine. He sees Andre shaking his mother's shoulders as the wave crushes him in light.

When he wakes up, he doesn't know what he's doing on the kitchen floor, and the top of his head feels like it's on fire, and his hair is sticky and wet. He sees his mother is still flat on her back, breathing shallowly in the living room, and when he remembers what happened, he is not sure if he was passed out for an hour or only a few seconds. His father is not there. Andre is on the telephone. He says their address, two-two-two West Linden Drive, Edgefield, Indiana.

"My mom is having a heart attack," he says.

Henry moves to her on his hands and knees. She is frightening to him, breathing like she is. Some of her breaths do not sound like breaths. Some of them sound like moans, like she is possessed. Frankie is still sobbing upstairs, quietly, now, like he is singing a sad, repetitive song.

Henry doesn't want to touch her. Her skin is blue under the lamplight, her eyes glazed over, staring like a doll's. He wants to put a blanket over her, hide her skin and her eyes. "Mom," he says, trying to get her to blink or to move in a way that he will recognize.

She hears him. He can tell. Her head moves just slightly to one side. But he still can't bring himself to touch her. So he pictures another version of her, the version of her sunbathing, with her painted toes, a smirk on her face. He imagines this mother and is able to put his hand on top of hers.

Her eyes fix on something above Henry's head. Andre is no longer on the phone, but still holding it in his hand as he stands behind Henry. Then, she looks back and forth between the two of them, her breath coming in gasps. In this instant, Henry can see awareness in her face. She stares at him hard, and he watches her throat flutter.

"They sent the ambulance," says Andre.

"You have to hang up the phone."

"What?"

"You have to hang up the phone," Henry says again, "in case they call back."

"Oh," he says.

The receiver clicks into place.

They watch their mother jerk once, like someone yanked an invisible cord that was tied to her sternum. She sucks at the air and looks at Henry as if pleading for him to keep this from happening.

"I don't know what to do," Henry says.

Then she's still, her throat stops fluttering. And Henry can feel the absence of her. She is empty and limp.

He pulls his hand away and clutches it close to his chest. His heart is racing. He can't imagine what will happen next. Nothing, he thinks. This is where it ends.

Andre sinks down beside them. "What happened?'

"I don't know," says Henry.

Andre shakes their mother, and shakes her, and Henry has to look away.

BEFORE THEIR MOTHER'S MEMORIAL, HENRY'S father burns her clothes in a barrel outside their house where they normally burn trash. He puts only a few things, including her flower box full of cosmetics, in a drawer, to keep them safe. His father tells him and his brothers this only because he wants them to know they are not allowed in the drawer—it is in his bedroom, where they are also not allowed.

Eventually, Henry's curiosity will overcome him and he will look in the drawer. He will find nothing there but socks and shoeshine and think his father has thrown away the last of her.

At the funeral home, Henry kicks his feet in his seat until his father lays his hand on one of his knees and tells him to stop. Frankie sits beside him, and Andre sits next to Frankie. Relatives and friends of his mother, some of whom Henry has never seen, take turns looking into her casket. Henry watches as their Aunt Jenny peers in, her hands clasped in front of her as if she is being careful not to get anything dirty.

Watching his aunt stare into the coffin, he wonders if it is strange for her to see her dead sister, if she feels like she is looking at her own body. They looked alike, Jenny and his mother, both with dark, reddish-brown hair and skin that always blushed and only tanned below the neck. They had the same nose and the same lines extending from the corners of their brown eyes.

Aunt Jenny comes and touches their father's shoulder but she doesn't look at him. She kneels down and kisses Henry and Frankie on the cheek. Frankie is doing his coloring books and doesn't look up, but Henry appreciates the kiss and almost asks if he can sit with her, before he remembers this would hurt his father's feelings. Jenny moves over to Andre and takes his hand. "I'm sorry," she says. "This shouldn't happen to children."

Henry thinks this is true enough, but Andre squirms. "She's the one that's dead. Nothing's happened to us," Andre says.

"I know. I just mean that this is all so unfair. To everyone, including you," she says. When Andre doesn't respond, she begins stroking his hair. "You call me if you need me. For anything, okay?"

Henry hangs on to these words—"This shouldn't happen to children"—for the next several weeks and compulsively thinks of all the stories he knows where exactly *this* happens. He will make a list at school one day and then commit the list to memory and toss the paper in the trash before anyone finds it and asks him about it. He will recite it in his mind sometimes: mother of Cinderella, mother of the Skywalkers, mother of Snow White, mother of Batman, mother of James-and-the-giant-peach. It will become a chant that calls forth a parade of beautiful young dead mothers in his imagination. Mother of Henry always brings up the rear. He has to watch all the others go by before he can picture her face.

Aunt Jenny leaves and joins a cluster of old people that Henry doesn't know. He thinks they might be his mother's aunts and uncles, but he doesn't know what that makes them to him, and he doesn't care enough to try and figure it out. These people don't know about the gun, or the man who had run from their house as their father shot at him. They only know Rylan Bell is dead from a heart attack (so young!). Only Jenny does not seem shocked, does not say "so young!" When an old woman in black, with a neck like a dinosaur, says this to Aunt Jenny, Jenny only nods. Then the old woman shakes her head and says, "Those boys have only got Andre now." Their aunt looks away.

Henry isn't sure what happened to the man their father chased, but he was working up the courage to ask Andre, who probably knew because he had spent the last few days talking with their father, in dark rooms, in quiet tones.

Their father told them before the memorial that they would bury their mother tomorrow. And where will she stay until then? Are there catacombs of coffins beneath this place? Will they keep her somewhere comfortable? The room they're in is cozy enough, with dark-green carpet and floral wallpaper. There are bouquets everywhere and a flowing fountain in the lobby. It's nice with all the people around, chatting quietly. But at night, there are no people and probably no sound. They will probably keep her in the catacombs below.

And then the horrible thought occurs to him that she might be afraid in the basement, in the dark. He tells himself, no, she won't be afraid, her body is empty. Her spirit is in heaven. But if her spirit is in heaven, where is her mind? Is it still in her skull, thrashing around, fearful, trying to get her mouth to say, "Help me, I'm still inside"?

Andre leans over Frankie and whispers to Henry, "I'm going to look at her now. Come with me."

Henry shakes his head. "No, I don't want to right now."

"Come on, just come with me," he says.

Henry doesn't answer. He stares straight ahead and hopes Andre won't make it a big deal. He doesn't want to feel her mind trying to claw its way out of her head, or look at her blank face and see nothing trying to claw its way out. Thankfully, Andre just shrugs and walks to her casket by himself. His brother puts his hands on the shiny white sides of it and leans in. He stays in this pose for a long time, and the warm chatter in the room cools as people turn to see what he's doing.

Andre leans closer and kisses her on the mouth. When he stands up straight the spectacle is ruined by how casually he points to the door, indicating to their father that he wants to go outside. Their father nods his permission and Andre leaves. The talking starts again.

His father is getting agitated. He pinches the bridge of his nose, then rubs his forehead. Today, his hair is pulled back into a short ponytail, and his hands are cleaner than Henry has ever seen them. All scrubbed, except the shadow of dirt in the creases of his knuckles. Henry tries to see his mouth to know if he should keep quiet or if he can ask for something. He's not sure yet what he wants to ask for, but he suspects he might need something soon, and there is no mom to ask now. Before, she did everything for him.

But before Henry can think of what he might ask for, his father asks something instead: "You want me to walk up with you, Henry?" His voice is low. Quiet, but not exactly kind. Henry sits up straight in his chair and meets his father's eyes. To Henry, he looks old. The lines around his eyes, which, on his mother, looked sort of nice, make his father appear tired. Henry wants to give him the right answer but can't.

"I don't think so," he says.

And here he finds another problem—not only did his mother do everything for him, but Henry did everything for his mother. He performed for her, did chores for her, brushed her hair, helped her with Frankie. He is not used to doing things for his father—he cannot even bring himself to walk up to his mother's casket for him.

"No? Are you sure?" he says. He lowers his eyes and seems to be counting the buttons on the front of his shirt. "It's the last time you'll get to see her."

When his father touches his back, Henry feels a little sorry for him, because it seems like he is trying. So he tries, too.

"Do you want me to walk up with you?" Henry asks. His father doesn't answer. Henry pokes him with one finger.

His father faces him. The poke is obviously a surprise. "No. You do what you want," he says. He puts his hands on his knees and somehow uses them as leverage to stand. "You should . . . I don't know. Do whatever you need to do." He says something else as he walks to the casket, but Henry can't quite hear him.

Frankie has colored a hole into the page he's been working on. Usually this would send him into a fit, but now he is just working around it. Henry flips the page for him.

"I'll be right back," he tells his brother.

Frankie looks up. "Where you going?"

"Bathroom."

"Can I come?"

"Sure."

He takes Frankie's hand and leads him into the foyer, where a man in a chocolate-colored suit points him up the stairs to the restroom. They open the door on the right, as the man told them, and enter the cleanest bathroom in the world. It's all white and gold and there are fake flowers on the back of the toilet. It's cold, though, because someone has left the window open. A lace curtain trembles from the pulse of brisk air coming in.

Frankie fumbles with the button on his small corduroys. Henry helps him with his pants, picks him up, situates him on the toilet. Frankie sighs as Henry pulls himself up on the sink and balances himself, one foot on the sink, the other on the back of the toilet, to shut the window. As he pulls it closed, he sees Andre out between a pair of fir trees on the far side of the yard.

Frankie sighs again.

"What's wrong?" Henry asks him, jumping down. Soft landing. No thuds to alert adults of climbing.

"It isn't going," he says.

Henry turns the water on for him. "Better?" he asks.

Frankie studies his crotch. "No."

"Well, hurry up. I have to go, too."

"I can't!'

"Think about going swimming in the lake," says Henry.

Frankie squeezes his eyes shut, presses his belly. "It's not going," he says. He sniffles and presses his belly again.

"Crap, Frankie, don't freak out. You probably don't have to go. Just get up and try later."

"I'll have an accident."

"No, you won't. We'll just come back later."

"I don't want to have an accident," he says.

Henry pulls off a piece of toilet paper and wipes Frankie's nose. He considers the perfectly white sink, then decides against it. "Okay. Just. Stay here, then. I'll go to the bathroom outside. When I'm done, I'll come get you. That'll give you plenty of time."

Frankie stops crying and blows his nose. Henry leaves the restroom, running down the stairs and out the door of the funeral home. No one notices him. He runs through the snow, which is clear up past his ankles to the trees where he saw Andre. He's still there, smoking a cigarette under the cover of the low-hanging branches. He's squatting, hunched over, his light-brown hair parted down the middle. His shoulders conceal most of him—he's only twelve, but as big as a few fourteen-year-olds they know. The smoke from his cigarette rises in big clouds, like he doesn't quite inhale it all.

"Hey," Henry says, turning to face one of the trees.

"What are you doing out here?"

"Pissin'. Frankie got nervous in the bathroom. He's still on the toilet."

Henry unzips, opens himself to the cold air. It smells crisp out here, like water. He thinks the ground must be frozen. How will they get her in?

"Why didn't you make him get up?"

"Because you know how he is."

"You could have just picked him up and moved him."

Henry re-zips his fly and makes sure his pockets aren't hanging out. "So. What did that feel like?"

"What?"

"Kissing her," says Henry.

"Go find out," says Andre. "Have you even looked at her?"

"No," says Henry and crouches beside him.

"Go away," his brother says.

Henry ignores him. He has more questions now than good sense. "Did Dad kill that guy?"

Andre snorts again. "I don't think so. I wish he did, though. He'd be in jail."

"You want him in jail?"

"Not exactly," says Andre. He drags on his cigarette. "But I'd settle for jail."

"Don't they put us up for adoption, then?"

Andre smiles and his eyes wander toward the top of the fir tree. He throws his cigarette into the snow. "We belong to the state of Indiana, then."

Henry stands back up. He wanted to ask about the agent, warn Andre of his suspicions. But this seems dumb, suddenly. And his brother makes him angry, walking around in his near-man's body and acting like a baby.

"Well, I don't want him in jail. I don't want to belong to Indiana. What does that even mean? It sounds retarded," Henry says.

"*You* sound retarded. He murdered your *mother*. And you don't want her to have any justice. You don't even want to *see* her."

"She had a heart attack," says Henry. He tenses, feeling his pulse quicken, and not just because he knows that any moment Andre is going to beat him to a pulp, but because he doesn't want to believe whatever Andre believes.

"Yeah, that's what happens when you get scared to death. You know how when you get scared, your heart beats real hard, like this." Andre demonstrates by jumping to his feet and thumping Henry on the chest three times.

"Yes," says Henry.

"Well, your heart can only take so much of that, right? He scared her. And being scared, that's what gave her a heart attack, *him* almost killing *you*."

"But he didn't almost kill me. I'm alive. I'm not even hurt."

Andre grabs him by the hair. "You're not? Then what is this?" His voice cracks when he says it. Henry squeals and pulls away. Beneath the hair is a long tender wound dividing his scalp, which burns when Andre pulls the hair around it. Their father's "warning shot" had grazed the top of his head, a fact that no one realized in the chaos of the moment, not even Henry. It didn't turn out to be that deep, and so it was easily concealed. There was a lot of blood the night he got it, though, so when he realized he was hurt, he rinsed his hair, and put a skull cap on before the ambulance arrived for his mother.

"That was an accident," says Henry.

"Yeah, it's always an accident. Listen, you little shit, if he'd aimed a quarter inch lower, you'd be dead."

Henry feels the choking sensation of tears and turns, stalking back toward the funeral home. Andre follows him.

"I'm going to make you look at her," he says.

"Fuck you, Andre!"

"I'm going to make you. I'm going to stick you right in there with her."

Henry is shoved, hard, and lands facedown into the snow. For a moment, everything is dark and silent and smothering. He pushes himself up with his hands and knees, but Andre already has him by the shirt and is lifting him up. He flips him over so he is lying on his back, staring up into his brother's face. Henry guards his head with his forearms.

"Don't!" he says.

Andre picks Henry up under his arms and then tosses him over his shoulder. "You're a little traitor. I'm going to put you in with her body and shut the lid before anyone can stop me. I don't know how long it'll take to get you out. I hope they never do. I hope they give up and just bury you with her."

Terror shoots through Henry. It seems entirely realistic that Andre could shut him in the coffin with his mother, and no one would notice he was buried alive with her. Just the idea of being underground, pressed against his mother, makes it hard to breathe. He has to get out of Andre's grip—or die.

He brings two fists down on Andre's back, one on either side of his spine. He kicks. He makes his body into a clothespin and snaps it shut on his brother's.

Andre grunts. His hold loosens, and then, to Henry's surprise, he sinks. Andre is suddenly on the ground, beneath him, looking confused. Henry is as confused as he is. Andre is so much bigger than him. Their fights are no contest—Andre hits Henry, and Henry doesn't even bother hitting back. He knows his efforts are better spent shielding himself from blows to the softer parts of his body. But here he is, and here is Andre, knocked to the ground by the force of Henry's fists and feet.

He knows he has to keep going or he'll be back on Andre's shoulder again, getting thrust into a coffin, so he punches him. He hits him in the nose and the cheek before Andre can raise his arms to defend himself.

"Stop, Henry! I was only kidding," Andre yells, and reaches to grab Henry's shirt again.

But Henry hits him twice more, in the chest, in the belly. The belly punch is the one that gets him. Andre curls into a ball and rolls on his side. Henry wins it here, for the first time ever, but he has forgotten his objective, so he doesn't know he's won. He keeps kicking Andre, the tips of his good shoes smashing into his ribs. This is all, all, all there is for a moment. No one is dead. No one needs him. No one is there to be afraid of.

CHAPTER 8

St. Louis
June 1990

ONE WEEK BEFORE THE CIRCUS was slated to leave for Galesburg, Adrienne had her MRI done. There was no question in her mind anymore that the tumor had grown back. What she wanted to know was how bad it was, how tightly it clung to her pituitary gland, how dangerous it would be this time to carve it out. In a few days, they'd tell her the answer to this, and, regardless of what the answer was, she would be saying good-bye to Caleb, and to Henry, her strange but welcome house guest. For the next six weeks, the circus would hit the road.

Adrienne could feel the effects of the tumor now, not just in her bones, but in her whole body. The surge of hormones made her ache. She got migraines that lasted for whole days and then, when they finally went away, the tips of her toe bones started hurting. If it wasn't an ache in her head or her toes, it was another type of ache—she would become aroused out of nowhere, would swear she felt the walls of her vagina sticking to each other, and believe only filling herself with something would relieve the pain this caused.

What an unexpected side effect of dying, she thought, *to want to screw like a teenager.* It was the opposite of what was supposed to happen to people with her disease, but it made sense to Adrienne, who knew her pituitary was being squeezed, flooding her body with the chemical desire to grow, grow, grow, just as it did when people went through puberty. She knew it confused

Caleb, too, the way she'd spend her day in the bathtub holding her head, too depressed to speak, and then suddenly pounce on him, kissing him until he struggled for breath.

The night before Henry came to stay with them, she had her husband pinned beneath her, and it was the first time in ten hours that she had not been in pain. It was a good moment, but he kept ruining it by looking uncomfortable. She moved her hips, splaying her palms on his chest. She tried to play with him, to bring him back to her.

"I love you, Caleb," she said. She dipped her head down and let her hair fall around his face. "This is what you'd look like as a blond."

"Adie."

"I think I prefer you bald. Maybe if it were a darker blond. And maybe if it were a little shorter."

"Jesus, Adrienne."

"Am I freaking you out?"

"No, I just feel terrible," he said.

At this rate, she would never get his pants off. She rolled away from him.

"You know I would never leave unless it was really important, right?" he said. His voice was soft and hoarse, and she could see his thoughts on his face: *Poor baby. Poor Adrienne.*

"Please, Caleb. Just let me be happy for a minute, will you?"

"Well, do you understand or not?"

"Not really. Give the reins to Azi. He knows exactly how things go."

Caleb sat up. "I can't. I know it seems like I could, but I can't."

Adrienne didn't understand, not at all, but when she saw Caleb looking so miserable, she couldn't send him on the guilt trip that (in her less charitable moments) she thought he deserved.

"If you say you can't, then you can't." She reached out to touch the dark black hair on his chest, one of her favorite parts of him, but he intercepted the touch, caught her hand and kissed it.

"Thank you," he said.

That night, Caleb sketched her on a piece of canvas. She posed seated on the couch with Richard on the perch next to her. She didn't think the proportions were right. Caleb said that was just the style he wanted to paint in, but she still felt self-conscious. The lips, the hands, the arms—they were all too big.

The next morning, Henry moved in with a prop trunk and a military-issue backpack. Richard eyed him with suspicion, once landing on his shoulder and tasting his hair. Henry slept in their guest room. The pack and all the clothes inside smelled like mildew, so on Monday morning, when Henry went to rehearsal and Caleb went to meet with Seamus, Adrienne dumped them into the washing machine. Hot water, extra soap. She even folded it all and did her best to pair each sock with its closest match. When he returned that afternoon, she handed it all to him in a neat pile.

He balanced the pile in one hand. "Thank you," he said. "You didn't have to do that."

"I thought it might be nice for you to have clean pants. And you all put in so many hours in the spring and summer. I remember. It's hard to find time," she said.

Having a guest in the house gave her energy. She still ached and felt sharp pains in the back of her skull to remind her, now and then, that everything was not quite well. But at least she was not in the bathtub crying.

Tuesday afternoon, Henry came back early from rehearsal. She heard him clamoring around in the guest room like he was rearranging furniture. She figured whatever he was doing was his prerogative, though Caleb had warned her to "watch him." He was a little nuts, Caleb said. But Adrienne saw nothing in Henry that made him seem like the bad kind of crazy. He blushed nearly every time she spoke to him, and she found this disarming. It was true that she was sometimes wrong about people, but if there was any meanness in his nature, he hid it well. And if his eyes darted from thing to thing a little fast, and if he never felt completely comfortable in his own skin, well, she could identify with that.

She turned on the radio and started boiling water for noodles. The phone rang just as she dumped the noodles into her hot water. She picked up the receiver and tucked it between her chin and shoulder.

"Hellooo?"

"Adie? It's me. How ya doin', girl?"

"Hi, Nancy. I'm doing great. How're you?" said Adrienne. She grazed her fingers ever so lightly over the little plastic nubs on the phone's cradle, as she entertained the idea of simply hanging up. Nancy had called twice recently to "warn" her about her ex-husband, but it didn't seem like a warning. It seemed like Adrienne was the butt of some kind of inside joke that only Nancy was in on.

"Oh, peachy-keen right now. Got a big party comin' up. Real rich girls at this one. We'll see how that goes. I'm making quiches," she said. Adrienne could picture Nancy right now, sashaying around the kitchen with her French manicure and big Kentucky hair. "Anyway, your man around? I got something to tell you. Personal stuff. I want you to be able to talk openly."

"He's at work," she said, peering into the guest room. Henry had left the door open a crack. She could see him inside, doing some sort of weird dance or something. Or maybe it was karate. Either way, he was totally absorbed, probably didn't even care what she had to say.

"He's leaving town, isn't he? If he hasn't already. I bet you get so lonely."

"I don't mind," she said. She could tell Nancy was fishing for information, but she wasn't sure why.

"Well," Nancy said. "Talked to Curtis again. He's looking into transferring to the St. Louis Southern Blue warehouse, so he's still planning to be in your neck of the woods. You won't be around, will you?"

"I won't," said Adrienne, gripping the phone so tight that her fingernails dug into her palms. She'd known Nancy since high school, and never liked her. She felt sorry for her, because nobody else liked Nancy either, and Nancy was unaware of this fact. She went right about her business, being obnoxious, while everyone talked about her behind her back and rolled their eyes when she called out to them in the hall. But now Adrienne was tired of feeling sorry for her.

"So you're not, deep down, hoping he'll drop by for a rendezvous?"

"You didn't tell him where I live, did you?" Adrienne whispered.

"Huh? No, I didn't tell him where you live."

But Adrienne could tell by the lift in her voice that she had. Adrienne was almost sure of it.

"Well, listen, I'm not gonna be here even if he did show up. I'm going to be on tour with Caleb," Adrienne lied.

Nancy said nothing for a moment. Adrienne wondered if she'd seen through her deception.

"Well, that sounds nice—" she said.

"It will be. Talk later, Nancy."

"Uh-huh. Bye then."

Adrienne placed the receiver back in its cradle. She couldn't believe Nancy. Sure, Nancy had done some mean things to her—when they were in high school, Nancy had chucked Adrienne's diaphragm out the window of a moving car. But even that Adrienne could at least find some humor in. Telling Curtis where she lived, on the other hand, didn't seem humorous.

She drained the noodles and found herself getting angrier, even though she knew it was ridiculous to be angry. After all, she had a tumor, the size and removability of which were currently uncertain. Compared to this, Curtis was nothing—a drip of spaghetti sauce on the carpet, a pimple, a minor annoyance. Or he should have been.

But Curtis had left her when she was down. Worse than down. She'd been going blind. Her tumor was growing, her drugs were not enough. One day, she was at the post office, and as she filled out the address on her package, the letters blurred, and for a moment, they disappeared. Later, the doctor, an old man with more liver spots than normal skin, said her tumor was strangling her optic nerve.

They did an MRI, and the doctor told her that her best chance was an operation. It was death on one side, death on the other. He explained that most pituitary tumors were fairly safe to remove, but Adrienne's was particularly large, and blood vessels had taken root around it, making its removal a greater risk for hemorrhage. It was even likelier that the surgery might blind her.

On the other hand, if he did not take it out, the tumor itself would kill her if it kept growing, and if it didn't, the hormones that the tumor squeezed into her body eventually would kill her, too. A young body responded to these hormones by growing large, as hers had when she was a girl. But an older body, already strained from sustaining its own size, would become deformed, eventually growing beyond what her heart could keep supplied with blood.

She was the loneliest she ever had been in that hospital room, four white walls and two doctors and three MRIs, all saying the same thing. Take out the tumor or die. Or die from the taking of it.

Curtis knew all this and asked for a divorce only days before her surgery. He didn't move out, but he took her hands in his and told her he wasn't digging this marriage thing. He wasn't ready for it. He was sorry. Shouldn't have signed on for this so young, he said, because he realized he couldn't live with this pressure, this constant obligation to love her sick body. There was another girl. He was not obligated to this girl, and so when he was with her, he felt happy. And how could he justify denying himself happiness, when life was so short? Adrienne had taught him that. Life was so short.

The worst part was that she'd never seen this coming. They had matching blue ten-speed bikes that they rode all over town. They made everyone suffer their public displays of affection, kissing and clinging and petting. He had this soft blond hair and she liked to stroke it whenever she was tired or nervous, like children do with their blankets or teddy bears. She could not believe he would leave her, let alone days before her forehead was supposed to be cut out by a little buzz saw, days before her brain would be exposed and the tumor removed. It shocked her, not because she thought Curtis was such a good man—she knew he was not—but she had thought they were good together. She thought they made each other better.

After the surgery, she had come home to find him sitting on their couch, as if nothing had happened between them, as if he had not had an affair and asked for a divorce. She set her small suitcase down, and he looked at her head, shaven an inch back from her hairline, with such genuine pity and remorse that she nearly went to him and begged him just to pretend to be a good husband—just to love her and not mention his affair. It was what she wanted, at the moment, more than anything. She wanted to forgive him, so that she could touch his hair and have some comfort.

But he was wearing a blue T-shirt she did not recognize and was watching *M*A*S*H*, a show he did not normally watch. She interpreted these differences as being the influence of his mistress, and she asked him to leave before he could even say hello.

He'd looked stunned, stuck to the couch with his mouth hanging open for a moment. When he found his voice, he said, "C'mon, Adrienne! I don't have anywhere else to go. I mean, can't we be adults about this? I want to remain friends, I really do."

"You are *not* my friend," she'd said.

And then he stood and pursed his lips and waved his hand and made a whole pantomime of not wanting to say something, but then said it anyway. "I am your friend, Adrienne. I'm the one that paid for all this surgery. I got you this house. I've taken care of you. We've had good times. I might not want to be married anymore but I am your friend."

Adrienne realized then that he felt her life belonged to him. He felt he had saved her from being the lonely ogre-woman, maybe even felt he had saved her life by paying for her surgery. The way he saw it, they were even. But she had faced blindness and death alone, and there was no gift he could give her that would make things even between them.

So she screamed at him, and though she intended to say words, the words only came out as noises. When she finished screaming, she picked up her suitcase again and left, because she had no other choice. She could not bear to touch him to force him out, and he refused to leave. After that, she stayed alternately in Nancy's garage and a women's shelter before she found her job at the Caribbean Steakhouse, and with her very first paycheck she bought her gun. She didn't feel threatened by Curtis, not in the physical sense. But she felt robbed of power. Her body, big as it was, strong as it was, had failed her. At the thought of hurting Curtis, it wasn't the violence she couldn't bear, but the intimacy of doing it with her bare hands. And so she bought the gun, just to know she had it, just as a sort of talisman she could reach for to feel strong.

This all happened twelve years ago, and of course it shouldn't matter now, she told herself again, but when she thought about sitting in the hospital alone, it still made her angry. Worse than angry, really. Toxic, the boy in her guest room would say.

She emptied the seasoning packet on two bowls of noodles and stirred. From her guest room, she heard the ricochet of a cartoon bullet and rapid string music coming from the little color television she had hefted into the room before Henry came to stay. She knocked lightly at the door, holding the hot bowl of noodles in one hand.

"Come in!" he said. She pushed the door open with her elbow and saw him sitting on the floor at the foot of the bed.

"Here's some lunch," she said. "Not very fancy, but it'll fill you up."

He took the bowl from her and said thank you so quietly that it seemed like he hoped she wouldn't hear. "You're welcome," she said.

"You always have food with you," he said, nearly as quietly. It was a sort of surprised observation, not a criticism.

"Well, I eat a lot. Normally. And I don't like to eat alone. Makes me feel like the giant girl who eats all the time. Which is exactly what I am, but I don't like to feel that way."

She got her bowl from the kitchen, and he scooted over to make room for her, the blush in the tips of his ears returning. On television, a rabbit carried a stack of books, which he struggled to keep balanced in his arms. The tower of them kept bending from one side to the other, so the rabbit had to skitter from side to side to keep the weight even. Then the stack itself was shown, the frame following the books up and up and up, past the Empire State building and the top of Mount Everest, while a sound track of violas and cellos climbed the scales in the background. Finally, the top of the pile appeared, all the way up in space. An alien zoomed up in a spaceship, and took the top book. He read the title of the book, *The Drapes of Wrath* (the cover showed a picture of scowling curtains), and rejected the book, putting it back on the stack just a little off-center. Of course the pile fell and crushed the rabbit beneath a mountain of pages and spines.

Adrienne laughed, inhaling one of her noodles. "*Drapes of Wrath*. That's hilarious!"

Henry was not laughing, but he did look at her and smile. "Yeah, it's alright. I like the rabbit."

"I mean, I'm not a professional. But from a layman's perspective, *Drapes of Wrath* is pretty much gold," she said, trying to cough up the noodle stuck in the wrong pipe.

"I guess," he said. "It seems like a little bit of a stretch to me. But that's a cartoon for you."

She couldn't get enough of this kid, really. He was not watching the cartoon, so much as studying it.

"How old are you, Henry? Be honest. I promise not to tell Caleb."

Henry raised his eyebrows. "Yeah, right."

"Cross my heart. He already knows you're younger than you say you are. But I won't tell him how much."

The cartoon rabbit show ended. A commercial advertising fruit snacks came on.

"I'm twenty," Henry said. "Almost."

"So you're nineteen? You must've just graduated and come right here, huh?"

"No. I didn't lie about my experience. I was busking before this. In Indianapolis first, then in Chicago. I was good at street shows. But there ain't any money in it."

Adrienne was careful about the next question she asked. "So . . . how long did you do that, total?"

"Three years," he said, wedging his chin between his knees. He didn't elaborate beyond that. He lowered his eyelids halfway, as if meditating, and a silence fell between them that allowed Adrienne to see how her husband might find Henry a little unnerving.

Adrienne sighed and stood up to stretch her legs. "Well, I guess I'll leave you to it," she said. She must've hit a touchy subject, and figured she'd let him be.

She walked toward the door, but Henry asked, "What do you do?" She turned and saw that he was looking up at her. He didn't want her to leave.

"What do you mean?"

He nodded at the picture of her, in costume, that was displayed on top of the dresser. "Are you in the circus, or what?"

"I used to be. But I retired. Usually I make some extra money for us by selling makeup."

"Like an Avon lady?"

"Yes. Sort of. I set up parties and women go to them and try the makeup and buy it from me. Not Avon. A smaller company."

"That sounds like fun," he said.

"Are you being sarcastic?"

"No, I wasn't, I swear. It sounds nice. Going to parties sounds like a job to be jealous of."

"Oh, jobs only sound fun until you're actually doing them," she said, waving her hand to dismiss the idea. "You should know that. Mr. Circus Clown."

"I love clowning," he said.

"Do you? Is it fun, though?"

He shook his head. "Not exactly fun. Sometimes, I guess. But usually not. Usually it's something else."

"I see. Something else. Something more deeply gratifying than fun, right? Oh!" she said, remembering. "Speaking of Southern Blue, I have something for you!"

She went to fetch his present. It was a lime-green makeup bag, a gift-with-purchase if a customer ordered twenty dollars' worth of Southern Blue merchandise. She'd noticed that he stored his makeup the same way he stored everything, in grocery bags, and thought it might make him happy to have a bit of an upgrade.

"Here. I have a million of them. In fact, I use one myself. They're great! Lots of pockets to put stuff in and little elastic rings for brushes. I figured, it's green, so it's not too girly."

Henry took the bag. He unzipped it, looked inside and felt around. It had a green floral lining that she'd forgotten about.

"Oh, I guess it is a little girly on the inside. You don't have to take it if you don't want, I won't feel bad," she said.

"I love it," he mumbled. "There are like five different compartments here."

Adrienne smiled. Her head was starting to hurt again, and her energy was waning. Still, she felt heartened and resisted the urge to curl up on the couch and mope.

"Thank you," he said. He sounded so earnestly grateful that it embarrassed her a bit.

"It's nothing, just a freebie," she said, waving off the compliment.

"Still," he said, "it's really nice of you. When is your next makeup party thing?"

Adrienne opened her mouth to answer and found that tears were forming in her eyes. How stupid, she thought. She held up her finger to tell him to wait a moment. She turned to get a cigarette from the case in her back pocket and blinked the tears out of her eyes so he wouldn't see them.

"I'm sort of sick," she said, lighting the cigarette, "so I probably won't have one for a while."

Henry stared at her. She could tell he understood that this sickness was serious, but his face did not take on the same pitying scowl that Caleb's did when she talked about it.

"What do you have?" he asked.

"A tumor on my pituitary gland."

He nodded. "I would help you throw a party, if you wanted. Before we leave. Caleb would help, too."

"I know you would. That's nice of you. But that's not exactly how it works. I need a hostess. So, unless you know a ton of girls and want to invite them to your trailer and bake sugar cookies for them, that probably wouldn't work."

Henry looked like he was considering this for a moment. "I've never baked sugar cookies."

"I'm kidding. Really, you're nice to offer but I'm just not up to it. I'll see the results of my MRI on Thursday. Maybe the thing will be a nice normal shape this time and they'll take it out lickety-split. If that's the case maybe I'll feel better, but right now, I'm just a bundle of nerves."

Henry stood up and brushed the hair from his face. "Well. If you change your mind, you know where I'll be." He became Henry-the-character, then, bringing the back of his hand to his face to shield his stage whisper: "Here. In your house. Eating your food."

She swiped her finger under each eye. "You are welcome here, Henry. Life goes on. People have to eat and shit and work. I don't feel sorry for myself."

"I don't feel sorry for you either. I just want to pull my weight, and, you know, I'm pretty good at distractions. You may have heard: I'm a classically trained dumbass."

Adrienne smiled. "I had heard."

"I can show you some tricks. I can do what that rabbit did, if you want."

"I don't think I have enough books."

He put up his index finger. "It only takes one encyclopedia to give me a concussion. Don't worry, I can make it work. Come on. I'll even put my face on for you. For my hostess!" he said, with a flourish.

He charged out of the room, in full performance mode, and as he did he brushed against her. Now it was Adrienne who blushed. She could feel his strength and smell his Noxzema and musky deodorant. But really, what made her blush was his warmth. When he performed, he was all heat and light, like he saved every ounce of energy up for the moment he would be in front of an audience and then let it all burn at once.

CHAPTER 9

A FEW DAYS LATER, CALEB and Adrienne were at the doctor's getting the results from Adrienne's MRI, and Henry was looking for a way to get out of their house. He did not want to be there when they got home, did not want to see the two of them cry, or worse, try to act like nothing was wrong when they all knew there *was* something wrong.

What he felt for Adrienne was both new and familiar. When he was with her, there were butterflies in his stomach, but it didn't take long before the butterflies turned into something more like crows, beating their wings, scratching with their hooked nails. There was sex in this feeling, but also tenderness and dread. If he saw Adrienne crushed by some horrible news, he would not be able to keep himself from touching her, and if he touched her, Caleb would know something was up. Something *was* up. So to escape, he told Kylie that he would meet her at the music store before the show tonight.

For the most part, he liked staying at the Baratuccis'. It was an old house, like the one in Edgefield. He liked the doorknobs that looked like big crystals, the windows above each bedroom door. It settled into its foundation every night with comforting creaks. On the dresser in his room was a picture of Adrienne onstage with Richard, wearing a blue-green costume. The picture was bad, a ghostly pale Polaroid, but he could still tell it was her, her big Wonder Woman form, her bright smile. He picked the picture up and adjusted the direction it was facing, so it would be more symmetrical with the other picture, one of a younger, lankier Caleb standing in front of a beautiful mountain range, looking utterly bored.

In spite of the fact that Henry had actually been a perfect gentleman with Adrienne, Caleb barely spoke to him. Henry couldn't blame him. If Henry had ended up cooking himself in that trailer, Caleb would have been screwed trying to find a new clown at the last minute. If anyone in the media had found out, there would've been accusations of hazardous working conditions, and that would've been a mess for him. Worst of all, it would have been Caleb to find his body if he had died. No one wants to find a carcass already rotting beneath a sheet of plastic and a mound of blankets, even if that carcass, in life, was not particularly likeable.

He was sorry for doing it, that thing in the trailer, but he had needed to be in hell for a while. It wasn't fair for Andre and Frankie to be out there, suffering, while he went about his life, ignoring them.

He'd tried to pull it together. Caleb and Adrienne gave him a room and a job, and he wanted to keep them. He still meant to write Andre back, but he tried not to think about the fact that he wouldn't reply in time to see him when he came to the US. His brother had probably already come and gone.

THE MUSIC STORE HAD A homemade sign on the door that asked patrons to check their backpacks at the front, but it looked like everyone ignored it. People were meandering around in various stages of undress, all with backpacks slung over one shoulder. The guy at the counter wore Ray-Bans and a teal button-up shirt and saluted Henry as he walked through the door. Henry checked his backpack with him.

Henry moved through the aisles not knowing what to do with his hands. The walls were papered with promotional posters, long, glossy shrines to M. C. Hammer, The Black Crowes, Public Enemy—smaller, squarer advertisements for Soundgarden, The Flaming Lips. He wanted to flip studiously through the tapes like the other people there but he wasn't sure where to start. He didn't know a thing about music. Not a single thing.

And he didn't seem to know anything about fashion, either, because he was dressed too plain, and his jeans were torn to hell in a way that didn't look strategic, his Chucks held together with duct tape. He peered over the rim of a box of records so it would seem he was searching for something like everyone else.

He wandered a little more until he nearly tripped over Kylie, who he found crouching down next to a box of records with her eyes closed, a pair of headphones held flush to her ears with both hands. She bobbed her head like the guy at the counter but she furrowed her eyebrows as if she was reading something difficult, or praying. He tapped her on the shoulder. She looked up at him and smiled like she was surprised to see him.

"Hi."

"Hi," she said, too loudly, and bounced up. She took the headphones off. "You came."

"Why wouldn't I?" he said.

She didn't answer. He knew why—everything between them was awkward, and yet here they were, because it seemed neither of them had anywhere else to be.

Kylie slipped the headphones over Henry's ears and filled their silence with a jangle of minor chords and a voice that was all jagged around the edges, a man's voice saying that he did, he did, he did. At first, this man's voice annoyed Henry because here he was on an album, released into the world for everyone to listen to, and it didn't even sound like he was trying to hit the right notes. Henry didn't know a thing about music, but he knew about performing, and as the song went on, it became clear that the flat, angry notes were intentional. What he couldn't figure out was whether these sour notes offended him—whether they were meant as a big middle finger extended toward the rock star's audience, or something more vulnerable, an expression of grief that stretched a sympathetic hand to other grievers. It could have been both, but there was that jangling guitar assuring him it was neither—*it's just a song*, the guitar said. *Tap your foot.*

Kylie watched him listen out of the corner of her eye, while she sifted through a box of second-hand records. Occasionally she would pull the shiny vinyl out and examine it for scratches, her fingers holding it gently by its curved edge, while the man sang on.

When Henry took the headphones off, she replaced them on the hook for him and said, "It's awesome, isn't it? I mean, it's just devastating."

He thought then that this green girl might know some things he didn't. Not about staying alive, but about what she liked and what she wanted.

Henry picked up his backpack, and they left the store without buying anything. He and Kylie got a hot dog and waited for the bus. She asked him if she had mustard on her face, and he said no. Then she fished something out of her own backpack and handed it to him. It was a recordable cassette. A white note card was folded into the plastic case, on which was written a numbered list of songs in neat cursive.

"What's that?" he said.

"It's a tape, dummy."

"Of what?"

"Of something special. I had my mother get this album for me from a store in San Francisco because a friend of mine told me they were good. I made a copy for you at the library after I listened to it. I think you'll like it."

"Yeah?" he said, turning it over in his hand. "I don't have a tape player. It'll be a while before I can give it back."

"You don't have to give it back. I made a *copy* for you. And we can find a tape deck somewhere at Feely and Feinstein. They play that God-awful music over the loud speakers somehow. I guess that's a tape player. Or maybe the stagehands sit back there and turn a fuckin' crank." She mimed this, scowling, puffing at an imaginary cigarette with one side of her mouth, and Henry couldn't help but smile, couldn't help but want what she seemed to keep offering.

By the time Henry and Kylie arrived at the circus, children were already lined up to ride Tex. Some of them were too afraid to ride but let her eat peanuts out of their hands. A little girl with long black braids had just finished giving Tex her peanut. She was supposed to move along for the next child to have a turn, but she stood there openmouthed, staring at her own hands. She looked stunned at how the elephant's nose worked just like her own fingers, clumsy, small, greedy when presented with a treat. It seemed to Henry that the girl was astounded to have anything in common with an animal so large.

Lorne watched her with his arms crossed over his chest, smiling. When the other children started groaning for her to hurry up, it was their turn, Lorne said, "Well, hold on, now. Let them finish their conversation."

Not thirty yards from where the line of children ended, Jenifer and Vroni sat chain-smoking outside the blue-and-white trailers. They glared at Henry and Kylie as they passed, and Henry acknowledged this by smiling and waving at them. They continued to glare, sucking diligently at their cigarettes.

They were always together, known only as a unit. "The German girls," they were called, though "girls" was not exactly the right word for them. Without their whiteface, they looked closer to Caleb's age than Henry's, older even, since their bodies were so tiny and shriveled. They each had a pair of designer jeans, which they wore every day, along with brightly colored button-up shirts that they tied just beneath their breasts. Henry could count their ribs. Their hip bones were sharp as weapons jutting out just above the waistline of their jeans.

"Better shake a leg, clowns," said Vroni.

"Which one?" Henry said. "Right or left? What about middle?"

"You shake the middle one enough, Pierrot," said Vroni, smiling. Henry had this special ability, he thought, to make people smile even while they actively hated him. He wasn't sure why the German girls hated him, but they definitely did, and they hated Kylie even more. They thought Kylie, with her old Mercedes and new degree, needed to be taken down a peg. Behind Kylie's back, he'd heard them call her fat and slow and other words in German that Henry assumed were even nastier.

Kylie stared straight ahead as they walked by, and Henry thought that maybe Kylie had already been taken down a peg. He remembered the little star below her hip bone. He had been complicit with these German girls in stripping her of the dignity that a little money and a loving family had given her. Realizing this made him all the more disgusted by them.

"Bitches," said Henry, when they were out of earshot.

"Henry, you can't call women bitches," said Kylie.

"What about when they're being bitches?" he said.

"No. It's sexist. It shows disdain for all women, not just them," she said. "You can only say 'bitches' if you're another woman."

"Then *you* should call them bitches," he said.

Kylie grabbed his hand, and he realized he'd made a mistake. She'd interpreted his dislike of the German girls for a protectiveness of her. Or maybe she was reading him exactly right, that he did want to protect her. Still, he didn't want to hold her hand.

"I will. Give me a minute. We've said 'bitches' too many times and now it doesn't mean anything. Timing, you know?"

"Right."

The silence dropped between them again.

HENRY CHANGED INTO HIS COSTUME and went to the tent to see if there was anything he could do to help set up. On the way, children waved at him shyly, and Henry waved back.

In the tent, Azi hollered orders at stagehands, and they ran around like spiders in their black clothes, arms everywhere, setting up the ring, running through the light changes.

"Henry! Come help me if you have the time!" said Sue, waving him over. He went to her quickly, glad to have anything to do that wasn't figuring out what to say to Kylie. Sue looked like a lumpy rag doll sculpted into the shape of a woman by the force of a corset and hairspray. Henry knew Seamus's philosophy about letting the prettiest woman start the show, though he hoped that Sue didn't; she had never started the show, not once in the fifteen years she'd worked at Feely and Feinstein. Azi had told Henry this with a laugh in his voice. "She's a virgin. Has to be. If the ugly doesn't keep a guy away, those dogs will. They'll bite at anything that gets near her snatch." Henry thought Azi was wrong to say this in more than one way—for one, he didn't think Sue was ugly at all. Of course, he had the somewhat problematic tendency to think that most women were attractive, in some way, but Sue was no exception. For another thing, Sue was nice, and her dogs didn't bite.

"Anything that gets near her snatch, huh? How would *you* know that?" Henry had asked, and Azi laughed, too, but hadn't said anymore.

Sue's dogs were lined up obediently but barking diligently. Henry laid his hand on the head of one of the little gray poodles, careful not to disturb the sequin bows clipped near its ears.

"They're barking at the swan's patoot on her head," Sue murmured to Henry, dabbing primly at the sweat along her hairline with a blossom of tissue.

The lights in the tent kept going up and down and on and off as the stagehands ran through the cues, and Henry was about to suggest that the dogs were barking because they were about to have seizures. But then he saw what Sue was referring to: the contortionist, a petite Mexican girl who was even younger than Henry, had a new headdress, a massive black-and-white fountain of feathers, spewing from her small head.

"She just got it, and she goes on right before us. If the dogs see her come outta the ring wearing that, they're gonna get all nervous just before their act." Sue turned to Henry. "Do me a favor. The next time she walks by and they bark, go to all the females and lift up their ears and whisper, 'candy canes' to them."

"Are you . . . are you serious?"

"Of course," she said, tightening the strings on the back of her frilly corset.

"Which ones are female? They're all wearing bows."

"The two on the left. Jo-jo and Cantaloupe. Just whisper it, and don't be sarcastic about it, or it won't help. I will whisper to the males. They have a different command word."

They waited until the contortionist walked by again, and when the dogs barked, Henry kneeled in the sawdust and lifted their silky ears and said what Sue told him to say. The first dog, Jo-jo, whimpered for a moment and marched her front paws in place. Cantaloupe only blinked. The next time the contortionist went by, they were calm.

"You're good at this," he said to Sue. "Not like Lorne. I don't even think he likes animals."

"Well. Thank you. Though, you're wrong, Lorne does like the animals."

"He doesn't act like it. I know he hooks Tex. You just whisper random words in their ears and they behave."

"They're dogs. Tex is a big girl, and she's got a hide thicker than asphalt. She can handle it. Ask your friend Azi about Lorne if you want. You'll change your mind about him."

"Why don't you tell me?"

"Because Azi will enjoy telling you more than I will. He likes his gossip. And we've got fifteen minutes before they let in the patrons."

Henry left the ring thinking that Feely and Feinstein wasn't so different than Edgefield, where everybody told stories about everybody else's business, and the truth got buried.

WHEN HE GOT HOME TO the Baratuccis', it was dark. He took the spare key from under the mat and opened the door on a silent living room. Adrienne had kept the chain on the door undone for him. Richard eyed him from his cage, shifting from one perch to the other to get a better look.

Henry hadn't seen Caleb at the show. Light still came from under Caleb and Adrienne's door, but he could not hear the sounds of them whispering, as he had on other nights. His footsteps seemed loud, and he took care to walk silently after he realized this. The ticks of the clock seemed as obtrusive as a snare drum.

He noticed something propped against the wall next to the television that had not been there when he left. Taking off his shoes, he studied the thing. It was a canvas. He could tell that Caleb liked paintings because his house was full of them, all girls with long necks, flowers rendered in sunset colors, dark-suited men outlined in thick black strokes. But this canvas made Henry suspect that Caleb was a painter himself and this made him wish Caleb would like him more.

Henry pulled the canvas from its position leaning against the television and found that it had a hole in it, a big one. The painting was unfinished, colored in light shades all over. He could still see the pencil sketch in some places beneath the paint. It was a woman in a red robe, one breast exposed, her long hair obscuring the other. Perched beside her was a large hook-beaked bird.

Henry felt his face begin to burn. The painting didn't exactly look like Adrienne, but it was her, and she was nearly naked. It wasn't her semi-nudity that embarrassed him, though. It was that he'd stumbled upon something that must have been a secret between them. The hole in the canvas made him think that this secret was not entirely about the two of them making doe-eyes at each other and saying, "I love you, I love you. Get naked, my darling."

He carefully replaced the painting and walked toward the guest room.

Halfway down the hall, he heard a mournful voice come from the living room. It was slightly robotic but definitely feminine. "Please don't leave me," it said. "Please, please, please."

Henry went back into the living room and saw Richard, bobbing his head, blinking his lizard eyes. The bird opened its mouth just enough for Henry to see its tongue and begged him again: "Please don't leave me. Please, please, please."

TWO DAYS LATER, THE CIRCUS hit the road.

CHAPTER 10

Edgefield, Indiana
1983–1985

IT'S FRIGID IN THEIR HOUSE the night Andre runs; the heat's gone out and it's the middle of winter. Henry stands in the doorway of their bedroom and watches his brother fill a big bright-yellow duffel bag full of clothes and bars of soap and razors and socks. It is the middle of the night, and their father is dead asleep, but Henry woke up when he heard his brother unzip the bag to pack. Andre moves swiftly and quietly, as if he is stealing his own things. When he finishes, he slings the bag over his shoulder and walks to where Henry is standing, at the bedroom door. Andre hasn't told him what he's doing, but Henry knows, and he doesn't move.

"Move, little brother," he says. Henry knows Andre has been waiting to do this for five years, waiting to be tall enough and whiskered enough to be mistaken for a man. Counting the days since their mother died, planning his flight.

At twelve Henry can't pass for a man. His head comes barely to the middle of Andre's chest when his brother stands square with him. *Move, little brother.*

"I'm going to Chicago, I'm going to stay with Aunt Jenny," he says. "Don't tell Dad. If he shows up, I'll know who told him, and I'll beat your ass."

"When will you come back?" Henry asks, stupidly, full of stone-heavy dread.

"I don't know. You've got to be cool about this. I promise I'll catch up with you later." He touches his face to the top of Henry's head, and Henry feels his brother's warm, fast breath on his scalp.

This is against the rules, Henry thinks. Like wasting food, like staying out too long, like getting in trouble at school, and all the subtler rules that Andre broke to keep himself alive, and that Henry kept diligently, for the same purpose.

Andre pushes past Henry into the hallway, where the only light comes from under the door of the bathroom. The soft yellow glow and the hum of the refrigerator make it seem like Andre is leaving a peaceful place, and Henry can see him hesitating, drawn into the illusion.

Andre grabs the fabric of Henry's pajamas then and pulls him closer. He whispers, "Hey. Keep treading light, huh? Don't fight him but don't let him know you need him, either. He'll get you if you do."

Then he goes. The front door doesn't squeak. Andre must've gotten to it with WD-40. His brother is smart.

Henry doesn't know what to do. If he tells on Andre, the consequences of that betrayal would be terrible. If he does not tell, Andre might get kidnapped or murdered or thrown in jail. These thoughts keep him awake, tossing around. His pajama pants feel too hot, so he takes them off. Then, he feels like the top of his pajamas are choking him, so he takes that off, too. His long underwear ride up and strangle his balls. By morning, he is naked. He goes to the bathroom and sees in the mirror that his lips are blue, and his skin is white as a bone. He still feels uncomfortable. Shaking, he dresses himself in the loosest clothes in his drawers, pinches Frankie awake and makes him dress himself and brush his teeth. Then, he wakes up his father and tells him that Andre has gone.

At fourteen, Henry is awakened by the thudding of his heart every morning and a keen feeling of dread. He shakes it off as best he can, gets dressed, and walks Frankie to the elementary school before going on to the junior high. Frankie sits by himself on a curb, waiting for the bell to ring. He and Frankie are in the same boat, and Henry can't exactly figure out what made them so unpopular. It might be their generic tennis shoes and sloppy haircuts, but Henry suspects it's something more. Their classmates know all about their mother, and now, all about Andre, who never showed up at their Aunt Jenny's (according to her, anyway). He never turned up anywhere else, either. He has seen it happen to other kids before; people got to know too much private, unspeakable stuff about those kids, and it ruined their reputations. Sometimes that private, unspeakable stuff isn't their fault, and sometimes it is. It doesn't seem to make a difference.

"Why don't they like me, Henry?" Frankie asks sometimes. And Henry can't explain what he barely understands himself, so he jokes: "They're jealous of your long eyelashes. They can't stand the effect you have on older women." Or: "They're afraid of you. They know you are learning the Bell Brothers' Ultimate Kung Fu."

Like Frankie, Henry would be totally invisible if it weren't for Cassie Littrell and her loud mouth drawing attention to him. He's still playing the kinds of games with her that he feels guilty about in the morning. Her laugh is still like rusty nails dumped in a bathtub, but her hair smells like lilacs, and she doesn't fight with boys anymore. She drinks rum and Cokes, easy on the Coke, out of a plastic travel mug. Henry likes the way she doesn't wear makeup, and the way she doesn't seem to notice that she's his only friend.

Her friends are like her—they smoke cigarettes and pierce their ears with safety pins. They call him queer because he's got a mouth like a girl (Cassie told him this when he was little, and he finally accepts it as true). It doesn't bother him too much. If they say it too loud for him to pretend to ignore it, he'll make it a joke, bat his eyelashes, and say, "So you've noticed?"

But Cassie's friend Lee is the worst. He's a Miller, a cousin to their old neighbor, Will. He has a high-and-tight haircut and wears fatigues, as if he's already a marine, whiskerless and acne-sprinkled.

They play cards at lunch—blackjack, with no bets, of course, because none of them have any money. When Henry is dealing, Lee accuses him of cheating because Henry's dealt himself an ace and a jack three out of seven games.

"Dude, I couldn't cheat if I wanted to. If I could cheat, I'd be out hustling people at cards, not sitting in a junior high cafeteria."

"There's no way you're that lucky. You're stacking the deck," says Lee, throwing his cards at Henry. They fall on the floor, and Henry twists in his seat to pick them up.

Other kids are walking to their tables with their orange plastic lunch trays in hand. Cassie picks at a peanut butter sandwich she brought from home and passes her cards back to Henry.

"I'm *not* lucky, usually," says Henry, shuffling the deck.

"It's true, he's not," says Cassie.

"Then how come he's had three perfect hands? That's what I'm saying, it's not luck, it's cheating," says Lee.

"You wanna deal?" says Henry, offering him the cards.

Lee squints at him. "No, I don't wanna deal. You deal. I'm going to watch you and see how you cheat."

Cassie rolls her eyes. "You're a retard, Lee."

Henry deals the cards. He does it nice and slow and lets Lee cut the deck. Cassie finishes her sandwich and pulls her travel mug out of her backpack and takes a drink. When the cards are dealt, Lee stares over the tops of his cards at Henry.

"Hit me," he says.

Henry slides a card across the table to him. Lee picks it up and looks at it, looks at Henry, lays the whole hand on the table. "I bust. This is bullshit," he says, loud this time, so that some people turn in their chairs to see what's going on.

"You watched me. Did I cheat?" Henry says.

"I know you did," he says and throws the cards at him again.

Henry picks them up. "Fine. I won't deal anymore," he says. He really, really doesn't want to fight. If he does, his father may or may not be angry, and Henry doesn't want to risk it. It doesn't occur to him to stop cheating—he's not stacking the deck, but he has four high cards literally up his sleeve, which he plucks from the deck in between each hand. How could he resist?

With fingers that are so quick, so precise, and an opponent like Lee, who's such a prick all the time, how can he be expected not to cheat?

"I'll deal," says Cassie, holding out her hand. Lee swats it away.

"No, let him deal. I'm going to catch him. He's got cards up his ass or something, don'tcha, fag?"

"Yep, a whole deck. Plenty of room in there," says Henry, reshuffling. A girl sitting behind him laughs. He can't tell if she is laughing at Lee's comment or at his, or if she's just laughing because they make her nervous and she doesn't know what else to do. Cassie's usual line here is to announce to Lee what Henry did to her last night, to protect his manliness, but Lee interrupts her.

"Yeah, I bet. Plenty of room. Bet you could fit a few decks in there. Or a football team. Take after your mom."

Henry stops shuffling. "What are you talking about?"

Now everyone on this side of the cafeteria is watching them, and they are not giggling anymore.

Lee leans forward and Henry can see blue veins reaching up from his temple to the edges of his haircut. "I mean, you take after your mom," he says. "She's the one that taught you how to take a train, right? One dick right after the other."

He isn't afraid of Lee. Henry knows he can whip this kid for the same reason he knows he can cheat at cards and not get caught—because his body is smarter than his brain. All he needs to do is watch someone else do something and then picture himself doing it. This is how he learned to become a wheel for his mother and how to play basketball for Andre and how to juggle apples for Frankie. He learned these things fast, without much practice, because his body knows the urgency of things.

This is how he finds himself on top of the table, stepping across it, and thrusting his foot, heel first, into Lee's face. Even through the sole of his shoe, Henry can feel Lee's nose flatten and crack. When Lee tries to get out of his seat, he gets another heel in the chin, which forces him back into his chair. Lee can't see through the tears that have filled his eyes, so that's the end of it.

HENRY SITS THERE, IN MRS. Hancock's office, waiting for his father to come pick him up, his heart speeding up every time he thinks that maybe everyone knows—that maybe this thing, about his mom, is the thing that everyone says about him when he is not around. Do the kids in Frankie's grade know it, too? Do they ignore him, and then whisper behind his back that his mother was a whore, barely knowing what they are saying, repeating the things their own mothers talk about?

Henry had abandoned the idea that the man who their father shot at was a government agent years ago. Andre had shamed him out of this theory. But the notion that the man could have been his mother's boyfriend came to Henry only recently, and he was surprised he hadn't drawn that conclusion before. Obviously others had drawn that conclusion, too.

He can't bring himself to blame her for it. He knows now that things happened between his mother and father, on the other sides of walls, just before she walked into a room, in the dark when he and Andre and Frankie couldn't see. He remembers sudden whimpers, pleading whispers coming from other parts of the house, the look on his father's face when he had done something to Andre or Henry himself and gotten a rise out of her. At the time, these moments seemed uncomfortable, but ordinary. In retrospect, Henry understands the full implications with horror and guilt.

So she was with someone else. Maybe she was with a lot of someone elses, looking for a nice guy. Who cares? But it makes him furious that *other* people might have her figured for some kind of slut, running their mouths when they didn't know the first thing about her.

His father comes. Mrs. Hancock greets him with a handshake—she hasn't said a word to Henry except "sit" the whole time he's been in the room. She is a fat woman with icy-pink lipstick and black hair pulled back tight that explodes into a frizzy ponytail. After shaking her hand, his father leans down to make eye contact with Henry, resting his hands on his knees. He has a two-day growth of whiskers from getting home late from work and not showering or shaving before he goes to bed.

"I had to take off early to get you," he says.

Henry sits up straight and tries to look apologetic but doesn't speak. His father's mouth tells him that anything he says right now will be the wrong thing. Mrs. Hancock says that she is really sorry about all this and hands his father a form to sign.

Mrs. Hancock glances at Henry disapprovingly and then looks down at her forms. His father's voice and his body language announce plainly that he intends to beat the shit out of Henry, and she seems to approve. She thinks she knows how this goes, because she knows the fathers in this town, the controlled cruelty they dole out to boys. But she knows nothing. Just like the rest of them, the smug little bastards who spread trash about his mother, who leave Frankie out of kickball games.

At this moment, Henry hates Edgefield and everyone in it. It's all he can do not to fly at Mrs. Hancock and punch her in her icy-pink mouth. He follows his father out through a hallway of gawkers and meets all their eyes fearlessly, hoping one of them will say one word, one fucking word. No one does.

As soon as he slides into the passenger seat of the car, his father reaches over and slaps him. When Henry covers his face, his father knocks his hand away and slaps him again. He feels it in his teeth, but worse, it's insulting.

"Why would you do that? Why don't you use your brain, Henry? Now you can't go on school property, and I have to send Frankie to school by himself. The next thing you know, he's in a fight on the way there, and I gotta take off in the middle of the day to get *him*, too," he says.

Henry shakes with rage and holds his cheek. His father slaps him again, and for the second time today, Henry's body moves of its own accord. He lunges at his father over the arm rest that separates their seats and immediately gets a fist in his side. Henry loses his wind. He can fight, but he's no Jackie Chan, especially not in a car. If he had wanted to avoid this, he should have run.

But there is no space here to regret his decision, no space to think at all. His thoughts are unreachable, on the other side of a wall of pain. If he could get to them, he might be able to stop his father from hitting him, but the wall gets higher, gets thicker. He thinks he says, "Dad, Frankie doesn't fight; it will be okay," though it's probably just coming out as nonsense, just garbled, breathless begging. *Stupid, Henry.* He should have used his mind when it was still an option.

When Henry's head slams into the passenger window, he feels the glass shatter. It falls slow, though, like snow, and there's something not quite right about it. It's not really happening like this. There is no broken glass. He is in between worlds now, barely conscious. His face is pressed against the door, face smashed to the window, his neck crushed between the door and his father's hand. He tries to remember how to get back to the part where it was snowing glass, because there was not so much pain in that part.

Then, his father lets go, stops hitting. Full consciousness slams into Henry, and he feels the blood rushing hot to all his injuries. This is the worst part, but then it gets a little better, and a little better, until he can reach his thoughts again. The fuzz clears from Henry's vision, and he sees his father's face has gone white. He knows what he has done to Henry; the anger goes out, and shame slithers in. It cools your blood, sucks the color from your face. This shame is paralytic. His father doesn't move, but the car fills with the sound of his breathing. It's a terrible thing to hear.

Eventually, his father starts the car. Henry sits up and tries to put on his safety belt in a way that doesn't make it obvious that he hurts all over. Half-way home, Henry says he is sorry for kicking Lee in the face, and he really is, though he only says so out loud because it will help protect him, and Frankie, to apologize. "Sorry. I'm really sorry."

His father squeezes the steering wheel and nods.

He lets Henry sit by himself while he picks up Frankie from school, then makes Henry and Frankie double-decker ham sandwiches for dinner. This means his father is sorry, too. Henry eats it, even though it hurts to chew. He thinks, bitterly, that when he leaves here he will never apologize for anything again, not with words or with sandwiches, because apologies are empty.

They eat at the table, with the TV on. Frankie watches Henry eat, his eyes magnified by the lenses of his glasses. He looks back and forth between Henry and their father, swallowing bites of sandwich without chewing. Henry knows he hates ham.

119

After their father goes to bed, Henry pesters Frankie to put on his pajamas and brush his teeth. Frankie doesn't argue tonight, but he moves slow as molasses, eyes fixed on Henry, who stands in the doorway of the bathroom while he brushes.

"Celia Miller said you got into it with Lee," he says, after he spits a wad of foamy toothpaste into the sink.

"Huh? Yeah. I did. I'm suspended now. But I don't get to sleep in, 'cause I still have to walk some little punk to school."

"She said you won."

Henry takes his turn at the sink and knows just what Frankie means by this when he sees himself in the mirror. Half his face was swollen, his right eye purpled. The real mess is on the inside, in his throat and in his midsection, but his father was too angry to keep the visible parts intact this time. He passes his little brother a cup of water and brushes his own teeth, trying not to wince.

Frankie stands there with the cup.

"You should see Lee. Now *he's* fucked up," Henry says and laughs. "His face looks like a taco."

Henry knows Frankie can deduce the facts. But Henry will keep bluffing. Their father has never done anything like this to Frankie, and there is no reason Frankie should have to walk around fearful that he will, not while Henry can block for him.

As Henry washes his face, Frankie seems to cave in on himself, his skinny arms and legs drawn more and more tightly to the center of his body, until he is a lump on the floor. The water from his cup spills and pools around his downy, knobby knees.

Henry kneels down next to him and mops up the water with a towel. He taps his brother lightly on the cheek to get him to look at him. Frankie lifts his head. His brow is knit, the bridge of his nose raw from his glasses. Henry takes the glasses off.

"Hey, man. I'm fine. Alright? Quit being weird and rinse your mouth."

WHEN FRANKIE GOES TO BED, Cassie will come over and try to make Henry feel better, and it will annoy him. She'll say he won't have to put up with his dad much longer, and she'll say Lee got what he deserved. She'll graze her fingers over the backs of his arms until he sleeps. But in the morning he'll still know his body betrayed him when it carried him over the table and broke Lee's nose.

Henry is afraid he'll do worse one day.

Alien Encounters

The circus leaves St. Louis for Galesburg tomorrow, and I can't sleep. I just nodded off for half an hour and had a dream everyone was walking around wearing those helmets, the ones the Flying Delaflotes wear at the beginning of the show. The helmets were heavier in the dream. Me and Kylie, Azi and the Germans, Caleb and Adrienne and Lorne, we were all walking around with our heads dragging the ground. In the dream, it was kind of creepy, and I thought of how insects curl up like that when they're half-squashed.

Now that I'm awake, though, it seems kind of ridiculous. I mean, it was just so much ass. Giant ass and old guy ass, skinny, crazy trick-rider ass. Kylie's bubble ass and my assless ass, and Jenifer and Vroni's twin velociraptor asses. Azi's I-did-eighty-squats-this-morning ass.

So now I've got this idea for a show about an alien with a too-big head. He's the typical type, with a green body and eyes like big black tree seeds and no ears. Gecko fingers. But that head. It's just too big. The gravity on his planet just doesn't have the same power as ours, and now, here he is, on the street, trying to get back to his ship with his noggin scraping the sidewalk.

While he's pulling his head along behind him, he'll be asking people, "Hey, have you seen a ship? Hey, can you help me out here?"

He'll drag his head to the clown, who has been obliviously reading his news-paper while everyone else took off. The clown is respectable, in his bowler hat and a tweed vest, and he tries to be polite: "Well, what does the ship look like?" *he asks.*

"Oh, y'know, like a couple of plates stacked rim to rim," *says the alien.*

The clown in the tweed vest scratches his head.

"It has a lot of lights," *says the alien, bending at the knees, unable to get com-fortable.*

"Mmmhmmm. Mmmmhmm."

"Some landing gear."

"Of course, of course."

"You've seen it, then? Oh, thank goodness. This is really agitating, this situa-tion."

"Hmm? What 'situation'?"

Silence here.

"Oh! You mean, the situation with your fat head," *says the clown.* "Terribly sorry."

"Completely understandable."

More silence. The alien's gecko hand rubs the back of his neck, as the clown purses his lips and looks off to the side.

"So, you've seen it, right?" *asks the alien.*

"Your head? Yes. Very unfortunate for you."

"My ship."

"Oh, your ship. No, I'm afraid I haven't. I meant, I know the type. I haven't seen your ship specifically."

"So, you haven't seen it?"

"No, I have."

"You have?"

"Yes. Just not yours specifically."

The alien fully realizes now that he has gotten help from the wrong person. But it's too late to go back. The clown insists on helping.

The rest of the sketch will be about them finding the ship, a lot of physical gags where the alien's head bumps up stairs and the clown tries to shove him through doors too small for him. In the end, they'll find it, of course. The clown will send his friend up into space with good wishes. He'll go back to reading his paper, glad to resume his routine, though maybe once he'll look up at the sky, like he's a little lonely.

I think I would do the alien in this one. I make a good straight man.

If I had my way, I would have Christiakov be the clown. He plays that role well. The helpful dumb guy. But I'll probably have to settle for the second-best person to play the part, because there's no way I'll call Christiakov unless what I've got to show him is perfect. Proof that I wasn't a waste of time.

CHAPTER II

June 1990

ON THE WAY TO GALESBURG, Henry rode in the trailer, which was now fastened to a pickup truck by a hitch that Henry noticed was made in a factory near Edgefield. Not the factory where his father worked, but one where many other people from his hometown worked. Stuffed into the trailer with him were Caleb, the German girls, and Kylie. Henry's cot was folded into the wall and in its place was a bench where Henry and Kylie sat, their thighs touching every time the trailer hit a bump. Catty-corner to them was another bench where Caleb did crossword puzzles. Jenifer and Vroni perched like a couple of birds on the metal shelf that Henry had used as a makeup table and whispered to each other in German, turning their beady eyes in his direction before returning to their conversation.

Henry watched Caleb, trying to get a clue from his face about how Adrienne was doing. The news from her MRI had not been good, and Henry didn't know all the details, but her surgery was scheduled for the end of July. Caleb's face was pale and unshaven, and he did his crossword without looking up. Maybe Henry should have felt sorry for him, but he didn't. He liked Caleb but he couldn't believe he'd left Adrienne when she was clearly sick and scared. Not even his father, who was the world's biggest asshole, was

125

such a coward. When his mother had the stomach flu, he'd stood by her like a sentinel.

Outside, cornfields went by in a green velvety blur. Up close, Henry knew the stalks were short, leaves curled from the heat and lack of rain. The cows grazed in patchy fields, on weeds and yellow grass.

Kylie passed him a scrap of paper. *What's wrong with you?*

It was not a question that could be answered on a scrap of paper. What he should have done was write *Nothing* and hold her hand as she had held his before their last performance. But he didn't, because he was preoccupied with what seemed to be going on with Adrienne and dreading having to perform the farmer show *again*. So he just shook his head and handed Kylie her piece of paper back. The German girls giggled.

What Seamus had said was, "Henry, if it ain't broke, you don't fix it."

Henry had done his best to hold Seamus's stare, but the man made him nervous, with his weird violet eyes and low voice.

And so it was the farmer show for the rest of the season. It got laughs. It fit with the other acts. And that was that.

Henry had told Adrienne and Caleb about Seamus refusing to let him change the show, and Caleb had shaken his head and left the room, clearly unsurprised and not disappointed. Only Adrienne understood. She said that she was sorry, that Seamus had never let her do the things she wanted to do, either.

"He always wanted me dressed like a prostitute and holding some kind of phallic thing, like a sword or a boa constrictor. His taste is cheap."

And Henry looked at the long curve of her neck, and he nearly said, *You could never look cheap. You are the most beautiful woman on the planet.*

At a rest stop outside Peoria, the circus caravan pulled into the trucks and trailers parking lot so everyone could stretch their legs. Only Kylie got out, though; Caleb and Henry were determined in their misery, Jenifer and Vroni too deep in conversation.

Through the trailer window, Henry saw Kylie toeing the black-eyed Susans along the edge of the parking lot with her sneakers. Vroni pointed at her, and Jenifer squealed with laughter.

"Okay, what the fuck are you laughing at?" asked Henry.

"Henry," warned Caleb.

"Mind your own business, little Pierrot," said Vroni.

"Hey, where's your handler?" asked Henry.

"Probably with your fat girlfriend," said Vroni.

Then he was standing over them, one of his hands clamped over Vroni's arm. He could break them both in two, snap them apart at the legs like a couple of wishbones. They didn't seem to know this. They only looked up at him curiously.

"She's not my girlfriend," he said, and his hand clamped harder around Vroni's arm.

"Sit down, Pierrot," said Jenifer.

"Call me that again and I'll show you a sad clown."

"Henry," Caleb said. "Sit. Please."

Henry turned and saw Caleb looking up from the thin tablet of crossword puzzles.

"Please," Caleb said.

Caleb had a pamphlet between the pages of his puzzle book, the kind you get at the doctor's office. Information about thyroids or herpes or, in this case, probably brain tumors.

"What'll you do if I don't?" said Henry.

Caleb didn't say anything.

"That's right. That's what you'll do. Fucking nothing," Henry said.

If Adrienne were his wife, he wouldn't have left her for anything. In fact, just being her tenant for a week had made it hard to leave her. He'd felt so good the day that he had performed for her, when she was down and he had painted his original face on and balanced a small library's worth of books on his head. Her smiles were worth more than other smiles and being able to ease her mind helped ease his own. It was Caleb who should have been hungry for that approval; he was the person who was supposed to comfort her.

Caleb closed his crossword book, enfolding the medical pamphlet in it. "If you think you are the first person that Vroni and Jenifer and I have seen lose their mind in a circus trailer, then you have another thing coming.

Usually we've made it through at least one show, but hey, you're an amateur. I know it. This is what I expect from amateurs. So what exactly is it that you think I should do? Kick you off? If I did that to every performer that Vroni and Jenifer provoked, we'd never have a show."

This set them off again, the German girls, and they were back to cackling.

"Amateur?" said Henry. He looked for other words to follow this, but there weren't any. Amateur. It was a kick to the chest.

Kylie climbed back on the bus then with a handful of black-eyed Susans. When the trailer started rolling, Henry had no choice but to do what Caleb said and sit down. Almost immediately there was another note in his lap in Kylie's cursive:

What am I, then?

BEFORE THE GALESBURG PERFORMANCE, HENRY realized that he had grabbed Adrienne's lime-green makeup bag instead of his own when he'd packed. He had a brief moment of panic, mostly because his brother's letter was tucked in that bag, but he assured himself that Adrienne would take care of it for him, and Kylie let him use her makeup, which was better quality than his own and of which she had a pretty ridiculous abundance. He thought he was deftly avoiding the subject of whether or not they were dating, and he could tell she didn't want to press it while they were stuck in close quarters, dependent on each other for professional success. But when he had asked to use her makeup, she'd gotten so uncomfortable she ended up just shoving half a dozen tubes and compacts into his hands, and running off to the bathroom, as if desperate to end their conversation.

In Galesburg, they performed in an open lot next to a mall and couldn't quite get the lighting right in the tent. This was fine with Henry, who could see the faces of his audience clearly for the first time since he'd joined Feely and Feinstein. They were mostly small faces, children with loud, honest laughs.

The Galesburg show was a good show, even though Kylie wouldn't smile at him.

The Chicago show was a different story.

This was a big show, the biggest yet, and he'd worked, and starved, and worked some more to get here. He'd walked the streets with an apple in his hand trying to entice someone, who was always busy, into giving him five minutes of their life, so he could show them how an apple can be a world.

He'd left his little brother alone with his father because he wanted to do these things, and now here he was, taking a fake punch from a girl who probably should've knocked him out for real. He flipped backward, the icy white lights in his eyes, and in that blind moment it occurred to him that if he had written his brother back, Andre might have been here watching him right now.

According to Caleb, Chicago was the biggest show he'd do on the tour, and though the tent was not quite filled to capacity, Henry knew that there were more eyes fixed on him now than there had ever been before. And of these hundreds of eyes, none of them belonged to his brother. All he could think about, as he landed, legs-up, against the bales of straw, was how much he regretted this. If he'd written *something*—a couple words on a wadded-up napkin would have worked—he could have shown Andre how things had changed since they'd last seen each other.

The show went on and on, a bright blur, Henry trudging through the routine without listening for the audience's reaction. He was supposed to cry now and be interrupted by the sounds of stomach rumbling. But he found that the corners of his mouth would not turn down and he couldn't make his eyes squint. And then, when the stomach rumbling sounds came over the speakers, he couldn't snap his face into surprise. The Chicago crowd tittered in confusion. Henry felt their frustration building, but he couldn't give them what they were looking for. His muscles would simply not respond to his mind's commands. When he tried to look sad, he made a gasping noise instead, and when he tried to look surprised, his face went slack.

He caught a glimpse of Kylie. She wore her favorite nose, bulbous and shiny. She looked at him sidelong, and he saw a brief glimpse of her panic—but her jaw tightened with determination, and she turned toward the audience with a dramatic expression of woe.

Amateur. He was an amateur.

He fumbled on. When the carrot top sprouted from the ground, he only watched it, stupefied. He didn't lose his hat or spring straight up off the ground or close his own gaping mouth with his hand. He just stood and stared. Finally the audience began to laugh genuine laughs, but only because Henry looked lost. They didn't know if his behavior was an act or not. They didn't care.

Finally, the act found its end, and Henry ran backstage, where he bent over the bars of the elephant's enclosure and threw up into the straw. Kylie went straight to a corner to change into her clown garb, the white bodysuit with red marabou around the neck, wrists, and ankles. She did not ask him what was wrong or if he was alright, but once she was dressed, she stood and glared at him as she tied her hair in two ponytails, little brown pom-poms on either side of her head. His stomach kept heaving.

He heard the tent flap open and the voices of Azi and the German girls. Out of the corner of his eye he saw the shimmer of Azi in sequins and Jenifer and Vroni's whiteface. Henry heard the slosh of water, Chuck Delaflote following them with buckets to extinguish the fire at the act's end.

"What's wrong with him?" Azi asked. "He's not in costume."

"How should I know? He just started puking for no reason," Kylie answered.

Henry tried to lift his head and assure Azi that he would be ready in a minute, but the warm saliva gathering in his mouth told him he'd better not move.

"We're going on, Henry. You have to hurry," said Azi.

Jenifer dipped her head to look at his face. "Oh, *mein armes Kind!*" she said, patting his shoulder.

"Don't touch me," Henry managed to say, wiping the vomit from his lips with his sleeve and leaving a smear of white makeup on his shirt.

"Don't worry," said Kylie. "I'll get in on the act. You don't really need both of us out there." She picked up the fire extinguisher that Henry normally used.

Now it was Azi's crooked face next to his. Henry could smell the lighter fluid on his breath. "You're alright, then?" Azi asked.

Henry nodded. "I'll be out."

Azi and the German girls walked out into the ring then, Chuck right behind them. Kylie stood on deck, waiting for her cue. When it came, he heard her say, "Really, Henry. We'll be totally fine. Sit this one out."

He tried to move to get his costume, but the room still spun. The elephant's feet shifted in the straw, and Henry heard its loud sniffing, then felt the tip of Tex's snout, like a finger, poking him in the back. Then he felt the whole trunk lying on his shoulder. "Ah, God, you are so weird and gross," Henry told Tex. He did find her skin strange, but in truth, it was comforting.

Ambrosia was tied near the elephant pen. She also began inching toward Henry, her hooves clicking against the hard concrete beneath the hay. The shoes seemed to make it hard for her to lift her feet, but Henry might have imagined that, since things seemed to be moving in slow motion. He thought he might have imagined that she was moving at all, since she had never let him get too close, not even when he filled her water trough or offered her an apple.

But no, he wasn't imagining it. She was right there, craning her neck to smell his cheek. Lorne was right. She was a special animal. Henry thought he had never felt anything as soft as her nose. Her breath smelled surprisingly pleasant, and the puffs of it against his face seemed affectionate. It was consoling, but he wished for something more, for a human understanding.

Henry ran the tips of his fingers down the length of her nose. "You're too nice to make a joke out of," he said, and thought of Adrienne, who, like him, had spent time as a fool for the entertainment of others. Who Caleb had left and who might feel as abandoned as he did at the moment.

He heard Kylie's fire extinguisher: *shooooosh.* Shouts of laughter followed.

Christiakov was right. Audiences came for blood. So why had they even bothered? Why had Christiakov bothered training him, and why did Henry bother now? Why did he ruin his back and study his face for hours? Why did he bother analyzing the titters of the crowd, thinking, *This one has to be perfect. I'm a phony if this isn't perfect?*

Why was he doing this at all?

131

He still felt nauseous, but by putting his arms around Ambosia's neck, he was able to get to his feet. He couldn't get back in the ring. No, he was done with that, at least for tonight. What he had to do was get away from Feely and Feinstein. What he had to do was see Adrienne. There was a cacophony of inner voices berating him, telling him that he had done everything wrong, that he could never make it right. The one right thing he could think to do was to be with Adrienne. She did not want to be alone; he could be her not-alone. He could handle at least that much.

CHAPTER 12

CALEB LEANED AGAINST THE GLASS of the payphone that stood on the fairgrounds, about fifty yards from the circus tent. It was a strange, desolate place out here—the Chicago show was actually in a town called St. Charles, about thirty miles outside of Chicago, and the tent was set up in the same space that hosted Hog Fest and Mud Bowl and the Bacon Olympics and any number of other redneck events that probably drew bigger crowds than Feely and Feinstein had tonight.

The show had begun—they were probably well into the aerial act. He'd wanted to call Adrienne earlier, but she was at her doctor's appointment, discussing treatments, all the drugs that sounded to Caleb like dinosaur names: bromocriptine. Octreotide. In fact, all the words that Adrienne and her doctor used to discuss her condition sounded vaguely monstrous and otherworldly: adenoma. Somatotrophs. In a matter of weeks, they had gone from calling it "something else" to identifying the names of the cells that made up that something else.

Over the phone, Adrienne had cried because her wedding ring was cutting into her finger. It was red, she said, so red that it looked like it might be bleeding under the ring.

"It isn't, honey," he told her. "You're probably just puffy from the stress and the heat."

"No, Caleb. I'm *growing*. I'm growing again."

Caleb rubbed at his face. "Are you taking the octreotide?" he said.

"Yes." She sniffed. "The nurse gave me the last one at my appointment, but I've done all the rest."

The octreotide had to be injected beneath Adrienne's skin every eight hours. The doctor had started the regimen as soon as she'd gotten the results back from her MRI. He wanted to treat her "aggressively," he'd said. For now, the octreotide, then, another surgery to remove the tumor, then, they'd radiate the hell out of the thing, and then, another medication. With any luck, it would never grow back again. But for now, Adrienne stuck herself with needles. She didn't ask Caleb to do it for her—she'd done it for herself before, she said. Not only would she not allow him to give the injection, she wouldn't let him watch either and locked herself in the bathroom.

"You've got to give it a chance to work. So you went up a ring size. It's no big deal. It's a ring size."

"You didn't go up a ring size in a month," Adrienne said. "Honestly, Caleb, I've seen pictures of people who can't control this, and I swear to God, I'm going to have fingers like corn dogs."

He grinned at this analogy. "You won't let me see those pictures. So I have no idea what you're talking about," he said.

Then he told her he had to go because there was someone waiting to use the phone. He would call her tomorrow, on the road to Indianapolis. He was startled at the sadness he could hear in his own voice and hoped Adrienne could hear it, too, so she would know how he felt.

"Okay," she said. He heard a flap of wings. Richard was in her lap. "I'm sorry to cry on the phone. And I'm sorry about the painting," she said.

"Don't worry about the painting."

"I'm going to take off my ring. If they have to cut it off, I'll die. Those nurses will laugh at me, and I'll be so humiliated."

"Do whatever you need to. We'll get it resized when I get home."

"And I'm going to have your painting restored," she said.

"What, like it's a Rembrandt? No, honey. I'll just start over."

He said good-bye, then, and hung up the phone.

As Caleb walked to the tent he thought about how, once, he interviewed a performer, and instead of asking her questions from an interview form, he asked her questions that he wanted to know the answers to. He listened to her digress, divulge too much about herself, and he ended up loving her. That was the joke between him and Adrienne. She was the reason why he interviewed people the no-frills way that he did now—because he didn't want to end up married again.

He'd conducted this interview at Bill's Caribbean Steakhouse. Conall Feely was dead, and Seamus found himself in possession of his father's circus. He had just offered Caleb the position of circus manager, and Caleb's first task was to hire a new act ("Something kinda sideshow. But not too freaky," Seamus had said). He was directed to the steakhouse by a customer at the Hanky Panky Party Shop, who had spent a drunken birthday there and sworn he'd seen a giantess on their stage. So Caleb had thought, why not check it out? At least he could treat himself to a steak.

When he saw Adrienne, he knew she was exceptional in spite of the kitsch and the gimmicky parrot on her shoulder. She sang and danced and talked to the parrot and the audience. She told jokes and took on the personas of several different characters, relaying the memoirs of a giantess raised in the jungle, who finds out that her real father is a gorilla. The hug of her suit barely smoothed the contours of her crotch, and he thought of that part of her as magnified, bigger, and more accessible than a normal woman's. He wondered if any man had ever filled her, really, and he imagined being the one, the only one, who could.

By the time she had finished her act and met him at his booth, he was drenched in sweat. She slid into the red Naugahyde booth across from him, and sat sideways, stretching legs still encased in silky stockings across the booth. This was purely utilitarian—her legs would not fit under the table—and not meant to entice Caleb. But it did. Up close, she was even more unbelievable. He was afraid that she would not be interested in the job he was sure he would offer her, but he tried to look confident. She put her parrot down on the branch of a fake palm tree behind their booth and offered Caleb her hand.

"I'm Adrienne Lee," she said. "And this is Richard."

"Caleb Baratucci," he'd said. "And you have to cut me some slack because I'm a little new at this." He tried to discreetly tuck more of his shirt into his armpits to hide the darkening fabric. Luckily, he was a little handsomer then, or so he liked to think. He was always a little thin on top when it came to hair, but he got compliments on his eyes.

"Well. Then we're both new at this. And nervous. I do think we oughtta keep our voices down. My boss doesn't know you're here to poach me. And I'd like to keep my job here. In case you decide against poaching me, that is."

Caleb looked around. The people around them couldn't help but glance at them out of the corners of their eyes. Adrienne's boss didn't seem to be among them. Caleb's steak sat cold and nearly whole in front of him.

"I guess the first thing I should ask is why do you want to be in the circus?"

Adrienne Lee began pulling the pins out of her hair, massaging her scalp with one hand as she plucked with the other.

"Well. I have a very specific skill set. Which mostly involves not having any real skills and just being what I am. And what I am is a circus act, isn't it?"

Her curls fell down around her face, and he could see her youth, the girlishness that hid behind her size, her brassy singing voice.

"How old are you?"

"Twenty-four."

"How long have you worked here?"

"Not long. A few months, I think."

"And before that?"

She sighed, and he could tell he was steering his questioning down a path she didn't want to go.

"Before that, I was married. I'm a divorcée, and the truth is, I just want to get out of town. I'd love to go to St. Louis. My ex-husband's been trying to sweet-talk me back to him, and I think it would be best if I left town before I start thinking that would be a good idea."

"So you don't have . . . like a portfolio I could look at?"

She shook her head. "This is it, Caleb. This is what I have to offer," she said, gesturing toward the stage and then to Richard. When she said Caleb's name, his heart hammered its way into his throat. Above them, a yellow-and-red stained-glass lamp cast its mellow light on Adrienne's skin, and the place smelled of wine and the bloody middles of steaks, and of *her*, a scent he eventually came to recognize as magnolia powder. He felt drunk on these things, absolutely senseless.

"Would you really go back?" he asked, lowering his voice. He said it quietly, because even as he said it, he was unsure he wanted to expose himself like this.

"Excuse me?" she said, leaning forward to hear him better.

"Would you really go back to your ex-husband?"

Her face changed then. This question was not part of the interview, and it wasn't one of idle curiosity, and she knew it. She didn't say anything for a moment, thinking about it.

"No," she answered. "I don't think I would. He left me when I was down."

"I'm sorry," said Caleb. "I know it's none of my business."

"Do you know how a person becomes a giant?" she asked.

"Not at all," he said.

"By being sick."

He hadn't known. He felt guilty now for eroticizing her size but not enough to stop finding it erotic. How this was a sickness, and not just a manifestation of the elegant variety of nature, was not clear to him then.

"Listen," he said. "I'm going to tell you right now before you say anything else that I want you to work for me. For Feely and Feinstein. If you're sick, well, we don't provide health insurance, but maybe I could talk to Mr. Feely about . . . I don't know, maybe we could work something out. But, you can get away from your ex, and I'll provide a moving stipend. And by moving stipend, I mean, me coming to your house with a truck and helping you move."

"You're really selling this to me," she said, half-smiling, toying with a plume she had pulled out of her hair.

"You do have a skill set, Miss Lee. You're very funny. You're a good actress and a good singer."

She stopped fiddling with the feather then. Behind her, the big blue parrot with a man's name stirred, opening its wings as if to shield its mistress.

"That's a very nice thing of you to say. I hear people laugh sometimes and I wonder if they're laughing for me or at me. If that makes any sense."

"For you. I'm sure of it."

Adrienne agreed to come and work that season in exchange for a pitiful wage, and Caleb's aid in moving her stuff out of Nancy's garage.

The two of them remembered their meeting at the steakhouse over and over, together. In every retelling, Adrienne would ask, "Was it my size, or my sense of humor that made me interesting?" And he would answer firmly that her sense of humor was what made her show special, not her size. Then she would ask, "And was it my size that made me sexy to you?"

And he would answer, "No, it was your hair and your legs. And your talent."

She never quite believed him, and he was never quite being honest. If he were honest, he would say, "Yes, your height is shocking. You are shocking. People turn their heads to look at you not because you are beautiful, but because you are like nothing they have ever seen. And yes, the fact that you're like nothing I've ever seen is sexy." But this would hurt her, because she did not want to be a freak, did not want her height to be the factor that determined everyone's impressions of her. So he pretended, for her sake, that he only saw her as beautiful.

Now, CALEB WENT INTO THE circus tent through the patron entrance and found an empty seat in time to watch Azi as the fire-god. Vroni and Jenifer climbed up on his arms. He balanced them there, and they twirled fiery poi balls as Azi rotated his body. The girls fed him fire, and all the while Azi supported them on his shoulders. He was astonishing. He could have been a world-class athlete with superhero strength. Instead, he preferred to eat fire. The girls, on the other hand, were made for the circus only, had come from a circus family, and would keep on starving themselves and hissing at outsiders until they broke their hips and had to stop. He would have to explain this to Henry, he thought, who obviously didn't understand people like Jenifer and Vroni, people like Alastar Feely, who fed dogs to Igorots for a chance at a sideshow.

He didn't have a lot of emotional energy but Caleb still felt bad for the boy, who'd tried to change his act and gotten the mean stare down from Seamus. Henry couldn't understand why he didn't quite fit in with Feely and Feinstein. This inability to fit in was the whole idea. Caleb wanted him because he was exceptional and not like other clowns. He could have explained this to Henry, but instead, he tried to keep the boy at arm's length, hadn't spoken to him while he stayed in his house, didn't offer him a ride to rehearsal. Every day, Caleb watched him walk bleary-eyed out the door to the bus stop while he sipped his coffee in the kitchen. Meanwhile, the boy set the table for Adrienne every night during his stay and put the toilet seat down after he used the bathroom. One evening, when she was waxy-skinned and distant, Henry had even put on his whole vaudeville act for her.

In the middle of Azi's act, the girl-clown appeared with a fire extinguisher, wearing a clown costume and a fireman's hat. Vroni and Jenifer, the fire-god's consorts, teased her. They blew fire at her and she jumped, fell back, tumbled, and staggered into a defensive stance. They set her foot on fire (achieved with a little lighter fluid and flame-retardant boots). When she noticed her flaming foot, she panicked and fretted over it theatrically before dousing it in a bucket of water. She had her revenge when she extinguished the German girls' poi balls. It was normally Henry who came to the girl-clown's defense and extinguished the flames, but Henry never came out.

He knew immediately something was wrong. Caleb left his seat and circled around outside.

Backstage, it smelled like vomit. Lorne was nervous to the point of shuddering, as he was before every show, mounted atop Tex, and Tex, who was not nervous in the least, was taking copious, leisurely shits. The smell of them would have easily overpowered the scent of anything but human vomit.

The trapeze artists stood with their hands on their hips, rolling their necks. Sue talked sweet gibberish to her dogs to keep them still. Kylie returned from the stage, sweating from exertion and the heat of the fire, the marabou that embellished her costume adhering to the sweat on her neck.

"Where's Henry?" he said to her.

She wiped her neck with a towel and shrugged. "I have no idea."

"What do you mean you have no idea? Was he here for your act?"

"Yeah, he was here for our act. He felt sick or something. Didn't you *see* our act? He was completely off."

"What's that awful smell?"

"I told you, he felt sick. He ralphed in poor Tex's pen."

Azi carried the buckets they had doused their flames with toward the rear opening of the tent.

"Baratucci," he said when he saw Caleb, nodding his bald head. "What do you need?"

"I've lost a clown," said Caleb. There was no doubt in his mind that Henry was more than a little sick, or he would have gone on.

Azi set his buckets down, and Remy nearly tripped on one, then pivoted to avoid it, somehow finding a way to flip Azi off in the same motion. "Well, watch your step, man, goddamn!" said Azi before turning to Caleb again. "Yes. He looked bad. He said he would be out, but he didn't come. No worries, though. The little girl made 'em laugh."

From the ring came a ripple of approving "aaahs" as Lorne and Tex began their show. Caleb felt uneasy, and Azi noticed this, clapping him on the shoulder before taking up his buckets again. "He's alright. He seemed to want to be alone, and so he probably found a place to do that. A man has to disappear from time to time."

Outside, Caleb knocked on the door of Henry's trailer and when he didn't answer, he went in. It was stifling and the place was starting to take on the odor of urine and dirty socks. The boy's street clothes were in a wad on the floor, but his black-and-white Converse shoes were not parked at the door where he normally left them. Henry was gone.

CHAPTER 13

Edgefield, Indiana
1985–1988

THE GYM IS LOUD AND hot and the whole high school is roaring, bellowing, completely out of control. Being let out of class stirs them up like nobody's business, because they feel their strength when they're all together like this, power in numbers. Henry sits on the third-closest bleacher bench and keeps his arms crossed in front of him—the crowd makes him nervous and his stomach lurches. There is a curtain with a sign mounted above it that says HOOSIER YOUTH CIRCUS in curly letters. Rings are suspended from scaffolding, and curious objects are scattered on the floor.

A white-haired man wearing a tuxedo with tails and bright-green laces in his shoes steps to a microphone.

"I am here on the unofficial business of getting people to like me," he says softly into the microphone. The kids all shush each other to hear him better. "To get that business out of the way, everyone must clap for me. In fact, don't just clap. Scream your approval, if you please. Make me believe it." And of course, they do, because who could pass up that invitation? The man wears thick eyeliner, and something about the crisp, precise way he moves immediately causes the seventh graders around Henry to whisper, "He's gay." They don't say this hatefully, the way they say it to Henry—they say it with awe and disbelief.

"I am Instructor Christiakov, and I teach clowning arts at the Hoosier Youth Circus. Which means that I teach people to do things like this," he says and pulls an umbrella from the sleeve of his jacket. He twirls it, then throws it high into the air. He catches it, then mimes being pulled by the umbrella, which is caught in a gust of imaginary wind. The illusion is so complete, Henry thinks he feels a breeze. The man tumbles, as if blown over, but then rolls back onto his feet and does a series of front flips, the open umbrella turning like a pinwheel as his body spins. Without even seeming out of breath, he tosses the umbrella into the air again and catches it back in his sleeve.

"Before we start, let me take a little poll: What is the first thing you think of when you think of the circus?" he asks. There is a slight accent in his voice—he is a foreigner in every way.

Henry's classmates yell out their answers: elephants, ponies, clowns, high-wire walkers, weed, queers, bitches with beards.

Christiakov smiles at their answers, acknowledges them with a flourish of his hand. "Yes. Elephants and ponies and unexpected facial hair. This is all perfectly accurate, my friends. But I will tell you," he says, "I will tell you that a circus is really all about blood. The first circuses were in ancient Rome, and, I think you must have studied this by now, the Romans thought there was no such *thing* as a show without blood. So to be a performer means that you must really love other people, even bloodthirsty ones."

The gym is silent.

He leans in close to the microphone. "I very much hope that you enjoy the show."

The students of the youth circus perform. They're impressive, in their hot-pinks and electric greens and blues, doing half-turns on the trapeze, wrapping their bodies like Christmas presents in the ribbons of the Spanish fly. The clowns, made up like glam rockers, rush out and climb on planks balanced on rolling tubes. They stay balanced on them, all the while brandishing toy electric guitars and their tongues. None of the kids performing look afraid. Henry thinks he would be scared to screw up, scared of how this roomful of his mean-spirited peers might react to him. But these kids are baldly confident. They know they are talented, and Henry's classmates are caught up in the act. He sees the faces around him soften with curiosity and laughter, even the eighth graders, who think that everything that isn't death metal or firecrackers is for chumps.

He watches them closely, all their moves, their tricks, and it occurs to him: *There is nothing they are doing that I can't do. Not a single thing.*

After the performance, when Christiakov asks for volunteers to try out the unicycles, the rola bolas, and the low wire, Henry's hand shoots into the air. He wishes he could reach out and grab Christiakov's suit jacket and say, "It's me! It's me you want." He's not certain he won't be laughed at but he is willing to take the risk. If he can do all the things these circus kids can do, then why shouldn't he be able to blast into a room like they did, hypnotizing everyone into thinking they are happy? Why shouldn't he be able to make people look at him and see something good?

Christiakov picks four people, then another set of four, and, finally, he hears Henry's psychic message and points to him.

Nobody seems to want to try the rola bola—they all dash for the low wire. Henry runs to the rola bola and sets the plank on the pipe. One of the clown students spots him. He holds the board on the pipe with a hand on each side and puts his left foot on the board, barely touching it. He remembers how the other clowns did it. As the other kids slide off the low wire like silk off a clothesline, Henry's generic tennis shoes plant squarely on the rola bola. He looks up at the bleachers full of students and grins.

Beneath his feet, the piece of pipe is a wild thing trying to run off. He has to crush it with the weight of his right foot, then crush it with the weight of his left foot, until it is equally crushed beneath both feet and steady. After balancing for awhile, he asks the student spotting him if he can stack them.

"You can if you want," he says, sounding a little irritated. "Just don't fall and sue us."

He helps Henry stack the pipes three high, and stands close, arms on either side of him. Henry doesn't gauge the hop right this time, and the board flips out from underneath him. The pipes roll across the gym floor.

His classmates point at the rolling pipe and laugh at Henry but in a way that makes him think they are on his side. He feels a surge of closeness with them.

Then, he tries the unicycle. A student tries to help him get on, but Henry shakes his head. He's already seen someone ride in the program, and he gets it. Once he's up on the seat, he is off like a shot, pedaling around the gymnasium, arms out like wings. Like the rola bola, it is all about pressure in the right place at the right time. It's fun. And it's more maneuverable than an actual bike, so he can ride figure eights around the equipment, making sharp turns that tilt the bike and make it feel like he is defying gravity. It's so fun, in fact, that he forgets for a moment that he has an audience to show off for, a fact he remembers abruptly when he sees Christiakov gaping at him. The circus students are staring, too, and he dismounts quickly, afraid that he has broken some rule by riding too fast.

When the show is over and they are all released, Henry walks toward his last-period class with his hands in his pockets, wishing Cassie hadn't skipped that day. He might be in trouble now, but she would have been impressed by how fast he rode the unicycle.

Before he gets through the doorway of his classroom, he feels a hand on his shoulder.

It belongs to the clown teacher, Christiakov. Up close, he's much taller. His face is carved with soft lines extending from the corners of his eyes and mouth. Henry can't decide how old he is—he has white hair, but his face looks much younger than his father's.

"Sorry to startle you. I hear your name is Henry," he says.

"Yessir."

"A pleasure to meet you," he says and extends his hand. His palm is warm and dry, calloused like his father's, but clean, with no black in the creases of his knuckles.

Christiakov pulls a white card from his breast pocket and hands it to Henry.

"You should consider taking classes," he says. "You would certainly make a good acrobat. And you might make a good clown."

Henry cradles the card in his palm. *Luka Christiakov*, it says. *Master Clown. Hoosier Youth Circus.*

"I hope I hear from you. And if I don't, I'm still glad I got to meet such a talent. I'm sure you'll do something astonishing with it."

He leaves him, standing in the hall with the little white card between his fingers. When he is gone, Henry bends the card by flexing it between his thumb and forefinger, and then lets it spring into the air: *pop!* He catches it, slips it into his back pocket. The air in his lungs feels light, lifting him, so that when he walks to class, it's nearly a strut.

Finally, he has done something right, and someone was there to see it.

As SOON AS HE GETS his learner's permit, Henry calls Christiakov and drives his father's car to the Hoosier Youth Circus center in the adjacent county, alone. Driving by himself is against the rules, but it's a rule no boy his age follows in Edgefield. Who hasn't been driving tractors and four-wheelers for ages? His father doesn't think twice about it. He tells him to pick up some coffee while he's out and to get home by ten.

Henry hasn't seen Christiakov since the Hoosier Youth Circus did their show in his high school gymnasium several months ago, and he is nervous that the man won't recognize him. But when Henry sees Christiakov, standing outside the studio in a pair of vertical-striped pants, the clown smiles and says, "Phenom!"

Henry has arrived after classes have been dismissed, but Christiakov takes him into a small rehearsal space with inspirational posters on the walls and blue mats on the floors. It smells acrid, like sweat and rubber. Three other students are drilling an acrobatic routine with an instructor. They wave to Christiakov when he comes in but then return to tumbling.

That day, without a word about fees or scholarships, Christiakov teaches him to breathe and to stretch. This is how to get the poison out.

"If you expect to take a decent fall, or move particularly fast, or hold a pose, or anything out of the ordinary, really, you have to have your muscles in good working order. And you can't have your muscles working well if they're full of little toxic knots. Make sense?"

145

"Yes."

"Of course it does."

He does as Christiakov tells him, though some of the stretches make him look ridiculous and some of them downright hurt. He is a bit disappointed that Christiakov doesn't seem to think he's talented enough to jump right into the interesting stuff. He thinks that perhaps he was wrong, that this is not a good idea after all.

After he leaves that evening, Henry gases up the car and stops by the grocery store and picks up a quart of milk, a bag of spaghetti noodles, a box of doughnuts for Frankie, and coffee for his father.

The next morning, for the first time in memory, Henry awakens to the sound of his brother's breath and the twittering of birds, instead of being jolted awake by the explosive flutter of his heart. He lies there, unwilling to open his eyes yet. His body is sore, but he feels so much lighter. Calmer. He feels good enough to recognize just how shitty he felt the day before and the day before that, how shitty he's felt for so, so long. There is no churning in his stomach, no feeling of dread. He thinks it must be the stretching. *So simple,* he thinks. *Nothing to it. All this time.* His eyes well with tears.

His father seems to assume that Henry spent the evening on a date with Cassie Littrell, because at the breakfast table he asks, "Did you two have fun?" Henry says yes. Frankie eats his doughnuts and Henry and his father sip coffee together. His father thanks him for picking up groceries.

"You can use the car when you'd like, as long as you ask first," his father says.

"Oh. Okay. Thank you. I promise to ask," he says.

HENRY ARRANGES TO GO TO the Hoosier Youth Circus twice a week. Whenever he uses the car, he brings something home for his father that he knows he needs: a roll of tape, a bottle of windshield washer fluid, a loaf of bread. Sometimes his father gives him money if he wants something specific, but usually Henry uses his own. There aren't many regular jobs around, but Henry mows lawns, bales hay, moves furniture—whatever people will pay him to do. His father continues to give the car up without much questioning. He is more grateful for this small contribution of money and time from Henry than Henry ever expected.

Henry doesn't have to worry about tuition for the circus class or keeping his grades up for it, because he isn't officially enrolled. He can't pay for it, and Christiakov says he would be bored by the regular classes, anyway. When he asks Christiakov what he wants for private lessons, he says this is about art and scholarship, not money.

Part of Henry thinks he could just tell his father what he is doing. As long as he doesn't ask for money and keeps running errands, Henry suspects he couldn't care less if his son wants to be in a circus—and why should he care? It doesn't hurt anyone. He wants to tell him, in fact, but something keeps him from saying anything. Later, after he moves out, Henry will realize that he didn't tell him because he didn't want to take the risk. He didn't want to give his father the opportunity to try to take something Henry needed as badly as he needed this. Because, if he said no, what else could he want but to hurt Henry? Everything else could be chalked up to accident. Even his father's fury was a kind of accident, a force that had nothing to do with his father's real feelings or desires. But to say no to this, what else could it mean but that his father did not care about him, did not want him to be happy?

For now, the only person who knows where he goes in his father's car twice a week is Cassie, who keeps all his secrets, as he keeps hers. He's been thinking lately that they either know too many of each other's secrets, or too few. They can't seem to get away from each other. They have broken up more than once, but when something bad happens to Cassie, instead of going to her new boyfriend for comfort, she comes to Henry. It happens every couple months, Cassie showing up to school in tears. He'll find her standing by his locker like that, and he will not ask questions. To Henry, the reason for her crying seems much less urgent than the crying itself, and the crying itself he understands implicitly. When something bad happens to Henry, he doesn't cry, but he goes to her, whether they are together or not, whether they are fighting or not. They end up in bed and back in love, back to holding hands in the halls, back to sloppy kisses hello between classes.

She says she doesn't mind that he's studying to be a clown. She likes it, she says, even though she can't say "studying to be a clown" without giggling. She only wishes he'd take her out once in a while. She'd love to go to the bowling alley in the neighboring town, she says. She wouldn't say no to a dollar movie, a burger, to watching him get swallowed by ghosts playing Pac-Man at the arcade, if he asked.

She mentions the Pac-Man thing again, one Saturday while they lie side by side on his bed, making out. When she brings up going out, Henry gets annoyed. He spends all his money on gas and food, and he's explained this to her at least a dozen times.

"Take some from your dad," she says, sweetly, letting her hair hang down in his face. In the time it takes for her hair to sweep across his cheek, he goes from annoyed to beside himself.

He sits up, and when she moves, too, he forces her back down. "Are you retarded? Or do you hate me?"

"What?"

"You know he'd like fucking kill me, right?"

"I don't know," she says, her eyes darting back and forth. "Don't be mad."

You do know. He could kill me. He could. You do know, don't you?

He has the worst thought he's ever had, then, that he would like to push her off the bed. He thinks he would like to see the look on her face when she fell, thinks it would satisfy him to see her reel back into the dresser. As soon as he thinks it, he is disgusted with himself and lets Cassie go. She's already sensed the danger, though, and looks at him with the same fear on her face he saw when they were little, when she thought her sister would tattle on her for doing dirty things in the overgrown grass. This fear still softens her, makes her something exquisite to Henry.

She goes back to kissing him, deeper now, and Henry doesn't stop her, even though he is still angry. She is kissing him not out of affection but as a means of distraction, of self-defense. But he needs the distraction. He thinks, *She's fine. She knows how to deal with someone like me*, though what the hell that means, Henry doesn't want to consider any further.

CHRISTIAKOV CALLS HENRY A "KINESTHETIC genius," which means that he's a genius of movement. He teaches Henry some basic anatomy because he believes that if Henry knows what is inside his body, he'll be able to control it that much better—if he is aware of the tiny muscle groups in his face and his ears, for example, and if he knows where the muscles in his back are attached to his bones, he'll be able to call out to those muscles with his mind and move them as he pleases.

His teacher's hunch turns out to be correct. After Christiakov teaches him the muscle groups and tendons, Henry spends a session in front of the mirror practicing this skill, which mostly involves making faces at himself, flexing his biceps, and making his pecs talk to each other. Christiakov decides he has a sense of humor after all.

He teaches Henry to juggle irregularly shaped things, to fall, to walk like a drunk, to walk like a woman, to walk like a tough guy—how to look startled, smitten, hurt, embarrassed, how to cry, take a stage-punch, take a pie, and how to be absolutely, positively stone-still. When Henry messes up, Christiakov doesn't get angry, he doesn't yell. He says, "Again." Christiakov shows him videos of Charlie Chaplin, Abbott and Costello, Buster Keaton, Carol Burnett, Emmett Kelly, and Jackie Chan. Jackie Chan is one of the great clowns, according to Christiakov.

"I thought he was just a martial artist. And a badass," Henry says as Jackie battles an onslaught of goons on the television.

"Are you kidding? He's a clown to the bone, my friend," says Christiakov. "They call him a kinesthetic genius, too. You're cut from the same cloth."

Christiakov rewinds the tape, and Henry watches his routine in reverse: Jackie Chan pulls a blow, ducks, flips away from his tall, square-faced opponent, contorts his face to rage, then confusion, then laughter.

Christiakov, standing only a few feet from the screen, says, "Okay, now watch his face here."

But Henry is behind Christiakov, not really listening, mimicking the martial artist's moves in reverse, as if his body is on rewind. Christiakov turns when he hears Henry land the flip, in time to see him shuffle through Jackie's three facial expressions.

PHYSICAL MIMICRY IS EASY ENOUGH for Henry. Being funny is more of a challenge for him than being coordinated, but Christiakov still believes he will be a good clown.

"It's not about being a cheery little idiot, Henry. People get enough of that," Christiakov says one day. The two of them are outside the rehearsal space. Spring has made the days longer, and they try to enjoy the last few minutes of sun before it goes down for the day. Christiakov is drinking a glass of tea that smells like flowers and looks like piss on ice. "Being funny comes from understanding that the same pain you have, everybody has. If an audience can watch *their* pain in *your* body, they feel relieved of it for a while."

"That seems kind of shitty of them," says Henry.

"Not at all. It's very gracious. People are reluctant to give up their pain. They've earned it, after all. Which is why you must be careful with it—you don't want to disrespect their pain by being a mediocre clown. You've got to have some grace about it. You've got to tell a good story of that pain, or it's just going to cut."

Henry nods.

"Do you understand that, or are you just nodding because you want me to think you understand that?"

"No, I understand. I do."

"Good," he says and sips his tea. "Because I'm telling you, if you ever want to get a steady job, you're going to have to know more than just the rola bola and the unicycle. Circuses that are just a series of neat stunts—they're dead."

Henry looks around to see if any of the students are puttering around the studio. He hopes they don't overhear Christiakov, because what if they're like Henry and hope to do this for a living? What if they haven't heard yet that their rola bola skills are for a dead art?

"You'll be fine out there, I know you will. But if you want to find a place for yourself, I'm just saying, you're going to have to use your noodle."

The sun goes down, and they go inside. Henry has an especially important task to work on: he needs to create a face for himself. All clown faces are unique, and Henry has almost got his pinned down. He paints a jester's mask on his face, all white with high black eyebrows, little smile lines at the corners of his eyes—all the kind people he has known have these, and he wants them, too. He makes black lines extending up past his natural eyebrows and down to the apples of his cheeks. He looks like a joker from a deck of cards. It is simple and open, and Henry believes the face he's created is his own proof that he will find a place for himself.

BECAUSE HE HAS LEARNED HOW to stretch, Henry stops getting sick at the thought of his mother or Andre. But he still thinks of them. Sometimes, Henry will say her full name, Rylan Bell, out loud, just to hear it. He does this a lot in the car, on the way to the Hoosier Youth Circus. No one can hear him there, except, maybe, hopefully, her.

Christiakov doesn't ask questions about why he has never met Henry's parents or why he has bruises on his arms that never go away. Henry assumes that he doesn't really care about his parents, since they are not paying him, and he figures Christiakov believes the bruises are from tumbling. He's not perfect, after all, and some stunts result in inevitable bruises, no matter how well executed.

By the time Henry is only a few months from turning seventeen, his balance is uncanny. He can stand on one foot on the seat of a moving bicycle. He can walk on a line thinner than his finger as easily as a spider can stand on its own web.

Still, one evening, his father shoves him, and even though Henry can catch himself before staggering back into his bedroom door, he doesn't. The doorknob leaves a mark like a purple butterfly under his bottommost rib.

He doesn't have to put up with this anymore. But he still does.

HENRY BECOMES OBSESSED WITH THE idea of "air-clowning." Climbing and hanging from things is the only real challenge for Henry. "It's psychological," says Christiakov—the fear of the fall makes Henry nervous and clumsier than he ever is on the ground. But there's no reason that he should be less coordinated five feet from the ground or forty, so he practices with a hoop that dangles down from scaffolding. Over the course of a few weeks, Henry works on this exclusively. Christiakov gives him a routine and raises the hoop in increments so that Henry gets further from the ground each time he runs through the moves. On the hoop, Henry slips. He moves like a fat man. He can't concentrate on his face, so he isn't funny at all. He gets so frustrated, he'd like to hang himself from the scaffolding. Christiakov says nothing but: "Again."

But just when he is beginning to suspect that he is Christiakov's favorite, his teacher tells him that he is leaving, for a city near the ocean. Henry finds Christiakov already has a default favorite, a son. Christiakov says this son wants Christiakov to live closer to him.

He tells him this as he drinks his piss-colored tea outside of the rehearsal space. Christiakov leans against the rail and Henry sits cross-legged on the cement. Beyond the parking lot of the youth circus, some of the oak trees still have bright-red leaves clinging to the tips of their branches.

Christiakov says his son is planning his grandchildren, and Henry pictures him, the son, with his pearly-toothed wife in a white house with blue shutters and flowers clustered around the foundation.

"Where'd you get a *son*?"

"That's a very personal question, Henry. One answer is, magic. Another involves a long, boring relationship with a woman, of which I can tell you all the tragic details. Which version would you like?"

"Magic, thank you."

"Very good."

"But you have a job here. Doesn't your son understand that?"

"Yes, he understands that. He isn't making me move. I want to move. I want to make up for some lost time—I was *not* a good father to him, and now I'm grateful that he wants me around. Moving near him is the least I can do."

"I'm sure you were a good father," Henry says.

Christiakov shakes his head. "I promise you I wasn't." He pauses, seeming to consider the ice in his tea, then adds, "Although, I've never put any bruises on him. I have managed at least that much."

Henry feels himself blush. "No, I didn't think that you meant that."

"Of course you didn't," he says and sits down next to Henry. Christiakov's voice gets quiet then, and he says, "You need to get out of here, too. That's very plain."

Henry does not look at him. He looks at the cement in front of him, wishing to sink into it.

"And here I am getting personal, too, aren't I? We don't need to talk about it, as long as we are both agreed that when I go, you do, too. I'm not in the habit of telling my students to run away, but . . . I would hate to go and have something happen to you. I think you've always known you could come to me in a pinch. You have, haven't you? But since I will not be here anymore, you need to get out of the pinch."

Henry would be angry with Christiakov for assuming he knew so much, but he is too relieved. No adult, other than his mother, has ever insinuated that anything out of the ordinary or anything dangerous might be happening to his family. He feels vindicated. Even if he does not run away, he knows now that he has the right to.

He considers asking Christiakov to take him with him but quickly concludes that asking such a thing would be asking Christiakov to risk his whole life. A gay Russian immigrant kidnapping a teenaged boy? The town of Edgefield, as little as they cared for Henry, would find Christiakov and string him up.

Christiakov pulls an envelope from the inside pocket of his jacket. He's been preparing for this. "Here is a list of numbers. Every circus in the Midwest. My number is in here, too. You may use me as a reference. If you must busk for money, there's a list of places where you can do this safely, but I would caution you against doing it for any length of time. You don't want to announce yourself to the law too obviously. They'll ignore you if they can, but if they see you every day, they might feel obliged to take you in."

Henry folds the envelope and sticks it in his pocket. "Thank you," he says.

"There's a circus in St. Louis that I think might be a good starting place for you. You'll want to talk to a man named Caleb Baratucci. He is not as friendly or as charming as myself, but he is a good man, and he will look out for your interests."

Henry would rather look out for his own interests, but he says, "I'll find him."

"Good. In a week or two, you'll get a package from me in the mail. That'll be your cue to get out of Dodge."

Henry is finally able to look at Christiakov and sees that he is sad to be doing this.

"This is the only way that makes sense," says Christiakov. "I always make sense. I have not ever steered you wrong." He sounds as confident about this as he does about everything else he tells Henry to do, but Henry has already said he will go, and Christiakov is still making his case. Maybe he senses Henry's hesitation, or maybe he is just trying to convince himself that this is the right thing to do.

Henry tells his teacher again, yes, he will go.

He doesn't learn anything new at his last session at the Hoosier Youth Circus. Just practices the old stuff. This time, Christiakov doesn't say anything, or laugh, or smile while he performs. He says that he has to be his own audience, cheer for himself while he does his acts. He can't count on energy from the people watching his act.

"What I said about audiences wanting your blood—you remember, don't you? I wasn't kidding. They will. The only way to keep them from slaughtering you is to stay confident and stay in character. If you want energy, you have to make it yourself."

Henry does as he says. Christiakov waits until he is done reviewing everything he knows to uncross his arms and clap for him.

"A phenom," he says.

Henry bows.

On Henry's seventeenth birthday, Cassie comes over with a chocolate sheet cake, which she delivers to his bedroom.

Henry looks at her, looks at the sheet cake, looks at her. He takes the cake from her hands and puts it on his dresser. Her eyes are bright and green like a cat's, and her thin lips are curled into a smile. He turns her around, kisses the back of her neck and rubs her shoulders. He feels the lumps of poison in her muscles. Henry reaches down and catches the fabric of her skirt between his fingers, pulling it up until it bunches around her waist.

She turns her head and breathes right into his mouth, her too-sweet breath. He wants to tell her that he loves her and thank her for always being so nice to him. But their house is small and the TV is off, for once. His father and brother are in the kitchen making a birthday dinner for him. He can hear their conversation downstairs and he only assumes they can hear his.

When Henry and Cassie kiss, something goes wrong. He slips. Sometimes this happens, even to kinesthetic geniuses. His teeth collide with hers and slide upwards, slicing her lip.

"Sorry," he mumbles. He tastes copper, just the tiniest hint of blood. But like all tastes and smells from the past, this one grips a memory, yanks it out by the roots and tosses it into the forefront of his mind. He remembers chomping down on her tongue when they were little. The blood reminds him of her body as it was. Her poor bare pubic bone, her hair that clumped and smelled of mildew. He realizes something, then—she doesn't want this. She doesn't want sex.

They know too many of each other's secrets but they don't know the right ones.

He stops touching her, and she looks relieved. "Your lip is hurt. You want me to get you a washcloth?"

There is a reason she has come to school in tears, and the reason wasn't beside the point. Someone has been hurting Cassie. And he is complicit in it, because he has never taken the time to ask her, *Why are you crying?* Because he has not taken the time to ask why she relaxes when he pulls away. All along he has been afraid he would hurt her the way he hurt Lee, by succumbing to his impulses to push, to punch, to choke. Instead he has hurt her with negligence and willful ignorance.

He brings Cassie a rag, damp with warm water, and she holds it to her mouth. "It's really not that big a deal," she says. "Thanks, though."

He sits down on his bed. "Well. You're my girl."

Two weeks later, before Henry leaves for school, his father accuses him of having shoplifted the pair of tennis shoes he's wearing. They are black-and-white Converse All-Stars, stiff canvas and rubber. He knows better than to wear them because of course they would make his father suspicious. They aren't something Henry would buy for himself. But not only does he wear them, he threads them with red laces. He keeps them in the box they came in, trying to keep the store smell on them for as long as possible.

He tells his father they are a present from Cassie.

He believes this, because why wouldn't he? But Henry finds himself wanting to bait his father by telling him how he really got them. If his father knocks him out, he won't be able to leave, and it won't be his fault that he didn't follow Christiakov's instructions. He wants to stay to protect Frankie and because this is his home. He doesn't bait him, though. And in this moment, his decision is made. Henry believes that his father will try harder with Frankie. Perhaps he will see him as he once saw Henry: as a clean slate, another chance.

He checks Frankie's backpack to make sure he has his homework and the sheet Henry signs their father's name to whenever Frankie reads for the requisite amount of minutes in the evening. Inside the backpack, there are the potholders that he made himself with a plastic loom and colored loops that look like they are cut out of women's stockings. Presents for girls. Henry had given him a hard time about it: "Because girls have to handle so many pots," he said.

Frankie had glared at him. "Dickhead," he'd said.

His father should be leaving for work now, but he stays a little longer and watches Henry as he fixes Frankie's lunch.

"Do you want a sandwich, Dad?"

"No," he says.

His father watches him cut the sandwich into two triangles. "You're a good kid," he says. It's the first time that his father has said this to Henry.

His father looks embarrassed then and Henry realizes it's because he's staring at him.

The shoes came with an envelope full of twenty dollar bills and a note: *Time to rise, Phenom. Be safe, and write your acts down. What if I want to see them some day? Stop being so selfish.*

Henry's father leaves for work. As soon as the door shuts behind him, Frankie charges into the kitchen, and Henry walks him to school. He's eleven and doesn't need an escort anymore, but Henry likes to walk with his brother. Frankie lines up with his classmates and Henry stands there, watching, until all the children file in. He never even considers telling Frankie his plan, because he doesn't want Frankie to try and stop him. But as Frankie walks into the building, Henry wishes that he would look back at him. *If he turns, it will mean good-bye. If he turns, it means it's okay to go.*

Frankie doesn't turn, though. Frankie walks, with his funny little gait, with potholders in his backpack. Henry's backpack is full of clothes and food today, rather than books.

At first, Henry is stuck to the sidewalk. But then his mind makes allowances for what his body decides to do, and he walks, one foot, heel to toe, until he's rolling along, not thinking, riding his own stride. It's cold enough to freeze a speckle of spit on his lip but not windy, so not even the sound of air disturbs the silence of his walk. He makes his way up the highway, fields dusted with snow on either side of him, until he gets to the train tracks, where he waits. The trains inch through Edgefield. He will jump an empty car when it comes and ride it to Garrett, where he can catch a passenger train to Chicago.

He hears the whistle of the train, and he can see the engine, a yellow smudge in the distance. He is not sure where he will end up, but he knows where he will not be. He will not be in his father's house with Frankie. He will not be with Cassie Littrell. The wind nicks his dry face. He thinks, *This is lonely, staring at this train.* Still, he feels a sudden comfort. His mother would be proud of him, and the dead can travel.

Clown Car Skit

It's a Volvo.

The trunk opens and out pops the first clown, looking dazed, like he just woke up or got sober or something. In his hand, he is surprised to find a flower.

He staggers across the ring, trying to retrace his steps. How did he get in that car? Then, he is distracted by a pretty girl in the audience. He makes eyes at her. Kissy faces. He hands her the flower.

While the first clown flirts, the second clown pulls himself out of the car. He looks just as confused as the first clown and just as surprised about the two flowers in his hand. He sees the first clown and walks up to him, hoping he'll have some answers about what has gone on. Then, he sees the pretty audience member that the first clown was talking to. He is stricken stupid, just as the first clown, and hands her his two flowers.

This irritates the first clown.

And then the third clown emerges. Dazed. Three flowers. Dumped in love's lap, just like the two before him.

This goes on until . . . How many clowns did the girl in the motel say she saw come out of a car? Seventeen? Sure. Make it seventeen.

In the end, they will all try to pile back in the car, and fail, scratching their heads. How did they get in there?

There's something cute for you, Seamus Feely, you old fuck.

All I will need is a Volvo. And 142 flowers to cover a girl in.

CHAPTER 14

St. Louis
June 1990

Henry drove Sue's van cautiously, just a hair over the speed limit. He'd found the cassette that Kylie had given him in his back pocket (he hadn't washed his jeans since) and he'd had it in the tape player the whole ride.

The song playing right now was heavy and angsty and all about dying young, though he wasn't paying as much attention to the lyrics as the music, the eerie-sweet harmonies and the guitar that sounded like a revving engine. He listened to the song over and over, and the more he listened to it, the more certain he became that he was doing the right thing, that Adrienne needed him, that he needed Adrienne.

He had no idea what he would say to her when he saw her, but he had brought with him the makeup bag he'd accidentally taken, and figured that if she was angry or if things were awkward, he could say that he only came to switch them out.

When he arrived, it was 11:30 p.m. according to the clock in Sue's van. Standing outside the Baratuccis' house, Henry had a moment of panic wondering what he would do if she did not answer the door. But then he saw the flash of her eye at the peephole, and she undid the chain and let him inside. Richard was immediately at his feet, pecking at him. Adrienne put the bird in his cage.

"What are you doing here? Is everything okay? Is Caleb okay?" she asked. She was still waking up, her eyes watery, the folds of her pillow still carved into her cheek. She was wearing what was probably a man's big-and-tall T-shirt, though it was too short to cover anything below her ass. He could see the faint outline of her nipple beneath the dark fabric.

"Don't worry about Caleb," he said, and the words sounded sleazy to him.

On the coffee table, amid the clutter of half-empty water glasses and beauty magazines, there was a syringe and a square of gauze, polka-dotted with blood.

Adrienne arched an eyebrow. "Alright, then. Are *you* okay?"

"Yes," he said.

She sat down on the couch, her big thighs flattened against the cushions and joined together, obscuring his view of her underwear. She patted the seat next to her. He shook his head. There was a sour taste in his mouth from puking earlier, and his legs were cramped from driving. The audience in his head was still jeering, still telling him in moans and shouts that he could not do anything right.

He seated himself on the floor and began stretching as he normally did, by folding himself in half.

"Henry," said Adrienne, "tell me why you're *here*."

Henry sat upright and twisted from side to side to stretch his lower back. It allowed him a few seconds not to face her when he asked what the doctor had said about her brain.

"It's not something you need to worry about," she said. "I'm going to have another surgery, and until then, there's these drugs."

"Will they work?" he asked.

"Yes," she said, with certainty and softness in her voice. "They will work."

He could not turn back to face her but saw her reflection in the black television screen, saw she was not as certain as she wanted him to believe she was.

"That's good," he said.

"You could have asked Caleb, if you were worried about that."

"I don't know why I came. I needed to get out of there. Those German girls. They keep giving me shit."

"They give everyone shit. They're crazy."

"And I blew it tonight," he said. "And nobody really noticed."

"Well. That's a good thing, isn't it? You pulled it off."

He twisted back to face her. "No. It means that all my work is basically for nothing. They don't get it. I could get out there in baggy pants and do just about anything, and they'd laugh. As long as I looked like a jackass."

"I don't know if I'd go that far," she said. He shrugged and rolled his neck. He pulled each arm with the other and held it flush against his chest to stretch his triceps.

"I can *do* stuff, Adrienne. I can do . . . just about anything. No joke. People always think I'm exaggerating. You want me to do six consecutive back flips? I can do it. You want me to do it with shoe boxes on my feet? I can."

"I don't think you're exaggerating. I've never seen anybody do what you can do."

His arms fell limp at his sides, and he felt a release in his shoulders that was not due to his stretching, but to what Adrienne said. He'd known she would say that.

"I don't know why I fucked up tonight. I kept thinking about how I *wanted* to do something different," he said, lying down on his belly and then pointing his chin up like a seal. "And I kept thinking I should have told my brother to come and see my show. Hell, he might be in Chicago *right now*, visiting from . . . I don't know, some country. Some place in Europe."

"How do you figure?"

"He wrote me a while back, telling me he wanted to come," he said. "So he might have been here, if I just wrote him back."

He hadn't said anything to her about Andre before this, and he wasn't sure why he decided to now. Except, Henry's regret about Andre was not a ghost yet. It was immediate. And it animated all the other regrets he had about his brothers and made them immediate, too.

He stretched his feet, curling and uncurling his toes, rotating them at the ankles.

"I suppose you don't have his phone number," said Adrienne after a moment.

"Andre? No. He didn't give any numbers. I don't know if he even has a phone."

Adrienne leaned forward, her brow furrowed. If he wanted her sympathy, he had it.

"There's no one you could call who could get hold of him? Not your parents? Or friends?"

Henry shook his head. "I'm sure my dad has no idea where he is. Andre ran away when I was twelve. I thought he was dead for a long time."

"Jesus," she said.

His muscles relieved, he got up from the floor and sank into the couch next to Adrienne. He noticed that there was a pink indentation in the skin around her ring finger, instead of a ring.

Did she and Caleb fight? Was she not wearing his ring for a reason? He remembered the night Richard had begged him in his girl's voice not to leave.

He explained that Andre had left in the night when he was barely seventeen. He told her how Andre had planned his flight for years, since the night their mother died. He said it just like that: "My mother died."

"I'm sorry to hear that."

"And Dad was rough with Andre. He was rough with everyone, but especially Andre."

He didn't want to tell her that "rough" meant Andre and his father blackened each other's eyes when Andre was fifteen, because they got into an argument over a Misfits decal Andre put on his bedroom door. He knew how these details sounded to people—to hear it like that forced them to see his father as a monster and Henry as a coward and Andre as a miserable little victim. And this wasn't the truth, either.

Adrienne took his hand and enfolded it between hers, and the heat from her palms warmed his own. Her hands felt heavy over his, but she didn't squeeze. When he first imagined being with Adrienne, he thought he would have no confusion about whether she wanted him or not, because she was too wise for him to manipulate, too big to accidentally hurt. When she held his hands, though, he felt uncertainty about everything except the fact that he loved her, in spite of all uncertainties, in spite of the fact that she was Caleb's, and in spite of the fact that she might not feel for him the way he did for her. And so he was confused again. He had this love. He didn't know what to do with it.

"I'm sorry. You don't need to hear this. I need to shut up," he said.

She shook her head. "No, I worry about my things all the time. I want to worry about your things. You should have picked up a phone instead of driving all the way here, and that's a fact. Caleb is going to be livid. That's a fact, too. But I'm not going to say I'm not glad to see you. I've run out of ice cream, and Richard keeps saying Caleb-things—and I'm glad to see you."

Her false fingernails, which had been long and shellacked in red glossy paint when he met her, were all torn off now. Each nail was kinked in the middle, yellowed like old paper and just as thin. Her hands, always big, looked more swollen than usual.

What had she called this disease? Acro-magnolia? Flower of the brain. He wished there was a single useful thing he could do for her.

And then, as if she'd read his mind, she offered him something to do.

"Would you just give me one shot? I never used to be such a chicken," she said, "but on the last few injections my hand's been shaking. It's hard to even look where I'm sticking."

Henry hesitated. "I don't want to do it wrong," he said.

"You won't, it's easy. It doesn't even hurt that bad," she said. "I know that, logically, but it's the anticipation that kills me. I'll show you what to do. It goes just under the skin."

He agreed. She showed him how to pinch the flesh between his fingers.

"Push the plunger steadily, but not too fast," she explained. He kneeled next to her and poised the needle over the spot where he intended to give her the shot, mindful of the bruises where she had injected herself before this.

"Got it. You can turn your head," he said.

She turned and he punctured the skin quickly. He pressed the plunger, and it was easy enough to keep it steady, of course, because Henry's sense of balance was in his hands, too. He had polished his mother's nails with these even hands, perfect pink or red strokes of equal thickness, and she gave him compliments. *Good boy. You're a stick-in-the-mud, but you do fine work.*

"Thanks. It didn't hurt at all," said Adrienne.

The medicine rushed through the tiny barrel of the needle to the other, even smaller spaces inside, fat cells and blood vessels. He wished his kinesthetic genius extended to these small places and to other people's bodies so that he could show these cells how to move, how to wiggle free of guilt, and disease, and solitude. He would gladly rush through the barrel of the needle, climb the vascular vines to her brain, kick the tumor loose.

"What else can I do?" he asked.

"Nothing," she said, taking his hand again. She pulled him to his feet with an ease that he found surprising. Her giant-strength.

He felt the charge of blood through her hands, pulsing up from her wrists into her fingers. She felt so close. He wanted to keep her close. It was rare for him to be able to tell anybody anything about himself without some measure of regret, and it had been so easy to tell her about his family and his mistakes. When she began to pull her hands away, he held on, afraid if he lost physical contact he might lose this feeling, too. He put his hand on the back of her neck, as Cassie had done when she gave him his first ugly kiss in the empty lot in Edgefield. Adrienne looked amused rather than excited by this touch, but Henry knew he wasn't mistaken. It wasn't just him that did not want to let go. He leaned in, closing his eyes just before his mouth met hers.

Her hands flew up to his chest and she pushed, but not hard enough to convince him that she did not want to be kissed. He pushed back. Her mouth was soft against his, and he felt that she loved him.

But even being certain of her love, he could not open his eyes, and the kiss was not what he expected. He'd thought it would set him on fire, would burn him to the absolute ground. Instead it came over him like a breeze, nostalgic and gentle.

Adrienne shoved him, for real, then, and it was all he could do not to fall back on his ass. He saw her protecting her mouth with her hand and felt hollow and disappointed. Still, even in this disappointment, there was momentary peace: the cacophony of critics in his head fell silent.

165

CHAPTER 15

CALEB COULDN'T FIND HENRY, AND Sue couldn't find her minivan. Sue didn't seem too upset about it.

"Shoot, Caleb, I do this all the time. I just don't remember where I parked," she said. Her dogs were pulling at their leashes, always revved up after a performance, and Sue's makeup was sliding off, her white hair springing in little ringlets from her French twist. "I'll just wait till all the cars clear out. Right now I have to get the babies to bed. I'll find it in the morning."

Caleb tried not to jump to conclusions and went to bed, but when it became clear to him that he wasn't going to fall asleep, he peeled back his sheet, slipped his sandals on, and left the trailer. The grounds were dark, all the campers in bed except a couple of tent crew members. Caleb shoved his hands in his pockets and walked. It was much cooler outside the trailer without all those bodies packaged in one room.

They had undersold the show tonight, the Chicago show, the biggest show they would do this season. He had no idea where, when, or how they were going to recover the loss.

Mentally, he prepared the speech he would make to fire all of Seamus's employees—he imagined Jenifer and Vroni clinging to each other's bony bodies, crying from the phlegmy dark place in the back of their throats, from the same place they kept their German and all their emotions. He imagined Azi, all straight-backed and unsmiling, thinking of having to return to Nigeria, where he was born, and where he once had to pay a nurse for a clean blanket when he was in the hospital for third-degree burns. He imagined Sue, so phobic about being separated from her dogs, that she once ate nothing but stale crackers and expired milk for a week to avoid leaving them while she went to the store. When Caleb fired her, she would bite her fingernails down to the nubs.

And now the circus was only a part of his worries. What would he do if Adrienne's surgery went badly? What if she did not get better? The doctors said there was no reason to panic. They'd figure it out. But there were so many "ifs" when they spoke—when it came to his wife, even the smallest uncertainty made him panic.

They wanted to do the surgery the least risky way—go in through her nose, cut out a mere chip of bone, then cut the tumor out with the tiniest of blades—but if they couldn't remove the whole tumor that way, they'd have to take off her forehead again and poke around in there with her skull open.

So what would he do if things went wrong? Would he yell at the doctors and drop out of his own life, as he had when his father died? When he really let himself think about Adrienne's tumor, he couldn't help but remember his father's glassy eyes, the way he had stared at a fleur-de-lis on the wallpaper, with cancer all over, in his blood, his brain, his toe bones—everywhere. It was a daily agony for his father to swallow a handful of pills, but Caleb and his mother had made him do it. They'd forced him. Behind his stare, Caleb believed his father's encyclopedic knowledge of baseball and the world wars still existed. He was still himself in there, his mind a museum that was closed but still full of everything Caleb treasured. Caleb was young and he had been studying and he knew that nearly anything could be preserved with the proper care. But he couldn't figure out why taking care of his father, loving and preserving him, made him feel so terrible.

If he had to see Adrienne like this, tied to the world by a handful of pills and a wallpaper pattern, it would be so much worse than losing his father, so much worse than losing Feely and Feinstein. He could not rehearse for life without her, because there would be none.

167

Her surgery was scheduled for next Friday, a week from today, when the circus would be in Fort Wayne. She was panicking, too, he knew. He ought to be with her.

It was close to midnight by the time Caleb shook off the webs that had been spun between his calves and went back to their campsite. Lorne was awake, leading Ambrosia in slow, shuffling circles around the camp. When he saw Caleb, he waved, then dropped his hand as if he were embarrassed. Caleb hurried to wave back so he wouldn't feel foolish.

"Late for a walk," said Lorne.

"I wanted to get in my exercise."

"Heh. Agreed," said Lorne, pointing to the horse. Unlike Sue's dogs, whose puffed-out chests and lolling tongues made them appear almost arrogant, Ambrosia always seemed lost to Caleb, like she was wandering around in a nonsensical dream.

"Sorry about the show," Lorne said.

"Why is that?"

"Small crowd. Makes money tight. I know it has you under pressure."

"Crowds are always small."

Lorne nodded. "I know. Remember when Adrienne was still the Amazon Woman? Crowds was small then, but I can tell—they got smaller every year since."

Caleb sighed. "We know how to get by on a shoe string."

Lorne snorted at this. "An elephant can't get by on a shoe string. Camels and horses can't. They need pounds and pounds and pounds of shoe strings."

"Sure," said Caleb. He was tired now. He wanted to get some sleep, and maybe he could, now that Lorne was no longer snoring in his ear.

"I worry about the animals, Caleb. Money gets tight, they get skinny. Those ASPCA people don't come until they got their ears cut off or something . . ."

"We won't let them get skinny," said Caleb. Lorne spent all his time with animals and circus people, so he was ignorant about the institutions of normal people. He filled in his ignorance with works of imagination: when an animal bled, the ASPCA arrived like Superman; banks, in his mind, looked like they did on the set of an old Western. It shocked Caleb, whenever Lorne revealed such beliefs, that a person could be so innocent. But what reason did Lorne have to go to a bank? Like the ex-cons that raised the tent every year, Caleb paid him in cash. And what experience would he have with the ASPCA, other than that tragic one so many years ago, when he performed with his foster parents? While Lorne's way of seeing the world sometimes caught Caleb off guard, Caleb never tried to disabuse him of his beliefs. In a weird way, they seemed part of his aesthetic as a performer.

Lorne lifted his chin a little, and Caleb felt like he was being challenged. Caleb promised again that the animals would be well fed as long as they were at Feely and Feinstein. He said it with as much confidence as he could muster.

Lorne shook his head but left to take Ambrosia back to her stall.

On the way back to his trailer, Caleb saw Kylie sitting outside on the ground next to the porta-potties, with her chin propped on her fists, and knew that Henry had not yet been found.

CHAPTER 16

HENRY STILL HAD A RAGGED line of white makeup around his face when he arrived at Adrienne's house. He looked like he was being chased and she'd thought that this was an extension of one of her nightmares. In the dreams where people came into her home uninvited, the intruder was either Curtis or Caleb, or sometimes Jack from *Jack and the Beanstalk*. Now, the intruder was Henry.

It was hard to figure out exactly how he'd gotten there but she could fill in the gaps of his story with her own memories of the better part of her twenties. At Henry's age, Adrienne was also parentless, groping in the dark through medications and surgeries, clinging to Curtis like he was Jesus-come-again. So Adrienne knew that in life, there was chaos, and then there were bad choices, and then there was more chaos.

Henry's sudden appearance wasn't the surreal part. The thing that kept her wondering if she was dreaming was the way she had reacted to Henry's intrusion. Instead of shutting him down, kicking him out, sending him back to Caleb with a cool good-bye, she'd let him intrude. She had been isolated, and she wanted to hear a story she could connect to, she wanted closeness. Even Jack's giant had a harp to sing to him. She only had a TV and thick walls.

So she let Henry in. She let him talk.

There had been no closeness in Caleb painting her nude, with those boxy, misshapen features. The idea that he might find her newly disfigured body somehow beautiful or exotic, or that he might feel obligated to find the beauty in it—this made her furious. This was the thought that drove her fist through the canvas that night.

Now Caleb's painting was ripped, and Caleb himself was gone, and, just a few moments ago, Henry had kissed her.

He had driven many miles, in fact, to kiss her. If she could have designed her own antidote for sadness, she couldn't have come up with a more potent cure than the kiss of a man as pretty and young as Henry. Still, it was not what she wanted. What she *wanted* was for Caleb to do the driving, for Caleb to do the late-night secret-shame sharing and the kissing.

When she pushed Henry away, his whole face went slack and pale, but he looked directly at her. She guarded her mouth for a moment, then felt ridiculous. She lowered her hands and clasped them to her chest. No matter what she did with her hands, she couldn't seem to shake the pose of some sullied handmaiden on the front of a romance novel.

"Henry," she said, hoping that if she said his name, more words would follow, and those words would express, without ambiguity, that she was a married woman, with no interest in him except friendship.

Richard jostled the perch in his cage and filled the silence with, "I love you . . . I love you . . . peanut butter sandwich."

Henry sighed. He ran his fingers through his hair as if he'd like to have pulled it out. Adrienne thought about how other people might react in this situation, and none of those reactions felt right to her. To yell at him was hypocritical. To comfort him was confusing. To laugh was cruel.

"What do you want from me?" he said.

"What?"

He looked at her through his fingers. "I don't get it. I just don't get what it is you want."

"I want to be friends," she said.

"Ah, Christ. No, you don't," he mumbled.

"I do!"

He threw his hands in the air. "I lived in your guest room! You unwrapped my gum for me and did my laundry. And where's your wedding ring?"

"Keep your voice down. Don't you dare give me that you-led-me-on crap, Henry, just because you feel like an ass," she said.

"I didn't," he hissed. "I didn't say you led me on. I said you want *something*, and you fucking do."

She was about to say again that she wanted his friendship, but she stopped herself. She considered he might be right. She might want something else from him.

When she first saw this scarecrow kid outside Caleb's office, pulling tattered props from a trunk, she'd had a startling thought: *Oh, it's you*. She'd entertained the notion of fates and gods and reasons for things like airplane crashes and tumors in brains and webbed toes and the crush of hunger and pain in the world and she'd begun to think there was no reason for anything—that these things were all accidents. And then she'd seen him, a stranger, and it felt so not-accidental, like something she'd been waiting for, planning for.

Oh, it's you. Finally. It's you.

What she wanted from Henry, she decided, was relief. He lifted a grief so old, that she no longer registered it as grief, but simply as part of who she was. She was this: a member of a family of two that would never grow any larger. That was the fact. She loved her parrot, and she loved Azi and Sue, and sometimes she even loved Seamus; but only Caleb felt like family. She knew that her family was supposed to be bigger than that, but if the circus didn't feel like family, then she had been convinced only a baby would complete them. There, she was out of luck.

But the feeling that someone was missing had persisted. It was as if the babies who were supposed to join her family had gotten lost somewhere. It made her sad to think of them—they had wanted to come to her. But to call this sadness grief seemed strange, because she hadn't lost anything. She only knew it was grief when it was gone. She only knew it was grief when she met Henry.

Now, here he was, waiting for her to say something, his forehead wrinkled, his hands balled into fists. If she said this, about reasons-for-things and wandering babies out loud, would that tell him what he needed to know?

She was so wrapped up in trying to make sense of everything, she did not hear the knocking.

The knob was turning, clicking. She had not bolted the door after letting Henry in.

"Anybody home?" A voice, and the top of a head, covered in a thin layer of blond fuzz, emerged from between the door and the frame. The tip of a black boot.

The boot could have belonged to anyone. But the blond fuzz was familiar. It was Curtis.

Richard threw his beak up, opened it, and began to screech.

"Who is it?" Henry asked. He reacted to her face, drawing himself up fast. She sprang up, hurdled the coffee table. She landed hard on the wood floor and ran back to her bedroom.

Under her bed, in the hatbox, was the gun, a Sig Sauer semi-automatic with a faux wood handle, cowboy-cool and shiny as the day she bought it. When she picked it up, it didn't feel nearly as dangerous as it looked. It felt like a toy, a telephone, a toothbrush in her hand—like any other household object. She slid the magazine inside and it locked with a click.

HENRY WAS BETWEEN ADRIENNE'S GUN and her target, held in the grip of the man who'd just shown up—because Henry had frozen up, exactly as he'd done the first time someone had pointed a gun in his direction. The scar on the top of his head felt like someone had struck a match on it. He had a good hold on the man at first, but when Adrienne raised her gun, his grip went slack, and now the man had him by his collar, making the neck-hole of Henry's shirt into a noose that gradually tightened by twisting his fist.

"Adrienne," the blond man said, "look, you're flippin' out for no reason. I'm in town on business. For Southern Blue. I just wanted to say hi."

"Hi, Curtis," said Adrienne. "Get the hell out of my house."

"Didn't Nancy tell you I was coming?"

"Only forty times. I told her not to tell you where I lived. And here you are."

"Well, don't blame Nancy. She has a hard time saying no to me. Who's this little fuck-rag?" the man said, slapping Henry on the side of his head.

Adrienne stepped closer. "That is absolutely none of your business." Her voice became shrill. That animal voice. Henry remembered it, the same desperate pitch that had clawed its way out of his mother when she was angry and panicked—the voice she sent after their father to slash at him when she couldn't stop him physically.

Move, Henry, move.

He felt the man's body close to his. He was not much taller than Henry, and Henry was stronger. He knew he was. And faster. But he could not stop looking at Adrienne's finger on the trigger, thinking it would be so easy for it to slip.

Henry's collar cut into his neck as the man twisted it. "Adie, come on, girl. You can't kill me. I was there when that wasp got in the house, and you carried it out in a Ball jar all careful, like it was baby Jesus."

Adrienne shuddered—her hold on the gun seemed to weaken.

The hand on the back of Henry's neck felt hot and sweaty, and the feel of this man's skin against his own made the hair on Henry's arms stand up. There was a reason that Adrienne wanted to shoot him. This man had done things that he should not have to her. Henry heard it in his voice, in the layers of bravado and guilt.

He saw her shoulders relax, and she dropped the arm that held the gun, sliding the clip out. She set the gun on the table next to the syringe and held the clip in her hand. Adrienne wouldn't risk shooting Henry. Of course.

"See?" the man said. "What'd I say?"

"Shut up," she said. Her eyes were still wet, but her voice had lost its scrape. "I'd still be happy to shoot your dick off."

Finally, Henry's mind reconnected with the rest of him, and he bent his knees, ripped his collar and slid out of his shirt to get away.

The man tried to reach out and whack Henry in the head again, but Henry had his genius back. He dodged the man's swat, and the handful of empty air he caught humiliated him, forced him to take another swing. Henry jumped back onto the coffee table, his feet tearing the faces of the women on Adrienne's beauty magazines. He didn't hit the man. He wanted to let Adrienne take her swing. If she didn't get her chance to, she'd be thinking about this a long time, thinking she should have stood up for herself.

Come on, Adrienne. You don't need a gun. You're seven feet tall! Just hit *him.*

Henry stepped back onto the couch and bounced, up and over the lamp on the end table. His feet tucked beneath him like a bird in flight. But he was used to landing on soft mats, and his feet hit the ground too hard, sending shock waves of pain up through his heels. He staggered, and in that instant the man clocked him, hard. Henry saw the floor rising up to meet him and tucked into a roll. His back slammed into Richard's cage, and the parrot thrashed around, beating his wings, knocking his water bottle down. The cold water splashed across the back of Henry's hair, rolling down into his eyes.

Okay, then. No more dodging. He wasn't going to get beaten to death waiting for her to do something. The man lunged for him, and Henry prepared to go for the nose, the throat, the spots that make gentle blows painful, and hard blows lethal.

What he saw next was like something on pro-wrestling: Adrienne, the giantess, wearing a pair of fuzzy yellow slippers and no pants, grabbed the man by the collar, the same way the man had held Henry a moment ago. Instead of strangling him, she lifted the man by his shirt right off his feet, making it look as effortless as lifting a kitten by its scruff. The man's eyes widened, and he writhed in her grip.

"You bitch," he said, "you let me go, you fucking ugly sasquatch-looking bitch!"

And then she tossed him onto his face. He slid, stopping only a few feet from the open door. When he looked up there was a bright thread of blood hanging from his lip.

"I can't believe you can't take an apology after all this time," he said, trying to sit up and wipe his mouth at once.

"You called me a sasquatch. That's the worst apology ever," she said.

175

Curtis was quiet for a moment. He seemed fascinated by the blood he wiped from his mouth and stared down at his hands, studying it. When he looked up, he spoke quietly. "I hadn't gotten round to the apologizing yet. I'm moving up here. To work at the St. Louis warehouse. Nancy's coming, too. We're together. We're getting married," he said.

Adrienne put her hand on her heart as if she were getting ready to say the pledge of allegiance.

"I thought you would want to know. I'm going to be taking care of my family now—I've changed, and I hope we can be friends."

Adrienne's lips moved, but nothing came out of them. Henry didn't know who this Nancy was, but he had a pretty good guess about her. He had a pretty good guess about why Curtis talked so quiet, and his pupils were pinpricks in the middle of his blue eyes, like a dog's after it's finished off a rabbit.

While Adrienne still held her palm to her chest, Curtis noticed the syringe on the table. His mouth puckered into an *O* shape, a look of mock horror.

"You're sick again?" he asked.

Adrienne's hand curled up into a fist, then, and she looked like she might march over and stomp on his skull. Henry was rapt, hoping she would.

"Really? I pay all that money for surgery, and you got it again?" He laughed, and the hair on Henry's arms and neck stood up. "I tried to tell you they were ripping us off."

The blond man squirmed to his feet.

Adrienne moved in the man's direction like she might toss him again, but he bolted out the door. Henry chased him, not to catch him, but to be sure he ran far enough away. The neighbors' houses were lit, and he could see their silhouettes in the windows.

At the end of the block, the man vaulted into the driver's seat of a blue van and drove away.

Southern Blue, it said on the side of the van, in cursive letters. He didn't recognize the words, but he recognized the shape of them. He recognized the shade of blue.

When he was back inside, Adrienne turned the dead bolt and put her arms around him. He pressed his face into her shirt. It didn't matter what he did anymore. He felt as if he were dreaming—the gun pointed in his direction, that van. It was too surreal.

"That was my ex-husband," she said.

Henry wasn't surprised—the nature of their relationship was clear enough to him, after listening to them talk. But hearing her say it chilled him. She'd shared a house, a bed, with the man who'd just driven away. In that van. Why would her ex-husband have that van? The madness of the evening, the adrenaline that was still coursing through him, had scrambled his brain.

"He abandoned me the first time I had to have this tumor removed. I didn't want to have it removed, but—my size strains my heart. I can't let it get out of control."

Henry swallowed. The tumor was what strained Adrienne's heart, she had just said so. But it was his mother's heart that he thought of then. The heart that his father made race, until it could not anymore, until it started skipping every other beat just to take a rest, just to get some peace.

"You should've killed him," Henry said. He clung to Adrienne. Now this desire to touch her had even more urgency and had little to do with anything but protecting her. Still, he felt her arms peeling away. She took the gun back to her bedroom, and he followed. He watched as she placed the gun in a hatbox, and put the hatbox on the high shelf of her closet.

They returned to the living room, where Richard rattled his perch. "Poppa," he said. "Peanut butter and jelly."

"I would have backed you up. I would have said it was self-defense," he said.

"Oh, Henry. He's just an idiot. He isn't worth all that," she said. And Henry thought, what if it wasn't his scrambled brains talking? What if Adrienne's rotten ex had some connection to his mother's lover?

"I've seen a van like that before," he said. "Saw it a long time ago when it was new enough to have perfect paint. A man who drove a van with that symbol was there the night my mother died."

It was the second time he'd said it tonight, but this time it was not so easy. In his head, the march began: mother of Batman, mother of Cinderella, mother of Conan the Barbarian and the lost boys and all those kids in the wilderness in *Mad Max*. When he got to Rylan, mother of Henry and Andre and Frankie, the features of her face were even more generic than the last time he imagined them. He had no pictures of her except this one, the one in his head, and it was fading.

"It's a Southern Blue van," she said. "There are dozens like it. So I'm not surprised you've seen it before."

"Oh. Wait, you told me about them before." He remembered the makeup party that she was supposed to throw before she got too ill. "That's the cosmetics company you work for?"

"I hate to say I share anything with Curtis, but yes. He worked for them when we were married, and now we both do."

"Is he like a . . . door-to-door salesman?"

"He was, back when those existed. He works in the warehouse now. We don't go door to door. We have parties. It's a whole different company now."

"But it's the same van."

"Yeah. Maybe Curtis bought it off them when they replaced their fleet. Who knows?"

"Who knows," Henry mumbled.

"So . . . that guy. What did he do, anyway? That night," she asked.

"That night? He got shot at. He tried to talk to my mother, and my father chased him out with a shotgun."

"Oh," she said. "The way you were talking it seemed like maybe—"

"He didn't kill her. I mean, the guy didn't. She had a heart attack."

"A heart attack?"

"Yeah."

"Awful young for that," she said, quietly.

"That's what everybody said." He explained how his father had grazed his head with a bullet that night, shooting at the man. He showed her the scar beneath his hair. "He was the sort of person who can't stop themselves when they're angry. And, yeah, anybody would be pissed about a strange guy in their house, but he could have lost it over a cold cup of coffee on the wrong day, and who knew when the wrong day was gonna be? And we think—I mean, me and Andre think—my mom just couldn't handle it. Her body couldn't keep it up."

Adrienne took a moment to put together what Henry was saying, that their father hadn't shot their mother and neither had the man, but that his father was unquestionably responsible for her death. "I see," she said, nodding apologetically. "I shouldn't have asked."

"It's fine," he said.

They sat together until the birds outside were singing full force. Richard mocked them, repeating the notes of their songs from his perch in the living room.

When Adrienne insisted that Henry return to the circus, Henry groaned with dread. Caleb was probably going to kill him, and he was anxious about leaving Adrienne alone, even though she promised that if Curtis came back she'd call the police. But if he had to go, he didn't want to look like he'd been up to no good when he returned. He asked Adrienne for a safety pin to doctor the rip in his shirt. She brought him one from her sewing box.

He carefully pinned the rip, folding the fabric and hiding the pin on the inside of the shirt. "I'll convince Caleb to come back," he said.

"Henry, you need to worry about convincing Caleb not to fire you."

He picked the keys to Sue's van up off the floor, put them in his pocket. "Eh. I'll get him to come back, I promise. Might not have any luck with the other thing, though."

"Be careful," she said.

Halfway back to Chicago, he realized that he'd forgotten to swap makeup bags with her. Hers was still sitting in the passenger seat. Oh well. Kylie would keep sharing with him, if he asked, even though he hated asking.

He reached over and opened the bag with one hand, keeping the other on the wheel, and took out the container of powder that smelled like flowers. It was awkward opening it with one hand, and he got a lapful of powder, but also a rush of her scent, which was the purpose of opening it. He'd asked her what she wanted with him, and as he smelled the powder spilled in his lap and thought of the inch of flesh pinched on her thigh when he gave her the injection, he got it: why she had picked up Curtis and flung him. Why she'd done Henry's laundry and given him the stupid makeup bag. Why she told Caleb he'd better let Henry stay in their guest room, or else. The intimacy between them was not the intimacy of lovers, but the intimacy of walking into your house at night, of seeing a certain face, and knowing you were home. Oh, yes, he got it now, what she wanted with him, but he didn't get it like a slow injection. He got it like a bullet through the skull.

He was her favorite.

CHAPTER 17

THE BOY STEPPED OUT OF the minivan he'd stolen and he looked like hell, with his shirt pinned and a red ring around his neck. The first thing he did was return Sue's keys to her. She asked why he'd done it, and Henry said something that Caleb couldn't quite hear, because the boy had his hand near his mouth, half covering it.

Sue took her keys. "Well. That's not a reason. Caleb is beside himself. And here I thought we'd get along," Sue said, shoving the keys in her denim purse. She turned and stalked away, calling her dogs to heel.

Then Henry walked toward Caleb, his hands shoved into his pockets. And Caleb couldn't help but picture Henry kissing his wife. He couldn't help trying to imagine the things Henry had said and done that had led up to the moment where he caught her off guard and smashed his clumsy baby mouth into hers. It made Caleb want to tear himself apart, this imagining. If she found this kid attractive, then how did she also find Caleb attractive, who had to shave twice a day to keep his stubble down, who had more than an inch of gut sticking out past his belt, and who couldn't boast, really, of any true talent but a good eye and a discerning taste? How could she love Caleb when it was this boy who had been there when Curtis turned up?

On the phone this morning, she'd said she pushed Henry away. Caleb believed she had. But there was this sad quality to her voice like perhaps she regretted not letting him kiss her.

Not only did Caleb want to tear himself apart, he wanted to do the same to Henry. He wanted to dismember him. Finger by finger. Tooth by tooth. All the parts that had touched his wife, he wanted to jerk from his body.

When Henry stood in front of him, though, he found himself incapable of saying anything. He made an awkward gesture in the direction of the trailer they both rode in. Caleb stepped inside, and the boy followed him in and shut the door.

Caleb opened a briefcase on one of the little benches in the trailer. He took out a form and fastened it to a clipboard. He sat on the bench and laid the clipboard in his lap, filling in the blank spaces with a mechanical pencil, keeping his eyes down and his mind focused on the page, the job, the procedure. It was not easy, because he had spent the last three weeks sharing a kitchen, a living room, and a bathroom with the boy. He'd told Adrienne it was a bad idea, and she had thrown in his face that he was the only one wearing a suit. Well, that was true. But now the kid was tangled up, not just in the circus, but with everything that Caleb cared about, and Caleb still had to wear the damned suit.

"I meant to get back before anyone missed me," Henry said.

Caleb looked down at his notes, written on the thick black lines of the form. The employee in question showed a lack of respect for his colleagues and his superiors. The employee in question misused the property of another employee. The employee is an excellent clown who will be impossible to replace on such short notice. It wasn't even worth it to try. Why waste himself on this? Why waste himself firing and hiring and searching, why throw his energy into shaping this show while Adrienne was at home, sick, needing him?

Caleb printed and signed his name, wrote the date out long form just to keep his hand busy. *July second, 1990.*

"She wanted you," Henry said. "She wants you to come back."

"Don't talk," said Caleb. *Or I will kill you,* thought Caleb. *I'll take you apart starting with your mouth.* Henry had no family that Caleb knew of. The circus was *Caleb's* family. In spite of the suit, in spite of the office, and the fact that he hadn't been born particularly talented, beautiful, or freakish, he was one of them, and Henry was not. *Better yet, Henry, talk a little louder and I won't have to lift a finger.*

Caleb tore the yellow and pink carbon copies from the form. The white form he slipped into a folder, for his own files, and he folded the pink form into one of the briefcase pockets to give to Seamus. The yellow copy was Henry's. Caleb stood and handed it to him.

"We've just had a discussion about your conduct," he said. "You can imagine the details of it. The broad strokes are on that paper."

"Okay."

"Don't ever tell me again what my wife wants."

IN INDIANAPOLIS, CALEB MET SEAMUS in a hotel restaurant bar while the circus set up at the State Fairgrounds. Seamus occasionally came to see a tour show and check in with Caleb. It often happened that the show he saw was the Indianapolis show, and Caleb suspected that Seamus had a woman in this town that he liked to visit and felt like he was killing two birds with one stone. He was efficient like that. It was four in the afternoon, and when Caleb joined him, Seamus was watching highlights from a ball game on a large television above the bar. The bar was empty except for Seamus, Caleb, and a young man in a suit sitting at one of the tables. Seamus sipped a black beer and the sunglasses perched on his head held his black hair back, revealing shocks of gray that grew from his temples. He shook Caleb's hand and went back to watching the television.

When Caleb was a kid, he and Seamus Feely and the other boys in the neighborhood played baseball in backyards and alleys, a pretty elegant system, really, of home games on the west side of the neighborhood and away games on the east. They had about four even and regular teams, and a paramount sense of sportsmanship. No fights, no bloody noses, no trash talk about anybody's mama, even if she was a hairy Italian, even if she was the gap-toothed Irish ringmaster's wife.

Caleb wasn't the best athlete—he was the catcher, and not much of one to begin with. When he burnt his fingers trying to weld two pieces of old copper pipe together (he was sculpting a crucifix for his mother's birthday), he was an even worse catcher, because the ball kept hitting his fingers, even through his glove, making the wound hot and fresh again, forcing the blister open. Seamus told him, with absolute professionalism, wearing his rolled-up jeans and ball cap, his violet eyes menacing even then, set in his plump little-boy's face, that if he could not catch the ball, then there was no point in being on the team. Caleb had, also with professionalism, agreed and gone home for the day.

That night, he stayed awake in his bed, anticipating the moment in which he let another easy-out slip over his mitt, and Seamus would tell him to leave and not come back. He decided on what to say: "I only hope you'll have me back next summer, when my fingers have healed." He mimed, in the dark, relinquishing his catcher's mitt, which belonged to one of the other boys.

The next morning, he told his mother and father about Seamus and what he had said. His mother said, "Oh, good grief, Caleb, don't let the little mick kid bully you. Just wait till your hand heals and go out and thrash him, why don't you? You don't need to play ball *every* day."

His father bandaged his fingers together. He did it tight. To see that they were secure, he made Caleb wiggle them at the lowest knuckle. He flicked the bandaged fingers and asked if it hurt. When Caleb said no, his father had nodded, patted his cheek, told him to pretend like it was one big finger instead of two bound together, and he would catch just fine. And he *did* catch just fine, even though it was still a bit painful.

While Seamus watched the game in the hotel bar, Caleb studied his fingers. There weren't even any scars from that soldering accident, which almost left him friendless for a whole summer. "That Bonds is really something else, don't you think?" said Seamus, indicating the TV.

"Yeah," said Caleb. "He's a home run machine, I hear. Haven't had much time to watch the games, though."

On the television, Bonds swung, hit, and zipped through the bases, all the movements seeming so familiar to him that he could have been brushing his teeth.

"Oh, you should make time. It's a great season. Cards don't have a snowball's chance, but that's alright," said Seamus.

"Maybe with you."

The sports segment was over, and it was back to the anchors, on to the weather.

Seamus turned to him and smiled. "He's cheating, of course."

"That right?"

"Bonds? Oh, yeah. He's juiced. Don't get me wrong. He's talented. But talent is only a fire. Talent needs something to burn."

Caleb nodded. He ordered a Diet Coke from the bartender. The restaurant had dark furniture, dark carpeting, dim lighting, all designed to make the place feel restful. But the carpet was tacky and the furniture felt slightly sticky, covered in a film of nicotine and sugar from spilled cocktails. The place was more depressing than anything.

Seamus waved a hand at the TV, indicating he was done talking about it. "Sorry. I get caught up in these things. How are you? How is the tour so far?"

He wanted to tell him that he, Caleb Baratucci, had performed his life's miracle, and things were starting to turn around. But it wasn't true.

"Well. To be honest. Not so good," said Caleb. The bartender set the glass in front of him, and he took a sip.

"Surprise, surprise."

Caleb pinched the bridge of his nose. "We're in the red. Again. And it's worse than it's ever been."

"Hmm."

"Gas prices are obscene. It's costing us a fortune to travel."

"I see. How deep in are we?"

He popped the brass latches on his briefcase and handed Seamus a ledger bound in fake black leather. "Deep. No possible way to recover it. I haven't even factored in this round of paychecks, not theirs or mine or even yours, which we have to pay, and I've got no idea where that money is coming from."

"Well. Do we have to pay them just now? Could we pay them, perhaps, in a lump sum at the end of the summer?"

"What? *No.* Seamus, they have bills to pay, they have families, and you're low-balling them already. And what makes you think we're going to have the money to pay them at the end of summer? We don't have it now. Where do you expect this money to materialize from?"

"Well, what are we doing to *make it* materialize?"

Caleb was sweating. He thought of Azi, who had hooped glowing necklaces around his forearms as big as bread loaves and offered them to children for two dollars apiece to supplement his paycheck. And Kylie, who had two sets of clothes that weren't costumes; yellow tank top, sundress. He lost his temper a little.

"*You're* not doing anything. *You're* the artistic director. Did it ever occur to you that we might do better, or we might be more organized if you were ever around?"

Seamus waved his hand. "That's what I have you for. You're my eyes and ears. And anyway, the only newbies are the clowns. Everyone else knows the routine."

"The routine changes. I can't do everything."

"Caleb," said Seamus. "Why don't you get a real drink?"

Caleb was about to protest, but it was not a suggestion. Seamus ordered a neat whiskey, and the bartender laid it square in front of Caleb on a little white napkin.

"There," said Seamus, taking a gulp of his beer. "That should calm us down."

"Don't say 'us.' You sound like a dickhead when you say 'us.'"

Seamus laughed. "I'm sorry, Caleb. I don't mean it that way, you know that." He pointed at the whiskey. "You don't need to drink it straight if you don't want. You can mix it with your Coke."

Caleb shook his head and raised the drink to his lips. "This is fine."

"Good," said Seamus.

The bartender brought a basket of deep-fried mushrooms. Caleb sipped his drink.

"You probably remember how my old man loved the circus," said Seamus after he had eaten two mushrooms, chewing them deliberately, chasing each one with a gulp of beer.

"Yes. I do. He talked about it a lot."

"Yes. 'A lot' is an understatement—polite of you. It was the only thing he talked about more than soccer. And communism."

He ate another mushroom and asked for a second moist towelette.

"Remember," he said, "how he would have the freaks to dinner? The midgets and the fat lady? The albino?" Seamus shook his head and drew back the corners of his mouth. "Jesus. They scared me to death."

Caleb did remember the albino. The first time Caleb saw him, he knew there was something unsettling about the man that he couldn't put his finger on. His eyes had not been pink like a lab rat's, but pale blue. And he remembered the man leaning in to greet the boys, trying to be friendly but too conscious of the boys' repulsion to be really charming. Seamus hadn't seemed afraid. He had refused to shake the man's hand until Conall Feely pinched him, and then, during dinner, Seamus whispered to the man, too low for Conall to hear, "You're disgusting." The albino had ignored him and stammered through the dinner conversation while Seamus pecked at the man's shins with the toes of his shoes.

"You weren't very nice to them," said Caleb.

"Because I was afraid of them. And because my father liked them so much," said Seamus. Then his eyes wandered over the surface of the bar and he seemed lost in thought. "Thing is," he said after a moment, "I learned to love the circus, but never as much as him. He put everything into Feely and Feinstein, and I have put things elsewhere."

The setting sun was coming in bright through the windows. Seamus pulled his sunglasses down over his eyes, now watery from the sun. "I've diversified. And so if I lose the circus, it'll be a sentimental loss, not a monetary one. I know you'd feel bad about it, because I know how you blame yourself for things, Caleb, but there's really no need to feel guilty. You've been a wonderful manager. You've kept this going for much longer than you should have," he said.

Caleb had not rehearsed for the hollow feeling that was spreading inside him, the cold open area that was broadening just under his sternum. Seamus was not disappointed in Caleb, but as the conversation veered toward its predictable conclusion, Caleb discovered that Seamus's feeling about this was irrelevant to him. He also found that, even though he told himself that the loss of Feely and Feinstein was a blessing in disguise that would allow him to go home to his wife, he couldn't bring himself to give it up without an argument.

"It doesn't have to be a loss. I can save this for you if you'll just approve some changes in the way we run the show."

That's right, keep fighting, you idiot, so your wife can completely give up on you. Seamus was about to say something else, but he paused, raising his eyebrows. "Alright. How should we run the show?"

"Few things. Phase out the animals, except maybe Sue's dogs. We can't afford to feed them. I'd find something else for Lorne to do. And stop touring in the summer—stop showing up places whether they want us there or not. Let them invite us. Get rid of the tent. Then we would be more mobile and more accessible. More marketable with lower production costs. For the show itself, we should get some better lighting design. Some musicians. A story that ties things together, maybe."

Seamus considered this a moment, then shook his head and took the last swallow of his beer. He didn't purse his lips over the edge of the glass but opened his mouth wide and dumped the beer in. "You're right. But that would not be a circus, Caleb. What you are describing is a theatre company. I don't have any sentimental attachment to theatre, and I've told you already, I have been holding on to this for sentimental reasons. If you change all the things that make it a circus, then it's still a loss from my perspective. You haven't saved anything," he said.

"It would still be a circus."

"No. It would not be. My father's albinos and midgets were circus, and that poor elephant is circus, and those scary German girls are circus. Circus can't just be beautiful. It has to be weird. It has to be frightening. You of all people understand that aesthetic, your *wife* is circus, for Chrissakes. If people want to be awed and inspired and not thrilled and uncomfortable, then the market has spoken. Let them have their live musicians and storylines. But don't call it a circus. And don't ask me to produce it."

Caleb didn't know what to say. It felt like he had just been fired.

"Listen, you'll get your paycheck. And so will they. I'll be sure of that. But after this tour, Caleb . . ." He shook his head. "I think it's obvious that this is no good for anyone anymore. Not profitable. And unhealthy, really."

"Unhealthy?"

"Clinging to the dead. Very unhealthy."

"Circus isn't dead."

"No, not circus. My father." Then he added, "I'll sell it piecemeal. That should pay our debts. And if there's any money left over, Caleb, you'll have a part of it. I knew when I hired you that you would be the only real professional of all of us, and you were."

"Thank you," said Caleb, and he found himself tugging at the knot at his throat, trying to loosen the tie with his fingers. "Speaking of which. It doesn't seem to matter much now, but . . ." Caleb pulled from his briefcase the disciplinary measures form he had filled out for Henry. Seamus skimmed it and handed it back to him.

"Whose property was misused?" he asked.

"He stole Sue's car. Or, borrowed it without asking, I suppose," said Caleb.

"Well, yeah, it doesn't matter much, now. You can let him go if you want."

"That's a pain in my ass."

"Figured. Then keep him on until the end of the season. I imagine you're not surprised by this from him."

"I didn't expect *this*."

"Really? You told me he was freakishly talented. Seems like a given."

"He's worse than most."

"Not so. Take Bonds, for example," he said, wagging his finger in the direction of the television. "Like I said, talent is just a fire. It needs something to burn. And if your clown isn't on drugs, then he's burning something else."

Caleb shrugged. He did not want to continue a conversation about the boy. He'd done his job and now he preferred to pretend Henry did not exist.

189

"Maybe you should suggest drugs," said Seamus. "He's such a scrawny little bastard. Maybe steroids are the ticket."

Caleb tried to smile.

"At any rate . . . cheers," Seamus said and raised his mug. "To doing all that you can."

The circus was dead then, just like that, along with Mr. Feely and probably that poor old albino that Seamus had kicked under the table as a boy, and the tired old elephants that stood on their haunches and raised their trunks night after night for Conall Feely, goaded along by the hook.

FEELY AND FEINSTEIN'S INTERNATIONAL CIRCUS went on to Fort Wayne, Toledo, Detroit, and Toronto, but Caleb did not. He went home to his wife after Indianapolis, telling Seamus that if Seamus wanted to stay and act as manager, he could. Otherwise, he would leave his on-site duties to Azi and take care of checks and supply orders from a distance. Seamus didn't want to stay with the circus either, so he bought a cellular phone for Azi so that Caleb could give him instructions whenever he needed. If things fell apart, well, that's the way the old cookie crumbles, Seamus had told Caleb. It was their last season anyway.

Caleb thought the whole train ride home about how he would confront Adrienne and ask her what exactly Henry meant to her and what exactly had transpired between them. Who said what. Who touched who first. He wanted all these details. They seemed necessary to know if he was ever going to discover whether or not it was possible to love only one person forever. Because that was what was at stake here. The possibility of love. The reality of love. If she had done something that Caleb felt showed that she could, under the right circumstances, have loved Henry in the exact same way, to the exact same degree that she loved Caleb, then it was certain that love was not a creation between two people, as he always thought of it, but a random wash of emotion that could take hold of a person's senses for any reason, at any time.

When Caleb arrived at his house in Dogtown, his wife did not come to the door to undo the chain after he undid the lower lock. Their car was in the driveway, so he knocked, thinking she was probably sleeping. He didn't want to wake her up but he did want to get inside.

After he knocked, she still did not come to the door, so he pushed the door open as far as he could and slipped his hand in the opening to try and undo the chain.

Then he remembered the gun. He slowly retracted his fingers and decided it would be safest to announce himself.

"Adie," he said in a low voice. "It's me. I'm home. Let me in."

He heard Richard inside whistle and say "Poppa! Who's a sweet bird? Poppa!"

Still nothing. The smell of sour milk wafted out from the house. For a moment the stink of it was strong enough to make him gag. He had to take a step back. His heart fluttered, then flew, like a hysterical bird, up into his throat, flapping and stopping his breath.

The last time he'd felt this hysteria was when Henry locked himself in the unconditioned trailer and covered himself in blankets. Caleb took a deep breath and stopped himself from throwing a shoulder into the door to smash it open. He forced himself to reason: Henry was here just four days ago. She was fine then. And she was fine now. Just resting. Sick people need a lot of rest.

"Adie," he said again. "Let me in already. I'm sweating bullets out here."

He heard the parrot's feathers brushing against walls, his claws clicking against the floor, but he did not hear her heavy footsteps, the sound of her walking to the door to let him in. Still, he could smell, faintly, beneath the odor of sour milk, the magnolias and talc. Was she standing on the other side? Was she just refusing to open the door?

"Let me in, please. I came back to take care of you."

A car went by, and beneath the noise of the motor, he thought he heard her take a breath on the other side of the door.

"Please. Let me in. I won't leave again. I get it. I won't leave again."

He heard the scrape of the chain being undone and the brass latch falling limp against the door frame. *Clink.*

He waited for the doorknob to turn and the door to open for him but it didn't, so he pushed the door open himself to find that Richard had undone the chain and now perched on the highest rung of the hat rack, looking at Caleb with his lizard eyes.

Caleb called to Adrienne, finding in the kitchen the source of the rotten smell: a melted carton of ice cream on the counter. Dead flies were floating in a swirl of Neopolitan, and a cluster of living ones were settled on the sticky scoop left next to it. Caleb shooed them away.

He found her curled up in the guest bedroom, naked beneath her black robe. She was awake, but dazed, her hair unbrushed, held back in what was probably a ponytail a day ago. Now it was only a handful of hair held back from the knots of blond encircling the rest of her head.

It had only been three weeks since Caleb had seen her, but he could see the difference in her face, especially around her mouth. Her lips were always large but now they looked thicker. Her chin looked larger, too. The changes were subtle and probably wouldn't even be noticeable to someone who wasn't Caleb, who hadn't spent hours studying her face. For a moment, he could only stare at her. He knew immediately that this was at least part of what she had tried to avoid by not answering the door, and he could not help but linger on this new face. She had expected this, and he felt ashamed for having missed the opportunity to surprise her by being a better person than she'd assumed he would be.

"How did you get in?" she said. Her voice was hoarse and quiet.

"Richard undid the chain."

"Good bird. I didn't know he could do that. I was trying to come, Caleb. But the room is spinning right now."

He sat down on the bed next to her and kissed her hand. "You're dizzy?"

"Yes. And nauseous."

"You've been taking your medicine?"

"Yeah. I've been doing okay. Today was just a bad day."

"Have you checked your blood pressure?"

And just like that, they dove right into Adrienne's blood, heart, brain, health, tumor. There was no room for petty things like a question of fidelity.

"No."

"Why not?"

"I don't know. Should I? I'm not thinking straight."

He dug through their night table drawer and found the home-test blood pressure cuff that the doctor had given them weeks ago, when Adrienne had gotten her tests results back. He wrapped it around her arm and affixed it with the Velcro.

"I'm sorry," she said.

"It's alright," he said. He pushed the button and the cuff inflated.

"I'm really sorry, Caleb."

"No. Don't be sorry. You're sick. I shouldn't have left. I shouldn't have left you to figure this out on your own."

"I told you to go."

"I shouldn't have listened to you," he said. "Look, two-twenty over one-ten. We should get you to the doctor. I don't know how accurate this is. Could be higher than that."

"I have an appointment tomorrow for my surgical consultation. They'll take care of me then."

"We should go right now."

He undid the Velcro on the blood pressure cuff, and Adrienne shifted so that her head lay in his lap. Richard made his way into the room, scooting his beak along the floor. He flapped his clipped wings and hopped, which gave him just enough lift to reach the bed.

"Adie, we should go."

"Wait. Let me just be still. I've missed you so much. Why are you home so early? Why did you come?"

"I came for you."

"No. Why else?"

Caleb sighed. He began working the rubber band from her hair. Blond strands entangled it, and he untwisted each strand one by one to avoid hurting her. "The circus is going to fold," he said.

"I knew it," she said.

"Well, so did I. But I thought if we had a strong season, if I got some new talent in and kept things running smoothly it might, I don't know, resurrect the thing. Change Seamus's mind. I tried to keep it afloat."

"I know you did. Why didn't you just say that?"

"Because it wasn't a good enough reason to leave you. I knew it."

"And because I would've let the cat out of the bag."

"Yeah."

"You're right. I would have. Your people . . . they could have been looking for other jobs."

Caleb was quiet while he finished extracting the rubber band from her hair. "Would you like me to brush this before we leave?"

"You can if you want."

"Let me get a brush."

"Don't move yet," she said.

"Okay."

"Do you have to let them all go? Or is Seamus going to grow a pair and do it himself?"

"What do you think?"

"I'm sorry. You poor thing."

"Don't feel bad for me, feel bad for them! I have management experience. They have . . . I don't know what they have. I think some of them have the loony bin."

"You mean Henry?"

"No," he said. "You were right. Henry has nothing. And that's his own fault."

"Did you fire him, Caleb?"

"No."

She turned her new face up toward him and smiled. Her face became familiar to him again, in spite of her swollen lips and the unhealthy blush caused by the too-fast rush of blood.

"I knew you wouldn't."

"It was too much effort."

"No. That's not why."

Caleb went to the bathroom to get Adrienne's brush and makeup bag in case they wanted to admit her to the hospital. When he opened the bag to shove in her toothbrush and toothpaste, he found a tube of white grease paint and a set of small makeup brushes with wooden handles, none of which belonged to his wife. All her cosmetics and accessories were Southern Blue brand, and these were not. At the bottom of the bag, Caleb also found a crumpled envelope with a smudged address. Recognizing the letter as Henry's, Caleb felt a jolt of jealousy.

"Adie?" he called to her. "Why do you have all of Henry's shit in your makeup bag?"

"Huh? I don't."

"You're wearing whiteface regularly now?"

"I bet he swapped our bags. I gave him one that looked like mine. I didn't know; I haven't touched my makeup since you left."

Curiosity overtook Caleb, and he found himself taking the letter from the envelope and reading it. At first he thought the letter was written by a child. The letters were too neat, as if the writer had to think about how to shape each one consciously. The spelling was atrocious. As he read the letter, though, it became apparent that it was written by a grown man. The boy's brother. There were several references to their father and mother, and while none of them said so directly, it was clear to Caleb that their mother was dead and had been for many years. It was also clear that the brother was afraid of their father.

The letter asked Henry to go with his brother to their house. The brother, whose name was Andre, had something he needed to do, and quietly, in every line, was his fear of doing it. Caleb was still so angry with Henry, still hot with jealousy. But this letter, and the memory of Henry grasping for it on the day Caleb found him giving himself heatstroke in the trailer, dampened his anger, turned it into a bitter kind of pity.

He replaced the letter in the envelope and set it next to the sink. The letter was old. The date which the brother proposed for meeting with Henry had passed. But Caleb didn't think it was right to throw the letter away, or to destroy it. He thought of what Seamus had said: that talent needed something to burn. Whatever Henry set alight night after night when he performed, Caleb realized then, it had everything to do with this brother—and it was burning out.

CHAPTER 18

ONE NIGHT AFTER CALEB HAD left, somewhere between Indianapolis and Detroit, Henry overheard Lorne say that Henry behaved unnaturally—that, mark his words, the boy was the one who would put the nail in Feely and Feinstein's coffin.

The rest of the circus seemed to believe this. They hid his things. His costume went missing hours before a show, and he tore through his trunk looking for it. He got so frustrated trying to find it that he bloodied his knuckles punching the lid of his trunk. The costume later turned up in the contortionist's backpack, and she returned it to him without a word. He wore white gloves during that performance to cover his injuries, but the blood seeped through, a dark spot on his second knuckle. The gloves went missing the next night.

After performing for a surly audience in Fort Wayne, Henry found dog shit in his bed. When he asked Sue about it the next day, she burst into sobs, causing her mascara to dissolve. The contortionist came and comforted her and wiped the black tears from her face, looking at Henry like *he* was the one who had done something filthy.

Henry found his mirror shattered. His alarm clock went off at strange times. He had no idea if they had planned it, or if it was an unspoken understanding, but there was no doubt they were attempting to punish him for what they saw as his betrayal of Caleb. They sought to drive him out of his mind. And it was working. He got paranoid, constantly checking all his belongings to be sure they were clean, checking his trunk to be sure his costume was there, assuming that every whispered conversation was about him.

He found it hard to sleep, but when he did, he dreamed an old dream, the one where the stars were whizzing past him like a snowstorm—where his mother was Princess Leia and they were hurtling through space, riding in a ship. Her hair curled like ram's horns about her ears. She was holding baby Frankie, slipping a finger into his mouth, sliding pink gel over his gums, as Henry had watched her do when Frankie was teething. Then it was Henry's own tongue gliding over her knuckle, her oval nails. It was as real as anything, her skin, her body, touching his again. But as close as they were, he still could not make out the features of her face. Between her Leia buns was a flat, smooth nothing. When he awoke, the taste of her finger in his mouth disappeared, and she was gone again.

"Rylan Bell," he said, hoping that the sound of her name would bring back the memory of her face. He took a deep breath. He was going to say her name again, but he was afraid to wake up his bunkmates. He lay quietly, then, trying to picture her, until the sun came up.

That morning, Azi and Henry were still in their beds while everyone else had gone to breakfast. They were quiet, watching the dust float in the sunlight for a moment, listening to spoons against bowls and the chatter of the performers as they got their breakfasts off the meal truck.

"I'm sorry about the shit in your bed," Azi said, when he finally sat up and pulled on his socks.

"Thanks."

"It's not you, really. Something's up, though. They all know it."

"With what?"

"Caleb left."

"Adrienne is sick."

Azi shook his head, mashing his heel into his massive boot. "That's not the whole story. He met with Feely in Indianapolis. They're not telling us, but I think we're all out of a job."

Henry sat up in his cot. "How do you know?"

"I don't," he said. "I'm guessing. Been thinking about it a lot."

Azi finished tying his boots and glanced in the mirror, swiping his hand over his head as if smoothing hair he didn't have. "Don't talk about this," he said, and left Henry alone in the trailer.

In Detroit, Henry and Azi watched the Delaflotes rehearse their flying before the show. Every time the Delaflotes paused, Azi would stop speaking to him. Caleb had left Azi in charge so if it seemed like Azi and Henry were buddies, the circus would turn on Azi, too, and then nothing would get done. Remy and Chuck passed Lola back and forth, a jagged bolt of black lightning in her tights and leotard.

"She's a fox," said Azi, as Lola arched her back, hanging by her legs from the trapeze.

Henry smiled. "You know anything about her? Sue said you know about everyone."

"Hm. Sue. She should talk. No, I don't know about Lola. Except she's a fox."

"She's French. I know that."

Azi snorted. "She's French-American. When Feely and Feinstein folds, I'll have to go back to Nigeria. She can stay here."

"You can marry her and stay here, too. Be one of those strong men that pull cars and locomotives and shit."

"I'm not that strong, kid."

"You don't want to go back?"

"No. But I don't have a choice. I don't have a green card. Caleb applies for me and the application disappears—they stick it in a box and bury it and forget about it. I think if you start digging anywhere in the country you'll find a box with someone's green card application in it. That's what they do with them."

"My teacher had one of those. He was Russian. But he was here for a long time."

Now Chuck was the one being passed from hand to hand. Lola could catch, too, she and her brothers being not too different in size. When she caught him, and their hands and elbows collided with a slap, Chuck grunted, and Lola made a sharp "ah" noise. They did this every time.

Azi asked if Henry's teacher was really Russian.

"Yes," Henry said, and then Azi didn't say anything else for a minute. When the Delaflotes were in the air again, he asked if Henry was trained in a school, like Kylie.

"We practiced in a school," said Henry, "but I wasn't a student. Not officially."

"You stole your Russian circus education."

"Yeah. I guess so."

"Then you've always been as you are."

"How?"

"Lucky," he said.

Chuck slipped from Remy's hands and plummeted into the net. Henry studied the fall—it was nothing like the kind of falling a clown would do. Clowns rolled and tumbled, compromised with gravity by working with it. Flyers surrendered to it, went limp and heavy as if they had died on the way down.

A clomping of hooves came from the left side of the tent. Lorne led Ambrosia in by her bridle. He wore riding boots and muddy overalls over his costume. He stopped before he reached the middle of the ring, surveying the space, then climbed onto the horse and dug his heels into her. She raised her head and broke into a high-kneed trot. Her shoulders flexed and her white mane rippled like a silk flag.

"What do you know about that one?" asked Henry.

"Man or horse?"

"Man."

"Lorne's not so bad," said Azi. He pulled something from his pocket and started fiddling with it. They were little packets of explosives, the homemade version of those little poppers kids threw on the Fourth of July.

"Is he like Vroni and Jenifer? Circus freak by birth?"

"You ought to be careful who you call a freak, kid," Azi said, making the little packets snap between his fingers. "Caleb isn't around anymore."

Henry snorted. "Like Caleb gives a shit about me."

Azi looked up from his explosives, fixed Henry with eyes that were so black they seemed without pupils, without centers. And Henry remembered that though Azi was his friend, he was also what he was: big as a bear, pyromaniacal.

"Caleb likes you. I've known him a long time. You should be grateful for such a friend."

Ambrosia reared up, took two steps on her hind legs. Lorne struggled to hold on to the reins.

Azi went back at the sawdust and gunpowder in his palm and sighed. "Lorne isn't circus by birth. He was adopted by Bulgarian trick-riders when he was thirteen. I guess his mother wanted a kid, and his father's balls were shot from all that time bouncing around on top of a horse. So Lorne can ride. But he isn't great at it. He isn't great at anything."

"If he isn't great at it why is he here?"

"He loves the animals. Let me tell you, he told me this thing, about when he was in the circus with the Bulgarians, one of their horses got attacked. These boys rushed it with jackknives and yo-yos and took its eye and its lip. Broke its jaw, its leg . . . who knows why? Who could explain such a thing? But Lorne, he went after those boys. Chased them for *hours*, he said. And Lorne, he can't lie about this stuff. Trust me, that guy doesn't have the kinda brain that can make something like that up. When he got back, his parents told him that they had called the ASPCA to take the horse away and fix it up, and he believed them. He believes them to this day," Azi said and shook his head. "*Hours*. Can you believe it? Over a horse. He never caught them."

"Doesn't that just mean that he's crazy? What would he have done if he caught the kids?"

Azi waved his hand as if Henry was being ridiculous. "The *reason* his parents told him that the ASPCA took away that horse is because he was too tenderhearted to know they probably shot the thing in the head soon as the crowds were gone. And he still is."

ON THE CIRCUS'S LAST NIGHT in Detroit, Henry prepared to run away. Azi and the others were afraid of what would happen to them if the circus disbanded, but Henry, after the second broken mirror and the shit in his bed, was ready for another end.

He went to the trailer where Sue, Kylie, and Lola Delaflote slept. He planned to snatch Sue's keys again. He figured he would just drive and see where he ended up. If it was somewhere good, he might consider staying there.

He slipped inside their trailer without a sound. It was dark except for the light of a neighboring campfire coming through the windows. The dogs, three piled at the end of Sue's bed, and three on the floor beside it, lifted their heads when he entered. He cringed at the jangle of the tags around their necks. To keep them from jumping off the bed to greet him, he sated them with scratches behind their curly ears, while their pom-pom tails beat the bed in muffled rhythmic thuds. They licked the sweat from the palm of his hand.

Sue's keys were on the floor, in a cluster of personal items that included her canvas wallet and a pile of pins she used to restrain her hair. As he bent to pick them up, his gaze fell on Kylie's bare arm, which was slung over the side of the bed opposite Sue's. The tips of Kylie's fingers grazed the floor and her shoulder blade jutted out from beneath a thin blanket.

He noticed she looked stronger. Her arms were still lean, but her biceps were more defined, and her forearms were thicker. What had she been doing to get this way? Push-ups? Pull-ups? Handstands? Maybe she'd decided to cushion herself a little more, provide her skeleton with a shield of muscle. Whatever she was doing was working to make her a better clown. She was doing well. Getting a lot of laughs. Getting hurt less.

At the base of her neck was a silver clasp, a shining circle with tiny letters that read Tiffany & Co. Maybe also a present from her rich grandfather, or her parents. Seeing this didn't fill Henry with the kind of envy or bitterness it might have a month ago—because so far, no loaded, doting family had shown up to see Kylie perform. He kept expecting people with monocles and fur coats, or at least designer jeans and fresh facelifts, to rush her after the show and shower her in praise. It had not happened yet.

He had the urge to touch her fingers.

Like he'd suspected from the beginning, it was best to keep his distance from her, that they would both do better work and be happier if he let her be. Still. It was hard for him not to imagine that she was lonely—that, like him, she wouldn't mind if she woke up to someone holding her hand and admiring her. He knew this was the kind of thinking that got him into the whole Adrienne mess. Still.

He left the keys on the floor and slipped back out through the door. Because, if he left, Adrienne would be disappointed. And what if, without Henry to compete with and hate, Kylie slacked off? And what if, somehow, the shit in his bed made him a better clown? What if this was exactly where he belonged, after all?

He paced back and forth outside the trailers, grinding his teeth. The energy that made him want to run or destroy something was the same energy that propelled him though his acts, through his stretches, the energy that Christiakov had told him to make for himself. Now it had nowhere to go.

He walked away from camp and found himself climbing a tree, just to keep moving. The limbs creaked and there were spiders and ants that scurried over his hands and feet as he bore himself upward, but he climbed fast, another rehearsal for his angel act.

Near the top, Henry heard a pop like thunder, and the branch beneath him broke off, separating from the tree with a burst of splinters. The only reason he didn't go down with it was that he had a firm grip on the branch above him. He hung there, thinking of letting go, thinking of Jackie Chan, of the epic fall. *It would be a simple thing*, he thought. *Lift two fingers and that would do it.*

But it wouldn't be epic if there was no one there to see it, would it? You could hardly call that art. You would have to call it a theatrical suicide, suicide with a quirky punch.

Not that again.

Then he *would* be Pierrot, a sad idiot, a stock character.

He pulled himself back onto his branch and sat until the urge to fall or run or hurt someone subsided. Until it seemed foreign and distant, and really, kind of stupid.

CHAPTER 19

THE FIRST TIME ADRIENNE HAD surgery to remove her pituitary tumor, they'd entered her skull through her forehead. She couldn't describe to Caleb what it looked like or felt like, even though she had been conscious for the surgery. That time, the surgery had been invasive and risky, the tumor probing its way into her "cavernous sinus," which sounded to Caleb like a spacious place with plenty of room to house a tumor and a surgeon's instruments while he dug the thing out. This was not the case. A cavernous sinus was a *bad* place for a tumor to get to, a place where a surgeon and his instruments had to be especially precise. Doing a surgery like this, Caleb figured, would be like recreating a Van Gogh with a child's watercolor brush, knowing that if your stroke was off by half a millimeter, someone could die.

This time, they would not open her skull, but go right in through her nose, pluck the tumor out, and stitch her up.

"Trust me," the doctor had said. "Your surgeon will walk into the operating room whistling, because he knows you're an easy fix, another feather in his cap."

And this time, she'd follow up with her appointments. She would let herself be monitored for any future growth, because if she pulled what she did last time, and didn't get her GH levels checked regularly, she'd end up right back here again.

There was no need to be afraid, but Adrienne couldn't seem to hang on to Caleb's arm tight enough during the surgical consultation. He had to turn to her once and say, "Honey, you're hurting me."

In pre-op, the surgeon smiled at them, and it seemed the doctor was right; he looked like he would go into the operating room whistling. Caleb tried to be comforted by this, but it was unnerving, the idea that a surgeon was a *person*, one who might wake up with a Madonna song in his head and whistle it right before he sent a camera and a blade up his wife's nostril.

Just before they took Adrienne to the operating room, Caleb told her that he loved her. He said that he would never, never leave her, and then was told politely by a nurse that he could head to the waiting room now. Caleb squeezed his wife's hand in defiance, but Adrienne peeled his fingers away and the nurses pushed her bed down the hall.

For three hours, Caleb was welcome by the hospital to pray in their interfaith meditation center, to buy things in the gift shop, or to pace the mile-long footpath that flanked the hospital. He was also welcome to sit in the waiting room and eat five consecutive PayDays, which was what he chose to do. He thought primarily about spinal meningitis (the remotest and most horrifying risk of Adrienne's surgery), and about love, and how he would live if he lost Adrienne. He wouldn't have her forever, maybe twenty more years at the most, but Jesus, if he could get even another month of her, his healthy, joyful wife, then he would damn well make something of it.

As THE CIRCUS WENT NORTH, the heat subsided. The sun ceased to be an enemy and recast itself as the cheery white light that illuminated the streets of Toronto in August. The performers took the bus into the city. They passed the sign that said BIENVENUE À LA CAPITALE DE L'ONTARIO.

Henry was looking absently out the window, trying to interpret the sign when someone tapped his shoulder. It was Vroni. She offered Henry a white jelly bean from a bag she'd bought at a gas station.

"The white ones taste like semen, anyway," she said.

He thanked her and pretended to eat it, using the same sleight of hand he used to pull quarters from behind people's ears to get it discreetly into his pocket.

Bienvenue.

The Toronto show was supposed to be at an inside venue that no one at Feely and Feinstein had been to before. The circus was told that there would not be anywhere to park their trailers all night, so the performers made camp at a nearby park and caught the bus to get into Toronto proper. Only the larger props and the animals were driven into town separately by Lorne.

The performers were already exhausted and anxious about the unfamiliarity of this setup—they always parked right outside their venue or had plenty of places to park where they pitched the tent. Then, somebody read the map wrong, and they got off the bus too early. The performers groaned when they realized this, rubbed their heads and lower backs.

After a ten-block walk hefting along their own trunks and backpacks, they arrived at the Green Lion. Henry felt like he had wandered into somebody's garage. It didn't seem like a performance space, but a private place. He smelled salt and beer and a hint of motor oil. The floor was concrete and on the walls were pictures of shows that had taken place on this stage, ticket stubs from carnivals and concerts in frames, and props—a knight's breastplate made of macaroni noodles painted silver, a string of fake sausages, a white judge's wig. It was a funny place—funny in an aggressive, absurd sort of way. In the pictures, a magician in white blew a bubble the size of a beach ball and six girls dressed as different kinds of fruit posed for a still life in a giant bowl. There was a picture of what looked like a cabaret show, a Barbie-shaped girl in fishnet stockings inserting a giant key into a giant lock.

Azi was not pleased.

"The ceilings are too low," he told the Green Lion's manager, a man with a pinched face and a pair of round glasses. "There's no way we can fit our elephant in here."

The manager shrugged. "Sorry, man. This is what we're working with."

"That's half an hour of show, gone, right there," said Azi. "We can bring down the high-wire walkers. But there's no way we can set up for trapeze. Even the horse . . . the horse is questionable."

"I'm sorry," the manager said again. "I think there was some miscommunication. I was told this was a small circus."

This time it was Remy Delaflote who interjected. "We *are* a small circus," he said, reddening. "You were expecting, what, some kind of miniature show? Flea circus?"

The manager looked as if he wanted to laugh, but he squeezed his lips together with his hand and nodded, looking at the floor. "Are you Mr. Baratucci?" he asked.

"No," said Azi.

"Well, see, I was fairly clear with Mr. Baratucci about what we could accommodate. Could I speak with him?"

"Mr. Baratucci had to take a leave of absence."

"I'm sorry there's been a misunderstanding," the manager said, "but certainly there are plenty of acts that don't require a horse or an elephant. Besides, there's another show here tonight. No one will notice if your performance is a little on the short side."

The blood drained from Remy's face and the other performers shuffled their feet and looked at the posters on the wall or the frayed luggage sitting beside them. The thing that made them feel the most pathetic was how hard the manager was trying to be polite. He said no one would notice if the program was short, but the fact was that no one would notice if the program happened at all.

Azi put his hand on Remy's shoulder.

"If Caleb had known—shouldn't he have told us? We could have gone home. Sent the animals, too."

Azi shook his head. "Honestly, he probably meant to. His head is not in this right now."

The Green Lion's manager clapped his hands together. "I'll call the other act right now and see if they can set up earlier." He walked away.

Azi studied the ceiling, the rows of chairs, the width of the stage, as if calculating what this space could contain. Henry knew he was thinking how he might rearrange it, so that they could fit in all the important parts, and the show would feel complete.

But Henry also knew it wasn't the lack of space that was getting to him, not really. It was Caleb doing un-Caleb-like things that made everyone suspicious, and it was looking like before it was all over it would be Azi who had to answer for them. Henry exchanged a furtive glance with the fire-eater.

"Alright, people," said Azi, stepping in while Remy seethed. "We have six hours before the show. So go and put your stuff down backstage, get some food, do your prep, take a nap . . . whatever you need to do. I'll see you all at five. No later than five."

Henry left the Green Lion and stepped into the sunlit street. The Delaflotes passed him, talking in vicious-sounding whispers. The only words Henry caught were "Baratucci" and "new gig."

He shielded his eyes from the sun and walked north up the street. He thought about the evening's show—without elephants or aerialists, there would be more pressure on himself and the other performers to make the audience feel satisfied. Still, he found himself in a good mood. Maybe it was the breeze. Maybe it was the French.

In a city park he watched a street clown in suspenders and baggy shorts performing with a man's tie. The man had a little boy around four with him, probably his son, who was giggling. The clown had his wrists twisted in the tie, then he tried to wear it as a belt, then as a jock strap. The man was only half-watching the clown. Mostly, he watched the boy, who was in such a fit of laughter that there were tears forming in the corners of his eyes. Some people on the street slowed down or stopped, but their eyes were also on the little boy. The boy was trying to calm himself down—his laughter was the frantic sort, as if he were being tickled. But every time he got a grip on himself, the clown would do something new, and the boy would start up again with an involuntary shriek. The clown started pestering the father to help him with the tie, who, still watching the boy, instructed the clown to first wrap the tie around his neck, then make a knot. When the clown tied the knot too tight and turned purple, the boy's knees failed him and he sank into a sitting position on the sidewalk. People continued to gather. The clown became a mirror of the business man, mimicking his every move, the flicks of his wrists and even the blinking of his eyes.

There were no acrobatics and no props except the tie, but the act was flawless. Henry could almost hear Christiakov: "Everyone is involved emotionally," he would say, "the little boy, the father, the onlookers, the clown himself. Everyone has something at stake. Tension is building and being released every second."

The boy couldn't stop laughing, but the joy of laughing released that tension. And the father was invested because the clown made him the hero in this skit, a role the clown would not let the man slip from. And the people watching, all these fanny-pack tourists and French-Canadian granola hippies, they knew that they were witnessing something of true value.

"Henry. Are you getting this, Henry?" said the Christiakov in his head. "Are you taking notes, Phenom? Burn this into your brain."

The audience would remember the show for a long time, and the father would remember it longer. The boy, though, would remember this for the rest of his life.

The tie had become the world.

Henry felt a presence beside him and turned to see Kylie, arms crossed in front of her, watching the show.

"Hi," he said.

"This is incredible," she said, not looking at him.

"Yeah. I know. He's a genius."

Kylie sniffled in the cool air as the wind from the lake picked up. Henry figured she was done talking to him, but after a moment she spoke again.

"So, do you think it's over?"

"Do I think what's over?"

"Feely and Feinstein. Don't lie and say you don't know either. Just tell me. Is it over or not?"

Henry watched as the crowd disbanded, leaving quarters and dollars in a sand bucket that said TIPS.

She had demanded that he not lie, and he felt bound by this, so he told her the truth. "I think so," he said. "But you didn't hear it from me."

Henry had no money with which to tip the clown so he robbed a wishing well a block north. Kylie waited for him, and after Henry left the clown a handful of wet pennies, they walked the city, looking for other street shows. People were out enjoying their Saturday, weaving in and out of the pubs and shops and smelling like peppermint schnapps and perfume. Most of them were Kylie's age or slightly older, the boys all with grins that showed white, sticky-looking teeth, and the girls all with gold earrings and permed hair as they clung to the waists of their boyfriends. In and out, in and out and around—Henry watched their feet, the way they couldn't move in straight lines. They leaned toward the people they were with as if they had no choice, as if the bodies next to them pulled them with a force as strong as the gravity that held the bottoms of their shoes to the pavement. Henry walked and sometimes he imitated their lean and their step, though he had no one to lean into.

Kylie did not hang around his waist. In fact, people who saw them would have probably thought they didn't know each other at all, that they were two strangers that just happened to be walking up the same street at approximately the same pace, with the same long, pointed gazes at anything that was not one another—the ice cream vendors, the hungry birds, the thin fissures in the sidewalk. When Henry did a funny walk, Kylie ignored him just as she would have ignored an overly excited child.

Still, she let him buy her a hot pretzel with the rest of the money he'd scraped from the bottom of the wishing well. They found a bench and sat together while she ate. She kept her eyes on Henry, as if she thought that any moment, he might snatch the pretzel away.

He smiled at her, and it was his charm-you smile, the best one he had. *Things are going okay*, he thought.

Then, with a full mouth, she asked, "Did you fuck Caleb's wife?"

"What?"

She rolled her eyes and chewed faster. "Caleb's wife. They said you and her had a thing."

"Who said that?"

"Jenifer and Vroni. Lorne. Remy Delaflote."

"Really?"

"Lola. Sue."

"Sue?"

"Yep. And Azi thinks so, too."

He wanted to say "Never! I would never even think to do such a thing!" But he had thought to do exactly such a thing.

It was clear that Kylie had been waiting to ask this question a long time.

"No," said Henry. "We didn't. I didn't."

Henry read suspicion in the muscles of Kylie's face, but then the expression began to soften, revealing a sort of a hope. A bit of salt stuck to her lower lip. If he kissed it away, she might give in, at least for a moment, and like him again. But he thought better of this.

"She loves Caleb," he said.

Kylie licked the salt from her own lip. "She rejected you."

He felt his face burn. "Yes."

Kylie was quiet for a moment, as if unraveling the implications of this. If Henry had been rejected, then he'd made an advance. If Kylie asked him what that advance had been, he would have to tell her. If he was going to keep on with this terrible, kamikaze honesty, then, after he told her, he would have to go back to that wishing well and drown himself.

"Do you really think she's pretty? I think she's strange-looking," said Kylie. He couldn't tell for sure, but it seemed like she was trying to make him feel better.

"I do. I think she looks like . . . I don't know, blond Wonder Woman? Or a really tall Suzanne Somers."

"Her hands are like a gorilla's," said Kylie.

Henry shrugged. "I don't care about that."

"You don't?"

"Do we have to talk about this? I feel like a dick," said Henry, realizing that at some point during their conversation, he had folded his legs up beneath him, and they had fallen asleep.

"You *are* a dick."

"Okay. That's fair."

"I just want to know . . . why Adrienne and not me?"

Another honest question that deserved an honest answer. So Henry tried to get a grip on it, the slippery truth. "I never thought 'Adrienne and not Kylie.' I never thought about the size of anybody's hands—"

Kylie waved her palms and said, "Wait. We should stop talking before you say something stupid. It messes up our on stage chemistry when I hate you."

But Henry persisted, braced himself for her frustration. "I'm trying to answer your question, okay? I never thought about anyone's size. It's not like I don't like you. I like you! I thought you were cute and smart, right away, and your body is like . . . it's amazing, right? If you trained better, you would be really something—you have all this potential," he said.

She covered her face with her hands. "It's like you can't help being a jerk."

"I *can't*, and I knew you were someone who I would be a jerk to, but by the time I figured that out, I'd already been a jerk to you, and I couldn't find a way to undo it."

"So you were a jerk to Adrienne instead?"

"No, I was an idiot to Adrienne. Those are your two options with me. Jerk," he said, holding out one hand, "or idiot," he said, holding out the other.

Kylie raised her eyebrows. "Well. At least you know it," she said. She paused for a moment, assessing his face. "Huh. I don't really feel better," she said.

Henry couldn't think of anything else to say, and apparently neither could Kylie. They sat in silence on the bench until Henry felt so awkward, he had to do something stupid, so he started singing. His specialty was early-eighties bubblegum pop so he went with "Girls Just Wanna Have Fun."

Kylie looked at him in mortified shock. "Henry! Shut up!"

He continued a few more bars, just to watch her face grow pink, just to see her looking around to see if anyone else was listening. They were, of course. Then, just before the chorus, he said, "Why should I stop?"

"Because that song reminds me of junior high, which was terrible. And it's musically uninteresting," she said.

Henry grinned. "You only like music that sounds like it's sung by a tone-deaf monkey and recorded in a high school gym."

She stood and brushed the salt off her pants and tossed the wrapper in a waste basket. Henry stood too and wobbled as he took a step. One of his legs was completely numb. He had to grab on to the bench for support.

"If you do ministry-of-funny walks all the way back, you're going to be late, and Azi is going to murder you," said Kylie.

"I'm not being funny, my leg is just asleep," he said, rubbing his calf.

He took a tentative step, and the pins and needles exploded all through his leg, making him giggle involuntarily. Kylie frowned and threaded her arm through his—not around his waist, but it was a start.

"Come on, Tiny Tim, we gotta hurry," she said.

He remembered that in Detroit, she had looked much stronger, and now, touching her, he could feel it, too. He thought, with her new strength, it would not be too burdensome if, for just a few steps, he really leaned on her.

AFTER THEIR PERFORMANCE AT THE Green Lion, the circus was angry. The Delaflotes and Lorne sulked about not being able to perform, but everyone seemed to feel betrayed by Caleb, and maybe that was why the general opinion of Henry had improved. Caleb had betrayed the circus, which vindicated Henry for betraying Caleb. When Henry returned to his trailer that night, Jenifer and Vroni didn't hiss a single insult at him as they crossed paths.

On his bed he found a white envelope, addressed to him in Caleb's handwriting, and his heart dropped. *This is it*, he thought. *This is my pink slip.*

Tearing open the letter on its side, Henry found a familiar scrap of lined notebook paper within. It was his brother's letter. He swiped his finger inside the envelope, looking for an additional note from Caleb, but beside the letter itself, there was no message.

Ultimate Kung Fu

The clowns walk in with makeup like characters from a Chinese opera, with black ponytails that sprout from the backs of their heads like dark cacti. It's all cummerbunds and wrists wrapped with tape and bare chests in the costumes. It's all Bruce Lee and Jackie Chan and Steven Seagal in the movements. And for God's sake, this act has to have people who can do the movements. Otherwise, it's pointless to even stage.

One clown raises his hand, open-palmed: universal kung fu sign for Come at me. *He is clearly the bigger and stronger of the two.*

The other clown does the same. No, you come at me. *This one is wiry and small, and has the more intense ponytail.*

You.

No, you.

These two kung fu masters are brothers. Let's say they are enemies, but not by choice. They've been fighting on different sides in a war, and they haven't seen each other since they were children.

In the time they've been apart, one brother has become a master of Possum Style kung fu, while the other brother has become a master of Cobra Style. They are both masters in their way. The thing is, they don't want to fight in the style they are masters in. They want to fight in the style they fought in together, when they were kids: Mad Monkey Style, the Ultimate Kung Fu.

Of course they discuss all this in detail for the audience before they start fighting.

That's all part of the kung fu, talking about using it.

Then, the fight starts. The bigger clown steps forward and delivers a big graceful spin kick, which the little wiry one blocks handily, and counters with a headbutt. The big one flies across the ring and lands hard.

They run toward each other, arms hanging to the side, limp, like orangutans, until they meet center stage, throwing punches in Mad Monkey Style. Their blows come faster and faster until it's a girly-looking slap fight.

They both realize this and try to recover their dignity.

I tricked you. I threw in some Mall-Fight Style, and you fell for it. Fool! *Says the smaller one.*

The bigger one has no imagination and can't think of a clever comeback.

They keep going like this. They run up walls and up each other to turn flips. They yell hi-ya! *and* Take that! *and insult each other's kung fu and manhoods and hairstyles. They whip around like a couple of fighting spaghetti noodles, striking and dodging until both slump against each other, heaving and panting, still hurling insults.*

Your mother is a bearded bag lady!

Your mother looks like the Crypt Keeper and a hammerhead shark had a baby!

Then silence when they remember they share a mother. And is that the turning point of the show? Let's say it is. Let's say in the end the brothers put aside the war and remember that they are brothers and decide forever more to watch each other's backs with Cobra Style and Possum Style kung fu. Let's say they retire the Mad Monkey Style forever and make amends while they sit side by side, sweaty, but without so much as a split lip between them. Because they were so evenly matched.

And because, you know, this is comedy.

CHAPTER 20

WHEN THEY PULLED THE PACKING out of Adrienne's nose, she thought for sure some of her brain would come with it. The packing was saturated with fluid, having soaked up the wetness inside of her head, from her nostril to her frontal lobe. And even though it had been several weeks since her surgery, it seemed the packing had been soaking up her thoughts as well because as soon as they tugged it from her skull, her mind's pace quickened, and all the fragments became real, whole memories. They were just facts before this, disconnected bits of time and action—Henry's mouth and Caleb's hand and Curtis's collar folded into her hand before she flung him. Now that the packing lay like a long slug in the dish beside the nurse's instruments, Adrienne began to remember the events prior to her surgery as meaningful, as something that had bearing on her past and her future.

On the way home, riding next to her husband, she understood that he had left the circus to be with her. She had punched through his painting, and he'd come back. A boy had kissed her, and she had not stopped it. And Caleb still came back. He was here, now, driving her home from the hospital and asking her how it felt to have the cotton out of her brain and saying things like, "Are you okay? Do you need a pillow? Do you want the window down? Your hair up? Really, is your nose okay?"

She gave him short, calm answers to these questions. Nothing hurt. She didn't need any air. Her hair was fine.

The things that were bothering her had nothing to do with physical pain, but rather the disturbing feeling that she had lost time, had just come out of a sort of haze. What really haunted her was the conversation she'd had with Henry right before he'd left their house on the night he'd kissed her.

She asked Caleb, "Do you know about Henry's mother?"

Caleb's body immediately tensed. "I know she's dead."

Adrienne had told Caleb almost everything about the night Henry showed up at her door, except the part about him recognizing the Southern Blue van, and the things he'd told her about his mother. It wasn't worth mentioning at the time, because it seemed to have nothing to do with Henry driving down and kissing her. As it turned out, dead Mrs. Bell, thought Adrienne, had everything to do with Henry driving down and kissing her. Dead Mrs. Bell had left a woman-shaped emptiness on the horizon where Henry's eyes were continually focused, and Adrienne had accidentally stepped into this shadow.

She told Caleb about Mrs. Bell, now, how Mrs. Bell had dropped dead in her living room, right in front of her sons.

"That's terrible," Caleb mumbled. He furrowed his brow, then glanced at Adrienne in a pleading sort of way.

"I know you don't want to talk about him, but this is really bugging me. Henry thinks it was his father's fault or something, I guess, since their father was a lousy husband and made her anxious. But that's a bit colorful, isn't it? Being scared to death. Dying of a broken heart. Physically, though, it just doesn't seem too likely."

Her mind restored, she had a more viable theory to explain Henry's mother's death. Like Curtis, it seemed the man at Henry's house that night made sales calls for Southern Blue cosmetics. During their marriage, Curtis had made a great deal of money selling door to door. But any idiot with a calculator could figure out he wasn't making his whole living from the commission he got hocking mascara and bath salts.

THE CIRCUS LURCHED DOWN THE highway toward Indiana, accelerating out of rest stops and gas stations and going from zero to eighty in a matter of seconds, only to stop a few miles down the road so that someone else could use the restroom.

Someone, who was not Henry, let the cat out of the bag about this being Feely and Feinstein's last season, and like any dying creature, the circus's parts all conspired to slow its death.

But they blamed it on the chili dogs they had in Toronto.

Only Kylie and Henry had avoided sickness. Kylie bought a little bottle of vodka that smelled like hairspray and she nipped at it while she and Henry played a slow game of go fish.

Earlier that morning, Kylie had shown Henry an idea she had been working on for an act: the climax was a sort of human slinky where Kylie would wrap her legs around Henry's middle, and he would do a sort of back walk-over—but she was attached to him, so that meant that she was doing a front flip with Henry's midsection as a starting point. Using the force of her flip, she could pull Henry over her, to his feet, and the centrifugal force would do the rest to propel them across the stage. They had rehearsed the actual stunt a few times, and it was not nearly as technically difficult as Kylie's description first made it seem, but it required enormous upper and middle body strength that challenged even Henry. There were no mirrors for them to use to gauge how they really looked, but Henry could tell by the rhythm of the movement that they resembled, as Kylie had hoped, a human slinky.

"Wow," Henry said. "I bet we look so weird! People will love this."

The slinky stunt cemented the peace between Kylie and Henry. Not only did they avoid getting ill, but now, as they rode to St. Louis, they seemed to be radiating health.

As the circus continued to stutter-step its way down the interstate, the clowns kept their card game going, distracting themselves from the moaning and gagging coming from the cots that flanked them.

"Do you have any sevens?" asked Kylie. Henry handed her a card. She offered him some vodka, but he shook his head.

"I don't get you. All underage people want to drink," she said, looking at her cards.

"I don't," he said.

"Your parents drunks or something?"

"No," he said.

"Do you have any twos?" she asked.

"Go fish," he said.

As she reached for the deck, he pulled the two from the air next to her shoulder.

"Just kidding," he said.

Kylie raised her eyebrows and snatched the card from Henry's hand. "You know, I think I've got your number."

"Of course you do. I just handed it to you."

"I mean your metaphorical number, you shit. I've figured you out. I know what your problem is," she said. She arranged her new pair neatly in front of her and organized the cards fanned out in her hand.

"Enlighten me," he said. He couldn't keep the sarcasm out of his voice, but he wasn't angry. He was curious, wondering if she really did—if she knew him well enough to reveal something true about him.

"I don't think I should say."

Vroni began to roll around on her bunk and groan. This went on for a few minutes before she said, "I'm going to shit everywhere. I hate this place, and I'm dying, and I'm going to shit all over it!"

When no one responded to this, not even her sister, who lay prone next to her, rubbing the tops of her feet against the sheets for comfort, Vroni lay back down.

Then it was quiet, except for the occasional sniffle from Vroni, the snap of cards being laid on a table. Henry held up five fingers, and Kylie mimed the casting of a line.

THEY STOPPED TO REST IN a state park in Indiana, even though they were only a couple hours from St. Louis. They all decided they'd had enough of starting and stopping and smelling vomit.

After traveling all day, Henry had so much nervous energy that if he could have found a way to crawl out of his body, he would have. He insisted Kylie come with him to the playground to work on the slinky bit. They saw Lorne guide Tex out of her pen and lead her in large circles on top of a hill north of the playground. Back and forth he went, exercising each animal. The rest of the performers fell asleep or were still out at the community restrooms, getting sick, or taking showers.

After practicing the slinky twice, Kylie and Henry rested against the monkey bars. It was finally getting dark and cooling down and it chilled the sweat on their foreheads. Henry was about to suggest they call it quits when they heard Ambrosia's whinny, high-pitched, like Henry had only heard horses make in Western movies. It was a startling noise, exploding in the air above the purr of cicadas.

"What was that?" asked Kylie.

"I don't know," he said, and shrugged. He felt a heat under his skin, like terror or embarrassment, or both. This expanding thing took the place of his breath, and he felt hot all over.

They heard the horse whinny again, and this time Henry could hear the muffled thud of something heavy colliding with her body. Kylie heard this, too, and strode toward the hill, her chin tilted up like a child trying to see over the head of the person in front of them during a show.

"It's just the horse making noise, Kylie," he said, but she ignored him.

They heard another muted thud, another bellow. Then there was Lorne's voice, but Henry couldn't make out what he was saying. Kylie moved faster up the hill, and Henry followed her, not because he wanted to stop whatever was happening, but because he wanted to stop Kylie from seeing it. For something to cry out in some unseen place stirred a familiar sense of fear and dread in Henry, one that made him want to go the other direction. But Kylie had no such sense—her knee-jerk reaction to what sounded like a creature in pain was a desire to help.

He managed to grab her arm at the top of the hill, and she turned around, outraged. But Henry shook his head desperately, begging her to be quiet. She closed her mouth, pressing her lips tight together, as if it were a great effort.

On the other side, at the bottom of the hill, Lorne was standing square in front of the mare, the great-great-great-granddaughter of the Horse of a Different Color. He held a thick wooden club in his hand, which he often used to lead Tex. They watched as Ambrosia nodded her head, up and down. *Yes, yes, yes*, would have been the message if she were a human being, but she was a horse, and the nodding seemed stricken, as if she had lost her mind: *No, no, no*, it said.

Lorne appeared hypnotized by this headshaking. He watched her without moving for a moment, then dropped the club, stroked her nose to calm her, and whispered something, his cheek against her long forehead. She stopped thrashing her head, but only as long as he whispered to her. Then, still nodding, she followed his lead back into the horse trailer. Lorne glanced up the hill before he shut the gate on her, but he gave no indication that he recognized the two figures at the top.

While the mare shook her head at Lorne, Henry kept shaking his at Kylie. Between Henry and Ambrosia, everyone was kept quiet.

CALEB WAS AWAKE LATE WITH his classifieds. He sat down to them refreshed, with a cup of herbal tea and a handful of saltines.

He could work at J. C. Penney. Why not? Circle. The Law Offices of Sellers and Nash. Circle. First Bank? Circle, circle, circle.

He saw "Assistant to the curator of the City Museum," which excited him. He circled it, but then crossed it out. It required a degree. Caleb didn't have one.

Just like that, he felt tired again. He scratched out his circles around the ads for sales clerks and bankers. Why would he want to be a banker? Because he was good with money? Because he liked to be in charge? Yes, he liked these things well enough. But not for the same reasons bankers liked them. He liked them because he liked to create, and he was part of his own creation. At the circus, he was the straight man in the chaos, a necessary part of things at the circus. At a bank, he would be a straight man among straight men.

He covered his face in his hands as if to rub out the exhaustion. The circus would return soon. He would have to face them all. He would have to face Henry, who had meddled in his life, and in whose life Caleb had now meddled. He kept thinking about what Adrienne had said, that Henry's mother had died in front of him, when he was very little. Caleb's father had died in front of him when he was twenty-two, and he had yet to recover from it. A dead parent didn't really excuse Henry from anything, but it was no wonder he was a wreck, someone who did things like run off in other people's cars and kiss other people's wives.

Someone knocked at the front door.

It was late. *If this is Curtis*, he thought, *I'm going to tear his asshole out through his mouth.* He walked quietly to the door and looked through the peephole. The young man on the other side was tall, wearing one of those Carhartt jackets that farmers wore. His head was down, so Caleb couldn't see his face, but he could tell it was no one he knew.

"Can I help you?" He called.

"Yeah, um—sorry to wake you up, er—disturb you," he said. The guy got fidgety the moment Caleb opened the door. He swiped his hand over his unshaven face.

"Do you need to use a phone or something?" asked Caleb.

"No, I was wondering if there was a Henry Bell who lived here," the man said.

Caleb recognized, then, the man's stance. Like Henry, he looked wary, as if any moment he would need to shed his Carhartt coat and sprint down the street, or scale the house, or explode.

So this was Andre.

Caleb invited him in.

CHAPTER 21

WHILE FEELY AND FEINSTEIN HAD been on the road, their plot of ground in St. Louis sat dusty and desolate as an uninhabited planet. And when the grounds repopulated with trailers, and the performers spilled out, all aching and crusty-eyed from travel, the desolate state of the grounds was not much improved by their presence. They brought no energy back with them. There were no departing hugs or see-you-next-years. Instead, everyone gathered their things doggedly and then milled around, waiting.

Caleb arrived at dusk, parked, and tugged the hem of his sleeves so they would emerge just so from his suit coat. He'd spent the whole day in pajamas, dreading this evening, but this was the Caleb they expected, put-together Caleb, white-collar-blue-button-clipboard Caleb. He owed them that, at least.

When he stepped out of the car, twenty-seven necks twisted his direction, and only then did he realize that he looked dressed for a funeral.

SEAMUS HAD CALLED HIM RIGHT after Adrienne's surgery. He said he still planned to sell the circus piecemeal, but it occurred to him that Caleb might want to "make a bid." Caleb went to the bank, and learned he could, in fact, get a loan, a decent one, to buy Feely and Feinstein, but only if he was willing to put up his house for collateral. The risk was crushing to even think about. If he failed to bring Feely and Feinstein back to life after he bought it, the debt would bury him and Adrienne. He was willing to take the risk on his own behalf, but he did not want to take it on Adrienne's behalf. What he needed was a partner, someone to share the financial burden, and the seemingly infinite labor, and he could not think of anyone that fit this bill. He told Seamus this, and Seamus said, "Well, that's the pits. I can give you till December, but I guess it's unlikely anything will change between now and then."

"Right," said Caleb.

"That's the pits," said Seamus.

Now, Azi came to meet him.

"Baratucci. They know," he said.

"Not surprising," Caleb said. "Adrienne knows, so I'm sure everyone under blue heaven does. Can you walk into the rehearsal building? They'll follow you."

"Of course."

Caleb needed acoustics for this message.

Inside the rehearsal space, the mildew smell had improved since the summer had been so hot and dry. Instead of that familiar mustiness, when he walked through the door Caleb was greeted by the sour odor of the unwashed clothes the performers carried with them. Packed and ready to go. They clustered around the center of the room, as if having an intimate conversation, but none of them were actually speaking. He thought Lola Delaflote tried to smile at him. Only Lorne hung back from the swarm of performers, sitting with his back against the wall, his hands folded in his lap, staring up into the rafters.

Caleb unfolded a chair and stood on it. It was quiet, so they would hear him if he spoke, but he wanted to see their faces. The German girls were diffused, daffy with fear, dressed up in suits instead of their normal designer jeans and tube tops. The suits were pale pink and stylish, made for a pretty woman to wear when she accepted an employee-of-the-month award at a luncheon. Jenifer and Vroni did not look like they were headed to a luncheon, though. Their sharp shoulder blades jutted from their backs, and their gangly hands stretched too far from the pink cuffs, gnarled and bird-like. He never found Jenifer and Vroni intimidating, but these suits made him shudder.

"Hey," said Caleb. "How's everyone feeling?"

They all looked at him. The clowns hung close to each other. Azi's was the only expression that bore Caleb any sympathy.

"I'm sorry I couldn't be there. I could have told you not to eat anything with the word 'dog' in it outside Chicago."

Remy Delaflote snorted. "Cut to the chase, Baratucci."

"Don't be a prick, Remy," said Azi.

"The chase," Caleb began to say, but he wasn't sure how to continue. He had rehearsed this many times. Now the words to deliver this news were gone. "Look, I wasn't making a joke. I have it in my notes, the okay places to eat hot dogs."

"How is Adrienne?" asked Sue, using the gentle voice she used with her dogs.

Caleb stared down at his clipboard. "It's hard to know, yet. But she seems to feel better."

"That's good," she said, and Caleb could see the wet streaks on her cheeks. "I miss her around here."

Remy walked out of the rehearsal space. The metal door swung wide behind him then slammed back into the frame, shaking the walls. The performers held their breath.

Caleb remained standing on his chair. The German girls slumped then. The daffy look left their faces, and the clowns stepped aside so that Azi could put a hand on each of their sharp shoulders.

Caleb pulled a stack of envelopes from under the clip on the clipboard. "Well. I have paychecks. If you know what I'm going to say and you'd like to walk out in a huff, I hope I've got the correct address on file."

He stepped down then and laid the envelopes on the seat of the chair.

"If you don't have a place in town and have to spend the night before heading off tomorrow, of course we'll comp your stay in a motel, as usual," he said. Seamus had made no offer of this sort but Caleb thought it was the least he could do. "And, as you all seem to know, this check is your last. Except for you, Lorne. You can stay and take care of the animals until we have them sold."

Lorne looked sidelong at Caleb, like Caleb's comment wasn't worth the effort of turning his head.

"I know you're not happy," Caleb said. "This is not a happy time for anyone. However, I would like to say that you've all been a pleasure to know and that I tried hard to keep this from happening."

It came out a bit too measured, like he had to choose his words carefully because he didn't want to come off harsh. Instead he had to choose carefully because any sentiment he had for this job, any meaning it had for him would seem trite in comparison to what it meant to Azi, or to Vroni and Jenifer, or to Henry. To tell them that the end of Feely and Feinstein was the undoing of his life's great project would be patronizing, even though it was true.

Caleb stood at the door and shook their hands as they filed out. He told them best of luck, promising them glowing references. Vroni was the only one who refused to keep a stiff upper lip. She sobbed while he held her hand, shaking there in the doorway. Jenifer spoke to her quietly in German.

"Hey, Vroni, it'll be alright. Listen. There are openings at Culpepper and Merriweather. I will post all the info to you," said Caleb.

She cried harder, still holding on to Caleb's hand. "We're an *act*," she moaned. "What do you think I am, Baratucci? Don't you *see* what I look like *alone*? I need an act."

"Of course, that's what I meant. They're looking for acts," said Caleb and pulled her toward him, cupping the back of her head with his hand. Her thin hair was soft in his palm, so soft that he felt if he touched it too long, it might disintegrate. She was right. She had no business being alone.

Azi and the clowns stood behind her. Kylie and Azi were polite and tried not to watch as she smeared Caleb's jacket with her dissolving makeup. Henry couldn't seem to avert his eyes, though.

"I don't get it," the boy said.

Vroni peeled herself off of Caleb's shoulder. Her face, which was crumpled with weeping, hardened into a snarl.

"You're a circus performer, and you don't know how to go from one outfit to another? You did it once. Just . . . do it again."

"Wow. You are such a prick," Vroni said.

"You say that now, but one day you'll wake up at your new circus and think, whatever happened to that prick clown I use to know? I shoulda made out with him when I had the chance."

Vroni tried to stifle her laugh and ended up spitting on Caleb.

Caleb looked down at the wet spot on his jacket. "Thanks, Henry."

"Everyone is welcome!" said Henry.

Vroni wiped her eyes and finally shook Caleb's hand. "I'm sorry, Baratucci. Really."

"Don't be sorry," said Caleb.

"See you in the funny papers, Pierrot," she said, then linked arms with Jenifer and walked outside. The wind was beginning to pick up, and the dirt stirred in little tornadoes around the women's pink heels.

When the clowns went to say their good-byes, Caleb asked them to stay just a while longer to help him with some cleanup. In reality, he wanted to invite them to stick around for awhile. If the others knew, they might feel cheated, but Caleb felt guilty about having hired the clowns, only to fire them after one season and send them back into the fray with hardly any experience. He wanted to send off Kylie and Henry on the best possible footing, because he discovered them. The others were circus from birth, but these clowns (and his wife) felt truly *his*, their talent first legitimized by his approval. Caleb still hadn't quite shaken the jealousy he harbored toward Henry. And yet the part of him that felt responsible for the boy won out.

Which was, of course, why Henry's brother was waiting for Henry back at Caleb's house, a fact Henry didn't know yet.

Azi, who, besides the clowns, was the last to leave, embraced Caleb.

"Baratucci," said Azi.

"My friend."

"You must make Feely sorry for this."

"Impossible. Seamus has no soul."

"He has desires. You're smart. You could find a way."

"Not a chance. *You* make him sorry."

"No time. I have to find a gym. I've gotten fat. No one but you would let me take my shirt off in a ring like this."

Caleb laughed. "Azi, you have muscles I didn't know existed. I'm envious to the core."

"You should see the guys out there, Caleb. They keep raising the bar for what a strong man looks like. It's not all WWF anymore, where you can have a shred of fat and your pants up to your belly button."

"You're not a strong man anymore. You're a fire-eater."

"Whatever I am. There's a standard for half-dressed men."

"I know."

"I'll call you in a month. See if anything has changed. See how your lovely wife is doing."

"I'll look forward to it."

Azi left the building, collecting Vroni and Jenifer. If they didn't get steady work, it would be hard to stay under the radar. An undocumented Nigerian fire-eater was harder to find than an undocumented Nigerian fire-eater with the two skinny blond human props.

Caleb knew he would hear from Azi in a month, and probably for many months afterward. He would check in, good as his word. Eventually, there would come a time when he would not hear from Azi, or anyone else from Feely and Feinstein. But he did not want to think about that.

When Azi had gone, Caleb turned to Henry and Kylie. "So, listen. I feel terrible about hiring you for one season. I'm not that kind of boss, y'know, but this was out of my hands. So if you wanna stay at our house for a while until you find a new gig, you're welcome to. Just . . . probably not more than a few months. I mean, you'll have to be reasonable about it. And you'll have to help out with food and cleaning and things of that nature. But it's not a big deal. I can help you find work."

Henry stared at him for a moment in disbelief, then gathered himself. "That's really nice of you. Considering."

Kylie stood up on her toes and wound her arms around his neck. "You are amazing, Caleb." Caleb staggered back, unprepared for her hug. "I was like thirty minutes from using the last of my money on a plane ticket back to California—and I really didn't want to. I just know if I go back, my parents will suck me in and I'll end up in school for a math job," she said.

"Ugh, math jobs! How bourgeois," said Henry, but Caleb saw he was smiling at Kylie, and his teasing seemed warm.

He gently pried Kylie from his neck. "We are happy to have you. Henry? What do you think? If you don't, then at least come to dinner. Your brother has tracked you to our door and he wants to see you."

The smile fled from the boy's face. "What?"

CHAPTER 22

ON THE WAY TO THE Baratuccis' house, Henry didn't intend to speak. He knew if he did, he would almost certainly say something that would remind Caleb that he had tried to fuck his wife. And if Caleb remembered this he might change his mind and not take him to Andre. He wanted to see his brother, but he was also picturing Andre about their father's size, a grown man who had nursed a grudge for nine years. The letter said, *Just think of all the times you left me alone. You and Mom. You could have helped me, but you didn't.* While the words on the page had seemed honest, harmless things, face-to-face the same words could come out in a different order, could multiply until they became a dark mass above them, crushing them, forcing Henry and Andre to fight their way out from beneath their weight. A part of him was afraid, and it would be this part of him that did the talking if he talked. So he just zipped his lips.

Kylie rode with them, leaving her Mercedes at the circus grounds, where it had been all summer, the dust settling on it like a coat of brown suede. She sat in the front with Caleb, staring out the window, while Henry tried to disappear in the back. Caleb's voice cut through the quiet.

"I've been talking to him," he said. "He says *you* were the good brother."

"I was," Henry said cautiously. "He was the troublemaker."

229

"Interesting. I guess it's all relative. He also said you were a good basketball player."

"Yeah."

"No baseball, though?"

"No. We didn't have enough people for a team. It was just me and Andre and sometimes a couple of his friends. Never enough people to cover the bases."

They passed the music store where he and Kylie had once met, the movie theatre, with its pink neon sign.

Henry took an audibly deep breath, trying to slow his heart.

"Hey," said Caleb, glancing at him in the rearview mirror. "Adrienne says you haven't seen him in a long time. But I don't think you need to worry. He came all this way to see you."

Once they were at Caleb's house, standing in the living room with its comforting smells of Pledge and French toast (breakfast for dinner, Adrienne's favorite), Kylie lugged her trunk to the guest room.

Caleb put his hand on Henry's shoulder. He steered him into the kitchen. There was no trace of French toast except the smell and no sign of Adrienne. Sitting at the table, though, slouching, was a man-sized version of his brother. He was the bigger, wider-shouldered, squarer-chinned version of Andre-the-boy. Same brown eyes and dust-colored hair—their father head to toe.

Andre raised his head and stood, smiled, and extended his hand toward Henry. "Hey, little brother," he said.

"I can't believe you're here."

"Good to see you," he said, and gripped his hand.

"Yeah. Thanks for . . . coming all that way."

"Oh, not a problem," he said. While he moved with more patience now, he grinned in an ornery way that Henry found familiar. "Not a problem at all."

Andre asked if Henry wanted to walk with him up the street, and so they left through Caleb's back door. As they headed up the alley, Henry could feel Adrienne watching them through the screen door, as if she needed to know, at least, the direction they were headed. Henry figured she had found his letter and sent something to the return address, inviting Andre on Henry's behalf. Now she probably wondered if this was entirely wise. Henry knew that, whatever he really was, he *looked* like a "nice kid." His brother looked like a man who had seen a thing or two, and he was two sizes bigger than Henry.

The days were getting shorter, and on some evenings the wind would pick up and it would feel like fall was already there. The future came on like this, subtly, with a little change in weather, a little extra speed in the wind.

They both walked with their hands in their pockets, down a steep hill that had them moving faster than normal, their strides aided by downward momentum.

"So my brother is a circus clown. Of all the things I thought you might be up to, this never occurred to me."

Henry stabbed his hands further into his pockets, braced for a volley of insults.

"Did you finish high school?" Andre asked.

"I'm a clown. It doesn't require a diploma."

"I just imagined you would, is all," he said. And then he added, "You really should at least get your GED. I did. If you don't have that, you just look like a lazy ass."

They were nearly running by the time they reached the bottom of the hill, where they came to a green-brick pub. Andre grabbed the door handle and jerked his chin toward the opening, indicating they should go in. A dark greasy smell and the clatter of conversation emerged from within. Henry shook his head.

They went to the deli instead. Andre bought a six-pack of Miller, a two-liter of RC Cola, and a bag of Doritos.

Henry picked out a poor boy wrapped in cellophane. Andre took it from his hands and laid it next to his RC and beer. "This too, please," he said and pulled another two dollars from his wallet.

"I have money," Henry mumbled.

"Nah, I wanna treat ya," said Andre.

When they returned to Caleb's house, they stayed in the yard. Henry sat down on the grass, but Andre remained standing, popped his beer open with a lighter and slurped the foam that seeped out.

"I met this guy who dragged the river," he said. "It was in a bar by the touristy part of Prague that I go to when I have a little extra money and want to hear people speak English. Anyway, the guy told me all about his job. He told me that he pulled out all kinds of trash. Crazy shit. Toilets. Cradles. Whole sandwich bags full of cocaine. I asked what he'd pulled out that day and he said, a body. 'Young,' he said, 'like boy. No hair on the face. Stabbed here.'" Andre impersonated the man's accent and pointed to his side and his neck.

"I started to freak out a little when you didn't write me back," said Andre, pulling open his bag of Doritos. "Kept picturing you floating in a river."

Henry had never imagined Andre in a river. He was always in a hole, beaten to death by their father, or some policeman, or gang member. He'd pictured him bloated, his body one big bruise, buried.

Henry's fist closed around a clump of dandelion leaves in Caleb's yard. He yanked them from the ground.

"It gets so gray there," said Andre, almost as if he were talking to himself. "You just think about stuff. Sometimes I think I'd like to live in a place that wasn't totally fuckin' gray and depressing all the time. Like Florida."

"Yeah. Why don't you?" said Henry

"I don't know." He shrugged. "I make good money at the factory. I don't know if I could make good money in Florida. And . . . I don't know. I don't think I'm done with the gray shit just yet. I think I need to be there. It's good for me there."

There were lines around his mouth like parentheses, a ring around his head where a hat usually sat. As he raised his beer to his lips, Henry saw a beaded bracelet peek from beneath the cuff of his brown jacket. Dangling from the bracelet was an oval shaped picture of a woman, wearing a crown on her head, encircled by a holy sunburst, painted and shellacked, set in cheap-looking metal. There was something about it that seemed deeply private and sorrowful.

What business did Andre have with the man who dragged the river?

He wanted to ask Andre this, but his brother seemed to notice that Henry's eyes were resting on the talisman at his wrist, and he spoke before Henry got a chance to.

232

"What about you? Why the circus, man? You could be a *professional athlete*, if you wanted. About as easily as I could go to Florida, anyway."

"I *am* a professional athlete," said Henry.

"Yeah, okay, so you're a professional athlete who makes no money and isn't famous. Why? Why don't you go out and be Michael Jordan or something?"

Henry thought about it. It was a good question, and he'd thought about it before but hadn't come up with an answer yet that he imagined would be good enough for other people. What he told his brother was an answer half-formed, mulled over during nights spent awake in trailers and in moldy apartments and underneath the tables of fast food restaurants—spoken to himself when he climbed trees, in the same low voice he used to say his mother's name.

"I like to make people laugh. It makes them like me. It makes them like each other, too."

Andre stared at him, shoved another chip in his mouth. "Sounds kinda gay," he said.

"Yeah. It is. Kind of gay, I guess. Gay like living in Europe."

Andre put his hand to his face. "Stop, you're hurting my feelings," he said.

Henry ignored him. "And anyway, did anyone ever say, 'Hey, you wanna learn how to be Michael Jordan?' No. But someone was like, 'Hey, you wanna learn how to be Buster Keaton?' And I was like, 'Yeah. Why not?'"

Henry flopped backward on the grass. Andre finally sat down next to him, folding his legs in front of him.

"Who's Buster Keaton?"

Lying on the sharp, long crabgrass in Caleb's yard, watching finger-shaped clouds drift across the sky, Henry explained to his brother who Buster Keaton was, and then he explained who Luka Christiakov was, and how he had learned to be a clown, and how he kept it a secret from their father, and how he got away with it.

"Good. Fuck him. That's good. All this time I was worried he would get to you."

Andre's shoulders relaxed. Henry closed his eyes and tried to envision the same thing he knew Andre was envisioning: a past in which Henry really did have the upper hand, in which, at twelve, he learned to outsmart their father, overcoming him with his superior wit like some kind of Robin Hood.

Finding he couldn't bring himself to unravel this fantasy for his brother, Henry opened his eyes. Henry had the same fantasy about how things were going for Frankie.

"Do you have a house in Prague?" he asked.

"No. An apartment."

"Do you have a girlfriend?"

Andre laughed. Henry watched as he pulled a flattened red-and-white package from his jacket pocket, pinched the package open and drew a cigarette from it. "No," he said, lighting it. He pulled on the cigarette, and the ember brightened. His brother seemed to be considering something carefully, inhaling and peeling the corners of the label on his beer.

"There is this one girl," he said. "Well, actually, there are two girls, but one of them, one of them is like . . . a mermaid. She has this real long upper body." Andre framed his own torso with his hands, one at his neck and one at his crotch, the one at his crotch still pinching the cigarette between its two fingers. "And she's skinny on top, and her boobs are kind of small, but nice . . . like scoops of ice cream. But her butt is huge, and then her legs go back to being skinny. I'm telling you, if she had a tail, she'd be a mermaid."

Andre tore the label from his beer now and crinkled it into a ball. He held it in his fist for a moment before flicking it across the yard.

"But she's not your girlfriend?"

Andre shook his head. "No. She and the other one, they're more like friends. We hang out together sometimes. And sometimes if they get into trouble, I'm there to help them out."

Henry twisted to face Andre. "What kind of trouble?"

His brother looked straight ahead, took another long drag from his cigarette, and the smoke floated from his mouth as he spoke. "Well, you know. Men over there are even bigger assholes than they are here. They give the girls a hard time, sometimes. And I take care of it."

Andre still didn't look at him. It took Henry a long, awkward space of time before he figured out what kind of trouble these girls might be in with men. "You're a pimp?"

Andre laughed again, nervously now. "No, no. I never take their money. They offer it to me, but I never take it. I don't do it for the money. I do it for the girl. I do it for Ice Cream Boobs." He took a deep breath and exhaled a gray cloud. "But sometimes . . . the guys I go after. They have money. And I take it if they have it. Give it to the girls if the dude didn't pay them or something. I keep the rest. I figure . . . I figure that's fair."

An image flashed through Henry's mind of his brother bloodying someone's face, smashing it beyond recognition. He thought of him taking a wallet, dragging a motionless body into a river, and tried to reconcile this image with the face in front of him.

Andre pushed him, and because Henry was stuck in these murky thoughts, he lost his balance.

"Quit looking at me like that," said Andre. "If you're thinking I'm running around killing people, I don't. I never killed nobody." He took a drink of his beer. "Not even if they really deserved it. Which you know they do, little brother. You know sometimes they deserve it."

Henry settled back on the grass. Night had crept in while they'd been talking. Henry could see the faint shapes of the moon and a bright star. *Here, this is the same sky we watched for lights as children*, Henry thought. *Of course. Of course you don't kill people.*

"You remember the UFO?" Henry asked.

Andre hesitated. "Yes," he said.

"I used to look for it. I waited for it," Henry said. "To beam me up, I guess."

"Did you ever see it?" asked Andre. "After I moved away? Did it come?"

"Naw."

"Oh. So it never came back."

"It probably came back. I just never saw it."

Andre rubbed the back of his neck, seeming distracted, and Andre-as-a-man looked more like Andre-as-a-boy than he had since he arrived. Henry reached over and poked him. Andre whacked his hand away.

"You're making a joke out of it. It was as real as anything I've ever seen and I've never met anyone who completely believes me about it, because no one has ever seen what I saw."

Henry rolled over so that he was lying on his belly. "Dude, *lots* of people have seen what you saw. There's police reports and blurry pictures and—"

"Yeah, but they didn't see *exactly* what I saw. And besides, half those people taking blurry pictures really are crazy. Which means that the sane ones still probably think I'm crazy 'cause that's the sane thing to think when somebody's like 'Oh, I saw a big fucking alien ship last night and it talked to me.'"

"It talked to you?"

"Sort of."

"Oh. Well, I never saw it but I still believe you. There's weird shit in the world."

"Pretty sure that's what Mom said, when I told her. First she said, 'It was probably a plane.' But when I swore up and down it wasn't, she said something like that: 'There's weird shit in the world. Weird shit and bad shit and you just gotta shut your ears and hum. 'Cause it ain't goin' away.'"

"Sounds like her."

Andre snorted. "Yeah."

From inside Caleb's house, Henry heard dishes clanking against each other as they were pulled from a cabinet.

Andre put his beer down, then. He pulled Henry up by his shoulders so that he was sitting upright on Caleb's lawn. "Look at this," he said. He touched his tongue to the tip of his nose.

"Yeah, that's great, Andre. You should join the circus, too."

He sucked his tongue back in. "The reason I can do that is because of the UFOs. 'Cause I told you, and you didn't say anything. And I told Mom, and she told me to *hum*. But then I told Dad, and *Dad* got pissed because he thought I was . . . I don't even know what he thought. Like I was trying to make a fool of him? Make him believe something that wasn't true and then laugh at him? Who knows?"

"I get it," Henry said, pushing his brother away. Andre didn't try to hold on to him. His hands fell limp at his sides.

"That little string of skin under your tongue that keeps your tongue attached to the bottom of your mouth? It got cut clean through. I guess on my teeth," said Andre. His hand hovered around his jaw as if he still had to protect it. "He hit me that hard."

Henry put his hands over his face. He couldn't look at Andre. "I know, I know, I know," he said. When he lowered his hands, Andre was still crouching there. Patient. He'd been prepared for this reaction.

"Will you chill out?" he said. "It's fine. You were like . . . seven? I get it. What were you gonna do about that, y'know? I get it. But sometimes I think, like, what the fuck? What the fuck was that all about? I didn't tell anybody. I didn't even bother *mentioning* it. My mouth was all messed up. Nobody said anything."

Andre stood then and straightened his jacket.

"Well, what do you want me to do about it now?" said Henry, in a voice that was louder than he wanted it to be.

"I don't know," Andre said. "Nothing."

The screen door of Caleb's house swung open. Inside, Kylie stood, holding the door open with one freckled arm. Andre startled but recovered and smiled at Kylie, teeth and all. Kylie did not smile back. Henry wondered if she might have seen Andre jerk him up from the ground.

"Adrienne told me to ask if you guys needed anything," she said.

"No. We're just jawing," said Henry.

She glared at his brother. "Okay. I'm sleeping on the couch."

"You should sleep in the guest bed," said Henry.

"That's where you're sleeping," said Kylie.

"Nah, I'm fine on the couch."

"You're a light sleeper. I'm not." She could not seem to keep her eyes off Andre as she spoke, and Henry swore that, for all the times he'd pissed off Kylie, she had never looked at him with the kind of distrust with which she watched his brother.

Henry conceded to sleeping in the guest bed, but she still lingered, propped against the door frame.

"Listen," she said. "I told Caleb about Lorne and the horse. He's going to find a place for the animals as soon as he can, but he won't say anything

237

to Lorne before that. He doesn't want to make him more . . . agitated, I guess."

"Oh."

"I don't like it. I'm afraid he'll go after her again."

"We'll check on her," Henry said. "Thanks for letting me sleep in the bed."

She reluctantly withdrew the arm that held the screen door open. "Yeah. No sweat."

When she was gone, Henry looked back at his brother. He was smirking, drawing another cigarette from the package in his pocket. "No introduction, huh? Is that the giant's daughter?"

"No. My costar. Kylie."

"Costar," he mumbled. "You queer."

"Shut up, Andre."

His brother shrugged. "She knows how you sleep. I guess that's costar business, huh?" His lips pressed around his cigarette. He seemed amused by Henry, even if he was still angry.

Andre would not stay long. He would be going back to working in the factory in Prague, to championing prostitutes, one with the body of a mermaid. Henry tried to come up with something that his brother wanted to hear, so that Andre would leave still feeling a little amused, a little curious. So maybe he would come back again.

"I believed you," said Henry. "Everything you said, I believe it, even though I never saw the UFO you saw. I've seen things. I know they're real. I just didn't know what to tell you at the time. You were scared of it, and you weren't scared of anything. That freaked me out."

Andre smiled, then lowered his head. All around them things hushed. Children and dogs went inside for the evening. The sky had become a dark, velvety blue, and it was a quiet few minutes between the end of the evening sounds and the beginning of the night ones: trucks starting and music drifting from car windows, the occasional howl of a cat.

"Remember that thing I asked you about? When I wrote you?"

Henry had known this was coming but he wasn't ready for it. Andre had asked if Henry would go back to their house with him, which Henry assumed meant he wanted to visit Frankie and their father. Henry's heart sprinted at the very idea; as if the prospect of seeing his brother and father again wasn't frightening enough, putting Andre and his father together in a room would be inviting disaster.

"I hate to ask. I don't know what happened after I left. What reasons you had to leave. But I have to get a hold on this. I can't stop my mind from trying to get to her. It keeps reeling and reeling, like a fishing rod. It's just a habit now. Get up in the morning, turn the reel. Have breakfast, turn the reel, walk to work, turn the reel. Eventually, you'll get to the end, right? She'll be on the end of the line. But she's not," he said.

Andre remembered the beer he'd abandoned and took it up again, disposing of about half of it in one swallow. "You can reel and reel until your arm goes numb, and she won't be there," he said. "But I can't stop reeling. My mind won't stop. I can't remember what she looked like. I can't remember what she sounded like. But when she stopped breathing—I remember that. I wake up at night, feeling that . . ."

Emptiness, thought Henry. Like a sky without stars. His brother woke up to this emptiness, in a dark, foreign city, touching the cold charm at his wrist.

"If I could just get one thing. One little picture. I feel like I could stop," he said. "And her stuff is still there. I know it is."

When Henry didn't reply, Andre polished off his beer. He studied the bottle in his hand, waiting.

Henry had been positive that when his brother asked this, his answer would be no. He could not leave Frankie twice. He'd done it once, because he was told by the only man he'd ever trusted, that by doing so, he could save his own life. He had been uncertain, since that day, whether his life was worth saving. Not sticking up for Andre, that was one thing. Cutting out on Frankie, that was entirely another.

When Henry still didn't answer, Andre assumed that he wouldn't. "Okay," he said and gave a little laugh. "I can't say I blame you."

He held up a finger, stored his cigarette between his lips, and fished around in the breast pocket of his jacket. "I brought this for you," he said, pulling a folded-up postcard from his jacket pocket. He handed it to Henry.

He unfolded the card. There was a picture on it of what looked like a chandelier in a church. Henry pulled the card closer to his face and saw that where the lights of a chandelier would be, here there were human skulls. The arms of the chandelier were made up of pelvic bones, each hung with a femur that dangled from the arc of pelvises. There were other bones that decorated the chandelier, too, pieces of spinal column, fine collarbones and ribs. There were pillars on the floor of this church made of bone as well, tiered skulls capped with fleshy sculpted cherubs. Drooping from the ceiling of the building was a garland of skulls and what looked like humeri, upper arm bones.

"Is this the church you play football outside of?"

"No. That's in the city. This is in Kutná Hora," he said. It was strange to hear the name of this place coming from his brother's mouth, in the original accent he learned it in. "It looks normal from the outside, but on the inside, it's all made of the bones of people who died of the plague. It's psycho that someone would think to make something like that. But it looks kind of cool."

All those people, Henry thought, taken apart and rearranged, sculpted into one body, one home for God to live in. His brother saw this and thought of him. He had brought him a gift.

"I'm glad Adrienne got hold of you," Henry said.

"It was the guy."

"What?"

"It was the guy who wrote me. Caleb? He's not too bad."

"Oh. And you came right here?"

Andre looked perplexed. "Well. Yeah. I mean, what if I never found you again?"

THE BROTHER LEFT FOR THE night, back to his hotel, and Adrienne was glad to see him go. He was not a frightening person, not like Curtis, but the brother stirred the air in the wrong direction.

She hadn't gotten a chance to speak to Henry since he returned, because he'd been with his brother all day. She had a head full of things to tell him that she'd been mulling over since the night he'd ditched the circus and driven to see her. About his family. About the two of them. She had the words now to explain that she had hoped someone would come into her life who needed her, not as a lover, but as a guide. How she wished he would be that person. She also had the words to tell him, gently, that he may be wrong about what caused his mother to pass away so young. Adrienne had held these words in for weeks.

That evening, she, Kylie, and Caleb sat in the living room while Henry showered. Caleb was thumbing through a manila file folder containing names: names of the owners of venues they had rented, names of other circus managers, names of performers he hadn't hired. Kylie and Adrienne read magazines and channel-surfed.

When Henry walked out of their bathroom with a wet head and tired eyes and waved "good-night," Adrienne almost waylaid him.

"Hey, Henry," she said.

"What?"

Caleb's head whipped around and he caught her eye with a look that said *What are you, crazy?* And he was right, of course.

"Never mind. Sleep well," she said.

Henry raised an eyebrow. "You're a head case sometimes," he said. "Night."

Henry went to bed and the rest of them sat like that for about an hour before Kylie passed out cold on the couch, a beauty magazine across her chest. Adrienne felt obliged to leave the room so that she could turn the lights off for Kylie but found that feeling of obligation not unpleasant. She had plans that involved leaving anyway, so she ushered Caleb to the kitchen to work, and left the house, clicking off the lamp as she went.

She met Azi at a diner, not three blocks away, where they sat down for a cup of cheap coffee and a long chat.

More Notes For A Show About An Angel

If you want to be a great clown, at some point in your career, you have to take an epic Humpty Dumpty–grade fall. In Project A, *Jackie Chan falls sixty feet from the big hand of a clock tower, just like Harold Lloyd in that other movie that I can't remember the name of (sorry, Christiakov). He's dangling on the hand of the clock and he's got that face, the corners of his mouth pulled back in a grimace so you can see every tooth in his mouth. He must have been scared to death. He must have known he was going to break something taking a fall like that. But he's in character even after he slips. He doesn't look truly scared. He looks clown-scared.*

That's why when Jackie Chan gets up in the morning, he thinks, Today is a great day, because I am fucking Jackie Chan and I am amazing! *Because he sucked it up and fell, because he's pulled every muscle in his body and broken every bone, and now he's famous, he's rich, and everyone loves him.*

And I've been thinking: I don't like watching kung fu movies because I like to see people get hurt. I like watching them because I like to see people come back from it. You fall from a clock tower, you get pummeled by gangsters, you get bruised and dirty—and then you stand up, you get your fists of flame. You've got tears in your eyes and a howl in your mouth, and you kick some ass. Seeing this, it gives a person a certain feeling. It's like being set yourself free, like everything that weighs on you is just the silly preamble to an amazing comeback.

Maybe people feel this way about comedy, too. What if your theory is wrong, Christiakov? What if people don't want blood, but they need it to get that other thing that sets them free?

CHAPTER 23

THE CIRCUS KIDS SLEPT, AND Caleb sketched.

He'd started to think of those dark lines in Beckmann's paintings not as lines but as shadows. It was this quality of Adrienne's, the quality of light and shadow that she carried with her, that he loved, and it was why she would have been a perfect subject for a Beckmann painting. So he had photographed her and Richard in candlelight, and that was the photograph he drew from now.

The sketching, this time, was a means to an end. It helped him focus on what needed to be done. He wasn't going to spend another moment thinking he was not a real artist. He was a real artist, and his art was the circus, putting together the pieces, making it whole and beautiful. What could you call that but art?

When he finished his sketch, there were many dark areas, but the bright crests of skin and the sharp curve of Richard's beak made the picture dramatic. Adrienne's head tilted upward so that there were black shadows in the space between her eyes and eyebrows. She looked like she had the night he saw her do her cabaret show as the Amazon Woman, a spectacle of otherworldly beauty.

He could still do this. He could still revive Feely and Feinstein. After all, he had found the boy's brother. When Andre had appeared in his doorway, he'd known, briefly, what it felt like to create something unambiguously good, and why people did it. He'd created something out of thin air, something even more complex than a painting, and he wanted to do it again, for Feely and Feinstein.

CHAPTER 24

As KYLIE FELL, SHE ECLIPSED the white industrial lights that hung in the rehearsal space—head tilted up, arms held straight out to the sides—and the scaffolding she launched herself from shuddered behind her. Henry caught her, righted her, and lowered her stiff body to the ground. She was still more of an actress than an acrobat, thought Henry, but she knew how to fall.

They were working on Henry's angel show. Adrienne had dropped them off at the circus grounds with a warning: don't get caught here by Seamus. Though it had only been a few days since the end of the season, the only person who had permission to be on the circus grounds now was Lorne.

They knew that they would not be able to perform the show until they found new work—*if* they were even able to find new work together—but Kylie indulged him. Or, maybe she secretly wanted to see if her newly nurtured acrobatic skills would allow her to try what, only two months ago, she had said would be impossible for her.

The act came slowly, because Kylie was still unsure what Henry wanted, and even when he succeeded in describing a particular movement to her, she seemed baffled about how to approach it. "I'll break my arm," she kept saying, or, sometimes, "That's physically impossible." The fall frightened her, and so she looked rigid in the air, too focused on landing safely to make the fall itself funny. Her body dropped from the scaffolding over and over, and Henry had to take deep breaths to stop himself from getting frustrated. He wondered how Christiakov had never wrung his neck, how he'd managed not to lose patience.

"All great clowns eventually have to take an epic fall," Henry said, when she was again poised on the scaffolding.

"This is hardly epic," she said.

"It will be," he said. "You still want to be a star, right? That's what that little tat you got's all about, right? Your next stop is Ringling Brothers'."

As soon as he said this, he wished he hadn't. He sounded arrogant, and the reference to Kylie's tattoo was taboo, a violation of their unspoken agreement not to dredge up the night they had seen each other at their worst.

For the moment, though, she didn't seem angry. She stretched her arms to the ceiling before opening them, slowly. She was concentrating, and Henry could see the energy rolling from the center of her body outward. It lingered around her, this energy, and when she pitched herself forward it seemed to slow her descent. Her arms and legs spun like pinwheels, cartoonish and exaggerated and gorgeous.

She landed in his arms, still light. When she drew a breath, her weight returned to her, and Henry was reluctant to put her down.

"That was exactly it," he said.

"I guess," she said.

"No, it was perfect."

"You'd say anything, wouldn't you? You'd say or do whatever to get the results you want."

"Maybe."

She reached up and put her hand on the nape of his neck. "You wanna know about the star? It's motivation, like you say. But not in the way you're thinking."

Henry let the weight of her hand pull his face closer to hers. His hair fell softly on her forehead. "Then in what way?" he said, and now he really wanted to know. He couldn't know for sure what he would do with this knowledge in the future, couldn't be sure he wouldn't one day exploit it to hurt her. He didn't *want* to hurt her, but then again people did things all the time that they didn't *want* to do. If he waited to be certain that he was a good person, he would be waiting forever. He would lose the chance he had to know her, in this particular slice of time, when she was so beautiful, and his intentions toward her were as tender as they had ever been toward anyone.

"It represents a failure," she said. "Actually, there are two of them, now."

"How have you failed?" he asked.

"The first is for something back in school. I screwed up a performance. Spaced on all my cues. It probably wasn't a big deal. But it felt terrible. It was more than I could bear, actually."

"They're like a punishment?"

"I don't think so. I just had to do something with that feeling. Guilt or shame or embarrassment or whatever that was. Every time I would even think about it, I'd feel sick. I'd want to hide. It made me not want to be a clown anymore. I had to do something with it, so I could forget about it."

Henry understood this implicitly. It was crushing, how well he understood this.

"Did it work?" he asked.

"Like a charm."

"I don't want to know why you got the second one, do I?"

She rolled her eyes. "Sure you do. You'll love it. Your head will blow up like a balloon."

"You think things about my head that aren't true." His arms were starting to quaver from holding her so long, but he didn't let go.

"The other star is because I got to this crappy two-bit circus and this *kid*, this self-important little hick kid is a better clown than I am. This *kid* is running the show. And whatever, so it's a boys' club, and I'm not a boy and that's a real pain in the ass, but the fact is that you're more talented and more dedicated than me," she said. She arched her back and propelled herself out of his arms.

"I'm not funnier than you," he said.

She froze. She had no doubt been expecting something cruel from him, and he had almost delivered it before he stopped himself. It was on the tip of his tongue, something like what he'd said to Vroni. He caught Kylie's hand as she moved away, reeled her back to him. He knew what to tell her this time. He had an answer.

"You didn't fail. That second star has to be for something else. I need you. I'm a stick-in-the-mud."

"I don't need you to say this," she said, but she wasn't pulling away.

He hugged her. First with one arm, like they were pals, and then, he thought, *Fuck it*, and held her with both arms, laid his forehead on her shoulder. Kylie *did* know something true about him. She felt it, the same as he did, the desire to be special, the frustration of wanting someone's blessing who was not there to give it or who refused to give it. It was easy enough to say, "I will stop wanting this," but nearly impossible to put the brakes on such a desire. She knew this as well as him, whatever kind of car she drove, whatever school she went to—she searched their audiences for a face she would not see.

"I'm sorry," he said.

She didn't say so, but Henry thought she must have forgiven him, to let him stay so close. And this closeness was different than it had been with Adrienne, and different than it had been with Kylie in the beginning. Different, even, than it had been with Cassie.

MAYBE IT FELT DIFFERENT TO hold Kylie because they were accomplices. They had a secret agenda, here, at Feely and Feinstein's grounds—besides practicing, besides getting so close to making out that they had to hold their breath when they finally pulled away from each other to keep from sighing, out loud, awkward and obvious in their disappointment. They were there to check on Ambrosia, or, if Henry wanted to put it in more devious terms, to spy on her master.

But they weren't good spies. They slinked along the edge of the trailers, quiet as they could, toward the animals' pens. Out of the corner of his eye, Henry saw Tex ambling up the narrow dirt path that flanked the trailers, led by Lorne, who spotted them immediately, and waved. In his other hand, he held the long wooden baton, the one that he had used to take a crack at the horse.

Tex's gait sped up when she saw Henry, her trunk swinging in front of her like a jaunty metronome. When she got close enough, she reached out with her trunk and patted his shoulder. Then she tried to pat his face, which was less successful, and made Henry laugh in spite of himself. "Hi, Tex. How's it going, big mama?"

"Not supposed to be here, Henry," said Lorne. He seemed like he was trying to smile. It was not quite a success, and he just looked like he was baring his teeth.

"I know. We're just not ready for the season to be over. We were rehearsing a little," said Kylie.

"Hmmm," said Lorne. Tex extended her trunk to greet Henry some more, but Lorne nudged it down with the baton. "You should find somewhere else to practice. There's not even a payphone here if one of you gets hurt."

He sounded sincere, but Henry couldn't drum up any warmth for Lorne. How could he stand there with that baton in his hand and pretend to be a nice person? "Why would that make any difference to you?"

Lorne shrugged. "I just think you should take care. Don't worry, I'm not going to tell Seamus, if that's what you're thinking. I'm not like that."

Then he walked on, leading Tex to a slab of concrete where he sprayed her down for her bath. Tex lay down, resting her big head against the concrete, flapping her ear when water threatened to trickle too deep inside of it. When the water began to pool around her, she dipped her trunk in, and sucked up water to squirt at Lorne. Lorne splashed her back, kicking the water up with his rain boots, laughing and saying something that Kylie and Henry were too far away to hear.

They continued watching Lorne hose down the elephant. They both seemed loopy, Tex rolling around now while Lorne chattered on at her, chuckling intermittently at his own jokes.

Kylie motioned for Henry to follow her, and they headed to the animal pens while Lorne was distracted. Ambrosia was fine. Clean as ever with her trough full of hay, her metal bucket of water. The clowns wondered if they hadn't had some sort of mutual hallucination. They decided that was the best thing to believe.

CHAPTER 25

A FEW DAYS LATER, ADRIENNE gave Henry a cardboard box to put his mother's things in, if he found any. She handed it to him warily, saying, "Now if you're going to do this, you should be prepared for what you find. Who's to say your dad didn't hide her things to protect her secrets? Women have secrets, Henry. You can't be surprised."

Henry took the box. "I know women have secrets. Tampons. Hair removal cream. I'm prepared."

Adrienne raised her eyebrows. "Alright," she said. "As long as you know about the tampons."

She almost let it go, almost rolled with the joke, because Henry's eyes begged her to roll with the joke. But she found she couldn't.

"Honestly," she said, "I've been thinking about you and your family. And I've been meaning to talk to you. You know, when you grow up, and your parents are alive, you learn by degrees that they aren't perfect. They're just human."

Henry looked up and sighed, resigned to being lectured. "Yes. I mean, I don't remember thinking my dad was perfect, ever, but I get what you're saying."

"Right. So . . . if you find evidence that your mom was only human . . . I mean, you were so little, weren't you? She must've seemed like an angel to you then. And because she's gone, in your mind, that's still who she is. If you find the wrong picture or the wrong piece of junk that she hung on to, she might not be that anymore," said Adrienne. She was still trying to find a kind way to say it, one that wouldn't make Henry want to shoot the messenger.

Henry must have been able to tell that she was circumnavigating the truth with this vague warning, that she was nervous about his reaction. He didn't say anything for a moment, and Adrienne had learned that this didn't mean he'd dropped out of the conversation, but that he was measuring his words.

"She's my mother. Doesn't matter what junk I find," he said.

"I suppose that's a good point," she said. "But that's not exactly what I mean. Of course you love her, but . . . you remember what I told you about Curtis."

He nodded.

"He's got that van because he still works for Southern Blue. He doesn't sell door to door anymore, but he did when we were married. And you know, it was pretty common for the door-to-door guys to sell drugs, too, back then. I don't know who came up with it, but it was a good delivery system for people who lived out of the way and wanted to be discrete."

Henry squinted, as if trying to process the connection between Adrienne's warning and this confession about her ex-husband. He seemed to be coming up blank. Even clearheaded, she knew he could not envision his mother as a person who could self-destruct.

"I'm saying that Southern Blue salesman came to your house more than once. I'm saying your father chased him out of the house at night, didn't he? Isn't it weird that he would have come to your house at night?"

"Oh," said Henry, finally seeing Adrienne's implication. "But he—well, I just thought they were sleeping together."

Adrienne held up her palms. "I wasn't there. I don't know for sure what happened. All I know is that Curtis sold a boatload of methamphetamines. And that generally, women in their twenties don't die just because their husbands stress them out. You know? You see why I'd think this?"

Henry stared at her, then into his empty box. "Yeah, I see."

"I'm not trying to jump to conclusions."

"I mean. It shouldn't matter . . . except, if that's true . . ." he said. He didn't finish his thought, and Adrienne didn't push him. He cleared his throat. "See you when I get back?"

"There was another thing I wanted to talk about," she said.

Henry's eyes widened and he took a step back. "Oh, God, please, don't."

"It's about when you kissed me," she said.

"Jesus Christ, I *know* what it's about, and I'm saying please, please let's not talk about it. Can we just say that I'm stupid? Can we just say that I have awful judgment when it comes to girls? And leave it there?"

"No. I wasn't even going to criticize your judgment," Adrienne said. It was hard not to smile at his melodrama, or the real embarrassment that his act was designed to cover.

"If you say you want to just be friends," he said, "I will jump out this window."

"We're on the first story. It's a four-foot fall."

"Don't push me; I'm at the end of my rope."

"We're friends, Henry," she said.

At this, Henry dropped his box and opened the window. Adrienne reached for him, tucked him beneath one of her arms and locked him there with her other arm.

"You've broken my heart," he said. "Now you're breaking my rib cage."

"Listen, I'm trying to tell you, I'm a good friend. I'm a better friend than most people ever have. I'll stick my neck out for you. I already have. A million times! And I'll keep doing it. And eventually, you'll see. You'll see I'm not going to stop."

She realized she was squeezing his torso pretty hard, and he wasn't saying anything. For a moment, she wondered if she hadn't gotten a little overzealous and made him pass out. She'd done that with a cat, once. But she felt him tremble, a small laugh escaping him.

"Adrienne, I know, alright? I already know all this. You're like the best friend I've ever had. Like, I've done nothing but fuck things up from the moment I got here, and you've done nothing but tell me I'm great," he said.

She sighed. "I know you don't think I'll stick around. But I will. You're going to see."

"I believe you," he said, earnestly, now, quietly. The change in his tone convinced her that he understood.

"Please," said Henry. "This sort of actually hurts."

IN EDGEFIELD, THE AIR TASTED like it did the day Henry jumped on the back of a freight train and abandoned the town. The leaves had just started to turn, and the air was light and fresh-feeling in his lungs. Different from the air in the city.

Henry played Kylie's tape in the rental car as the cornfields gave way to uneven sidewalks, old brick buildings in various states of restoration. The music carved minor chords into their eardrums while Henry watched Andre become more and more restless. He drove erratically, starting and stopping too suddenly, like he couldn't predict when he would need to push what pedal, like every stop sign took him by surprise.

When they arrived and Andre cut the engine, Henry felt no nostalgia about the house they were parked in front of. It could have been any little house in a small town. The white paint peeled in strips, a jagged pattern that revealed the gray wood beneath. Two trucks sat in the driveway, trimmed in orange rust. Tree branches and helicopter seeds littered the yard, and black-eyed Susans slumped against the side of the house, their season almost over.

They knocked on the door of the little house. A TV blared inside and the evening news trumpeted its call letters. A thin boy answered the door, wearing a white T-shirt and round John Lennon eyeglasses. The sparse brown hair on his legs hung over his white sports socks, which were pulled all the way up to his ankles. He looked, in general, like he'd just got out of bed.

"Hi, Frankie," said Henry, quietly.

Andre said nothing. He hung back, arms folded so that each hand clutched the opposite bicep.

Frankie looked Henry and Andre up and down, as if counting every button, evaluating the location of their eyes, ears, and fingers, scrutinizing the laces in their shoes. He seemed to decide that they could not be his brothers. They were imposters. He leaned against the doorframe and crossed his arms. "What do you want?"

To this, Henry couldn't think of a thing to say. This was the boy who, as a toddler, wrapped his arms and legs around Henry like a chimpanzee, who wailed, and smelled like the lavender lotion that their mother slicked over his limbs before bed. The idea that Frankie would really want nothing to do with him hadn't crossed his mind before. Of course he was angry with him. But would he really not let him in the door?

They heard their father's voice. "What are you doing, Frank?"

"Nothing," Frankie shouted over his shoulder. Henry returned Frankie's scrutiny. His skin was pale, and there were blue shadows beneath his eyes.

"You should come out for a second. Tell him you're going for a walk," said Henry, still in a low voice. He saw an opportunity here. If he could get Frankie to find their mother's things and bring them out, then no one would need to talk to their father. Henry would then take Frankie out for a hamburger to put the flesh back on his bones, and blood back into the flesh, and he would tell him to do like Kylie's beloved Talking Heads song says and *run, run, run away.*

"I don't want to come outside," said Frankie. His eyes were owlish behind his thick round glasses. What his little brother meant was, *I want you to leave.*

"Hey, help us out, man, would you? We're here for Mom's shit," said Andre. He knew their father was within earshot but didn't seem to care. "We know it's here, somewhere. You gonna let us in, or what?"

Frankie stared at Andre for a moment. "You're here . . . because you want to pick some stuff up?"

Henry shuffled his feet. Andre had been gone for nine years, and Henry had been gone for three, and he understood how this must sound completely ludicrous: *We just need to pop in and grab some things.*

Frankie uncrossed his arms and stood to the side, and Henry and Andre walked in. The house smelled yeasty and stale. Henry wiped his feet on the square of carpet in the entryway.

Everything was the same except the television, which was sleek, black, and foreign made, and the equally sleek black VCR below it, positioned awkwardly on a shelf too small to hold it, a garden of wires sprouting from its back. The carpet was the same trampled moss-colored shag that his mother had died on. The walls, half-covered in faux wood paneling, seemed to squeeze closer together as Henry entered, funneling him toward the southmost corner, where his father sat in his faded blue chair. Henry stopped at least seven feet from him, but they were so close, sharing each other's breath in that room, which was much smaller than Henry remembered.

His father wore an open work shirt and pajama pants, as if he'd given up halfway through changing his clothes. He needed a haircut and a shave—he had a purposeful-looking moustache and an accidental-looking beard. The wrinkles around his eyes were not so numerous as they were deep, like someone had cut them into his skin. He was still a big man, though his shoulders seemed a bit narrower than they were the last time Henry saw him.

Seeing Henry, his mouth dropped open. The shape of his father's mouth was always how Henry judged his safety in his presence, but this drooping jaw was not a familiar expression to Henry. His father started to stand but sank back down into his chair, his mouth still wide open, when Andre followed Henry in. There they were, in one room, all the living Bells.

"I'll be goddamned," said his father. "I'll be. Andre."

He stood up, made it all the way to his feet this time.

"Hi," said Henry, though their father was staring straight at his older brother.

"Henry," he said, squinting. He tried to keep the tears gathering in his eyes from falling. "Goddamn. It's like I'm seeing ghosts."

"Sorry to drop in out of the blue," Henry said. Already, the apologies tumbled out like they were nothing, when the one Kylie got from him had to be wrenched, dragged, forced through his lips.

His father seemed to choke. "Out of the blue. What does that matter?" He kept his eyes fixed upon Andre, whose breathing sounded heavy. Then, their father spread his arms, palms facing toward them, and Henry couldn't decide whether the gesture meant *Welcome* or *I surrender*, or both. "Should I put a frozen pizza in the oven?" he asked.

Henry looked back at Andre, eyebrows raised: *Should* he put a pizza in the oven? That would be okay, wouldn't it? It wouldn't take very long.

Their father moved even closer to Henry. Henry saw all his whiskers now—the patch of bristles beneath his lower lip was gray. He was close enough to smell: metal and water and oil from machinery. Faint body odor mingled with Speed Stick. He was glad his father didn't try to touch him, but this dry metallic scent gave him the sensation that there was order in the world.

"I'll put in a pizza," Henry volunteered.

He expected Andre to say no, to demand their mother's things, to start swinging. But he didn't. So Henry pulled a pizza out of the freezer, and Frankie was beside him before he could even take the plastic off the pizza, chopping a head of lettuce for salad. Henry leaned against the stain-mottled countertop and watched Frankie chop, then cut some onion into thin, uniform slices. The kitchen was small, but they were practiced at maneuvering in it.

There was a half-wall separating the kitchen from the living room, so while Henry stood in the kitchen, he could still see Andre and his father on the other side of the half-wall. Andre stood with his hands in his pockets. His father busied himself picking up the room, refolding the newspaper and stacking the wooden coasters.

"Can I smoke?" asked Andre, though he made it clear it was more an announcement than a question by pulling a cigarette from the pack.

"I'll open the window," their father said.

Once Andre got a lungful, his shoulders relaxed a little, and he offered up the information that he had been living in Prague. He didn't ask how their father had been or say hello. He simply started stating facts.

Their father nodded. "Oh yeah? Where's that? How do you like it?" He moved a throw pillow from one end of the couch to the other.

Andre told him about the job, the money, the architecture of the city, the green river, the language that sounded like the murmurings of witches around a cauldron. Their father laughed at this, a low-pitched chuckle.

Frankie looked up from a bisected tomato and saw Henry staring into the living room. "You can go talk to them. I don't need help. Besides, you're not helping. You're just standing there."

"I want to talk to you, too," said Henry.

"Whatever you wanna do, man."

Henry slid the pizza in the oven and walked out of the room, angry at Frankie and annoyed at himself for it. Whatever Frankie could muster to punish him, shrugs and silence and fuck-you stares, Henry knew he had it coming. Still, he found himself wanting to shake the tough-guy out of him.

"What about you?" asked his father, when he joined them in the living room. It was all so polite, but the three of them were fidgety as criminals, all standing, all eyes darting. The air was toxic, could curl the paint from the walls. "What do you do these days, Henry?"

Andre answered for him. "Henry joined the circus."

AROUND THE TABLE, THEY WERE seated close enough to touch elbows. It turned out all four were ravenous. Their napkins, pocked with pepperoni grease, accumulated between plates, and they had to heat another pizza after polishing off the first. They ate all the salad, too, and half a bag of pretzels dragged through sour cream. Both Andres, the senior and the junior, sucked down two cans of beer, and Frankie dug out four paper-wrapped pies, folded into moon shapes and shellacked in sugar. When those were gone, they picked at a bag of stale mini marshmallows. They said "more, please," and "pass the . . ." and nothing else. This didn't feel like peace to Henry, but it was worth prolonging, worth taking another marshmallow and letting it melt in his mouth. Frankie frowned at him, but his mouth was full of mini marshmallows, too.

When their father stopped eating, the rest of them followed suit. His inevitable question—"Why are you here, now?"—came out strained. Their father had no aptitude for the delicate language required to ask this question in a nice way, but Henry could tell he tried.

"So," his father said, "it's Wednesday. You have nothing to do on a Wednesday but come to Edgefield?"

Henry looked at Andre, and saw that his brother was reluctant to break whatever spell had been woven out of politeness and fear and love to keep them all sitting amicably at a table. Andre still had no imagination. He only foresaw one possible outcome of this visit and that was the retrieval of his mother's memorabilia. Maybe he considered that he might have to break one or two of their father's bones to get it, but nothing beyond that. It never crossed his mind that it would hurt to say that he wanted physical things rather than to see them again.

Frankie didn't seem to realize there was a spell at all. Or maybe he wanted to watch them all get a cannonball to the heart. "They want Mom's stuff," he said, and Andre's expectant silence confirmed that this was the truth of it.

Their father nodded and rose from his chair, slowly, gracelessly. He bumped his knee on the table and ignored it, though the force of it clearly warranted an *oh shit*. "Well. Write down your address, and I'll go through it and send some things to you."

"No. I want it now. I want everything you have," said Andre.

His father looked away, and Henry wondered if what Andre wanted was even there anymore. He recalled the empty dresser drawer he found the last time he looked for the floral box.

"Do you still have it?" asked Henry.

Henry could see the tiny ripple of clenched muscle near his father's ear. "Of course I have it," he said. "I still have to go through it."

Frankie began to clear the dishes, the pile of napkins.

"You've had twelve years to go through it," said Andre.

Their father was still and quiet, and Henry saw he was reaching for words that slid out of his grip. He had reached the place where he had no words, and Henry knew this because he had been here, too. It was a place where there was violence or nothing, and the nothing was too excruciating to bear.

"That came out wrong," said Andre. He might have thought a moment ago, with his quarterback's arms, his six feet of muscle, that he could speak his mind, but now he seemed to shrink.

Henry sucked in his breath, like he was blowing out a birthday candle in reverse. He breathed like he wished his father would breathe.

"I know how long it's been," his father said.

Andre stood up.

"Come around," their father commanded.

Andre couldn't back down now with any dignity, so he walked around the table to their father, swift, ready to fight. But he misinterpreted their father's meaning. This was not kung fu. Henry had, perhaps for the first time ever, gotten his wish: his father breathed. Henry saw it in his chest, but Andre didn't, and he was about to ruin it.

But their father cleared things up before Andre managed to take a swing. "No," he said, and touched Andre's arm. It was just the tips of his fingers that made contact, and it lasted not even a second, so brief that someone looking on might not have seen the touch at all and wondered what magic stopped Andre's rumbling forward.

Their father turned and walked to the door that led upstairs to the bedrooms. "It's in the attic. You'll have to hold the ladder for me so I can get up there."

Andre hesitated, visibly trying to shake off his adrenaline. He followed his father, slowly.

Upstairs, Henry stood at the base of the ladder while his little brother smirked at him. They were in the room the two of them once shared—shared not out of necessity, but because no one wanted to move into Andre's bedroom after he ran away. They thought, any day, he could come back.

Now, it was Frankie's room, and Andre and their father were in the attic above it, scooting around on their bellies.

Frankie's room was cleaner than the rest of the house. Pinned to one wall were pieces of fabric in different shapes, almost like a quilt, except Henry got the impression that Frankie was not a quilter. On another wall were columns of awards and certificates: honor roll, honor roll, honor roll, first place Academic Decathlon, first place Math League, medals for spelling and geography bees, accolades for leadership, student government. On top of his dresser was a lava lamp where an electric-green cell divided and reformed itself every fifteen seconds or so, and a pile of video cassette tapes. The furniture was the same, but Frankie had it arranged so that the lines of the bed led into the lines of the dresser. Everything was simple and bright, and all traces of Henry—his crumpled love notes from Cassie, dirty laundry, the bare mattress Henry stripped the sheets from to make a pair of pants to clown in—all this had been eradicated. Frankie's room looked like a page torn from one of Adrienne's homemaking magazines.

Seeing all this symmetry, and seeing how their father was indulging Andre, Henry thought he might come back and see his little brother and father regularly—attend all the ceremonies for these awards that Frankie seemed to be racking up, ask his father one or two things about his job ("How exactly do you make those hitches, and what are they made of, and how many pounds can they drag behind them?"). It seemed like his father and Frankie got along. Without three mouths to feed, without three boys kicking and spilling and occasionally yelling, his father appeared to have grown into a sort of sanity. The idea relieved Henry one second, made him burn with envy the next.

Frankie and Henry listened to the heavy limbs thumping around above.

"You should have been the one to get up there. Aren't you some kind of acrobat?" Frankie said.

Henry said, "Sort of. It doesn't really make me any better qualified to mess around in an attic. Can I look at your movies?"

"Sure."

Henry picked up the stack and examined them. They were all kung fu classics he'd watched when he was Frankie's age. *Drunken Master*. *Way of the Dragon*. *Police Story*. All still wrapped in plastic.

"Wow. These are all yours?"

"Yes."

"Really? Where'd you get the money for them?"

Frankie swiveled on his heel, a nervous movement. He'd done a good job of being stoic since Henry walked through the door, but now he was antsy. "He bought them for me."

"Dad?"

"Of course, Dad," he said, rolling his eyes.

"Christ almighty," muttered Henry. "He really . . . he really does like you."

"Why wouldn't he?" said Frankie, a little loudly. He pushed his glasses up on his nose. "Can I ask you something?"

"Sure."

"Are you really in a circus?"

Henry didn't answer right away. He wanted to say something funny and self-deprecating because he felt exposed and needed to show Frankie he knew his job was a silly one, maybe even one to be ashamed of. But he couldn't think of anything.

An arm caked in brown dust extended from the hole above their heads. It held a stack of photos, still in a drugstore envelope. "Hey, asshole, help me out," said Andre.

Henry put the videotapes back on the dresser and ran to the hole in the ceiling to take the stack of pictures. The arm retracted, and he heard Andre shimmying away.

"So—do you like, wear a wig and have giant shoes and make animal balloons?" Frankie asked. He was doing his best to sound snarky, but Henry could tell he was genuinely curious.

"Sometimes."

"Oh."

There was the sound of more shimmying, a muffled shout, and Andre handed down two books that Henry didn't remember, and a floral-print box that he remembered very well. Henry stacked these things at his feet.

"I looked for you, y'know," said Frankie.

"What?"

"I had it sort of figured out. Cutting up the bedsheets. The towels with melting ice in them. I thought it was a sport at first, I thought you were going to practice. But I'd catch you sometimes. Making these weird faces and gestures. And, y'know . . . you juggled."

Henry kneeled beside the box, touched it, and felt an electric dread.

"I went to Chicago," Frankie continued. "I bought a paper and found all the theatre productions. I asked about you in the alleys behind all the little shitty theatres, and the bigger ones, too. I showed people your picture. I walked right into rehearsals. You wouldn't think a twelve-year-old would be able to get in places like that, but I think it helped. If you act confident, people are curious. They wanna know what your deal is."

"You must have the biggest balls in history."

"I didn't think about the circus."

"I was on the street. I was busking. You were close."

"Not close enough," said Frankie, swiveling on his heel again. The movement was awkward. The spin couldn't be sustained because he was using a heel and not a toe, and he nearly tripped every time. Henry could tell he was using the swivel to distract himself, to diffuse the power of the memory he relayed. "The cops caught me. Dad came and picked me up."

Henry cringed. Deep in his throat, just above his heart, he felt everything constrict. Frankie skipped the last part of the story, the part where their father beat Frankie, but Henry couldn't imagine their father, keyed up on fury and panic after his third son ran away, would have any other response. The vision he had, of coming home now and then, receded back into the guilty place it sprang from. It was a stupid fantasy. Thinking things were different for Frankie. Stupid.

"Idiot," Frankie said, not to Henry, but to himself. "Of course you were on the streets. How would you get in so fast with a theatre looking sixteen?"

"You were close."

"Stop saying that. You wouldn't believe how much school I had to miss. I had perfect attendance before. Goddammit, it would have been worth it if I could have found you. But no, I had to be an idiot. I got nothing out of that whole trip. Except *Police Story*."

"Which you haven't watched."

"I never watch any of them," said Frankie. "But he just keeps buying them."

"Why don't you watch them? They're the best."

"I dunno. I just don't want to," he said. The interlocking shapes on his wall, though, made Henry think that Frankie knew exactly why he wasn't watching them. He was a kid who could see a pattern. Maybe he wasn't Robin Hood, wasn't impervious, but he was smart. He thought of what Andre said the night that he left, about not letting their father know he needed him. How that was the big secret.

263

"You can come and watch the show any time," Henry offered. "You can come and . . ." He dropped his voice. "I could even come get you if you needed. I already wrote a phone number on the pad downstairs. If you call it, I'll get the message. You could stay with me."

Frankie shook his head like he found this idea mortifying. "Man, I don't want to do that at all. I just wanted to know where you were. You and Andre, you're both messed up in the head. I'm normal. I want to go to fucking high school."

"Oh, so you think that being a runaway at a circus isn't the best life for you?" Henry clicked his tongue. "When did you become a snob?"

His little brother smiled, then, as if relieved of the responsibility of carrying the depressing conversation forward.

Above, they heard what sounded like a muffled debate over whether or not they had found everything.

"Do you want to go through this?" said Henry, pointing to the box, then the pictures.

Frankie shrugged. "I hardly knew her."

Henry's heart sank. He knew this was true, that Frankie spent only two years of his life with her. But some deep primitive part of his brain must have loved her, after all the mushy carrots she scraped off his chin, after all the nights she rocked him and patted his butt to make him fall asleep. Still, for nine years, it was Henry who had pinched him awake in the morning and made his breakfast and walked him to school and tucked him in at night. It would make sense if Frankie missed him more than her.

As if to placate Henry, Frankie pulled a random picture from the drugstore envelope and slipped it into his pocket. "Maybe you ought to take those videos. Since I'm never going to watch them."

Henry shook his head. "Not watching them might be a good idea. Giving them to me isn't."

Frankie eyed the floor. "Doesn't matter. Whether I watch them, don't watch them, keep them, give them away. You like all that kung fu shit. You take 'em."

"I'm not taking your videos."

Frankie skinned one of his pillows and chucked the videos in the pillow-case. "Take them. Take them and we'll be even. We'll be good. You left—so what? I'll forget about it. I won't hold it against you for another second."

Henry took a deep breath. *Yes, a strategist.* That's what Frankie was. He knew exactly what Henry wanted most and offered it to him in exchange for what he wanted. Henry wasn't quite sure why he insisted on, of all things, Henry taking a pile of videos, especially when it was something that might set off their father. Maybe he wanted to show Henry he was strong. Maybe he wanted to be sure that Henry thought of him once he was gone. At any rate, Henry knew his brother's offer was bogus: it wasn't possible for Frankie to forget about Henry leaving. It wasn't possible for them to be even. Still, Henry gave Frankie the keys to the rental car and told him to put the pillowcase in the trunk. Not to be even, but because whatever Frankie wanted, Henry wanted him to have it.

Andre's legs dropped down from the hole in the ceiling, and Henry stood up to hold the ladder steady. Both men came down filthy, covered in dust and wads of cobweb and insect carcasses. They were finishing an argument they'd started in the attic, something about life on other planets, about what must be in the goo that life lifts itself from.

Frankie flew back up the stairs and when he saw them, he shucked another pillow. "You're getting shit all over my room," he said, holding out the pillowcase. "Take your clothes off."

Without pausing their argument or questioning Frankie's order, Andre and his father began by removing their shoes. Andre said, "Mars," and their father said, "Impossible!" They stripped off their shirts and unbuckled their belts and their clothes dropped softly into the pillowcase that Frankie held open. They gesticulated in their boxers and their holey socks while Frankie rearranged the two bare pillows.

Andre said, "All humans came from the sky, goddammit. Yes, they did. We're all children of extraterrestrials. And furthermore, those extraterrestrials that left us here come and check on us from time to time."

Henry wanted to write this all into a sketch because this was the truth he could never manage to tell about his family: they were naked and mean, trying to get information from each other about what they were, where the fuck they came from, and when the ones that loved them would come back to make sure their feet were still stuck to the ground, that the light from the stars still reached them.

CHAPTER 26

THERE WERE ONLY A FEW pictures. In one, a little girl held her mother's hand at a birthday party. In another, the girl was older, around thirteen, in a wide-brimmed hat and sunglasses smiling out at them from a porch where people had gathered to cook out. A yet-older version of this girl wore a cowgirl costume, which was less a costume, and more a set of underwear that suggested cowgirldom. In this picture, she licked the boot of another near-naked girl in a ten-gallon hat, somehow managing to grin coyly, even with her tongue out.

Once they got back to St. Louis, Andre and Henry rifled through her treasures, crouched in an alleyway in Dogtown, trying to shield themselves from the gusts of wind that pulled the pictures from their hands. Andre winced at the picture of his mother publicly displaying her lean torso and deep cleavage but Henry thought his mother's smile was just as sweet in the dark club as it was in the picture of the cookout. In fact, it was almost sweeter. He knew without knowing that his mother was a performer, and here she was, performing.

Only one of the pictures had anything written on it, which was also the only picture that featured any of her children. It seemed to be in the same subterranean place, only this time their mother was more clothed and less shellacked in makeup. Her shorts were rolled up, her hair loose and curled.

267

She held a baby with fair hair and fat thighs. On the back of the photograph was their mother's handwriting, a cursive full of extraneous curls and loops: *Rylan, 21, with Junior, eleven months.*

"That's me!" said Andre, snatching the picture from Henry.

Andre examined the photo as if to be sure it wasn't counterfeit. While he squinted at every dark corner of the picture and analyzed the handwriting on the back of it, Henry opened the floral box full of Southern Blue cosmetics.

False eyelashes and gold-ribbed tubes—*like bullets*, Henry thought, and shivered, because he had made this mental comparison before, long ago. Velvety bright colors were in every compact, and now that he had seen the pictures, Henry knew why he never saw his mother use *this* makeup. This was for the stage.

When he touched the round floral-print box nestled in the bottom tier, he felt the same thrill and panic he felt as a little boy searching though his mother's things.

He twisted the lid. There was no powder—no, of course there wasn't. There never was. There was plastic. He remembered the plastic, the blue smudges, but here, the sources of the smudges were apparent. Little round pills, robin's egg blue. He pulled out the plastic bag and shook the old drugs into his hand.

"What is this?" he asked Andre, who looked up from his picture with reluctance.

"Where'd you find that?" Andre asked, snatching it away.

"In her makeup kit."

His brother held the bag up to the light. Henry had a good guess about what these pills were, and judging by the way Andre's face fell, he had a good guess, too. The wind blew through the alley, and the bag fluttered between them. Andre's face reflected Henry's own reaction to the sequence of memories that surfaced now. What their mother had gotten done during the course of a day when they were children was considerable, wasn't it? The damn well was always going dry. She grocery shopped with at least one of them in tow and often all three. Sometimes she didn't shop. She just made food appear, and no one ever wondered how, because mothers did that sort of thing, right? She swung Frankie around, she made Andre go to school, and teased Henry until he smiled, and cooked and cleaned and fixed whatever their father told her to fix. And wasn't it strange that she rarely seemed tired? And weren't her good spirits always a little frenzied?

"Shit," said Andre. He opened the bag and ate one of the pills.

"Andre. Jesus, what are you doing? That could be anything," said Henry.

Andre wrapped one arm around his knee and went back to staring at his picture. "Pretty positive it's speed."

"But you're not totally positive," he said.

"Yeah, there's only one way to be positive."

He offered the bag to Henry.

"It's old," Henry said.

"Don't matter. You'll feel it. Maybe not as strong, but it'll get you high."

"Jesus . . ."

His brother sighed. "You don't have to take it. I'll tell you what it is when it kicks in. But, whatever it is, she took it." He shook the bag. What he meant was, this was a chance to be near her. If Henry took the pill, he would feel something his living, breathing mother had felt. But once the effects of this pill wore off, his mother would still be dead, and his body, his only home, full of poison.

Still.

Andre tipped the bag into Henry's open hand, and Henry put his hand to his mouth, dropped the pill on his tongue, worked up a wash of saliva, and swallowed.

"Okay," said Andre. "Let's divvy it up. I got to get on a plane."

"The drugs?"

"Hell no, we're throwing the rest of this shit away. I mean, the pictures and stuff."

Andre had two giant ziplock freezer bags to put things in. They claimed what they wanted, without disagreement. As they loaded the bags, Henry saw his brother smiling to himself.

"What?" he asked.

"You. I can't believe you took that. You're such a fuckin' mama's boy."

Henry sealed his baggie. *Biographies of the American Presidents* hung out by one corner. Certainly it was the book that inspired her to give Henry his name. He would read it, carefully, and look for clues, messages from her about who she thought he might be.

CHAPTER 27

He drove his brother to the airport in Caleb's car, which Caleb had given over reluctantly.

"Caleb, I swear on a stack of bibles—" Henry said.

"And I swear on an even bigger stack that if I don't see you in two hours I will find you and end your life," said Caleb.

At the airport, Henry helped Andre carry his bag to the ticket counter before saying, "I'll see you at Christmas or something."

Andre wasn't sure what shoulder to bow toward when Henry opened his arms to embrace him. They were a family of people who slipped out in the night, on freight trains, without explanations or apologies—not one that accompanied one another to the airport, seeing one another off with a hug or a promise of return.

"For sure, little brother," Andre said.

After his brother boarded the plane, Henry took the car to the circus grounds to get the last of his things out of the trailer. They had found a new place to rehearse, a gymnasium in a church's rec center, so he didn't plan to be spending much more time on the grounds. He'd left an old costume, a can opener, and a big spoon in his trailer, and though he knew it was easy to replace a thing like a spoon, he didn't have many possessions, and that spoon was his.

He realized that he was thinking about spoons kind of loudly. In fact, all his thoughts were loud, his mind narrating everything in a shouting tone: *The stripes of the tent are blue-green-yellow, the dirt is soft and my feet are sinking in it a little, and the wind cuts between my arms and my sides and it rolls over my shoulders and my legs are like scissors, slicing. This is because of the drugs. This is what new feels like. This is what my mother felt like.*

There are circles on the ground, the loudest voice of his thoughts interrupted, *different circumferences, all dark red.* In the dust, they looked like round patches of velvet. But the patches got bigger, and Henry's already pounding heart thudded even harder when he realized it was blood—sticky like blood, smelling like blood. The smell triggered his reflex to run, and he found his legs spinning beneath him.

Someone had done something.

A scream confirmed this, and Henry wanted to run away from the sound, wanted to ignore it, but no, there he went, right toward it, to do what? To stop it? To get murdered? He wasn't making decisions, he was just doing what the world forced his body to do, move, move, move. Move toward the sound.

Inside the stable he found the source of the screams and the circles of velvety red. It was the great-great-great-granddaughter of the Horse of a Different Color. Her cries sounded like a woman's, and when Henry saw her, he thought he ought to be relieved that she was just a horse. But the froth of saliva that gathered at the corners of her mouth stopped him from feeling anything resembling relief. The skin of her broad, flat nose was split and she stood on unsteady legs outside her pen, Lorne beside her, holding a club.

Lorne didn't see Henry and before Henry could gather his breath to yell, Lorne swung the club against Ambrosia's head. It landed on her jaw with a sickening crack. She whinnied, another wide-open, human-sounding scream, and when her mouth opened, Henry heard the echo of the crack resonating.

Her head shook from side to side. *No, no, no.* But she was not saying no, Henry realized. He recognized this movement, the thrashing of her head, the way she stomped. She was in pain, and in her stupid animal brain, she thought that if she could just move enough, she could escape her own body.

Lorne saw Henry then, but that didn't stop him from swinging again, this time hitting the horse's shoulder. She faltered, going down on one knee for a moment, but then somehow lifting herself again.

Henry wasn't sure what he did to close the distance between himself and Lorne, or how the club ended up in his hands. His actual memory of the movements, the motions, would be overshadowed by his much stronger memory of what happened inside him.

Inside, he became Jackie Chan.

Henry did three or four front flips and grabbed Lorne by the neck, using his feet. Lorne fell forward, and Henry, who could right himself faster than gravity could pull Lorne down, popped a heel into the chin of the forward-reeling man. He tossed Lorne into the air with a roundhouse, and as the man flew off in one direction, the club flew off in the other. Henry's head whipped to the side as he saw the club and he leapt for it, catching it mid-air. This was how he wound up with the club in his hand, and his foot on Lorne's chest. Or at least, he felt like this was how things went. He couldn't be sure.

He hit Lorne with the club. Managed to avoid his head. And Henry heard him say something that sounded like an apology, but Henry had heard it all before. He'd heard it coming from his own mouth. *You say,* I'm sorry, I'm sorry, I'm sorry, *when this is happening to you, but what you're really doing is asking to be set free from pain:* stop, knock me out, kill me.

Lorne tried to say something else, but Henry jammed the end of the club into his chest. Lorne had tears in his eyes, and he grasped at something invisible.

Henry stopped hitting long enough for Lorne to find his voice.

"It's not like you think. Call the animal welfare people, they'll take her now. They'll fix her. They'll find her a home—she's practically royalty. But if I waited—if I waited until Seamus sold the circus off, she'd be glue, Henry. This is mercy."

Henry knew he was supposed to see the logic in this, but he didn't, so he hit him again, this time in the stomach. "It's not mercy to break a thing's jaw! Put a *bullet* in her head. That's mercy."

Lorne groaned, curled up. "But she won't get to *live*," he said. "You want to put a bullet in someone's head, put it in Tex's. And make it a big one. Because *she* doesn't have a chance. Jesus Christ, Henry, please. I didn't want to do them both. I swear to God, I was trying to save her. Call the welfare people if you don't believe me. Call them right now."

Henry looked at Ambrosia, thrashing her head, jaw slack, white foam oozing from her lips. The blood kept trickling, wet and fresh from her ear. She would not be the same. Whatever was in her head that made sense of the world no longer worked.

"You've done this before," said Henry.

"Just once," whimpered Lorne. "At the park on the way back. I wanted to see if I could hit her at all. She forgave me."

Henry smashed the curve of Lorne's spine with the club, and he cried out even louder than Ambrosia had whinnied. The impact moved up the length of the club and stung Henry's hand. He hated and loved how this felt. It seemed he'd been traveling toward this for a long time, traveling to the place where he met the highest potential of his body.

It was here, in this. He didn't doubt this was justice.

This was what Andre must have felt when he went after Ice Cream Boobs's johns. Strong and vindicated. But Henry's mind kept going back to Ambrosia and her broken jaw and her suffering and it ruined the thrill of justice.

Lorne tried to roll out of Henry's way but Henry kept hitting him. He aimed for Lorne's head now with a clear picture of what would happen after he bashed his skull. Lorne would struggle for breath.

It was then he thought of Caleb's hand on his shoulder the day his brother arrived to see him. The simple way Caleb made them friends again, with this one movement of hand to shoulder. He thought of how his father had brushed against Andre's arm when they were in Edgefield, how this touch arrested his brother at the last second of his charge. He thought of these things, and he knew that killing Lorne was not what he'd been traveling toward. The delivery of justice was not the highest potential of his body.

The club came down without force, gave Lorne an innocuous *thunk* on the skull, barely enough for a goose egg to form.

Henry stopped. He still held the club but his arm was limp at his side and he didn't say anything.

Lorne's hand still guarded his face. Henry saw his wide eyes between the fingers that shielded them. When Henry still didn't make another move, the animal handler squirmed tentatively, trying to get up.

It wasn't easy for him. Lorne held his stomach and chest like he wanted to keep his insides from falling out, and got to his feet. Henry guessed he had broken more than one rib and maybe his collarbone. Nothing they could set at the hospital. They would hurt for a long time but not long enough to make things fair.

Lorne looked at Ambrosia, who still whinnied, high, urgent sounds, like a squealing violin.

"You'll do it, right? You'll call the welfare people?" he said.

"Yes," said Henry, because he knew this was what Lorne wanted to hear. If he heard what he wanted, he would go, and Henry desperately needed him to go.

Lorne nodded. If he concentrated more on Henry, and less on the horse, he might have doubted Henry's word. But he looked only at Ambrosia, until he limped away, cradling his side.

When he was gone, Henry led Ambrosia, staggering, into her stable and left her, frothing at the mouth. He drove back to Caleb and Adrienne's. It took too long, and he tried not to think about the horse, tried not to think about what he'd done, or what he didn't do, but his thoughts were still loud.

Caleb and Adrienne would know what to do. But when he arrived, they weren't there.

He paced the living room, then tore through the yellow pages with shaking hands. He called an emergency vet clinic. He explained that there was an accident, but when he described Ambrosia's injuries, her behavior, the vet tech got all quiet and told him to hold. *There's no time to hold*, he thought. But then there was the vet on the other end of the line and she had that sad and serious tone to her voice.

"Your horse is seriously injured," she began. She had this little monologue memorized, right down to the gentle, condescending tone in which it was delivered. She'd given it to at least a thousand people, people who were holding tightly, naïvely to a beloved pet that was clearly beyond saving.

"She isn't mine. She works with me," he said. He said this so the vet would know he wasn't some kid who couldn't face facts. But it sounded terrible and it wasn't true. Ambrosia belongs to the circus, and Henry was part of the circus. She was his.

"I see," the vet said. Her condescending tone remained. "Well. I can get there in an hour. And whoever she belonged to should be there and be prepared to let her go."

"Okay," he said, but as he said it, he decided against having this woman do in his horse. "Wait, never mind."

"Never mind?"

"I can get to her faster," he said.

He found the gun in the hatbox, slipped it between his hip and the elastic of his underwear, and pulled his T-shirt down over it.

WHEN HE GOT BACK TO the stable, Ambrosia was swaying. She was still trying to get out of her body, still trying to escape her pain, but she had less energy with which to do it.

Henry loaded the gun.

He touched the scar on the top of his head, the mean little white zipper line. It had bled and bled. He wondered if it would be the same with her.

When he got close, she started to thrash again. He wanted her to settle down. He wanted to have to pull the trigger only once. He spoke to her in low tones, touched her nose, avoiding her swollen jaw. She went back to swaying, and Henry knew this was as close as she would come to being still.

So he did what Lorne should have done. It was another simple motion, a gentle curl of the finger that sent a bullet into her hard, flat forehead. Instantly she crumpled, crushing her own legs beneath her.

He took the clip out of the gun, and lay beside her great still body, and stroked her limp neck, and breathed harder than he thought he had ever breathed, his chest heaving. His stroking turned to clawing.

WHEN HE GOT BACK TO the house, Caleb was in the living room, lying on the sofa, his feet elevated on the armrest. Adrienne wasn't home. He would never put his feet up like that if Adrienne were home.

Caleb sat upright when he saw Henry. He was startled. Henry knew he looked wild, knew he smelled like blood. There really wasn't that much, and he'd washed himself with the hose, but the smell remained, coppery and sickening.

"You alright?" asked Caleb.

Henry wiped his eyes. The drugs were still in him—he wasn't high anymore, but he felt all wrong. His mouth was sticky. The muscles in his legs were fluttering, and acid kept shooting up into his throat. "Is Kylie here?"

"No," Caleb said. His brow knit and he stood. "She's at the music store. Hey, you alright? Did something happen with your brother?"

"No," he said.

"No?"

Henry turned, put his face in his palms. He managed to ask Caleb to help him, though the request was muffled, directed into his hands.

He heard Caleb take a deep breath and remembered the gun, still tucked into the waist of his pants, the barrel parallel to his spine. He wore it casually, like some kind of punk.

Caleb moved closer, his bare heels thumping softly on the hard wood. "I'll help. Just tell me what to do."

He must have wanted to ask about the stupid gun and why Henry smelled like blood. He must have thought Henry was nuts—Henry thought Henry was nuts—but Caleb said nothing.

"You have to get rid of Feely's animals. If you buy the circus. Or even if you don't. We have to find a place for them," he said. He no longer spoke right into his hands but through his parted fingers.

Caleb sighed, aggravated, and it was the Caleb that Henry knew, Caleb the curmudgeon. He'd shaken off all his concern and fear. "You really hate animals, don't you? I asked, and you said no, and now here you go with this."

Henry's muscles stopped twitching. Because Caleb pretended that everything was normal, Henry felt, for a second, like himself again, until he thought of Lorne, doubled over, limping across the dust. He turned to Caleb and handed him the gun.

"What the hell is this?" asked Caleb.

"It's Adrienne's gun," said Henry.

"I know that. Why do you have it?"

"I used it to shoot the horse. She was dying. Lorne bashed her head in. I killed her."

Caleb looked down at the gun, turned it over in his hands, two whole revolutions before he said, "Did you see him do it?"

"Yes."

"Where is he now?"

"I don't know. He left the grounds. I didn't kill him."

Caleb raised his eyebrows. "I wasn't thinking that."

"I wanted to," Henry confessed. "I think I hurt him pretty bad."

"Well. I'd've done the same," said Caleb.

His throat knotted up. Caleb was wrong. He would not have seen real death as a possible outcome of any interaction he had with a person. Caleb might have shoved Lorne, kicked his sides blue. But Caleb would never take it as far as Henry had. For Henry, death *was* a possible outcome; his father was a killer, and that meant that Henry could be one, too, on the right day, in the worst moment.

No. Wait. That's not true anymore.

Henry couldn't catch the sob before it escaped him. The implications of his recently revised history were suddenly clear to him: his father was not a killer. Henry had him wrong. He'd had himself wrong. The handful of words his brother had said, *scared to death*, changed the whole scope of creation, set the landscape. And now the words were gone, undone, and the world was not the world—it was a flower, an apple, the open mouth of a monster. He could not guess on what he stood, because it was not his father's treatment of his mother that killed her but the drug that he could still feel inside him. His father wasn't innocent, but he wasn't a murderer, and neither was Henry. It was a sweet but unsettling surprise, and he couldn't do anything in the face of it but cry.

Caleb looked embarrassed. He cleared his throat, made an odd humming noise. He looked around the room for a distraction, an escape from the moment. Henry continued to cry. Eventually Caleb was forced to look at him, forced to laugh just a little at how pathetic it all was, because what else could he do?

"Hey. You're okay. It's done. It'll be okay," Caleb said.

There was certainty in Caleb's voice that Henry had not been able to find in his heart—it relieved him, and the relief felt like exhaustion. He stopped crying, too tired to continue doing anything at all, including stand. He leaned back and was glad there happened to be a wall there.

"Careful," said Caleb. "You wanna chair or something?"

"Nah," said Henry, sinking to the floor.

Caleb squatted down next to him. "You sure? You look like shit."

He knew he did. He could feel the snot and tears drying on his face, the heaviness of his eyelids.

"Promise me about the animals," he said.

"I promise," said Caleb.

CHAPTER 28

September 1990

CALEB WATCHED HENRY AND KYLIE perform at Washington University. The buildings all looked to Caleb like medieval libraries, and they were performing in the shadow of one of those buildings. They'd charmed a student group into inviting them to campus to perform, and here they were, doing their angel routine. They couldn't put out a bucket for change, but the student group had promised them a hundred dollars in exchange for the show.

It was a pantomime, all done without speaking. The noises they made were only that: shouts and sighs and whistles. Kylie played her angel with a crooked walk and a lazy smile. Henry, the tramp, seemed to be trying to help her back up to heaven, but she resisted—sometimes by making her body seem limp and heavy as a sack of sand, and sometimes by outwitting the tramp, hiding, making excuses. She was glad to be free of heaven, euphoric about the change of scenery.

Caleb was the one who suggested asking schools if they would host their performance, and it was Caleb who suggested offering the show for a hundred dollars, just to build a portfolio. Next time, Caleb would suggest they ask for two hundred. They'd drawn a small crowd, even in the wet, chilly weather, and the people who'd come were staying, even though they were hugging themselves like their sweaters and jackets were not enough.

280

The audience was made up of mostly students, but there were a few children, too, little brothers and sisters, or sons and daughters brought by the college kids. The students were too brainy to laugh too hard. They were marveling at the physical challenge for the players, they were analyzing the themes of the show. All that thinking distracted them from laughing. The children, though, laughed plenty.

Sure, they could charge two hundred dollars. They were worth it.

He hadn't told the clowns, per se, that he planned to manage their careers, and he hadn't committed to anything but a short-term stay at his house. But Caleb couldn't picture cutting them loose with anything less than a secure gig and a web of connections. He couldn't imagine not sticking with them, helping them navigate the mess of show business. But without Feely and Feinstein, his resources for helping them were limited. Adrienne's medical bills were astronomical. Kylie and Henry were furnaces; in Caleb's estimation, they must burn about six thousand calories a day. In the last week, they'd gratefully eaten whatever Adrienne put on the table, but Caleb could tell it was not quite enough.

They had less than they'd had in a long time, right when they needed the opposite, an absolute windfall, in order to save the circus and find homes for the animals. Caleb had promised that he would help Tex and those pungent, smug-seeming camels, and he meant it, even though he didn't have a plan or the authority to do anything. It surprised him that he would ever make a promise without thinking it through and be so assured that he would be able to keep it. It made him feel powerful, but a little frantic, and he had the sinking certainty that this was not the last time he would make such a promise to this boy, who was not exactly a boy, but a young man who had waited as long to hear a promise like this as Caleb had waited to make one.

Kylie swooned, and Henry caught her. She feigned death. When the tramp looked helplessly at the audience to figure out what to do, she peeked at him with one eye, and closed it tight again when he looked back at her. The children laughed, and just like that, Caleb knew how to keep his promise to Henry, and how to keep working on his life's project. If there was anyone who had the capital and the heart to help Caleb revive a dead circus, it was the man who had sent him Henry, Luka Christiakov.

281

At the hobo's insistence, the angel swapped her halo for his hobo's jacket. She didn't want to be in heaven, so he volunteered to take her lot. Now the angel masqueraded as the tramp, and the tramp masqueraded as the angel. The trouble, it seemed, was that the tramp was really still just a tramp. His wings didn't work. Henry plucked two children from the audience, both about eight years old: a dark-eyed white boy with two lines shaved into the hair above his temples and an impish-looking Mexican girl in neon-pink everything. He stood them so they faced each other and demonstrated how they must hold hands, weaving their fingers together, and they were too old not to be shy about this, but they did it anyway. Henry nodded his approval and showed them how their hands would be his catapult, launching him into the heavens. The little girl let go of the boy's hands.

"That won't work!" she said, outraged. Kylie's angel-gone-hobo shook her head vigorously in support of the little girl's statement.

Henry patted her head, condescendingly. *There, there. Yes, it will.*

"You're nuts!" the girl said, and Caleb laughed loud enough for the rest of the audience to glance over their shoulders. Henry's eyes darted in his direction, though they quickly returned to the little girl. Caleb knew Henry had figured his laugh into his calculations of what must happen next, what he must play up and play down, what he'd do to win favor, what he'd do to surprise.

After two leaps that missed the catapult created by the children's hands, Henry released them back into the audience. He started to climb up the side of the building then. Hand over hand, he scaled the facade, using as footholds the grotesques and the places where the mortar had receded between the stones.

The student group that had hired them glanced around nervously, biting their lips, whispering in each other's ears. This was ad libbed. This was reciprocity for Caleb's laughter.

The children clutched their parents' jeans. When Henry rose above the second story windows, the adults started to cling to their children, too. They had not pictured this happening in a show the student group had billed as "traditional mime." Kylie ran back and forth below him, spreading her skirt as if the flimsy thing would act as a safety net if he plummeted. The real safety net was a cluster of bushes with waxy soft needles. It was not much of a barrier between life and death. But, perhaps stupidly, Caleb found that he trusted Henry. This was the punch line to a thrilling joke, and the best thing, really, for Caleb to do was to stand back, and shut up, and have a sense of humor about it.

The mothers and fathers and Caleb waited for Henry to turn to them, to cue them that he had arrived, that he had gone up as far as he would go.

The children held their breath.

Adrienne missed Henry and Kylie's show at Washington University (again) because she was out selling cosmetics to a bunch of smiley twenty-five-year-olds, who all had their first grown-up jobs and were trying desperately to look like women instead of girls, so their bosses didn't do things like wink at them and say "You remind me of my daughter." They didn't have to tell this to Adrienne. She just knew, and that was why she could sell to them—because she knew what they wanted. That was her art. Figuring out what people wanted and giving it to them.

When she arrived back at her house, she had a thousand dollars' worth of orders in her purse, the commission for which would translate to a couple of weeks' worth of groceries.

It would not pay the mortgage.

It was certainly not the money that Caleb needed to buy Feely and Feinstein.

She had her lunch, and afterwards, instead of smoking, she injected herself with octreotide, like a good girl, to keep the tumors away. She was on a lower dose now, just once a day, so she didn't have such a hard time finding a place to stick the needle.

Today, she found herself with a strange sort of housekeeping task ahead of her. It was one she had researched and planned since Seamus's call. She'd listened while Caleb suggested at least a dozen different ways to come up with the money, none of which were realistic. It didn't even take a person with Adrienne's particular gifts to see that Caleb wanted to buy Feely and

Feinstein more than he had ever wanted anything. It was, after all, *his* creation. Seamus had a claim to the circus in name only—it seemed to Adrienne that he was more like a pushy benefactor than an owner, asking Caleb to sculpt the statue of David, and then standing behind him the whole time, insisting that he put a moustache on it.

She checked her watch. She had to pick up her husband, Kylie, and Henry at the campus in one hour, after which they would go directly to Richard's appointment with the vet. She popped a stick of Big Red in her mouth and clapped her hands together once. *Get to work.*

Adrienne began by vacuuming the living room and going through Kylie's suitcase to look for anything that might be important to her. She took out her jewelry box and a folder full of papers and stashed it in the trunk of her car. She didn't go through these things, but she thought that if Kylie owned anything of importance, it would be in one or the other of these places. After that she did the guest room. Henry's valuables were just as simple to find: a stack of VHS tapes wrapped in plastic; a letter that looked like a dog had chewed on it; a notebook; a ziplock bag full of his mother's pictures; and a book of American presidents.

She knew she had to work fast, and she would not have dreamed of going through Henry's mother's things before—but now that the bag was in her hand, she couldn't resist opening it. She leafed through the book, and Henry's namesake's page was marked with a photograph of a stripper licking another stripper's boot.

"Good grief."

She put Henry's things with Kylie's, in the trunk.

Preserving Caleb's precious things, and her own, proved a little more difficult. Kylie and Henry came in with backpacks. But this had been her and Caleb's home for years, time with which to accumulate many things of sentimental value: a paper rose that she gave Caleb (she didn't know how many Valentine's Days ago) laid on top of a bookcase; their Christmas ornaments had been collected one by one, chosen carefully by the two of them to represent in some way the events of the year in which they were purchased. The first year they were so poor that they couldn't afford a Christmas ornament, and so 1979 was represented by a light bulb Caleb had painted and wrapped in pipe cleaners.

Keeping a light bulb from shattering for twelve years was not easy, and now Adrienne was certain that the thing wouldn't make it to their next Christmas. There were so many objects she wanted to save, but things like ornaments and dried roses did not make the cut. If she counted roses and light bulbs, she might as well count the china and the framed pictures, the countertops and the drywall. She might as well save the whole house for its sentimental value, and she'd already decided against that.

Once the car was loaded, she started the real work—the work that she'd needed to go to Azi to learn how to do. At least, she'd learned the science of how to do it from Azi, the materials to use, the bare pyrotechnics. The criminal savvy she'd borrowed from Curtis. She'd gone to see him at the warehouse one day and apologized for having perhaps overreacted the night he came to her house. But mostly she was there to ask him questions that she knew he would answer with lies. She wanted to see how this was done. How to not let the cat out of the bag, how to not feel guilt so she wouldn't look guilty.

After she'd studied his lying long enough to learn what she needed to know, they'd parted amicably for once. Even though she still thought Curtis was a shit, she did, sort of, forgive him. When he left her, he was doing what had to be done, what anybody might do in his situation, which was push the dead away. She understood his fear, his reasoning, and it seemed now to her that Curtis probably did love her, which was why he had to push her so hard. Dead people couldn't be allowed to linger in the front of the mind, thrashing around. They'd just drag you into death with them. You had to keep dead people with you some other way, keep them in dreams, keep them in ziplock bags. Be honest about what you could afford to carry.

From beneath the bathroom sink, she took out a jar of cotton balls that had been soaking in rubbing alcohol. She unscrewed the plate on the circuit breaker and stuffed the wet fibers in the spaces between each breaker switch. The alcohol made her light-headed, but the smell was pleasant and familiar.

It was funny, she thought. As soon as she got her home the way she wanted it, she had to burn it down. She'd told Caleb she didn't care if they put the house up for collateral and lost it, and he'd tentatively agreed to apply for the loan, but she was concerned that even if he applied, he could be denied. Or Seamus would want too much for the circus, and it would look suspicious to collect a pile of insurance money right after applying for the loan. If she was going to try this, it had to be now.

She scratched the side of her nose and felt the smallest soreness—under this cartilage, things were still healing, bones were still fusing back together, and Adrienne worried. She worried that this plan wouldn't work, that Caleb would be left with nothing. If her tumor grew again, he would not even have her. Even if her tumor didn't grow back, the strain on her heart from powering a body so large would shorten her life, without question. She ached to think of Caleb with nothing—no circus, no wife, and no house. It was the only thing that caused her to second-guess herself. It made her consider pulling the cotton out of the breaker, forgetting it, and doing things the normal way.

But Adrienne figured that most people don't get what they really want the normal, safe way. She had always hoped to be more beauty than freak, but here she was, with her big, shaking fingers soaked in alcohol, trying to start a fire that would look like an accident. Nothing could have been more freakish. She was grinding bones to make bread.

She lined the lower lip of the circuit box with the cotton, pieces drawn long, their filaments stretched so that the fire could burn fast once it reached these, sparking on a thin wisp that waved the flame on to the next thin wisp before it got to the denser stuffing above. Azi had said that it mostly mattered where the fire started. If the breaker box was the origin, the fire would appear to be electrical, though he warned her that her insurance would investigate, and they would be looking for any scrap of evidence that might indicate that the fire was set. The rubbing alcohol was difficult to detect as a catalyst, he told her, and the cotton would burn to nothing. "But you'll want to get out of the house before it burns," he said, "so you'll need something to slow down the process a bit . . . probably a candle, but not the kind with the little metal wafer at the bottom for holding the wick . . ."

She placed a yellow birthday candle, with its base burned to a flat pancake of wax so that it would stand on its own, on the shelf below the bare circuits nestled in cotton.

Was it too late to stop?

No. But here was the match in her hand, and here she was striking it.

She screwed the front of the breaker back on, hiding the flame she'd planted.

Before she left, she got Richard and put him in his small cage. He and her purse full of Southern Blue orders were the only things she took from the house for herself.

This Is Number Seven

Every song I sing to her, she hates.

We're on the circus grounds, because where else would we be, and I start in with
"Come On, Eileen."

And Kylie, who's sitting on a lawn chair across from me, throws one of her
shoes at my head, like she couldn't care less that I've got a broken collarbone and a
cast up to my elbow. She doesn't mind picking on the infirmed.

I guess it is a little bad. I only know about half the lyrics.

"Sing anything else," says Kylie. "That song is terrible."

I keep it up. "Oh, you have a dress . . . Oh, my hots I confess . . ."

She hates all my acts, too, so I've decided to let her write them. I'm throwing
in the towel on the writing. I said I would write five, and this is number seven,
and I'm done. But I gave it a shot, Christiakov. Maybe soon I'll be able to show
you a waterfall of pages, but you'll just have to take my word for it that they're acts,
because I won't let you read a word.

There aren't any trees on the grounds, but the leaves are still blowing through
from somewhere, tumbling through the dust like orange and yellow pinwheels.
Caleb is sitting on a lawn chair looking all worried about the money, about Feely
and Feinstein, about the black skeleton of the house in Dogtown that some suit is
investigating right now.

Adrienne doesn't fit in a lawn chair. She stands. I guess she looks worried, too, but she smiles when I sing.

Number seven is my mother's act.

I can see it: she dances to the strangest, darkest songs, not the bubbly disco that the other girls dance to. They like her because of this and because she moves like she does, shoulders jerking, legs kicking high, then coming down, the momentum pulling her into a fury of pirouettes. And then she slows, glides toward the floor, a raindrop down a window pane, a sultry, snaking path. She is where I got this genius, Christiakov. She knows every muscle in her body, and she uses it to tell you the story you want to hear. She is just scary enough onstage but if she talks to you, she's so sweet and interested, like you are the center of the universe. She makes you special, even though you are nothing, just a fat ugly guy in a strip club, or a boy who thinks he can make himself into a wheel.

I used to think I didn't get enough time. I used to think it would take me my whole life to tell her, sufficiently, how I loved her; and too-bad-so-sad, she wasn't around for my whole life or really for much of it at all. But now I think what I got was enough—*because it's possible to show love in a matter of seconds. Hand on a shoulder. Head in a lap. Fingers through hair.*

This is the highest potential of the body.

Caleb is trying to start a fire from scratch like a boy scout, trying to scrape a spark onto a pile of dry leaves and sticks. Adrienne rubs his back while he does it, and says, "That's never going to work. It's too windy." And for a second everyone thinks, Trust her, she's good at this.

Caleb tosses a match and the contents of Adrienne's lighter on the pile. It flashes up.

The fire throws a yellow glow on our faces, and looking at Adrienne with that bright mask on, I still get a little jealous of Caleb, what he has—the most beautiful woman in the world. But here, he's got his hand on her calf, which is where it should be, and he knows it, and I know it.

I feel light right now, like I felt at that first show when the laughter came down and settled around us like snow. Inside, there's nothing toxic. In fact, it feels like there's nothing at all, no bones, broken or otherwise, no muscles. No heart or breath or blood.

Kylie bites her nails. Before I started singing, she was staring into space like she was trying to figure out some unworkable problem. She and Adrienne and Caleb don't seem to feel light. Whatsamatter? You got tacks in your shoes? *my mother would've asked them.* You got bubblegum in your underwear?

I have more love than sense. I have more love than anything. I can think of my brothers and father without losing this love—something about seeing them in their own spheres, knowing they exist there, with or without me. I have already sent a letter to Frankie, telling him to walk at graduation. You can't possibly start annoying people too early about this sort of stuff.

"Come on . . . ta-loo-ra."

"It's not funny anymore, Henry," says Caleb.

"Shhh, it'll come back around again," I say, and it does, because that's how you work the running gag. You stick with it, until the last too-ra-loo-rah-aye, and I do. I stick with it until Kylie comes after me and I have to explode out of my lawn chair and run, kicking up the dust and leaves, cutting through the dark, past the animals, the Feely and Feinstein sign framed in burnt-out light bulbs. I'll let her close the gap between us, let her catch me once we forget why we're running. When we're breathless and the movement is its own reason for itself, I'll take her, and all the rest of them, to lightness. I'll show them how it's done.

ACKNOWLEDGMENTS

THIS BOOK BEGAN AT CALIFORNIA State University's Summer Arts program. I was an office assistant for the program and became obsessed with a certain clowning arts class after being tasked with ordering supplies for the course, including a preposterous number of red rubber noses. The earliest chapters of this were researched and written at Summer Arts, so I would like to thank the program, in particular Jim Spalding, Kelley Lansing, and Joanne Sharp, for encouraging me to write on the job and observe the clown class. I also wish to extend my gratitude to Hugh O'Gorman, David Shiner, and the students in that course for allowing me to observe. In addition, I'd like to thank Megan Ivey for kindly allowing me to interview her regarding her experiences as a clown.

I have had the benefit of wonderful and encouraging writing teachers. Bill Starr and Mark O'Hara have left a lasting impact on my writing life, and the writing lives of so many of their students. I also want to thank Steve Lattimore, whose teaching shaped me immensely as a writer. I owe a debt to my fellow writing students, teachers, and guides at Fresno State; Steven Church, Connie Hales, Alex Espinoza, Daniel Chacón, Lillian Faderman, and especially Steve Yarbrough and David Anthony Durham have been sources of endless writing support, kindness, and patience. I would also like to thank

Jill McCorkle and my Sewanee Writers' Conference workshop for helping give this novel shape and bringing me back to the world of writing as I was untangling the world of first-time motherhood.

I am so grateful to my writing group, Candace Duerksen, Carol Vitali, and Kristin FitzPatrick, who read this entire book, a chapter at a time, in its roughest form. I am also unbelievably grateful to Tiffany Crum for reading it (more than once) and for answering an endless number of neurotic questions about writing and publishing, sometimes at five in the morning.

I want to extend my thanks to my agent Jordan Breindel and my editor Chelsey Emmelhainz for believing in this book's worth, for seeing in it what I saw, and helping me shape it so that others could see it that way, too.

I am deeply appreciative to my mother- and father-in-law Jo and Kenny Martin for cheering me on, and for providing me with my husband, Jonathan Martin. Jon, like most writers' spouses, is the first reader of every piece of writing I produce, and I am grateful to him for weeding out the real trash, for moving across the country with me while I got my MFA, and for navigating everything with me, every day. I also want to thank my son, Audric, whose existence threw a new light on these chapters and helped me revise from the point of view of a person with an insanely high stake in the life of another.

I am lucky enough to have an incredible family, nuclear and extended, and I want to offer my profound gratitude to all of them for their support. I especially wish to thank my brothers, Michael Schulte, Bill Schulte, and John Schulte, who have all encouraged my writing and listened to me complain about it pretty much their whole lives. Finally, I owe the greatest debt to my brilliant and hardworking mother and father, Patricia and Edward Schulte, who told me that I could do or make anything I conceived of, which is what parents are supposed to say, of course, but my parents meant it. They were unflinching about it, they said it without caveat, believed it from the bottom of their hearts. This has sustained me through this book, and everything else.